Cana... ....

New York Public Library's "Books for the Teen Age" List

Shortlisted for the Ontario Library Association Silver Birch Award

Shortlisted for the Dog Writers of America Fiction Award

"I was thoroughly entertained by
this captivating novel. It is a boy and his dog story,
a time travel tale and a grand adventure
all rolled into one book ..." VOYA

"... a beautifully resolved ending.
DogStar is a novel about the great love between
humans and animals." VANCOUVER SUN

"More plot twists than a Hardy Boys adventure
in cyberspace ... The authors expertly bring to life
a time and place for their readers with
fully-developed characters and lots of
background detail." NORTH SHORE NEWS

"... *DogStar* grows on the reader,
and Patsy Ann's doggy grin lingers long after
the book is done." QUILL & QUIRE

"A time-travel adventure story with
emotional appeal for dog lovers." BOOKLIST

A SIRIUS MYSTERY

THE GOLDEN BOY

BEVERLEY WOOD & CHRIS WOOD

POLESTAR
An Imprint of Raincoast Books

Raincoast Books gratefully acknowledges the ongoing support of the Canada Council for the Arts, the British Columbia Arts Council and the Government of Canada through the Book Publishing Industry Development Program (BPIDP).

Cover and interior design by Teresa Bubela

LIBRARY AND ARCHIVES CANADA CATALOGUING IN PUBLICATION

Wood, Beverley, 1954-
    Golden Boy / Beverley and Chris Wood.

(A Sirius mystery)
ISBN 10 1-55192-953-8
ISBN 13 978-1-55192-953-8

    I. Wood, Chris, 1953- II. Title. III. Series: Wood, Beverley.
Sirius mystery.

PS8595.O624G64 2006   jC813'.54   C2006-901524-4

Library of Congress Control Number: 2006923726

Raincoast Books   *In the United States:*
9050 Shaughnessy Street   Publishers Group West
Vancouver, British Columbia   1700 Fourth Street
Canada V6P 6E5   Berkeley, California
www.raincoast.com   94710

Raincoast Books is committed to protecting the environment and to the responsible use of natural resources. We are working with suppliers and printers to phase out our use of paper produced from ancient forests. This book is printed with vegetable-based inks on 100% ancient-forest-free paper (40% post-consumer recycled), processed chlorine- and acid-free. For further information, visit our website at www.raincoast.com/publishing.

Printed in Canada by Webcom.

10 9 8 7 6 5 4 3 2 1

For Dax & Acadia

Table of Contents

One

A 'FAMILY' HONEYMOON

"... AND THEN we'll fly from New Zealand to Australia and see the outback," Amanda said, making a fan from the colourful brochures on the table.

"Kangaroos and wallabies!" Rory burst out. Her flawless face, a younger version of her mother's, glowed with excitement. "Guys, this is such a great idea!"

"We're pretty excited about it too," agreed Johnny Tanaka, reaching across to take his new wife's hand. "Your mom and I want this to be a family honeymoon."

Slouched in his chair, arms folded over his chest, Tomi kept his head down and his thoughts to himself. *Your family, maybe*, he grumbled silently. *Not mine.*

"What about you, Obaacha?" Rory turned to the older woman at the table.

Tomi bristled. It drove him crazy how easily his new "sister" had adopted the Tanaka family nickname for her new "step-grandma."

"I've already written my cousin Michiko in Hokkaido," the petite old lady said, drawing a skein of rust-brown wool from the knitting bag parked at her feet. "I'm going to get a train pass and visit all my relatives in Japan. I'll finally be able to catch up with what's going on in their lives."

"So how long do we have to be away?" asked Tomi, his voice sour.

"Oh, what a grouch!" Rory rolled her eyes. "It's not *have* to be, it's *get* to be!"

Oh jeez. She's so freaking chipper it's toxic!

"We'll be gone almost four months," Johnny Tanaka said.

"The plan is," Amanda leaned forward, "we'll put this house up for sale when we go ..."

What? Tomi's head shot up. His dark eyes burned.

"... and by the time we get back," his stepmom carried on, "the new house will be ready. We'll be able to unpack from the trip and move right in to our new rooms."

Amanda and Rory and even Dad had been bubbling over about the "new house" for months. Tomi had been ignoring it for just as long, secretly hoping something awful would happen to make it go away. He'd worked even harder to ignore what might happen to *this* house, the one he'd lived in forever. The house where he could still see his late mother's shadow in every room.

"So that means," Tomi's father gave each word heavy importance, "we need to pack up everything that's here, before we leave." He fixed a look on Tomi and raised his brows meaningfully. "And that means *everything*."

"No problem," Rory's bright voice chimed in. "I've barely *un*packed." In fact, she and her mom had left a lot of stuff in storage since the wedding nine months ago, waiting for this moment.

Tomi's chair shot backward, striking the kitchen counter with a loud crack. He stood abruptly.

Rory and her mother traded looks. Johnny Tanaka closed his eyes and seemed to be counting, breathing deeply. Obaacha frowned disapproval over her knitting.

For a moment Tomi's mouth worked as though he were going to say something. But only a wordless groan escaped as he spun around and stormed from the room.

TOMI DRIFTED down the wide service alley. The bare cement walls on either side belonged to low-rise industrial buildings. They had small offices out front and truck bays and dumpsters here in the back. Today being Sunday the buildings were mostly silent, the parking lots empty. No one was around to keep Tomi from boosting himself up and peering into each uncovered waste bin. He'd made some of his best finds in these dumpsters.

Today, they produced only a few odds and ends that might be useful for something in the future. After a few minutes he sucked in his breath and squeezed into the narrow space between a chain-link fence and a wall of sawn lumber stacked higher than his head. His nearly empty backpack collapsed with a faint sigh.

Beyond the narrow gap between the wood and the fence was a graded gravel lot. Tomi followed the fence another twenty steps or so to a line of billowing willow trees. He pushed through a curtain of narrow green leaves and scrambled over a tangled bank of thick roots and mud-caked driftwood.

Sunlight glittered through the leaves ahead, making him squint. Then he was there.

He dropped onto a natural bench of deep moss between two ancient willow trunks. No one else knew about this place, tucked away at the very back of the River Side Lumber Yard, right beside the river itself. It was one of Tomi's favourite secrets.

Here, he could feel close to nature and alone with his thoughts. The neat suburban streets of Delta, with their painted curbs and traffic lights, their crosswalks and rules, were left behind. Soft green leaves filtered the traffic noise drifting over from River Road. At his feet, grey-green water slipped past on its restless journey to the Pacific, now only half a dozen kilometres downstream. Across the moving expanse of water, big brown booms of logs, like floating islands, waited to be sawn into boards. Looking up and down the river, Tomi felt as though he could have been in a jungle in Africa or South America.

Both those continents were on the list for the coming trip. Globetrotting on Dad's airline pilot pass might have been something to look forward to, Tomi thought, if it had really been a family trip. And if he could look forward to coming home afterward to his own room in his own house. The house he'd shared with Dad *and Mom* until the ghastly night the young policewoman had shown up at the door, blue and red lights pulsing in the foggy street behind her. His stomach clenched and he squeezed his eyes tight shut.

Instead, this whole "family honeymoon" just seemed so ... *phony*. Really, it was all a big scam to trick him into forgetting that once they got in the taxi to go to the airport, he'd never see home — his own home — again.

A jet thundered low overhead on its final approach to Vancouver International Airport. Tomi gazed up at the plane's white belly. Sections opened up and two sets of rubber tires swung down and locked into place. Angrily, he kicked at a chunk of moss. It fell into the swirling grey water, bobbed to the surface and drifted off downstream.

I could run away and just hide out. He looked around. There might be room here for his little two-man tent. There was plenty of driftwood for a campfire. *They'd never find me.*

His stomach growled. He'd have to figure out something to do for food.

THE EVENING sky was turning purple as Tomi slipped into the lane behind the Tanakas' house. It would be dark soon. Tomorrow was Monday — garbage day. Every back gate sported at least one garbage bin or box. Tomi worked his way slowly up the lane, checking out each one. You never knew.

He went right past his own house with his head turned away, doubling back only when he reached the far street. Eventually, he could no longer avoid it. He stepped reluctantly toward his own gate. There, unnoticed on his first pass, a stack of cardboard boxes was half hidden behind the garbage cans. Tomi pried open the top one, and found old clothing, some of it his father's, some of it a woman's.

The next box held kitchen things: stained baking trays, split and scorched wooden spoons, the old can opener that stopped working ages ago.

Amanda must be throwing out stuff that she thought wasn't worth taking to the new house.

The idea gave him a painful jab in the stomach. Then he opened the last box, and felt a stab of real hurt. Jumbled together were old holiday decorations, a handful of books, a pair of black-and-white china Scottie dogs, some shoes and a purse he recognized as belonging to his mother. Every single item held a memory, reminded him of a specific moment with his family — his *real* family.

It's like she's throwing out my whole past!

Tomi lifted out a battered old cigar box. His fingers caught on the lid and he pulled it open. Inside were a litter of dust bunnies, a scuffed half roll of Tums, several ballpoint pens smeared with sticky blue ink and a half dozen old keys. Tomi's heart leaped at the sight of one of the keys. It was obviously much older than the rest, with a wide head and a round shaft that looked like a miniature wrench socket. Tomi snatched it out of the box and held it up. The fading light glinted on tarnished metal.

He recognized this key. Mom kept it in her jewellery box. Stacy (short for "Anastasia") Tanaka had known very little about her parents or other relatives. Her dad was an Irish–Canadian miner from Ontario who died underground when Stacy was just a toddler; her mother had been born in the Yukon. In family lore, Anastasia's grandmother was a romantic figure from a noble Russian clan, but that was about all anyone knew. She had died long before Stacy was born. Mom always laughed about the mystery and joked that the little key was "all that's left of the Russian family fortune." But it was about the only family heirloom Stacy Tanaka owned, and she'd never, *ever* have just thrown it out.

See, this is what happens! Tomi wished Amanda were there so he could yell right in her face: *You're throwing stuff out and you don't even know it's important!*

Heart pounding, he clutched the key in his fist and went into the house.

"WHERE HAVE you been?" Tomi's father fired the question at him from the living room the moment he stepped in the back door.

It was only six-thirty. *What's the big deal?* "Around," Tomi muttered.

"For *five hours?*"

"I was scouting."

"'Scouting'? What does that mean?"

Tomi headed for his room but Johnny Tanaka caught up with him before he reached the stairs. "What's in your backpack?"

"Stuff," Tomi grunted. "Just stuff I found."

Johnny Tanaka took the backpack from his son's hand and zipped it open. Reaching in, he pulled out a coiled length of stiff nylon cord and placed it on the telephone table. Exploring further he came up with two brass hinges, a pair of metal tubes that slid into each other, a handful of nylon cogs and gears and what looked like a piece of a computer. "You mean dumpster-diving." His voice was hard and scornful. "And this is for ... what?"

"My machine." Even to himself, Tomi sounded defensive.

"Oh, for God's sake," his dad rolled his eyes and heaved a deep sigh. "You don't participate in any sports, you don't have any friends, you're failing in social studies, you're barely making it in English, you won't do your homework, but you've got all the time in the world to build a damn gizmo that does *nothing*. Don't you *get it*, son? You want to be a dumpster-diver your whole life? How often do we need to have this conversation?"

It's not a conversation. Tomi scowled silently. *It's a lecture.* Johnny returned his son's things to the boy's pack and held it out.

"Tomi," his father tried again, in a softer voice. "You know I don't have anything against this ... hobby of yours. It shows some real engineering talent. But talent's no help if you don't have the marks to get into college. Your mom and I —"

"She's *not* my mom!" Tomi interrupted.

"I'm sorry. I know that. She's not your mom. But she does care about you and so does Rory. They both just want to be your friends, if you'd just give them a chance."

Tomi frowned. *How about they just* not *be my friends instead,* he wanted to say.

His father's tone was very gentle now. "You know it's going

to have to come apart sooner or later. We can't leave it here when we move."

"Then maybe we shouldn't move!" Tomi gave his father a scorching look and turned to take the stairs two at a time.

At the top of the flight he spun left. A hallway ran back along the stairwell. One door had a big yellow KEEP OUT sign taped to it. Tomi jerked it open and slipped into his darkened bedroom. He let his backpack slide to the floor, sagged his body against the door and released a long breath. *Why are you making me do this? If you want to make a new family with the Bobbsey Twins*, be my guest. *But why drag* me *into it?*

He took two steps forward and yanked hard on the little plastic zebra that hung from a string in the middle of the room. Dozens of tiny lights popped on, casting weird shadows over the walls amid a maze of spokes and stalks and wheels and pulleys that filled half the room. The free-form junk sculpture arched right up to the ceiling over Tomi's bed, creating a sort of a cave around the bed and his desk.

Tomi tapped his hand on a button and a whir came from beneath the bed. A chain started to move, running up and around a gear, which was actually the front sprocket of Tomi's old bike. As the chain crawled over its teeth, the gear began to turn. A long rod ran through the centre of the gear; now it began to turn as well. At the far end of the rod, a lever began popping up and down. With each upward motion it opened a little gate at the bottom of a jar of marbles, setting one marble free to run down a length of garden hose.

With a creak and a sigh and a gentle rattle, the whole machine came to life like a miniature, animated Jungle Gym cum roller coaster. Every lever and gear and cog began to turn or spin or lift or bob. Some parts rocked back and forth. Others waggled and pumped, looking like robots riding unicycles. A succession of billiard balls rolled and turned down a slalom track, clicking open gates and reversing other gears as they fell, only to be carried back to the beginning again up a little elevator made from pieces of a motorized toy truck.

He crawled under the canopy of moving parts and lay back on his bed, staring up. The machine was Tomi's pride and joy. It was what he thought about and planned at his desk all day at school, the reason for his scouting expeditions and very nearly an obsession. He'd started it years ago, when he was first old enough to put a couple of pieces of Lego together. But the time and attention he lavished on his mechanical creation had really spiked since that night three years ago. *"Mr. Tanaka, I'm so sorry. There's been an accident."*

Tomi brushed the back of his sleeve over his face. With a start he realized that his clenched left hand still held the little antique key. He opened his fist and held the key up. Someone had taken a lot of trouble to make this key: a thin tracery of something that looked like gold was inlaid in the silvery metal.

Tomi pulled a fine chain from around his neck and over his head. A little oblong of green jade hung on it, a good-luck pendant Dad had brought home from a flight to Hong Kong.

Tomi opened the clasp on the chain and slipped off the jade. He threaded the chain through the hole in the key, redid the clasp and returned the chain to his neck.

He lay back again on the pillow. His deep brown eyes were drained of tension now as he ran them over each part of the whimsical machine above him. The tightness in his gut had given up its hold. He breathed lightly again.

He watched an old baby-carriage wheel spin on its axle. *If I put a longer rod there,* he thought, *I could start a whole new section up over the dresser.*

Two

THE DOG

ROWFF! The white dog barked a second time. The animal stood at eager attention, skimpy white tail stiff and quivering slightly with anticipation. Its small black eyes were locked on a blonde woman wearing a print dress and an apron. The woman was methodically spooning the steaming, sweetly fragrant contents of a large bowl into a row of pie shells on a counter. Behind her, a younger version of herself was sitting at a table, making notes from a book. She had a cup of coffee and a half-eaten muffin before her.

Whatever the woman was spooning out was thick and sticky, dropping off her wooden spoon in slow, lazy, heavy dollops. To the dog it smelled as sharp and sweet and wild as the green-roofed caverns of berry canes in the long days of summer.

A clear bead of saliva formed at the corner of a pink-fleshed and white-furred lip. It grew and sparkled in the light. Then again, *rowff*, the bark bursting out with such energy and impatience that the dog's two front feet lifted off the ground and the drop of saliva flew across the room.

"All right! It's coming! This is the last one," the woman scolded. She scraped the spoon around the inside of the bowl to gather just enough thick, syrupy fruit to fill the last pie shell. When she was done, the bowl was still streaked and puddled with bright red filling.

"There you go, you silly old thing," the woman said at last, bending to place the bowl on the floor in front of the dog.

With the faintest of grunts, the white dog dashed forward and buried its head in the bowl. For the next several minutes the kitchen echoed with the sound of pottery scraping across the linoleum floor and the eager slap of the long, pink tongue as it methodically explored the bowl's rim and inside surface.

Suddenly, the white dog raised its thick head. Its two sharply pointed ears turned this way and that, as though casting about for a sound momentarily heard and then lost again. Pink stains smudged the white chin and jowls nearly as far back as those alert ears.

The dog gave itself a shake. The motion began at the heavy white head, making the pink-shelled ears flap like flags in the wind. It worked its way back past grimy shoulders and scrawny hips until the dog's tail was a blur and its two back feet skittered over the floor. With a final snort, the dog composed itself and trotted to the door.

With a single forceful nudge of its high-bridged nose, the dog shoved open the screen and slipped outside. A spring pulled the door closed again with a slap.

The older woman leaned down to retrieve the bowl. "Now that's strange," she said, straightening up again.

"What's that?" The younger one looked up from her book.

"Look." The first woman held the bowl out for the second to examine. One whole side was still heavily streaked with red filling and nearly a third of the puddle in the bottom remained untouched.

"Maybe a boat's coming in," the young woman mused.

"I guess so," the older one answered. "But even then, she doesn't usually leave anything behind."

"I hope she's not sick."

"Me too."

THE WHITE DOG paused for barely a moment, then turned and set off down the street. It certainly didn't look sick. White feet flashed back and forth beneath its ample little body. Its ears were turned forward, its skimpy tail held high. Now and again the black nose flared and the deep muzzle lifted at some passing scent. But not for an instant did the dog break its pace.

It trotted steadily along as though late for an appointment, passing between several houses and following the curve of a road that led out of town and up a hill, where green walls of forest descended to banks on either side.

At length the dog trotted across the broad timbers of a bridge. From below came the chuckling sound of water flowing. Then the animal turned away from the road and followed a rutted track. At last it ducked into the deep shadow between two tall, square stacks of heavy timber, and disappeared from sight.

Three

REPORT CARD

TOMI'S CLOCK radio clicked on. The raspy rock lyrics of his favourite band filled the darkened room: "It's hard to say it, time to say it … goodbye … goodbye."

His hand swept out and banged down on the snooze button. *Don't remind me!*

For weeks now, Dad had been dropping warnings that "D-Day" — Departure Day — was looming just as soon as school ended. For just as long, Tomi had been ducking the obvious. He was no closer to being packed for the Great Tanaka Family Honeymoon today than on the day it was announced. He'd also blocked out every heavy hint that he should start taking apart his machine. He'd even added a few pieces.

But now the last day of school was actually here. D-Day minus one. It felt like the last day of Tomi's life.

There was a knock on the door.

"Who is it?"

"Me." His father opened the door and stuck his head in. He wore his pilot's uniform. Light from the hall glinted off the gold bars on his epaulettes.

"What?" Tomi said.

"I hate to start the day this way," his dad said. "But the clock's run out. I've got a layover flight. The agent comes tonight to get the house listing signed and tomorrow we leave for the airport hotel. We *all* leave." He ran his eyes over the wires and rods and gears arching across his son's bed. "Son, I've given you every chance I can. But if this thing's still here by five o'clock," he sighed like someone who hated what he had to say, "then it's coming down — with or without your help. Are we clear?"

Tomi rolled over in bed and pulled the covers over his head.

His father sighed again. "I love you, kiddo," he said.

Tomi heard the door close. He rolled onto his back and gazed up at the tracery of wheels and axles, cams and cogs that reached from wall to wall. Each piece held a memory: he knew where he'd found it, and what had been going on at the time. How long had he been building the machine? It seemed like forever. Since he'd been, what, seven? Six? Almost half his life.

He remembered how delighted Mom had been when he first showed off how it worked. She'd laughed and clapped her hands and told him what a crazy, wonderful invention it was. And now that — the word that came to him rhymed with "witch" — was throwing Mom's favourite things out like they were garbage. And he was supposed to wreck the most important thing in his life so they could all go on this stupid trip.

He felt hot tears come and rolled back onto his stomach,

burying his sobs in the deep pillow. *I won't. I just won't.*

The radio clicked on again. The morning rock-jock was laughing his deep, nothing-ever-bothers-me laugh, riffing on the last day of school: "And now the top ten reasons for not bringing your report card home."

Oh, jeez. Tomi's heart managed to sink even lower.

"ABOUT TIME!" his grandmother greeted him twenty minutes later. "I was about to call the police to report a missing boy." She planted a bowl in front of his place at the table and moved the cereal boxes within reach. "Orange or cranberry?"

"Whatever ... cranberry," he sulked.

"Hey, *ototo-chan*," Rory greeted him over a cup of green tea and an open textbook. Rory was sixteen and still writing final exams.

Tomi scowled. His stepsister's eagerness to learn snippets of Japanese, and the easy way she'd fallen into referring to him with the Japanese word for "little brother," really ticked him off.

"If you don't watch out, Rory's going to speak better Japanese than you do!" Obaacha teased, putting a glass of cranberry juice near Tomi's cereal bowl.

"Fine by me," muttered Tomi under his breath. He lifted his spoon and dug into the fruit and flakes.

Rory leaned forward, narrowing her blue eyes to examine him more closely. "Hey, li'l bro'," she said. "You're looking a little puffy 'round the eyes. You haven't been ...?"

Tomi bowed his head in shame and embarrassment,

raising one hand to hide the top of his face. "None of your business," he muttered.

Rory shot a glance at the older woman then brought her gaze back to Tomi. Her eyes softened and when she spoke again her voice was gentle. "Hey, Tomi, if you look, you might just find a donut 'round the hole. This trip could be a lot of fun. See some neat places, stay in nice hotels. Mom says we'll probably fly business class on the long hauls. What's not to like?"

You! Tomi sniped silently. *And weird food ... and people I don't know ... and languages I can't speak and no TV or computer ... no machine.*

Obaacha placed a brightly decorated lunch box at Tomi's elbow. "Rory's right, you know," she said, cradling a steaming cup of *cha* in her hands as she sat between them. "Your grandfather dreamed all his life about taking the kind of trip you're grumbling about. Hong Kong, Paris, Rio de Janeiro. He read all the travel pages, all the famous journals, and he'd always say, 'One day.' Then one day he just ran out of time and the only city he'd ever seen outside of Lethbridge was Calgary."

"Then why didn't he go?" Tomi said, giving his words a sarcastic edge.

"Because he *worked*," his grandmother answered him evenly. "To put food on the table." She raised her thin eyebrows. "And to give your father choices he didn't have." She sipped from her cup. "And because people couldn't always just pick up and go, the way you kids can today. When *I* was thirteen, I wasn't even *allowed* in Vancouver!"

"The 'big bad city'?" Rory teased gently.

"More like 'big bad government,'" the old woman said.

"Don't get her started!" Tomi snapped. He'd heard all about how the police had rounded up the Japanese when Obaacha was a little girl, sending them away to concentration camps in the Interior. It was all so much ancient history, as far as he was concerned.

"If you forget your past, you forget who you are." His grandmother fixed Tomi with a severe look.

Not now, Obaacha. The old woman's insistence on knowing your family roots often irked him. It still hurt to recall the one time he'd seen a serious fight between Obaacha and his mother. It was over how little Mom knew, or seemed to care, about her ancestors.

Like anyone cares who I am anyway, Tomi thought.

Rory tried to change the subject. "Isn't today your last school day? *That's* gotta be a good thing!"

Tomi shot her a scorching look.

"Your father always liked the last day of school," Obaacha said. "Because he found out how well he'd done in all his subjects." She gave Tomi an expectant glance.

Tomi's temper boiled over. "Well, I'm not *him!*" he yelled. He shoved his lunch into his pack, pushing aside his mp3 player and the little tool kit that he took everywhere with him. He bolted out the door.

SOMEWHERE inside the beige brick building an electronic bell trilled. Thirty seconds later the first of several sets of double doors burst open, releasing a wave of twelve- to fourteen-year-olds bubbling over with a new sense of freedom.

Well, most of them. Tomi Tanaka's face wore a closed, sullen look as he emerged, shrugging his backpack over one slumped shoulder.

"Shoulda studied, huh?"

Eh? He squinted into the sun and spotted Rory.

"How'd you know?"

"It's all over your face," she laughed. "Don't ever play poker, kid, they'll eat you alive. So, how bad is it?"

Tomi swallowed hard. "I flunked history."

Rory's lips pursed.

"And geography."

"You're not serious? Geography *and* history? Your dad flies all over the map. Obaacha's a total history freak. Ohmigod, did you, like, fail the whole year?"

"No!" Tomi glared. Then he shrugged. "Barely. My math's pretty good. It pulled my average up. If I want a better mark I can go to summer school. History in July and geography in August." He watched Rory's face.

The older girl's blue eyes grew wide as she took in what that meant. "Oh *ototo-chan*, you are soooo dead."

"You guys can still go! I can go to summer school by myself."

"As if!" She gave him one of her patented I'm-sixteen-and-you're-not looks. Then her nose wrinkled. "Anyway, you'd really rather do that than travel the world first class?"

"I'd rather not do any of it!" Tomi exploded. "Why do I

have to learn this stuff anyhow? Whatever happened way before I was born has got nothing to do with me. I just want to be left alone."

"Well, you're going about *that* the right way," his stepsister said.

"You're a big help."

"Hey, Tomi," Rory fixed him with a straight-on look. "I know you hate me, I get it that you're pissed about what happened to your mom. But at least you got to *know* your mom." She threw her head back, looked skyward a moment and let out a long breath. She met Tomi's eyes again. Now she wore a been-there-threw-away-the-T-shirt expression. "Look Tomi, stuff happens. You do what you can with it." Rory waved at a group of older teens gathered around someone's car. She looked back at him, her eyes kinder. "You're going to be okay, Tomi. But not 'til you decide to be. Anyway, catch you later!" She turned away to join her friends.

"If anyone asks, you didn't see me," Tomi called after her.

Rory gave him a thumbs-up.

THE SUN was sinking low toward the mountains north of the city by the time Tomi turned the corner into the alley. It was the time of day in Vancouver when the light from over the Strait of Georgia seemed to kiss everything it touched. With a catch in his throat, Tomi longed to open the door and hear his mother's voice, singing along to one of her old CDs — Springsteen maybe, or that Lightfoot guy.

Coming up to the fence gate he frowned at the pile of boxes in the garage. *The witch must be throwing more stuff out.* On any other day, Tomi would have been on the boxes in a flash, picking through them for anything he could use. Today he couldn't get his heart into it.

Then he saw something poking out of the top box and blood roared in his ears. It had taken him months to get that section of the machine right, so that the five little Transformer superhero guys flew around just so when the old dishwasher timer kicked in. Anger and hurt boiled like acid in his gut.

With a pounding heart he tore open the next box. Like the first one, it was filled with motionless fragments of his marvellous invention. With each piece he recognized, the wound in his chest seemed to rip open a little wider, until he couldn't bear to search any further.

A sound brought his head up. Amanda stood at the door to the house, another box in her arms. Her face showed surprise, and worry. "Tomi! I'm so sorry, Tomi. But I couldn't find you and the agent's coming and you hadn't —"

"You!" He threw the word that rhymed with "witch" in her face like a rock. "Go on! Go on your damn trip! I hope you don't *ever* come back!"

Lost in a storm of hurt and anger, Tomi turned and ran down the alley.

THE SPICY SMELL of fresh-cut cedar brought Tomi back to the here and now with a jolt. He must have walked faster or longer than he'd been aware. He was already at the River Side Lumber Yard. Overhead, gulls wheeled and screamed.

He thought of his secret spot with its soothing view out over the grey-green river. It was the perfect place to hide out. *No one'll ever find me there.*

He jumped the shallow ditch that ran along River Road and climbed the far bank, squeezing through the gap between the fence and the first row of stacked lumber.

Something white flashed against the dark wood off to his right. He turned but was too late to get a good look. Tomi's sneakers crunched on the tarry gravel that surrounded the cubed stacks of sawn timber. He looked down each alley between the stacks for whatever had made the white flash.

There! Oh, it was only a dog, a white dog. Kind of a medium-sized dog, with a wide head, upraised ears like sharp triangles and a thin white tail. Tomi looked around for the dog's owner. He couldn't remember there ever being security dogs here before.

No one appeared. Tomi and the white dog seemed to be alone in the sprawling yard of scented sawn cedar. And was there something wrong with the dog? Tomi could see what looked like blood on its face and forequarter. Was it hurt?

The dog hung back in the shadows between two rows of lumber. Cautiously, Tomi stepped toward it. Head down, the dog turned and retreated between the stacks. Tomi thought he saw it limping on the sharp gravel. It didn't seem dangerous, anyway. All else forgotten, he followed the white dog farther into the cool, sharp-smelling shadows.

For the next several minutes, the wounded dog seemed to play a game of hide and seek among the stacked wood. Tomi glimpsed its white coat just long enough to follow the animal deeper into the maze of timber, only to lose it again around another corner. Past a row of boxcar shapes protected under white plastic, he stepped out into a long, sunlit alley, lined on the far side with more piles of heavy timber. Looking along it, he saw the skimpy white tail disappear once more into a narrow side-opening. Running to catch up, Tomi found the spot, a skinny gap between the rough ends of one pile of timber and the next.

There was barely room to squeeze through. Tomi turned sideways and bent into an s-shape to keep from snagging his backpack against the wood. "You dumb dog," he muttered as he felt the end of a plank scrape his shin. "You don't appreciate this, I know you don't."

An awkward moment later, he came out again into bright sun. This time, the dog hadn't gone on. It sat right there on the gravel, not two metres from his feet. It was facing him, mouth open and soft pink tongue draped across impressive ivory teeth and pink-and-black lips. The dog might as well have been laughing out loud at him.

"Good dog," Tomi murmured, holding out one hand and taking a step toward the animal. Now he could see that "it" was actually a "she." And she wasn't hurt after all. Up close, the stuff on the dog's face and shoulders was the wrong colour for blood — more like raspberry jam.

A gentle *whoosh* sounded somewhere to his left.

Without any warning Tomi felt himself yanked down roughly.

He landed awkwardly and painfully on his bum on the gravel. He hadn't even been able to reach out to break his fall. Invisible hands had tied his arms to his sides with a hard, brown rope.

Four

THE LUMBER YARD

POINTY GRAVEL ground through Tomi's jeans into his behind. From his painful position, he looked around, craning his neck to find the source of whatever had pinned his arms to his sides.

Over his shoulder a tall figure stepped out from between two stacks of lumber and carefully pulled on the rope, keeping the loop tight over his arms.

Oh, jeez. Security!

He squinted into the sun, but didn't see the crisp white shirt or military-style shoulder flashes of the security guards at the mall. This person wore a skirt. It was made of some kind of soft leather patterned with beads. Below the skirt was a pair of well-scuffed black rubber boots. Above it was a no-nonsense shirt of sturdy blue material, and above that, a face tanned as leathery as the skirt. Fog-grey eyes examined him suspiciously beneath salt and pepper hair pulled into a bun.

With even deeper shock, Tomi realized that jutting up from behind the woman's left shoulder was the handle of a rifle.

The woman stopped several metres away from him. The sun was behind her, making her face hard to read.

She kept the rope between them tight. The loop bit into Tomi's arms just above his elbows.

"You," she called out in a strong voice that was a long way from friendly. "You. Jap?"

Tomi squinted up at her in confusion.

"You hear me? *Nihon-go*? Nippon? Hey?"

He found his voice at last. "No, I'm Canadian!"

The woman frowned. "Don't look Canuck to me," she said crossly. "Look like one of those Japanese they got working down at the cannery."

"What cannery?" Tomi's face burned and he felt his temper rise at the woman's tone, and the offensive word. "Anyway, who are *you*? And what's with the lasso?" Shifting his weight, he got his knees under him, ready to get to his feet.

Before he could, the woman gave the rope a hard yank. Tomi hit the ground again, this time on his side. Gravel scraped his cheeks.

A swampy, sewer-breath smell smothered him. He had almost forgotten the white dog. Now the thick white head loomed over Tomi's face, powerful jaws opened wide. Tomi flinched.

But the crushing bite never came. Instead, he felt the warm, wet lap of a soft pink tongue over his cheeks and forehead.

"What's this, Patsy Ann?" the woman said in a new voice. "Don't tell me this is a friend of yours." Moving closer, she looked down, examining the prone figure at her feet more closely. "He's young enough, anyway," she added, seeming to speak to herself. She stepped back a pace or two and let the rope go slack. "Right then, on your feet," she said.

Tomi shrugged off the loosened rope and scrambled to his feet, fending off the pink tongue as he did so. By the time he regained his footing the woman had dropped her rope and backed another step away. Now the rifle was cradled in her dry brown hands, barrel pointed at the ground. She held it like someone who'd held a rifle before.

Panting, the dog sat at Tomi's feet, settling her white haunches heavily against his right sneaker.

"What are you doing then, skulking around my yard?" she said.

"I wasn't *skulking!*" Tomi responded. "I cut through here all the time to get to the river." The woman's eyes narrowed. "But then I saw this dog," he nodded down at the animal. "I thought she was hurt, so I followed her to … to try to help her."

The woman's head tipped to one side and her brows came together. She leaned forward to look at the dog at Tomi's feet, then straightened. "Hmph," she huffed. "Never seen real blood maybe. That looks more like pie preserves, hey Patsy Ann?" She considered a moment. "So, you off a fish boat then? One of the Jap boats over here after our salmon?"

Tomi felt himself bristle again, along with a new feeling that sent a chill up the back of his neck. Obaacha had made sure her grandchildren knew the shameful story of how the Canadian government had seized every fishing boat belonging to Japanese pioneers.

But that's gotta be … well, how old is Obaacha? Like, more than half a century ago! This lady wasn't nearly as old as Obaacha. Maybe she was crazy. Escaped from some mental home, armed and dangerous. "No, ma'am," he said, speaking very carefully now. "My dad's a pilot. I live just over there, past River Road."

His look followed his gesture, and shock struck again. Tomi squeezed his eyes shut and shook his head. He opened them slowly but the view hadn't changed. Looming above the stacked lumber he had come through barely five minutes ago was a green wall of trees that rose steeply toward a distant blue peak. For a moment, the gravel beneath Tomi's feet seemed to give way and he wondered whether he was going crazy himself.

The mountains across the harbour, north of Vancouver, were like this. But they were miles away. He couldn't possibly have walked *that* far, even zoned out as he'd been in his black mood. Down by the Fraser River, the land spread out flat on either side of the flowing stream. Or it was *supposed* to.

Tomi's mouth opened, but nothing came out of it.

The woman regarded him closely beneath furrowed brows. Now it seemed like she thought perhaps *he* was crazy.

A sharp bark broke the strained silence. The white dog nuzzled Tomi's thigh, then rose and trotted over to the woman, lifting her black nose to nuzzle the tanned fingers cradling the rifle stock.

The woman looked from dog to boy. Her brows knitted like someone trying to decipher a foreign language. "If you're not Japanese, you Indian maybe?" she asked. "What? Tsimsh'an?

Haida? You're tall enough to be Haida," she suggested.

Tomi recognized the names. They belonged to some of the First Nations who lived on the Pacific coast long before the first pioneers from Japan or anywhere else. He sighed heavily. *Whatever.* "My great-great — four or five greats ago — grandparents came from Japan. On my dad's side," he explained. "Mom's, well ... Okay that's a little sketchier. What's it matter, anyway? *I'm Canadian!* Japanese-something–Canadian."

The dog barked again, skinny white tail whipping back and forth. She pushed her berry-stained muzzle against the rifle again.

After a moment the woman shook her head, then swung the gun back over her shoulder on its strap. Tomi let out a breath.

"I expect I'll regret this," she muttered. Louder she added, "Right then, off you go, back to ... wherever you're from. Just don't let me see you 'round my wood yard again, or I won't be so tolerant the next time!" She kept her eye on him while she began coiling the rope in her hands.

Once more Tomi opened his mouth, but couldn't find words. He hitched his pack higher onto his shoulders and stepped away from the neat rows of stacked lumber. The white dog trotted out a little way ahead and turned back to look at him. With no better thought in mind, Tomi followed her.

TOMI WALKED steadily away from the lumber yard toward where the river must be. Struggling to get his bearings, he did a quick 360 while he walked. In the brief moment he faced the woman, he saw her still watching him, both hands now on her coiled lasso.

Turning to face forward again, he saw an opening in the trees where water puddled in deep tire ruts. Trucks must have driven into the yard here, loaded with heavy logs.

The river's got to be around here somewhere, he reasoned.

The Fraser ran like a moat across the suburb where the Tanakas lived. If you walked toward the distant mountains you literally couldn't miss it. Tomi thought he must have lost his sense of direction while he was chasing the dog around the maze of lumber. This must be some back side of the lumber yard he didn't know. *Wild security though.*

Through clumps of brush and young fir trees, he caught the glitter of sunlight on waves. On most days as clear as this one, when Tomi looked past the river, he could see a blue line of distant peaks along the horizon. Sometimes he could even see lights twinkle at the ski runs on their summits.

But this water looked too blue, too wide and too distant to be the river. And the mountain beyond it seemed too close. Following the green slopes with his eyes skyward to the summit, Tomi searched for the white splash of the snowboard slope where he'd gone with Dad and the Olsen twins — "Our last taste of Vancouver for a while," Dad had joked.

Why couldn't he see the slopes?

The short track led away from the lumber yard to a road

that might have been a serious street somewhere if it had been paved. *A new subdivision going in?* Tomi looked for a street sign but none offered any help. The dog was ignoring him now, her white nose sending up snuffling noises from the tall weeds where the track met the road ... or street ... or whatever.

To his right, Tomi saw that the way led downhill. Reasoning that downhill must lead to water — and therefore the river — he turned in that direction.

He came to the river about five minutes later. Or rather, he came to *a* river. But this dark stream was barely wider than the back alley at home. The road crossed over it on an old-fashioned timber trestle. It was a far cry from the broad sweep of the Fraser River, wide enough for ocean-going ships to travel on, or the soaring modern arches that were the only way across it.

But this creek must run into the Fraser, he thought. If he stayed on this road, sooner or later he'd have to spot a landmark — any landmark — that he knew.

He turned at the sound of a car engine behind him. A moment later Tomi stepped quickly to the side of the gravel as an ancient-looking pickup truck roared past, leaving a cloud of white dust hanging in the air. He listened as the sound — more like a Quad or lawn mower than a truck — faded away downhill.

It was then that he first noticed how quiet it was. There was the occasional cry of a bird, the continual low creak of insects, the sound that trees make when they dance with the wind. Now and again the wind also brought the rumble of heavy machinery from somewhere a long way off. But even when Tomi stood stock still, he heard no traffic noise, no cars moving in herds from stoplight to stoplight, no truck diesels winding up through their gears, no muted *thumpa-thumpa* from an over-amped car stereo, no sirens — none of the usual suburban soundtrack.

The weird, tummy-turning sensation he'd had back at the lumber yard returned.

How long had he been walking? He pitched his head back to look up. The tingle gathered in a spot behind his neck. Surely the sun was getting low when he'd got back to the house. Low enough for the beams to shine right in the corner where his machine lay in boxes.

So how can it still be way up there? *What time* was *it?* He checked his watch. 7:47. That couldn't be. He hadn't even gotten home 'til 7:30. The blowup with Amanda had to have occurred an hour ago, easily. He shook his wrist. *Dead battery, probably.* No more cars or trucks came by, and he kept walking.

He turned a corner and got the feeling again.

Only this time it came on like a full-body shower in something cold and creepy off a DVD nightmare.

Not that anything in the view before him was obviously creepy. Ahead, the gravel road ran a short distance down an open slope to a medium-sized town. Late afternoon sun cast clear, warm light over streets of small houses. A few buildings stood three or four stories above their neighbours. These were brick, and resembled the old buildings in Vancouver's historic Gastown district more than any of the city's new cool glass towers. Beyond them, blue water stretched away to either side. On the far side of the water was a mountain.

A causeway cut across the water to the far shore. Toy cars and trucks crawled along it in the distance. A handful of boats traced white wakes across the blue harbour. One of them slowly pulled a brown raft of logs behind it. Between buildings, Tomi could make out the funnels and high profiles of three or four ships that must be tied up for unloading at the harbourfront.

These elements were all familiar to him. He could see any of them on any day in Vancouver.

Except that Tomi was absolutely, totally, completely, right-down-to-his-toenails, *ohmigod how can this be happening* dead certain he had never, *ever,* seen this place before in his entire life.

Now his stomach really did churn. Abruptly, he collapsed against the high dirt bank.

The white dog trotted over to his side and sat down, resting her broad head on his knee. *Jeez, what's your head* made *of, dog? Cement?*

Tomi leaned over to look at the dog. Her eyes were small almonds in her none-too-clean white face. But what Tomi saw when he looked more deeply almost took him aback. In the dark depths seemed to glow a warm, reassuring intelligence.

It's going to be okay! that look said.

What did that crazy lady call her?

"Hey, Patsy Ann," he said. He rubbed his hand over her head, ruffling behind her erect ears. The dog turned into his hand, pushing closer. He bent close to her ear. "Patsy Ann," Tomi whispered. "Something tells me we aren't in Kansas anymore."

The hot pink tongue lapped out and swabbed a wet kiss on his hand.

Tomi sat there for a long time, trying to think. Had he hit his head? *No, not even when the crazy lady lassoed me.* Eaten something that someone might have put something in? *Not unless Obaacha spiked my ham-and-cheese on six-grain.* Was he really asleep and only dreaming all this? He raised one arm to his mouth and bit down hard on a soft part. *Yeouw.* Surely you couldn't feel that much pain in a dream.

Anyway, this just didn't *feel* like a dream. For several long minutes he stared hard at the dog, half hoping to see her turn into something else, the way people do in dreams. Right now, he'd even be happy to see her turn into Amanda. But the white dog remained stubbornly a dog. With a twinge Tomi realized how happy he would be right now to see Rory come down the road and hear her teasing, tirelessly cheerful voice.

But the road remained empty.

He shivered. Looking up and around him, he realized that the shadow of the distant mountain had crept up over the road as the sun slipped behind it. *I've never felt cold in a dream either,* Tomi thought.

Okay, like Dad says, be rational! *Think it through.*

The lumber yard. That's where things had gone seriously sideways.

Pushing himself back to his feet Tomi set off again. Turning his back on ... wherever the heck it was ... he retraced his steps up the road. Patsy Ann fell in at his heels.

The ascent was steeper than it had seemed coming down. Even in the cool air of deepening dusk, Tomi began to sweat. When he crossed back over the trestle bridge, the water below was a menacing black rush in the shadows.

They came to the rutted lane that led to the lumber yard. Tomi slowed and moved into the shadow of the trees along one side. He didn't want to encounter the rifle-toting lady again, thank you very much. But this was where he'd last been even remotely sure where he was. If he could just slip back into the maze of lumber stacks unnoticed and unlassoed, maybe he could find his way through whatever space-warp led back to River Road.

As he neared the rows of sawn lumber, Tomi crouched lower into the weeds that lined the track. Peering ahead, he could see no sign of the tall woman with the gun and the attitude. In a low rush, he sprinted across the gravel and slipped gratefully into the shadows between two tall stacks of lumber.

Again, he found himself squeezing sideways in the narrow space to make his way. *There was an alley. The wood was covered in white plastic,* he remembered. If he could just find that alley again.

He followed one narrow, dark, cedar-spiced crevice until it ended at a wall of raw logs lying in neat stacks like so many giant telephone poles. He turned right, following the stack until it flowed into another just like it.

Where the two stacks met, there was room — barely — between the logs in one pile and those in the next for a kid to manoeuvre. Between Tomi's feet, Patsy Ann squeezed through a narrow chasm where one huge log lay nearly touching the next.

There were more stacks of lumber on the other side of the gap. More dead ends and lefts and rights through neat stacks of sweet-smelling sawn wood. The route led only to more miniature mountain ridges of logs, volcano heaps of sawdust and rough piles of bark slashings. Tomi looked up. Beyond rose the damn mountain *that shouldn't be there at all!*

He cocked his head and listened. How long had it been since he'd heard a plane go by? He couldn't remember. Had there been any since his encounter with the crazy lady? He shook his head. *No jets for … what? A couple hours?*

That just never happened on River Road. A nervous chill came over him. Was the airport shut down? They only did that if there was a really big threat, or a crash. His stomach clenched, the way it always did when he heard a plane was in trouble. Especially when Dad was flying.

He shivered. *All right, which way?* In the deep shadows between the raw stacks of cut wood, the sharp smell of sap was strong. It was almost cold. He followed one lane to another, then another, but they all seemed to lead nowhere.

He had lost all notion of where anything was — the river, the crazy lady, River Side Lumber, South Fraser Intermediate, home. Something faint and wet caught and burst in his face, and he reached up to wipe the cobweb from his cheeks.

For the first time, Tomi began to feel a sensation that he didn't want to call by name. He tasted something nasty in his mouth. *Where the hell* am I?

He turned a dank corner and saw, against the wall of yet another alley, a warm light gleaming on damp red planks. He sprinted to the break in the stacks where the light was shining through. He stepped out into the light and emerged on the far side of the lumber yard.

But the sight he'd been hoping for — the streetlight over the ditch with its buzz-cut bulrushes, the comforting traffic along River Road and, beyond it, the street that ran past school toward 24th Avenue, where the Tanakas' house was the fourth on the left — was not what he saw in front of him.

He stood in a floodlit gravelled yard. A treed slope rose steeply to one side. Looking up, Tomi could see where the shadow cast by the distant hills hadn't quite reached the top of the mountain. Up there the sunlit trees glowed a warm green. To his right, a low shingle roof cast deeper shade over some kind of machinery. To the left, two dark windows with small glass panes stared from a moss-covered wall half hidden under overhanging trees.

Facing him was a larger and prouder structure: a fine-looking house made of oiled logs, with a high slate roof and yellow light shining through half open windows. From inside came the sound of music, an old-fashioned band like the ones Obaacha sometimes listened to.

A soft weight shouldered heavily against Tomi's leg, making him stagger. He frowned down at the white dog.

Patsy Ann barked, the sound startlingly loud in the quiet yard. Tomi's heart raced. "Hush! She'll hear you." *Crazy lady.*

The white dog trotted a few steps toward the house, then turned and looked back at Tomi, dark eyes meeting dark eyes. Again she barked, the sharp noise echoing off the hard wall of stacked lumber behind him.

Oh, jeez ... "Hush!" He was almost begging her now. "Be quiet, can't you?"

The dog erupted in a quick four-legged jump and midair twist that left her facing the house. The pointed ears were turned toward Tomi, the skimpy tail quivering with excitement.

Yet again the dog barked. And again. With each outburst the tense white form seemed to pop off the ground. The door of the house flew open. Silhouetted against the warm lamplight Tomi recognized the same tall figure that had stared down the length of a lasso at him earlier in the day.

Five

PRISONER

"PATSY ANN!" the woman said in surprise. In two strides she crossed the porch. Looking past the dog, she saw the boy and frowned. "You again!" she said. "I thought I —"

Another sharp bark cut her off.

"I ... I'm sorry lady," Tomi stammered. "I didn't mean to come back here, really! I was just trying to find my way back ... back home. And somehow I got turned around ... or something. Then Patsy Ann started barking and ..." his voice trailed off.

The woman stepped down off the porch and tipped her head to one side as she examined the boy more closely. Then her eyes dropped to the dog. Patsy Ann barked again, the sound gruff and insistent. The woman's face didn't become exactly friendly, just more ... thoughtful. "You're lost?"

"Yes, ma'am."

"Nowhere to go for the night?"

Tomi's stomach lurched, but the answer was obvious. "No. I guess I don't. Unless ..."

"What?"

"Could I maybe use your phone?"

The woman frowned in thought a moment, then agreed.

"Let's go to the office," she said, directing Tomi toward a small white building across the yard.

Inside was a counter and behind it, several desks. The desks looked unusual and the whole place seemed a little forlorn. But there was a phone on the counter: a funky retro handset, black, on a slender stand. When Tomi stepped up to it he was taken aback. The phone had no buttons. He looked back at the woman. She was standing at the door watching him closely, the white dog at her feet. "Um … how do you dial this thing?"

"Dial?"

"The number."

"Just pick it up. Tell whoever's on who it is you want to reach." The tall woman gave him a bemused expression, as though he'd asked when the next cow was flying out.

He picked up the handset on its heavy black cord and held it to his ear. There was a tone and a moment later a female voice chirped, "Operator. How may I help you?"

"I'd like to make a call."

"What number?"

"604-555-1723."

"604?" the operator repeated doubtfully. When Tomi said nothing she apologized, "I'm sorry, that's not a number. I can't connect you."

Whaddaya mean, not a number? That queasy, *Twilight Zone* feeling was back. "Yes it is. That's my number."

"Well, if it doesn't begin with 'Kodiak' or 'Glacier,' I'm sorry, it's not a number I can reach."

"Really." *Where the hell am I?* "Okay, thanks." He hung up the phone and turned to the woman in the door. He shrugged. "I guess I can't reach them right now."

"Them?"

"My folks."

The woman's doubtful look returned, deeper than ever. "And you're telling me that Patsy Ann brought you here? Twice?"

"Yeah, I guess she did."

The grey eyes glanced down at the white dog, then back up at the boy. Looking past him, the woman searched the gathering dark beyond the window glass. "I must be losing my mind," she muttered. "You can sleep in the bunkhouse. Only 'cause Patsy Ann thinks you're jake."

Jake? Jake who?

The woman tipped her head for Tomi to follow her. They left the office and walked briskly across the yard to the small building in the shadow of the trees. Reaching into a pocket, she pulled out a ring of keys and selected one. A moment later, she held the door open for Tomi.

He stepped inside. Patsy Ann followed on his heels.

The place reminded Tomi of the time he and Dad hiked overnight into the mountains and slept in a back-country trekker's cabin. The room smelled of old, cold ashes, of closed windows and damp bedding, of mice. Wooden chairs sat around a plain wooden table in the middle of the bare plank floor. Against the walls were three sets of double bunks.

The woman struck a match and lifted the glass of an old-fashioned wick lamp. A moment later a warm light filled the room, along with an oily, smoky smell.

"There's bedrolls in the trunk." She nodded to where it stood under a window. Turning at the door she looked down at Patsy Ann. "Well, what about you?"

Patsy Ann flopped onto her tummy beside the table.

"Hmph. Suit yourself," the woman said and walked out. The door closed behind her with a business-like click of the latch.

A moment later, Tomi heard the key scritch in the lock. He stepped over to the door and tested the rusty knob. The door rattled but did not open.

A cold feeling rose in Tomi's stomach as he stepped backward and dropped into one of the chairs. *I'm a prisoner! Why?*

And for how long? He thought about the time that had passed since he stormed away from the garage and Amanda. How many hours had it been now? Five? Six? Seven? He checked his watch. 7:53. *No way!* He shook his head in confusion. It felt like it must be after ten o'clock at the earliest. But there was still lots of light in the sky outside. So maybe his watch was right.

Tomi felt completely overwhelmed. The weirdness of the last few hours caught up to him, crashing down on his spirits like a load of falling logs. *How can this be happening?* As far as he knew, craziness didn't run in the family.

At least I've got a place to sleep. For now. He glared at the dog. Patsy Ann had curled up on one of the bottom bunks as soon as the door closed and was now snoring comfortably.

With nothing better to do, Tomi looked more closely around his rough prison. The oil lamp cast a wavering, smoky light that barely reached the walls. Puzzled, he squinted into the gloom. Something was definitely odd.

Getting up, he stepped toward one wall. Newspapers! Someone had tacked thick layers of newspapers all over the inside walls of the rough cabin. It took him a minute, then it hit him. Insulation! To keep the room warm. The same way homeless people in Vancouver sometimes slept with newspapers unfolded over them.

He moved closer. The newspapers were obviously old, with tightly packed columns of print. Heavy black headlines, in vaguely antique type, bled into the paper. Turning his head sideways, he made out the name of the nearest paper: the *Daily Alaska Empire*.

Alaska?

Moving along the wall he came to a different masthead: the *Alaska Labor Dispatch*. Next to that was the front page of something named the *Juneau Spirit*. A panoramic view out across a harbour covered nearly half the page. In the foreground was a wharf, beyond it a wide expanse of water against a dark mountain. In the middle distance, a ship nosed in toward the camera.

With a shock that sent him rocking back on his heel, Tomi recognized the view he had looked down upon just an hour or two earlier from the gravel road.

Juneau? Alaska? No way!

A memory flashed. Rory taunting him: "Ya never know!" His stepsister had read a book last winter. It was called something like *The Unexplained.* It had a whole chapter about people who'd disappeared from one place and mysteriously reappeared somewhere else thousands of miles away. He'd hooted with laughter when she told him about it and milked it for days, mocking her for falling for such guff. But ... *Juneau, Alaska.* How many hundreds of kilometres north of Vancouver was that?

How the crap did I get here?

If that's where he really was.

A whiffling sound behind him brought his head around. Patsy Ann stood on the bunk, giving herself a shake that started at her wide head and worked its way back to the tip of her tail. She jumped heavily to the floor and went to stand in the middle of the room, looking expectantly at the door.

A moment later Tomi heard footsteps outside, followed by the scratch of a key in the lock. The door opened and the woman came in. In one hand she held a metal tray. On it were a sandwich on a plate and a glass of milk. When she spoke, her voice was no longer so unfriendly. "Hope you people eat bread and corned beef."

You people? A growl from his stomach overcame his irritation. Beside the sandwich was a second plate, with a piece of pie. Biting his tongue, he gave a noncommittal "Thanks." After a moment he added, "Ma'am."

"Kasilof," the woman said.

Kasilof?

"Alexandra Kasilof." She stood straight, taller than Tomi, and gave him a deeply superior look.

He had his hand out without thinking. "Tomi Tanaka," he said.

The eyes narrowed. "Tanaka, hey? You *are* Jap, after all."

Tomi rolled his eyes. He started to say, "No. I'm ..." before he caught the faintest twinkle in the faded blue eyes.

The woman turned away. "We'll sort this out in the morning," she snapped back from the door. A moment later the key scratched again in the lock.

Tomi stood rooted to the floor, mouth gaping. He was back to the *crazy-lady* theory now. Somehow he'd been dropped into a Stephen King novel, captured by his own personal psycho.

A soft bark brought him back to the present. He turned. The white dog was sitting on one hip, both back legs off to one side. Her dark eyes were fixed on the table. Tomi followed her gaze to the sandwich and slice of pie. He had to laugh.

He stepped to the table and leaned over. He breathed in, inhaling salt and meat and sharp mustard smells. *If she really is crazy,* he wondered, *could she have ... Would she?*

Behind him Patsy Ann whimpered gently, then barked impatiently. Tomi lifted one edge of the bread. It was warm and moist. A little steam lifted off the spicy pink slices. Essence of hot smoked meat flooded his mouth with saliva.

Naaah. Eagerly he sank his teeth into soft bread, salty corned beef and just enough biting yellow mustard. The bread was fresh and very good. Sourdough. He savoured the tangy taste.

Sourdough ... west coast ... Alaska.

It just couldn't be.

He heard a scrabbling sound. The dog was standing on the floor, broad head lowered and dark eyes trained on him. She barked again, and a small spray of saliva sparkled briefly in the lamplight. As Tomi brought the sandwich back to his mouth, the heavy head lifted, its intent gaze never leaving the food. Tomi couldn't keep from grinning. On a devilish impulse he waved the stump of sandwich back and forth, laughing out loud as the white head swayed as though tied to the bit of food by a string.

"I guess you're hungry, too," he said. He ripped a chunk from the sandwich and threw it toward the dog. The small eyes never wavered, but the white tail quivered. The pink chin lifted, following the morsel's flight. Suddenly the dog lunged and caught the bite of sandwich. Teeth and gums snapped shut with a sound like a car door closing. A little grunting sound came from Patsy Ann's throat.

Tomi's eyes widened. He made a mental note never to get his fingers caught between the dog and a bite of food. For the next ten minutes he had fun tossing bits of sandwich for her to field. When they were done, he poured some milk into the plate and put it on the floor.

Taking the rest of the milk with him, he got up and drifted back to the walls. DEPRESSION DEEPENS, he read. VIOLENCE IN GERMAN STREETS. LINDBERGH BABY KIDNAPPED! FDR PUSHES FOR RELIEF. The thick black headlines meant nothing to him.

Then another photograph caught his eye. It was difficult to make out perfectly in the half light, but it plainly showed a dog — a white dog — sitting somewhere with water in the background. The dog was looking away from the camera, toward a large oncoming ship. Tomi got an almost electric jolt. He spun to look at the dog that was pushing the plate along the floor in pursuit of every last drop of milk.

Turning back to the paper, he squinted, struggling to make out the caption below the picture. "Patsy Ann, Juneau's Official Town Greeter, is now the most famous dog west of the Mississippi," it read, "more famous even than film and radio star Rin Tin Tin, according to traveller Gordon G. McKinley, recently arrived in the Territorial Capital from his home in des Moines."

Huh. But wasn't Alaska a *state*, not a territory? He looked a second time at the date printed beside the newspaper's name. "September 23, 1935."

He'd figured the papers were old. That was no surprise. But how could *this* Patsy Ann be the same dog who had her picture taken in 1935?

No way she's the same one. More likely Patsy Ann the XXIII or something. But the queasy feeling wouldn't let go of his stomach and Tomi couldn't stop seeing the date in front of him. "Hung up" would be the message on his pc at a time like this.

He opened the chest under the window and caught a sharp, nose-wrinkling gust of chemicals. But there were also blankets — thick and coarse, but warm-looking — and a few thin pillows. He threw a pillow onto the nearest bunk, pulled a blanket around his shoulders and flopped down. He closed his eyes.

This can't be happening. Someone must have drugged me. Thrown me on a freighter in Vancouver then thrown me off again in Alaska. Or I'm in a hospital somewhere and imagining all this.

He felt a soft blow to his thigh and the bunk springs sagged and jounced loudly, as the white dog landed beside him. Patsy Ann turned once and curled against him, her warm back pressed tightly into the curve of the boy's stomach and legs. Her head shared the same rough pillow with his.

It was very quiet. Tomi lay looking out at the flickering lamp, the view framed by the domed top of the dog's head and her pyramid ears. With a little wriggle, Patsy Ann settled herself even more closely to him. *Sure doesn't feel like my imagination.*

His eyes closed. His last clear thoughts were of the warm, furry sausage of solid dog, snoring gently in his arms.

Six

WATER WHEEL

THE SMALL room was crowded. On the walls, torn newspapers fluttered at cracks between rough planks. Wind battered against the thin wall. Above he could hear voices speaking in urgent tones. He strained to make out what they were saying, but the words were unfamiliar, the choppy syllables of Japanese. All the faces were Japanese too. With a start he recognized Obaacha — a younger Obaacha. She turned to face him and a horrid feeling came over Tomi, a feeling there was something he was supposed to remember, something he couldn't put a name to.

Then he was awake and the dream dissolved into the pale light of morning.

Tomi groped for his alarm radio.

His hand met thin air and then the rough rasp of unplaned wood. He sat upright, aware that the clock radio wasn't blasting out its usual chatter.

His hand struck the dry texture of paper. *Ohmigod.* Someone had tacked newspapers on the walls! *It wasn't a dream.* He looked around for Obaacha.

But the small room was empty. The lamp was long dead, sitting dark on the table. But clear sunlight shone through the windows.

The door opened and a shaft of sunlight pierced the room across to Tomi's bunk. He blinked in the light.

"Might as well come inside for breakfast," the woman — Castleoff? Klassikov? — said from the door. "You can wash up in the kitchen."

Tomi swung his legs off the bunk and sat up. Beside him, Patsy Ann lifted her head and yawned broadly. Tomi worked his lips over teeth that felt like the floor of a jungle and rose to his feet. Patsy Ann stood too and began a fore-and-aft stretch as methodical and disciplined as the exercise Obaacha did with her friends most mornings.

Tomi picked up his backpack and walked outside. He blinked in the bright, clear light of an early morning. The sun hung in a V of trees off to his right.

Behind him, the woman held the door, waiting for Patsy Ann to complete her Tai Chi. "If you're *quite* ready, your highness," she said as the dog finally ambled past her out into yard.

"Go on," the woman nodded toward the house.

Tomi looked at Patsy Ann, but she seemed to have lost all interest in him. The white dog was sniffing along the far edge of the yard, under the nearest block of sawn boards. As he watched, she trotted to the corner and turned into the tight alley between that block and the next. She vanished into the maze without looking back.

The knot in Tomi's throat strangled an impulse to cry out.

"Let's go," the woman said, an abrupt edge in her voice.

Tomi started toward the house.

A broad overhanging roof sheltered the porch. At this hour, sunlight reached deep beneath it. Varnished logs gleamed warmly in the rays. Through a screen door, Tomi found a warm kitchen smelling of coffee and gently sizzling bacon. Along the walls were broad, neatly ordered counters and the stove. A coffee pot and large black frying pan stood on glowing red element rings. In one corner was a curious white enamel cupboard set on legs; a stubby, barrel-shaped unit on top of it made a loud hum.

"Toilet's back there," the woman nodded at a closed door.

Tomi used it gratefully then came back out.

"Coffee?"

"Yeah, okay," Tomi said. "I mean, sure. Thanks, ma'am."

"There's the sink," she pointed to the deep porcelain basin. "And you can call me Mizz Alex, most everyone does."

Tomi washed his face and neck. He rubbed a finger over his teeth and wished for a brush. In the mirror over the sink, he watched the woman. Today she wore pants — not jeans, some kind of heavy grey material — and a sweater. In the strong light of day, she looked older, maybe even as old as Obaacha. Tougher, though. Her complexion was more like rawhide than Obaacha's rice paper.

She opened a cupboard, drew out two mugs and poured coffee. Then she opened the door of the curious white cupboard and removed a glass bottle of milk. Before the door closed with a snap, Tomi spotted several waxed-paper packages and bowls covered with the same material.

That's a fridge? It looked like something out of a science museum. *Time to update your appliances, lady.*

When he was done washing, Mizz Alex directed him to a chair. The woman cracked eggs into the pan, cut thick slices off a loaf of sourdough and placed them alongside the sizzling eggs. She assembled two plates of golden fried bread, eggs over easy and crisp strips of bacon.

They ate in silence. The woman watched closely as Tomi used his knife and fork. He was mopping up the last yellow puddle of yolk with a crust of sourdough when she spoke.

"Where did you say you're from again?"

"Vancouver," Tomi said. After a moment he added: "Canada."

The woman's face gave nothing away. "How old?"

"Thirteen."

"Where's your family?"

"We live in Delta." When the woman's brows rose skeptically, he added, "It's near Vancouver."

"Hmph. Then what are you doing in Juneau?"

Holy crap! Tomi pulled deeply on the last of his coffee. *So, this is Juneau.* "I don't ... I didn't really mean to be here at all," he started to say, as truthfully as possible. "I got out of school, and I had some things to think about ... at home, I mean. So I went down to the river to, well, just think about stuff. Then, like I told you, I saw Patsy Ann. And I thought she was hurt, like I said, so I followed her. Next thing I know, I'm on my ass on the gravel."

"Watch your language!" the woman rapped out. The grey eyes regarded him coldly. "That's no sort of an explanation."

Tomi threw his palms up and opened his eyes wide in a helpless gesture. "What can I say? It's the truth, ma'am. I mean, Mizz Alex."

"Hmph." The woman straightened in her chair. "Well, we'll see about that. Meantime, you can earn your night's lodging and pay off your breakfast. Come with me."

TOMI FOLLOWED her out the door and across the yard. Beyond the bunkhouse where he had slept, they entered a path that ran behind the lumber yard. Stacks of sawn lumber formed one scented wall of a cool, moist tunnel beneath the over-hanging evergreens. On the other side was a high bank, feathered with the fronds of giant ferns.

After five minutes, they came to a large, open structure, a broad roof of rusting metal held up by squared timbers, with no walls to speak of. The roof cast deep shade over the steel limbs and iron knuckles of heavy machinery. In the very centre, the arc of a huge disc rose vertically from the floor. Like a dark sun bristling with fierce teeth it towered above a series of ramps, gutters and chains designed, Tomi guessed, to guide logs past the saw's spinning teeth when it was in use, without removing any arms or legs.

Mizz Alex stepped carefully around the motionless blade. She ducked under a low-hanging chain and made for the back of the building. Tomi followed. The sound of rushing, cascading water came from somewhere ahead.

There was no wall to block the view out over a medium-sized pond. Its brown surface, dappled with green plants, stretched from the mill wall away to the eaves of the forest. Tomi saw another, even larger circular shape silhouetted against the morning light. This object was much bigger than the saw blade. Its construction reminded Tomi of the Ferris wheel at Hastings Park, except that where the Ferris wheel had swinging cars, this one had iron buckets of some sort bolted to its spokes.

Whoa. That's a water wheel!

Stepping closer, Tomi found a narrow catwalk running beside the big wheel. From there he could see the thing from top to bottom. It stood at least a couple stories high, the bottom of its arc just touching the surface of the pond. Through an open door, he saw stairs leading down to a gloomy room filled with axles and gears. The big wheel hung motionless. The machinery was silent in the cool darkness.

Mizz Alex caught his look. "That used to run this whole mill," she said. Tomi thought he heard a note of wistfulness in her voice. "If I could get it all going again, maybe I wouldn't have to sell up this way."

"Eh? Sell up? You mean you're closing down?"

"Pretty much closed already." She surveyed the rows of stacked lumber with a bleak look. "All prime, seasoned timber, and all wrong for the market. The mine's bust, so they're not buying any more heavy cuts. Lots of people boarding up and shipping out, but all they want are planks and two-by-fours." The woman sighed. "I sold the last of those months ago, and without the saw, I can't turn the one into the other."

She shook her head sharply. "Water under the bridge." Past the water wheel, a corner of the open structure was boxed in to create a kind of large cupboard or small shed. Mizz Alex produced her keys and began trying them in a large padlock. Tomi felt a sudden panic. Surely she wasn't going to lock him in *here* now?

The lock snicked. The woman lifted it off and pulled open the door. Inside, wrenches of every size hung on hooks against one wall. Below them was a broad workbench and underneath that, several toolboxes. In the shadows against the other wall were hand trolleys. They reminded Tomi of the ones at the building-supply store: flat wooden decks with wheels and steel handles.

Mizz Alex pointed around the mill and out to the yard. "Anything you see, any metal lying around loose ..." She bent and picked up a rusted bolt as big around as Tomi's thumb. She waved it at him. "Anything like this — big, little — make one pile in the yard." She pointed.

The old woman cast a bleak look around her. "Then ..." Her voice caught a moment. "Then you can start in on the rest," she said, seeming to gather strength. "Anything you can unscrew or unbolt or take apart any way you can, do it. Pile it all in the yard. If it's too big for you, leave it. I'll have to hire a whole gang of workmen sooner or later, I guess."

Tomi watched her take a last look around. The strong, proud face held such a forlorn expression that he looked away.

Then she turned and walked back down the path toward the house.

He was alone.

SHOULD HE make a run for it? Do what she told him to? Curiosity shunted the decision to one side. He stepped away from the boxed-in cupboard to the catwalk railing. Beyond it stood the great wheel.

Tomi's dark eyes glowed as he traced the parts of the giant mechanism. Looking down, he saw that the wheel hung centimetres above a flooded channel leading to the pond. Near the summit of its upper arc, a nozzle directed a powerful stream of water toward the wheel. Toward it, but not directly on it. The nozzle was pointed off to one side of the wheel so that the water fell noisily but pointlessly into the pond.

There's gotta be a way to move it. Tomi spotted a metal rod running from the nozzle back toward the wall of the enclosed shed. Looking along the catwalk, he saw a stubby handle sticking out from a slot in the wall. He stepped closer and gave the lever a push. Over his head, the nozzle creaked and swung into line with the big wheel.

A cold shower sprayed his face as the water rushing out of the nozzle with the force of a firehose struck the centre of the metal bucket at the top of the wheel. The big wheel seemed to shudder and groan. It began to turn, slowly at first, but then picking up speed.

Craning over the railing and looking past his feet, he saw the point at which the wheel's heavy axle led back under the floor.

As the wheel turned, so did the axle. *That's what makes everything else run*, he figured. *Or not, I guess.* How cool was it that you could use water to cut wood? *So why isn't the rest of the mechanism turning?*

He could hear the grind and rumble of machinery from beneath his feet. He thought he heard something else as well: a loose flapping noise, sort of like a trading card against the spokes on his bike, only more metallic. The wheel seemed to be going faster and faster as well. *Yikes!* He hastily pulled the lever back to its original position. The nozzle swung away from the wheel. With the loss of its energy source, the wheel coasted through two or three more revolutions and slowed to a stop.

This was the kind of problem Tomi loved. He couldn't care less about the pioneers or the history of Canada's confederation or last century's wars. He just loved to make things fit together and work smoothly. Things he could see. The more complicated, the better. He loved the feel of metal parts and the smell of oil, how one piece turned another and pushed the next and set the one beyond that spinning. The best present he could ever remember was the tool set in his stocking that last Christmas with Mom.

I wonder.

Seven

ORPHAN AND INDIGENT

TOMI RACED across the gravel yard and took the steps up to the wide porch in two bounds. He burst through the kitchen door, his broad face glowing and eyes dancing with excitement.

He pulled up short. A man and a woman sat with Mizz Alex at the big table. The man wore a dark suit and had a pinched face. The woman wore a dress and her washed-out hair was pulled into a bun at the back of her head. She reminded Tomi of Jughead's teacher, Miss Grundy. It was obvious they had all been deep in conversation.

"This him?" the man asked. Pale eyes set close over a narrow nose, he examined Tomi with evident distrust.

"He certainly *looks* Japanese," the woman said.

"I'm sorry, ma'am ... Mizz Alex," Tomi stammered. "I didn't know you were busy."

"Busy about you, as a matter of fact," the tall woman said. "This is Special Agent Nichols. He's from the FBI. Do you know what that is?"

Well, d'uh. But he only nodded. Why the FBI? Did he look like some Arab terrorist?

"And," Mizz Alex looked at the other woman. "I'm sorry,

what did you say your name was?"

"Sanderson, Ingrid Sanderson."

"From the Orphans and Indigents' Home. They're here for you."

"But I'm not an orphan." He felt fear rise. "And whatever indigent is, I'm not that either."

"No address and without evident means of support," Miss Grundy Sanderson's voice was as lifeless as an empty house.

"I'm not homeless. I'm just ... visiting. My family's waiting for me ..." *Holy Cow, it's* today. This was D-Day, the day the truck was coming to haul his whole life away. Later on, he and his family were supposed to check in to a hotel, have one last North American burger at the Flying Beaver, then set off on the Great Family Honeymoon. He had to get home. This guy sure acted like a jerk, but after all, he *was* a cop. Maybe Tomi should just —

"And where is that?" the FBI man asked, opening his pale eyes expectantly. He held a pen poised over an open notebook.

"Delta."

"Delta?"

"Outside Vancouver?"

"Vancouver." The agent sniffed. "This 'family' ... Fishermen? Cannery workers?"

"My dad's a pilot. My stepmother's a loans officer."

At the word "pilot" the agent scribbled a note. "Pilot, huh? In Tokyo maybe. No American airline's gonna hire a Jap."

Shock wrestled with anger. Was this guy for real? "We're *Canadian*, you jerk," Tomi blurted out. "And anyway, even if I was all Japanese, when did *that* become a crime?"

"You admit to being an undeclared alien, that's plenty enough." Nichols made another note.

"What, first I'm Japanese, then I'm from Mars?"

"I'd watch my attitude!" the bun woman snapped. "Before you make things any worse for yourself."

"I'd listen to the lady," the agent growled. "You're not American. That right there makes you an alien. And the Asian race is well known to the Bureau for its subversive and criminal tendencies." He looked across at the lumber yard owner. "He have anything with him? Any radios? Anything that might be code books?"

Code books? The room spun. Was the whole state of Alaska certifiably nuts?

"Just this," Mizz Alex produced Tomi's backpack.

"Hey," he stepped forward. "That's mine!"

"Step back!" the agent ordered, a hand going down to his hip.

Tomi watched the man unzip his backpack and remove its contents one by one, examining each item carefully before he put it down on the table. There wasn't much to find: along with the rest of his Grade Seven class, Tomi had turned in his last textbooks to Ms. Sandhu yesterday.

But there was his lunch box. It was illustrated with images of some of his favourite anime heroes, Japanese characters in black and red splashed behind them. *Ohmigod, Japanese!*

Nichols held the box in his hand, examining the symbols and pictures from several angles. His eyes narrowed. He opened the lid. From across the table Tomi could smell uneaten banana. Otherwise, the box was empty.

Next to come out was a comic book. It was a new *Superman*. Agent Nichols riffled the pages. Miss Sanderson sniffed. "It's garbage. But it's all the rage. Even some of our boys have got their hands on them."

Nichols nodded and reached into the backpack again. This time he brought out a small leather case about the size of a pocket book. He pulled at the zipper that ran around the edge to open it. Nested neatly inside were several small hand tools: screwdrivers of different sizes and types, an adjustable wrench, pliers and wire cutters. It had been Mom's best-ever Christmas present to Tomi — also one of her last. He felt a lump rise in his throat.

The agent was prodding and squeezing the lining of the little travel kit, as though he might find something hidden there. "What's a boy doing with tools like this?" he asked.

"They're just tools. I like to experiment with things, take them apart, see how they work. Toasters and clocks, old microwaves."

The agent's head shot up. "What did you say?"

Tomi gave him a baffled look. "Ovens ... or washing machines, anything that's been thrown away."

Nichols gave him a searching look, then reached into the backpack again. When his hand emerged it held a palm-sized square of plastic, about as thick as a slice of bread.

Two cushioned earpieces dangled from a nest of white wire. The mp3 player had been a Christmas present, too — from Amanda. *Take it,* Tomi thought, *just leave my tools.*

Nichols examined the player closely. He seemed puzzled by it. "What the ... ?" he muttered as he held it up at various angles to the light. His index finger flicked against the earpieces. "Some kind of communications device? Experimental probably. Sure not something any kid would carry. And look there," he pointed to tiny characters in the plastic beside the battery cover. "It's Jap, all right."

"Are you for real? It's an mp3 player. It plays music!" Tomi fumed, barely biting back the words he wanted to add: You idiot. "And I'm *not* from Japan. I'm Cana —"

"Yeah, sure you are," the agent cut him off. The backpack was all but empty now. When the narrow hand finished groping, all that it came out with was a white envelope. "South Fraser Intermediate School," the agent read the address in the upper left corner. He opened the flap and pulled out a folded piece of stiff paper.

His brow furrowed. "Looks like a school report card," he said, turning it over in his hand. "Here, look." He handed it to the bun woman.

"May 31, 2006," she read from the stamped entry on the front. "Must be some kind of school project? Or maybe a printing error."

"Don't be stupid," the man frowned. "Probably made a mistake converting from some Jap system. It's obviously a fake."

The Sanderson woman had opened the card and was reading the entries. "You'd think if they were going to forge it, they'd at least have given him better marks." She sniffed and handed it back to the agent.

He took the card and put it in the inside pocket of his jacket. "Probably didn't want him to stand out." Nichols got to his feet and began returning the rest of Tomi's belongings to the backpack. "You're coming with us."

Tomi's mouth opened but nothing came out. This was insane, unreal, like being dropped into a bad movie.

The agent stuffed Tomi's lunch box into the backpack and handed it to him, the zipper gaping open. He palmed the mp3 player off the table and thrust it in his pocket. "Not this. This is going to Washington."

Panic rising, Tomi turned to the third adult in the room. Mizz Alex's face looked troubled, but her head was down and she avoided his eyes.

The man grabbed Tomi roughly by the arm. "Let's go."

Patsy Ann! Where the crap was she when you needed her? "Okay, okay!" he found his voice at last. "Don't you at least have to read me my rights if you're arresting me?"

"You're not under arrest," the thin man growled. "Yet."

"You are a minor," the grey woman said. "Or at least you claim to be. And without a parent or legal guardian that we can find. That means you're my responsibility, until Agent Nichols decides otherwise."

Agent Nichols began to frog march Tomi to the door. "Thank you for the call, Miss Kasilof," he said over his shoulder.

"You did the right thing."

Tomi's brows shot up. He twisted in Nichols' grip to look back into the kitchen. Mizz Alex sat very still at the table, her tall figure bowed. *You. You snitched me out!*

The agent jerked at Tomi's arm. "Let's move." The grey woman followed them out, closing the door firmly behind them.

NICHOLS LED him to an antique car. It was very shiny and well kept and could almost have been brand new. Still, Tomi was surprised. Didn't the FBI on TV always drive big black sports utility vehicles? Maybe a Humvee?

That's TV, you fool, he told himself.

He slid onto the back seat. Without thinking, he reached over his shoulder for the seatbelt. But his groping fingers found only bare metal. Looking up, then down to either side, he could find no sign of belts or buckles. *Weird.* Didn't they have seat belt laws in Alaska?

They drove in silence. At first, they followed the same gravel road Tomi had walked down yesterday. But at the first houses, they turned. He waited for them to come to a proper paved street, but it never happened. They passed a couple of houses that were little more than small shacks, and a low-lying area where dead trees rose above stagnant water. In the distance he could see other buildings that might have been businesses, glimpses of the harbour, the distant mountain. It was all just as he'd seen it depicted in the photograph nailed to the bunkhouse wall.

Tomi shook his head hard.

There was something about all this that was even more wrong than ever. But it was not just the wrong place. Wrong place, wrong *time*. But that ... *Naaaah.* That was flat-out impossible. *No way.*

Still, an inner voice tugged: *Any more impossible than being in Juneau, Alaska?*

The car pulled up in front of a plain wooden building, a raw oblong of peeling clapboard walls. A faded brown tarp covered part of the roof. The yard was bare dirt except where tangled weeds erupted from what might once have been flower beds.

"We'll get out here," Miss Sanderson's empty voice spoke. She turned to the man behind the wheel. "Thank you, Agent Nichols. When should I check in with you next?"

Nichols shot a hard look at Tomi in the back seat. "Give him a few days, unless he lets anything slip. If he does, call me, night or day."

Freaking jerk! Tomi swore silently. He reached over the back of the front seat to grab his backpack.

A hand seized his wrist like a vice. The FBI agent and the boy locked eyes. Tomi's were blazing. "What about my stuff?" he asked.

The agent released his hand and let him lift the pack over the seat.

The woman pulled at his door. "Out you get, then," she said in a sharp tone. "Follow me."

The unpainted front door led to a bare lobby with worn

linoleum on the floor. Behind a reception window he glimpsed a small office. A bulletin board was pinned with signs reading NOTICES and RULES. On the opposite wall was the room's only decoration: a pair of dark photographs of men in suits.

Miss Sanderson led him through to a hallway. From somewhere, Tomi caught the drone of a voice. It reminded him of Mr. Eager, his least favourite teacher. They turned twice and stepped into the office. The woman pushed him into a chair and sat at a desk.

She rolled a form into an old-fashioned typewriter. For the next twenty minutes she peppered him with questions. "Age?"

"Thirteen."

"Birthday?"

"November fourth, nineteen ..."

"Twenty-five," the woman filled in, pecking at the keyboard. *Eh? Say when?* But the woman carried on.

"Place of birth?"

"Vancouver, B.C."

"Father's name?" And so it went. Tomi answered each question as briefly as he could.

"Race?"

Say what?

Bun-woman fixed her bleak look on him. She turned back to the form and typed something. "Religion?"

None of your damn business, he wanted to say. Instead he kept a stony silence.

The woman's face reddened with irritation. "None," she grunted as she hammered at the keys. When she ran out of questions at last, she rose and went to a closet. On the floor inside were two large cardboard boxes. One had the word "Boys" written on it in large letters. The other was marked "Girls." Miss Sanderson pulled out the first and beckoned Tomi over. "Two pants, two shirts, and two changes of socks and underwear."

The jumble inside the box looked like the clearance table at a thrift shop. Tomi poked through the contents.

"Quick now, don't just paw them over. Choose," she snapped, and turned back to the closet.

Tomi managed to find a couple pairs of jeans in his size, a T-shirt and a cotton pullover shirt, socks and underpants. None of them looked new, but at least they looked like they'd been washed.

The woman planted a thin towel, a cake of coarse yellow soap, a tube of toothpaste and a toothbrush on his small pile of clothes.

She led him back out of the office into the hallway. At the far end, Tomi could see a big room lit by a single large window. The metal frames of bunk beds jutted out from each side of the room.

Before they reached the dormitory, Miss Sanderson pointed to a door on the left and followed him inside. It was a bathroom. "Showers in there," she said. "Strip, clothes in the bin, there," she pointed again. "Shower, use the soap. Make sure to use plenty of it on your hair. Scrub. See if you can't scrub yourself pink!" Her thin lip twitched as though at a private joke. "When you're done, I'll be in the office."

Twenty minutes later he presented himself, damp but clean, in his rummage-box T-shirt and jeans. He had run his fingers through his hair and been grateful to brush his teeth. The rest of his "new" clothes were in his arms, his backpack over one shoulder.

The woman walked all around him once, reaching out to lift up his hair so she could look at the back of his neck. Tomi stood uncomfortably still for her inspection. *This must be what mutts feel like at dog shows,* he thought. Then she gestured him back out to the hall. They walked past the bathroom and into the room beyond.

Grey blankets were tucked — more or less carefully — under thin, sagging mattresses. At the heads of the beds, flat pillows of various degrees of cleanliness were lumped on yellowing sheets. Between each pair of beds was a closet with two narrow doors. The whole effect made the bunkhouse at the lumber yard feel almost luxurious.

Miss Sanderson pointed to the lower bunk of the bed on the right nearest the door. "That'll be yours," she said. "You'll be expected to keep it neat."

Tomi noticed clothes folded at the foot of the top bunk.

She followed his look. "John is your bunkmate. He'll show you the ropes. He'll be back from lessons with the rest of the boys any minute. Sister Agatha will enroll you in the morning."

Sister Agatha? "Sister? As in, a nun?"

"Of course!"

"I can't go to Catholic school. My whole family's Buddhist."

Miss Sanderson shot him a hard look. "We'll soon fix that." Her drill-sergeant eyes swept up and down the room. "I'll see you at dinner."

The door closed. The sound echoed in the long room. Tomi listened for the turn of a key in the lock. When it didn't come, his relief was so strong he almost felt embarrassed.

Eight

A FRIEND

TOMI SANK onto the bunk and wondered how everything had gone so sideways.

And where's the dog?

He suddenly felt like someone in the grip of a raging river, tumbling and rolling in the powerful water, unable to get his feet under him or to grab anything solid.

So, what did he know? Dad's rule in moments of crisis came back to him: "Facts, options, action." He fell back on the mattress. Over his head were the sagging springs of the upper bunk.

Facts ...

The low thunder of many feet pounding on hard floors rumbled up the hallway and broke against the door. It burst open and a wave of boys crashed into the room. In their arms were books and scribblers. Many were chattering in a language he didn't recognize, full of coughing sounds. The first ones into the room noticed Tomi and the hubbub fell silent.

Tomi counted nine boys, eight of whom looked to be Native kids. The youngest might have been six or seven. The oldest was maybe sixteen. One who seemed about Tomi's age peeled away from the rest and came over. He tossed his books onto the bunk over Tomi's head. The worn out springs jounced and complained.

"Hi," the boy said in a soft voice. Through eyes as dark as Tomi's own he examined the new arrival. He wore his black hair in a plain cut like Tomi's. His broad face was neither friendly nor hostile.

"Hey," Tomi said back.

The boy said something in the same unfamiliar language.

Tomi looked at him blankly. "I'm sorry," he shook his head after a moment, "I don't —"

"Look at him, dummy. He's not Indian." The only white kid in the bunch lounged on a bunk across the room. "Chinese more likely. Or maybe Jap."

"My dad's family's from Japan," Tomi found himself explaining. "I'm from Canada."

"Sure you are, bub, and I'm Rhett Butler!" the white kid mocked. He was bigger than most of the other boys, and one of the oldest. A pink rash crawled across his cheeks and forehead. It made the boy look like he was flushing even when he wasn't.

"I'm John," the first boy said. "John Paul. But mostly they call me JP."

"I'm Tomi."

JP nodded. "That's my bunk," he said and glanced briefly over Tomi's head.

"Hey," Tomi said. "I guess this is mine."

"Where you from?" JP asked.

"British Columbia."

JP nodded. "I got family in Prince Rupert."

"Family? I thought this was a place for orphans."

"That's only some of us."

"What about you?"

"My parents sent me. I got too many brothers and sisters. They can't afford to feed me so I come here."

"They just left you here?" Tomi asked in disbelief.

JP shrugged. "Better'n nothin'. Anyway, they didn't have no choice. I see them sometimes. They come visit." There was no anger in his voice, only acceptance. "You, how come you're here?"

Where to start? "I, uh, had a fight with my folks and blew off. But then I ... I kinda got lost. I'm not even too sure what happened myself." *As in, I have no freaking clue!* "But they're in Vancouver." *I hope. Or maybe they're in the air over the Pacific.* He felt his stomach lurch. *Or maybe they're not anywhere at all.* "But I can't get hold of them right now." There *was an understatement.* "So these guys seem to think I'm an orphan."

"Or indigent," JP nodded sagely.

A bell rang. Everyone dropped what they were doing and headed for the door. JP tipped a look at the boy in the bunk. "Coming? You want to eat, you don't want to be last."

For the first time, Tomi saw some light sparkle in the boy's serious brown eyes.

They beat the last stragglers down the hall to a pair of double doors. These swung open to reveal a room a little larger than the dormitory. Two long tables ran down its length, with benches set out along each. At the far end was a cafeteria-style serving line. The boys from the dorm jostled for position with an equal number of girls of the same ages.

Tomi fell in behind JP and picked up a tray. From a bucket he pulled a fork, knife and spoon stamped from thin steel. Plates were laid out on a counter of bare grey metal, food already on them. Ruefully, Tomi recalled the selection he'd often spurned at the school cafeteria. The only choice here seemed to be take it or leave it.

A rumble from beneath his belt prodded him into action. He grabbed a plate with a pool of brownish, vaguely meaty-looking slurry on it. An island of mashed potatoes and grey-green pea pebbles completed the fare. At least there was milk, in thick glasses, and bowls of Jell-O to round out the meal.

He followed JP to a place near the end of one of the tables and sat beside him. He could feel eyes following him.

Tomi was hungry. The stew may have looked unappetizing, but it was thick and well flavoured. He wolfed the meal down and found himself wanting more. He looked around. No one seemed to be going back to the counter. He leaned in toward JP and whispered, "What's the deal on seconds?"

JP snorted. "There's bread." He reached past the boy on his other side and pulled over a plate. On it were a loaf, bread knife and small lump of very pale butter.

"Thanks." Tomi cut a thick slice. He offered some to JP. "So, listen. How do I get out of here?"

"How old are you?"

"Almost fourteen."

"Can't."

"Why, can't?"

"You have to be fifteen. Then they have to let you go, or send you home if your parents want you back."

Oh, I'm pretty sure they want me back. They weren't the ones who threw me out. More like the other way 'round. He recalled this with a pang.

Tomi lapsed into silence. The rest of the room seemed to have lost interest in the new boy. Groups of girls, huddles of boys and a few mixed groups were wrapped up in their own gossip. Tomi pulled the bowl of Jell-O to him, holding it close to his chest to spoon up jiggling mouthfuls. His attention wandered. For the first time he noticed the pictures pinned to the walls. He recognized the guy with the crown of thorns and the beard. In some of the pictures he had children at his feet, in others sheep. In some there were other bearded men in robes. Around Tomi, the burble of voices rose as people finished eating, and he heard a few half-whispered phrases in the same unfamiliar language he'd heard earlier, with its machine-gun "kh" and "hx" sounds.

Thwack! The violent blow brought the room to silence.

Tomi whipped his head toward the sound. Miss Sanderson stood between the tables, a ruler quivering in one hand. A boy sitting at the table hunkered low in his chair, one hand reaching over his left shoulder to rub at his back. "English only!" the woman was saying. "You *know* that, Timothy."

Tomi turned back. His eyes locked briefly on JP's, then both boys dropped their attention back to their food.

The sound of conversation slowly resumed, but it had lost its energy. A few minutes later a bell rang.

"C'mon," JP said. "It's boys' turn to wash up."

Falling in with the others, Tomi helped clear the tables and carry the dirty dishes back to the kitchen. There, they fell into two teams. The blotchy white kid and a couple of the other older boys washed; everyone else dried. Tomi found a towel and joined the dryers.

On the way back to the dorm, he slipped in beside JP again. "Hey," he said, "do you know a white dog called Patsy Ann?"

JP snorted. "'Course. Everyone knows Patsy Ann."

"Whose is she? I mean, who's she belong to?"

"Belong to? She don't belong to nobody. She belongs to her own self is all."

"You mean, like a stray dog?"

"No!" The idea seemed to offend JP. "She's the Official Town Greeter!"

"Say what?"

"Every ship comes in, she knows. Before anyone. So she goes down to the water, then everyone else knows to go too. That's why she's the 'greeter.' But Indian people say she's a spirit bearer."

"Huh." *Well, she's special all right.*

Back in the dorm room, the other boys settled into their bunks. Some broke out books from lockers beside each bed. One or two opened scribblers and worked on homework. A group of four or five sat on adjoining bunks and began dealing out cards.

Tomi looked across the room and saw the white boy watching him beneath heavy-lidded eyes. Quickly, he looked away.

"Hey!" Suddenly JP's face hung upside down from the overhead bunk, black hair falling like a dark fringe below his upside-down face. "Want a comic?" In his hand was a brightly printed magazine.

"Yeah, sure. Thanks!" Tomi took the book, instantly recognizing the figure in blue and red tights on the cover. But the superhero in his hands was a little different from the one he knew — thinner, he thought. *You've bulked up some, Superdude. Hope they don't ask you to pee in a cup.*

Superman was delivering an armload of bad guys to jail by the time the Sanderson woman strode in. "Teeth and face! Teeth and face!" she said in a loud voice. Boys put down what they were doing, retrieved toothbrushes from their cupboards and straggled out to the bathroom.

Tomi retrieved his new toothbrush and paste and followed the others. The toothpaste was vaguely minty and seemed sandier that what he was used to. Ten minutes later, the lights in the dorm went out.

The restless shifting of bodies in neighbouring beds and the occasional muted whisper kept him awake a little while. But eventually he slept.

They were at the table in the dining room at home — all of them: Dad, Amanda, Rory, Obaacha, Tomi. He was drinking a Coke and there was a pizza box open on the table. Then they were in the car with Obaacha squeezed between him and

Rory in the back. They were driving through East Van and there, above the trees, he could see the roller coaster and other rides at the PNE. Then they were parking in the lot behind the horse track at Hastings Park. Everyone piled out of the car except Obaacha. She was upset, making a fuss, "*Ne*! You go! Go on if you want to, but I'm not going in there. Once was enough! Once was too much!" Her face was red with annoyance but also somehow younger, like the comic book Superman.

Tomi woke with a start and for a panicky moment wondered why there were so many other people in his room. Then it came rushing back. *Right.* With a sudden, stabbing longing, he missed home.

Then sleep captured him again.

Nine

NOSY REPORTER

WITHOUT appearing to move at all, the morning sun crept slowly across the boardwalk. At last it reached the white dog. She lay flat on her side, her back against the wall. All four legs stretched out straight in front of her. White eyelids fluttered and the grimy snout made little whuffling grunts. The stiff legs trembled. The black nose twitched, nostrils flared.

Patsy Ann's head jerked up. Her ears were held high, small black eyes squinted and blinked in the light. She got up, front end rising first, her back end taking a little longer. She stretched through her full Tai Chi routine. She made a thorough job of it, bowing down on extended front legs, then leaning forward so that her hind legs stretched behind her like a pair of fat drumsticks. Finally, she shook, briskly and energetically, so that her back paws danced right off the ground.

Her morning routine complete, Juneau's official town dog set off. She passed the meaty smells of Elder's Butchers without slowing down; Sam Elder and his son, Junior Elder, wouldn't be passing bones out from the side of the counter until much later. At the offices of the *Daily Alaska Empire*, her grimy nose wrinkled at the sickly sweet stench that billowed from the ink-stained back room where the noisy presses churned. At the Red Dog Saloon, the yeasty salt-and-beer scent drifting from the double swinging doors checked her pace for a moment, but bending low to look under the door, she saw only rows of empty tables and carried on.

With a quick glance up and down the silent street, she crossed to the other side and climbed up onto the high boardwalk. The sweet bread-and-spice smell was now a heady fog of mouth-watering scent. Stepping across the planks, she butted her nose hard against a door. Its glass pane rattled but the door remained closed. She barked, a sharp, impatient sound.

From somewhere inside a muffled voice called out, "All right! I'm coming."

Patsy Ann barked again.

The door opened. "My goodness, you're turning into a bossy old dog!" a young woman with auburn hair teased. "Is this what stars expect?"

Patsy Ann gave the girl a brief lick, and brushed past her through thick eddies of delectable aroma. She made for the back, almost breaking into a trot at the corner of the counter.

The back half of the building was a single large room. "Good morning, my dear," an older woman in a floury white apron sang out. Patsy Ann nuzzled the woman's kneecap gently with a cold nose. A big table filled the centre of the room. On it were mixing bowls and trays of pastries. Two ovens stood against the back wall, an unmatched set of heavy cast iron and cracked white porcelain raised up on legs above the floor.

Between the ovens was a door and on the floor near it, two bowls. One brimmed with cool, clean water. The other held a fresh, warm cinnamon knot.

Patsy Ann put it down in four or five mouthfuls, letting out a grateful little grunt with each bite. Then she drank long and noisily from the other bowl.

An old braided rug lay next to the door. On another day, Patsy Ann might have curled up there, basking in the warmth of the all-day ovens and the heavenly smells that rolled out of them. But today she had other matters to attend to. Dabbing another quick lick on the woman's leg, she retraced her steps out through the store.

The day's first human customer stood by the counter. He was a large man wearing a white jacket and billowy trousers in a black-and-white check. Patsy Ann registered the aromas of chopped ham, soup and braised meat that wafted from the stained jacket, but she barely turned her head.

"Look at that," the girl behind the counter said. "Something's up."

The man in checked trousers stepped aside to hold the door for the white dog. "Not a boat, though," he said, watching as she turned up the street. "Went the wrong way."

The many-stranded smells of downtown Juneau, the odours of people and kitchens, of city animals and sea salt and dead fish, fell away. Patsy Ann walked briskly, head down, tail out straight. The black nose twitched at different scents: sun on horses, tar on the gravel road, pine and hemlock trees dusted with yellow pollen. Soon she was panting in the warm morning, pink tongue lolling. Her pace slowed as the gravel road climbed toward green forest.

The growl of an overworked motor grew in the morning quiet. The dog carried on, not seeming to notice. The sound got louder and a truck pulled past her. A young voice cried something from the open window and the truck pulled to a stop in a cloud of white dust. The passenger door opened with a creak and a girl in a dress got out.

The girl knelt and clapped her hands. Patsy Ann broke into a half trot, lowering her nose toward the girl's hands. "Want a lift, Patsy Ann?"

Gratefully, the white dog got her front feet onto the high running board. The girl helped the dog up onto the seat, then squeezed in beside her.

"Going walkabout, you old thing?" the woman behind the wheel asked cheerfully, but Patsy Ann gave no answer.

The truck bounced on the rough road as it wound up through trees and clearings splashed with scarlet and purple wildflowers. After some minutes a small white building came into view, with a log house behind it and beyond both, rows of sawn, stacked lumber. Patsy Ann got to her feet and gave a bark.

"You too?" the woman asked, raising one eyebrow. She pulled the truck across the road into a gravelled lot in front of the white building.

"Sophie," the woman reached across to grasp the girl's arm before she could open the door. "Please, now, remember, this is work for me. This is a very important story and I need to concentrate. I have to trust you," she looked at the girl doubtfully, "to behave yourself and not to interrupt us."

"Yes, mother. I mean, *no*, mother!" The girl's eyes rolled.

Sophie's mother looked as though she might say something more about this, but movement beyond the truck's windshield caught her eye. "There she is now," she said. She grabbed a notebook from the dashboard and pulled open the truck door.

Sophie climbed down to the gravel. She watched her mother walk to meet the approaching woman, raising her reporter's notebook like a flag in front of her as she did.

Patsy Ann got there first, breaking into a run that brought her up against the tall woman's legs with a force that nearly toppled her. "Well hello to you too," Mizz Alex said, pleasure breaking through her surprise. She bent to chuck the animal gently under its muzzle. "Do you miss your little oriental friend, girl?"

"Mizz Alex," Sophie's mother began. Then she corrected herself. "Miss Kasilof, I'm Judy Carr, from the *Daily Alaska Empire*."

The tall woman straightened. "Yes?" she said, pronouncing the word slowly and carefully.

"Miss Kasilof, I'm writing a story about Juneau's future, about whether it even has one if the mine closes down."

The older woman's deeply tanned face was grave. Eyes sharp as splinters off a glacier shot from mother to daughter and back.

"You're one of our oldest ..." Judy began again, making her daughter cringe.

Mizz Alex's lip twitched and a gleam escaped from beneath the glacial gaze.

"... oldest businesses, that is," Judy rushed gamely on. "From one of our oldest business families, and ... Well, anyway, I'm sure you have a view."

Mizz Alex stood silent a moment more, then sighed and said, "Well, then, you might as well come into the office."

Patsy Ann followed Sophie and her mother into the small office. Inside, the dog promptly dropped her black nose in the direction of one corner of the room. Her ratty white tail stood up stiffly as she began snuffling her way around the floor, sneezing whenever her black nostrils vacuumed up a puff of dust or mat of fur from any of the several small creatures whose recent comings and goings she noted.

At the corner, the dog looked up. Sophie was wandering among empty desks, tugging out the drawers of one or two. Judy was asking Mizz Alex something about the "boom-and-bust ride," and whether Juneau might become just another northern ghost town. Mizz Alex's answer had something to do with fish and scenery and rich travellers from the Lower Forty-eight.

Sophie leaned over a desk near the back of the room. It was the only one that anyone seemed to use. Papers were scattered across it, several of them marked "Overdue" in bold rubber-stamped letters.

Patsy Ann's nose inspected a grey wire basket in the corner.

A fringe of newsprint lined the can. From it flowed the most tempting salty, oily, sardiney smell.

Sophie looked toward the counter. Her mother was deep in conversation with Mizz Alex. Turning her back on them, she reached out to the desk and slid a sheet of paper aside to expose one lying beneath it.

From behind her back came a clatter and sudden cry, followed by the smell of sardines.

"Patsy Ann! No!" Mizz Alex scolded. Kneeing the white dog aside, she retrieved a flat tin, its lid rolled back to reveal an odorous pool of oil glistening in one corner.

"Sophie!" Judy Carr spoke sharply. Sophie spun away from the desk and put on her innocent look. The glare with which her mother gestured her back to the front of the office suggested the act wasn't selling.

Judy bent to help the older woman retrieve the last of the waste paper. "So, just one more thing, Miss Kasilof. What about the dam?"

"What about it?" Mizz Alex straightened and put the basket on the counter.

"Well," the petite woman stood facing the taller one. "If Kasilof Lumber goes out of business, who's going to look after the Kasilof Dam?"

Mizz Alex appeared taken aback. "I ... I guess I hadn't thought about that."

"Hadn't thought about it?" Judy pressed on. "But if no one looks after it, what's to keep the dam from bursting one day? That much water could wipe Juneau right off the map!"

"I'm sure that won't happen," Mizz Alex said, her voice tight. "Now, if you'll excuse me, I have work to do."

Judy thanked Mizz Alex for her time, took Sophie by the hand and led the way back out to the truck. Patsy Ann followed at their heels.

The white dog walked to the edge of the gravel and stopped. She sniffed the breeze, black nose drawing little peaks in the air. Then without ceremony she dropped to the ground, stretching her chubby hind legs out behind her and resting her chin on her extended forelegs. The black eyes narrowed to mere slits in her more-or-less clean white face and a long, whuffling sigh escaped her chest.

Sophie opened the truck's passenger door and stood back to let the heated air inside the cab flow out. Judy slipped in behind the wheel and inserted a key in the ignition. Leaning back, she waved her notebook like a fan in front of her face.

"Mom, what's it mean to 'call a loan'?" Sophie asked.

Her mother gave her a sharp look. "To do what?"

"'Call a loan.' There was a letter on that desk away at the back. It said it was 'calling a loan.'"

"Did it now?" A thoughtful look settled over Judy's face. The engine growled to life and Sophie climbed in, tugging down on her dress to protect her bare legs against the searing hot seat. "It means somebody loaned you money, and now they want it back." Her mother's voice trailed away, seeming to leave some further thought unexpressed. She gave her head a brisk shake and worked the gear shift. "But Sophie, you really shouldn't go snooping around like that."

The truck backed out of the lot and turned down the hill. The sound of the motor faded and silence settled over the sun-bathed clearing between the road and the small white office. Patsy Ann's eyes closed completely. A little while later she rolled over onto her right side. Soon, gentle snoring could be heard above the insect buzz and muted rush coming from the direction of the mill.

Ten

BIBLE LESSON

"YOU CAN sit there," the woman in the long brown robe said. Sister Agatha had a warm smile, but it was hard to guess her age. She wore a robe with a full hood. Beneath it, a starched white collar surrounded her gently flushed face. Tomi couldn't even see her ears, let alone her hair. What he could see of Sister Agatha's face seemed kind, and her voice was encouraging as she gestured Tomi to an empty seat near the back of the classroom.

Tomi sat, feeling the stiffness of his unfamiliar jeans. The shirt he'd picked out from the box rubbed coarsely against his skin. *School! I'm back in freaking school!* He shook his head. He couldn't be in an orphanage in Juneau. *It's just not possible.* But he was getting a little tired of waiting for the guy with the microphone to jump out and spring the big "surprise!" on him. Meanwhile, this whole crazy place, these people, were beginning to seem a lot more concrete than anything about his last "real" day at school. *Why isn't school here out yet?* He wondered if it had something to do with being in Alaska. *Being so far north and all,* he thought.

He only half heard Sister Agatha rap on her desk for attention.

"Good morning, class," she was saying.

A half-hearted murmur that might have been "Morring-zizzster" ran through two dozen teenage boys and girls.

Sister Agatha smiled. "Who remembers our verse for today?"

A hand shot up from the front row. The teacher nodded and a girl with blonde hair in short pigtails sang out cheerfully: "Poke out your eyes!"

Sister Agatha laughed. "No, no, Zoe, not like that. 'If your eye causes you to sin, pluck it out; it is better for you to enter the kingdom of God with one eye, than with two eyes to be thrown into Hell.' That's from the Gospel of Saint Mark, 9:41."

Tomi frowned. In seven years in public school he'd never before heard a teacher mention Hell. Not inside a classroom, anyway. And eye-plucking? For the first time he noticed the small sculpture nailed over the blackboard. He recognized it: Jesus on the cross. He'd seen such statues before, at church weddings. But it was the first time he'd seen one so close-up, or with quite so much red paint lavished on its bloody wounds. *Ouch!*

"Can someone explain what Saint Mark means to tell us here?" the plump nun asked the class.

Tomi slipped down in his chair and avoided her eye. Three rows in front of him, Zoe's hand waved eagerly back and forth.

THE SUN crept across the sky. On the grass where the white dog lay, the line of shadow cast by the trees stole steadily forward, moving without seeming to move at all.

The shadow had almost reached the sleeping animal when a fly *zizzzzzed* past one triangular ear. The insect's body was big as a marble and its eyes changed colour as it turned, banking in the sunlight, and came back to settle on the peak of one pink-and-white canine ear.

The ear flicked away the fly. An irritated buzzing circled the dog two or three times and drifted away toward the trees. Patsy Ann rolled onto her elbows and shook her broad head. She got to all four feet, shook the rest of herself briskly, then sat down again. She sat at attention, her dark gaze directed intently at the spot where the road came up through the trees from town.

The white door opened and Alexandra Kasilof stepped out. In one hand she held a grey wastepaper basket. She upended the basket into a garbage can beside the door and fit the lid carefully back on the can. While she did this, she watched the white dog.

When she was done, she stood a moment, face raised to the warm sun. The rattle and grind of an approaching engine began to swell above the sleepy buzz of insects. "I'll never understand how you do that," Mizz Alex muttered, eyes on the white dog. She opened the office door and thrust the waste basket inside.

She turned back in time to see the second truck of the day swing into the gravel lot. This relic was rather different from the Carrs' pickup. Narrow tires on high, spoked wheels supported a cab that looked more like an old-fashioned carriage than a modern truck. Behind it stretched a flatbed of bare wooden planks. It pulled to a stop with a sour *pop, pop* of blue exhaust.

The driver's side door creaked open and hung trembling on sagging hinges. A man stepped out and walked around the front of the truck. Silver hair curled from beneath a blue peaked cap. White whiskers traced the line of a sharp jaw. The eyes in the sun-browned face were blue.

Warm delight softened Mizz Alex's usual stern expression. "Well if it's not Captain Ezra Harper," she called out. "I hope you're here as a customer."

"I'm not welcome as a friend?" The blue eyes twinkled.

"Oh of course you are." Mizz Alex took the old man's hand in hers for a moment, then released it and ushered him toward the office. "It's just that most of my visitors lately seem to be distractions — *unpleasant* distractions — and I could certainly use an honest-to-goodness customer about now."

"Business not too good, Alex?"

"It's the old wheel, or maybe it's the workings." Mizz Alex sighed. "I don't know. Something's bust or come apart or just plain worn out. I've no idea. Douglas always took care of that. It hasn't worked for months."

"Can't you —"

Mizz Alex waved her hand dismissively. "I've asked every mechanic in town and none of them will touch it. I suppose I could get a donkey-diesel. But the way things are, I doubt the bank would lend me another penny. And with the price of fuel, I don't know if I could afford that either. Nothing left really but to take it all apart and sell the scrap while I can."

"Well now, Alex," the old man cautioned. "In my experience even the worst gale ends in a calm eventually."

The woman dipped her head doubtfully. She reached for a pad, pulled a pencil from above her ear and said, "How can I help you today?"

"Cedar," he said. "Several planks at least a clean inch thick."

"*DogStar* need work?"

"Aye. I'm dreading it." The captain patted himself on the chest. "These ribs and rigging aren't getting any younger!"

"Isn't that so," the other agreed with feeling, and began writing.

A powerful bark interrupted them. Patsy Ann stood in the square of sunlight splashing through the open door. She stood stiffly, her skimpy tail quivering with tension. She barked again, and once more.

Both grey heads bent to one side. "Why Patsy Ann," Mizz Alex said. "What on earth is it?"

The white terrier put so much effort into her next bark that both front paws came off the ground.

"It's something, all right," said the *DogStar*'s captain.

With a comical little leap, Patsy Ann spun in place, took a few stiff steps toward the door and looked back. Then she barked again.

The Captain and the lumber woman exchanged looks. "Fine then," Mizz Alex sounded both mystified and resigned.

She put down her pencil and turned to the end of the counter. "I'm coming."

Patsy Ann gave a gruff little woof of satisfaction and trotted out the door. Mizz Alex and her customer followed.

The dog led them behind the office and across the gravel yard. Skirting the rows of stacked lumber, she trotted briskly across the open space toward the damp, mossy smell of captive water. The soft earth shook gently under her feet.

Beyond the last stack of sawn wood, the low building with the broad roof and open sides came into view. A breeze blew gently through the mill, bringing the soft rush of falling water and a sound that hadn't been there the day before: a rhythmic *creak, crick, creak.* The woman peered into the shadows.

"What in heaven?" the woman said. "I told him just to gather up loose ends." She cast about the yard for a pile of metal scraps, but saw only bare gravel. She strode forward into the gloom, Captain Harper a few steps behind her. Avoiding the giant saw blade, Mizz Alex stepped toward the boxed-in corner. The large doors hung wide. Tool boxes had been pulled out, lids opened.

"Why that light-fingered little brute. What's he done?" Looking past the storage space, Mizz Alex frowned into the sunlight reflecting off the pond.

A miniature rainbow wavered in the spray of water exploding off what seemed like an endless procession of small buckets, circling from right to left and down out of sight. More water dripped down the metal spokes as the big wheel turned. For the first time, the two humans noticed the heavy vibration throbbing up through the wide planks of the mill floor.

Mizz Alex's jaw dropped and her mouth opened wide. She rushed to the rail and peered into the shadow of the turning wheel. Grey eyes narrowed as she tried to make out the shafts and belts and pulleys that filled the space down there.

Patsy Ann barked again. Mizz Alex spun around. The white dog stood a little way off, not far from the big saw blade with its fierce-looking teeth. Beside her, a tall pole rose from the floor, like the handle of a hoe or shovel. Another bark.

"It's not possible," the woman said. She hesitated, then stepped to where Patsy Ann stood, gripped the wooden handle and looked down at the dog. She exchanged a look with the Captain, drew a breath and held it. Then she pulled hard on the handle.

There was a *ka-thunk* deep below their feet, and the whole building shook. A little shower of sawdust fell on them from the rafters. The blade groaned — and began to turn. Slowly it gained speed, turning faster and faster until the ferocious teeth around its rim were no more than a vibrating blur.

At Mizz Alex's feet, Patsy Ann barked with excitement.

Pushing hard, the woman shoved the wooden handle back to its original position. A softer click came from below and the blade lost speed. It spun ever more slowly until the teeth were once again visible and it lazily turned its way to a stop.

Heart pounding, Mizz Alex pulled back on the handle once more. Another hard *ka-thunk,* another shower of sawdust, and the blade picked up speed again.

"Oh, my God in heaven!" Grey eyes blazed as she caught the Captain's look. "He's fixed it! He fixed the mill!" An almost girlish look of delight came over her tanned face. Impulsively she wrapped her arms around the old man and gave him a powerful bear hug.

She pushed the handle again and this time let the blade spin itself out until it came to a complete halt.

"Oh, my ... oh, Patsy Ann!" She bent to rub her fingers deeply into the fur behind the white dog's ears. "Is that why you brought him here? To fix my mill? You really *are* an amazing dog!"

Patsy Ann grinned widely and gazed up at the woman. Holding Mizz Alex's gaze, she gave another bark.

"Got yourself a new hand, do you Alex?" the old man asked.

"Not 'zactly. He turned up the other night in the yard. Just appeared out of nowhere. Said he was Canadian, but looked Japanese to me. Just young. Couldn't account for himself apart from some shifty story about Patsy Ann." The Captain's white brows lifted. "I let the authorities worry about him. You have to be careful these days, what you read in the papers."

The old Captain nodded. "Patsy Ann brought him, you say?"

"Yep."

"The 'authorities,' Alex?"

"The Orphans' Home, of course. What else could I do with him? But then you know who turned up, who came out here with the woman from the orphanage?" Her fine face looked troubled. "That new G-man, Nichols! A real prune, too, I thought."

"Did you notice his feet?" the Captain asked. "More specifically, did you notice anything about his shoes?"

"The FBI agent?"

"No, the boy."

Mizz Alex gave him an odd look. "Let's go find your cedar for you."

Eleven

NICKEL BREAD

FISH. Sister Agatha drew the big block letters on the blackboard. "Very good," she said. "And what are some other things we do here in Alaska?"

Zoe's hand waggled in the air. Sister Agatha scanned the rest of the room, a hopeful expression on her face.

Two desks over, another girl raised her hand hesitantly. "Gold?"

Sister Agatha nodded. "Well, we *mine* things, yes Mary." She wrote the word MINING on the board. "Anything else?"

"Army?" one of the older boys suggested.

Sister Agatha made a face. "Well, yes, we have the navy up the road. And the military has a lot of other bases, to keep us safe. So, yes, that's another thing." MILITARY joined the list on the board.

Social studies. Usually Tomi's mind would have started wandering by this point. But this was *Alaska* social studies.

That *I-can't-be-here-this-can't-be-happening* feeling came back over him like an electric mist. Tomi looked around the room. It was small, barely bigger than the Tanakas' dining room. The desks were made of wood with iron legs like park benches, and the blackboard was actually black instead of green.

The class was a mix of older girls and boys, though it was hard to see how everyone could be in the same grade.

The door at the back of the room banged open. Miss Sanderson's dry voice clipped out names: "Ramsey. Wilson. John Paul. Billy Paul."

Tomi turned to see her pale eyes scan the room. Her washed-out gaze met his brooding one.

"Tanaka!"

The four other boys who stood up were all his own size or bigger. He took their lead, following the headmistress out into the hall. His mind raced. *What did I do? I haven't been here long enough to get into trouble.* He caught JP's eye; the other boy just shrugged.

Miss Sanderson gathered them in front of her in the hall. "Now then, some of you know how this goes. One or two of you are *new*," she fired a cold look at Tomi and John Paul. "So here are the rules. Now and again, some kind citizen requires a little extra labour for this or that chore. It is our practice to make our boys available for these sorts of odd jobs. If you are chosen, the benefactor will pay a reasonable wage for your efforts, and you will be allowed to keep part of this."

Say what? Tomi'd been with her right up to the end there. "Odd jobs," okay; "reasonable wage," okay; but ... "allowed to keep *part*" of the money? What was that about?

"Follow me." She led them to the office. Once inside, she directed the five boys into a line up against one wall.

A thin man in a pea jacket stood facing them. Stray silver

locks curled out from beneath a flat blue cap. A lined face and a beard bleached white by the sun showed the man's age. He stood straight as a mast and his buttons shone gold even in the gloomy office. He stepped across the small room and walked down the line of boys, examining each one from head to toe.

When he came to Charley Ramsey, he studied the boy coldly. "Aye, *you*. I've had you before." He turned away with a look of distaste.

Charley smirked.

The man returned to the beginning of the line, where Tomi stood next to jp. He stopped in front of them and looked back and forth between them. Tomi began to feel more than a little creepy.

What the heck is this — some kind of weird slave sale?

He looked up. The old man's eyes were deep set under thick white brows. They regarded him intently, as though something very important rode on what they saw. But Tomi thought they sparkled with a secret warmth. In the moment that he met the old man's gaze, he was amazed to see — *at least I think I saw* — one grey eye hint at a wink, a bare flicker of a lash out of sight of Miss Sanderson and the other boys.

Okaaay.

The man stepped back. "This one will do. He might know something about boats."

"Might. He's Japanese. Sign here." The Sanderson woman slipped a form and a pen across the counter for the old man to sign.

"Japanese–*Canadian*," Tomi objected, putting some heat into it. *What, are these people stupid? How often do I have to say it?*

"So he claims," Miss Sanderson took the paper back. She sniffed. "But really …" She tipped her head in the boy's direction. "Right then, the rest of you back to class."

When the other boys were gone, the old man held out his hand. "My name is Captain Ezra Harper, master of the *DogStar*. And you are?"

"Tomi."

The man's expression didn't change.

After a moment Tomi raised his own hand and took the old man's. Their shake was dry, firm and brief. "Tomi Tanaka."

"Mr. Tanaka."

Mister? That was unexpected. But nice.

"Have him back by six. I'll be here."

"Aye, Miss Sanderson, I'm sure you will," the old man said dryly.

Woooah? Was that a shot?

"If you please, Mr. Tanaka?" He gestured for Tomi to go ahead of him out the door.

THE OLD SEAMAN led Tomi out to a truck that looked like something from an Al Capone movie: long running boards below the doors, round headlights on pods above fenders that were little more than flat strips of painted steel. The bed in back was bare wood. More wood was tied on it: a dozen sawn planks, their unplaned surfaces as rough as short fur. Tomi detected the spicy scent of cut cedar.

Hmmm. He'd last smelled that at the lumber yard.

The truck door creaked as he opened it. Something white erupted from the shadows inside and Tomi stepped back. A waft of garbage-breath enveloped him. He caught himself and reached out to skiffle the fur behind the dog's pointed ears.

"Hey, Patsy Ann." He squeezed his eyes tightly closed and held his breath while the rough pink tongue slathered a kiss over his face.

He looked past the dog to where the old man was sliding in behind the wheel. *You ... her ...* Tomi's gaze returned to the dog as he pulled his own door shut. "You two know each other?"

This time there was no doubt about it. The old man's eyes definitely twinkled as he glanced down at the dog. "Herself and I? Aye, we're friends. Old friends."

"She's your dog then."

The man looked comically alarmed. "My dog? Oh heavens no. No, no, no. Not at all. But we do know each other, I'd say, about as well as two old shipmates can."

Tomi lapsed back into silence. *What if this guy's crazy too? What if all these people are crazy? What if I'm caught in the middle of their crazy game? Some kind of secret society that lives inside the lumber yard? Or maybe not so much crazy, just living in some parallel reality — like those people who dress up and have Civil War battles.*

The captain turned the key and stomped his left foot on the floor. The engine whined, burped, then kicked over with a bang. A blue cloud of smoke puffed up from beneath the hood. The truck lurched and Tomi found himself holding tight to the door with one hand and Patsy Ann with the other.

Tomi looked out the window as they drove. The rutted lane from the orphanage back to the main road followed the edge of a marsh he had barely noticed yesterday. His sense of having slipped into a period movie deepened as they approached the taller buildings that must constitute downtown Juneau. Tomi saw a few other trucks that resembled the captain's, more like horseless carriages than real pickups. The cars he saw were much the same: tall, dark and boxy, with high grills and vast chrome bumpers.

Pedestrians outnumbered people driving. The men all wore baggy pants and jackets, and hats. Almost everyone had some kind of headgear, whether an old-style fedora or a soft peaked cap. Not many ballcaps though, Tomi noticed. The women all wore skirts and dresses that came down well below their knees. None were in jeans, let alone the "low-riders" that Rory had begun to wear.

Some religious groups dressed oddly — conservatively — he knew. *Or else ... But no. NO, no, no.* He shook his head fiercely at the thought. *That just doesn't happen. Only if you go faster than light, and I haven't gone anywhere near that fast.*

The Captain spoke again. His tone was firm — not rude, but like a real captain, making it clear *he* was in charge. "Now then," the old man said. "Where is it you say you're from, lad?"

"Canada. Vancouver, B.C. British Columbia, that is."

"Aye," the seaman said in that dry tone. "I've heard of the place." He looked down, toward Tomi's feet. "And how old are you? Fifteen? Sixteen?"

"Nearly. Well, almost fourteen."

"What's your birthday then?"

"November. November fourth." *And you care why?*

"November fourth …?" the Captain pressed, making the date sound incomplete, like a question.

"Ninety …" Too late Tomi wondered if he should be telling his birth-date to a total stranger. It was the kind of thing every adult told you never to do. Then again, how much weirder could this get? "… two. Ninety-two."

"*Nineteen* ninety-two?" the Captain asked. He asked as though there could be other possible ninety-twos.

"Uh, yeah."

Without warning, the Captain pulled the truck in to the curb at a sharp angle. Through the windshield, Tomi read the name drawn in fresh red and gold paint on the window of the store in front of them: NATE'S DRUGSTORE AND FOUNTAIN. Beside him Patsy Ann lifted her head, sniffed the air, then climbed stiffly to her feet.

Captain Harper rummaged deep into his pocket. His hand emerged with a wad of green paper. Carefully he unfolded an American one-dollar bill. From inside its folds he drew a nickel which he handed to Tomi. "Take that in there, if you would," he nodded toward the drugstore, "and pick me up a newspaper. I need to step across to the hardware." He yanked opened his door and swung down to the unpaved street.

Tomi looked doubtfully at the coin in his hand, but by now the Captain was halfway across the street. A sharp bark rang in his left ear. He opened the door and stepped out.

Before he was able to close it behind him, Patsy Ann barked again. She stood at the edge of the seat, eyeing the ground but seemingly reluctant to jump that far.

"Okay, okay." Tomi lifted her down, groaning under her solid weight. On terra firma, the dog shook, then quickly gained the sidewalk. Trotting across it, she put her nose to the drugstore door.

"I don't think you're allowed in there, Patsy Ann," Tomi said. He held the dog's determined shoulders back with one knee and tried to sidle past her.

"Oh, that's okay," said a cheerful voice from behind a counter. "She's about due for a banana split, hey Patsy Ann?"

The store reminded Tomi of the place where Jimmy Stewart worked in that movie Mom liked to watch every Christmas, It's a Wonderful Life. A soda fountain counter ran along most of one side.

He heard laughter. Two girls sat on stools drinking milkshakes from tall glasses. They glanced over at the handsome boy with the longish black hair and Asian features, then quickly dropped their eyes.

"Mom said it's true." The one wearing a mauve cardigan was suddenly serious. "The Depression's finally catching up with Juneau. We have to watch every penny, she says."

"But Sophie, you have to! You promised." The other girl's voice came close to a whine. "It's only overnight. And besides, it'll be swingy."

"I know it will. But it's not just Mother. Dad says if they close the mine we're busted, just busted. We'll have to pack up and go." Sophie's gaze drifted back to the tall boy with the unfamiliar face.

"Oh, he's all wet," the pouty girl said.

A young man came to the end of the counter and leaned down to put a banana split on the floor. Patsy Ann gave a little grunt and buried her nose in the sweet treat. "Get you anything?" the youth asked Tomi.

"Just a newspaper."

"By the door. Five cents."

Holy cow. Wonder how much a split is? Tomi handed over his nickel and turned to go. Patsy Ann caught up to him at the door, as he pulled a newspaper from the pile in a wire rack. "You're going to get an ice cream headache, eating that fast," he said, and opened the door.

The white dog pushed past him onto the sidewalk. "Hey!" a voice boomed. Looking up, Tomi became aware of a rugged giant of a man dancing a clumsy jig on the sidewalk. Evidently Patsy Ann had walked right out in front of him, nearly knocking him over.

"She didn't mean to ..." Tomi started to say. But the man wasn't upset at all. In fact, he was bending down now to scratch behind the pointed white ears.

"Guess you couldn't hear me coming, could you, Patsy Ann?" the man said in a sort of affectionate growl. A huge hand disappeared into a pocket, then held something down to the dog. She took it with a ladylike little grunt. Straightening up, the man ran his eyes over Tomi. "Who's your friend, then?" He seemed to be speaking to Patsy Ann.

Clutching his newspaper, Tomi nodded a noncommittal hello.

The big man stepped back to get a better view of the boy. "You new to Juneau?" For some reason he was speaking even louder now, as though he thought perhaps Tomi was deaf. "First time Juneau?"

"Yeah," Tomi answered. "My first time here. Just visiting." *I hope.*

"Speak English pretty good, don'tcha?" The man said this like it was something unusual. "Where'dja learn that, hey?"

The man's attitude rankled. Then again, Tomi was a stranger here and this guy was the size of a football lineman. Across the street he saw Captain Harper come out of a store and step around a row of wheelbarrows lined up by the door. He took a chance. "Mister, I didn't *learn* it. I *speak* it. Just like my parents and my grandparents do." *Jeez. What cave did you crawl out of?*

The man sneered. "What? They come over in the *Mayflower*? How stupid do I look?" He stalked off, shaking his head. Tomi caught the words "Damn Japs" floating back to him.

Tomi was usually pretty slow to lose it, but the way so many people here spoke was really goading him. Obaacha talked about growing up with people like this. But that was so totally last century! He yanked open the truck door and half threw the paper inside.

Tomi held the door open for Patsy Ann. His dark mood deepened when she chose that moment to trot down the sidewalk away from them. Wearing his anger like a cloak, he barely noticed the Captain slip into his seat and start the engine.

The old man glanced at the boy's scowling face. "Anything in the news?" he asked mildly.

Tomi picked up the *Daily Alaska Empire.* The paper hadn't changed its old-fashioned black-and-white look since the antique issues that papered the bunkhouse walls. Scanning the headlines he read aloud:

KING AND BRIDE VISIT CANADA. *King?* PICTURES SENT THROUGH AIR: 'TELEVISION' CARRIES COLUMBIA–PRINCETON GAME TO DISTANT VIEWERS. *Eh? Howzat news?*

The Captain's voice was soft, almost gentle. "Look under the masthead. See the date there? Read that, lad."

"June 7, 19 —"

Tomi's mind went numb for a moment. "1939."

Suddenly he felt sick to his stomach. He'd suspected since yesterday. It was the only thing that made any sense. Except that it didn't make any sense at all.

Even now, he couldn't really believe it. He craned his neck to search the street beyond the window for something, *anything*, to disprove what he'd just read. Someone talking on a cell phone. A new car. McDonald's or FutureShop, a Starbucks, anything. They passed a row of wooden warehouses a lot like the old fishery buildings down in Steveston, only more rundown. The vehicles parked outside them could have won first prize in any classic-car rally.

He'd missed what the Captain was saying. "What?"

Captain Harper said it again: "You're not the first."

Twelve

BORROWED BOOTS

"SAY THAT again? Not the first what?"

The old man kept his eyes on the road ahead. "Not the first visitor. Patsy Ann has brought others before you."

"From Vancouver? Isn't she the town greeter? That's her job, right?"

"I suppose it is, in a way. And yes, some of them came from Canada. But," he shot a look across at the boy, "that's not what I meant."

They left the last of the built-up streets behind. Here the road followed the shoreline. A handful of small houses, cottages really, stood on the narrow strip of flat land between the road and the rise of the mountain, facing out over the blue channel.

It couldn't happen. It can't be. But it is! Tomi was suddenly anxious. "Where are we going?"

"We're nearly there," the old captain smiled. "I really *do* need a hand, to move my vessel 'round to the ways. That was my excuse for fetching you. But then, I have something to show you."

Tomi found the old-fashioned crank handle and cracked

open the window. He breathed in fresh air, glad for the oxygen and the clean, wild smell of salt wind. *The old guy* knows. *And he isn't freaking out.*

The Captain spun the wheel, and tires scrunched over gravel as the pickup rolled to a stop. Looking toward the water, Tomi saw rows of floating docks very much like those he knew around Vancouver. But those marinas at home were full of sleek white pleasure boats. Some of the very biggest even had their own helicopters.

These boats were no-nonsense working craft: flat skiffs made for carrying loads, fish boats with tall outriggers raised higher than their masts or wide decks stacked high with wire traps. The few pleasure boats among them gleamed with varnished wood.

Tomi stepped down gratefully onto firm earth. A breeze tousled his hair and the salt-and-fish tingle in his nose felt undeniably, comfortingly, real.

The Captain had parked toward one end of a gravel lot. He walked to the back of the truck and began loosening the ropes that secured the low stack of rough planks. "A little hard work always helps clear the mind," he murmured.

Yeah, right.

The cedar was heavy. With each of them taking an end, they managed four planks. The Captain leading, they followed a path that curved away from the parking lot to where a small shed stood at the top of a very short, very steep railway running down to the water. Wooden platforms made a series of shallow steps along both sides of the rusty rails.

At the first of these they put down the planks.

"Hauling her, are ya, Cap'n?" a voice behind him said.

A short fellow in greasy jeans and a T-shirt that might once, a very long time ago, have been white, stood in the door of the shed.

"Aye, Finn," the Captain answered. "Would you run the car down for me?"

"Sure thing." The greasy man disappeared into the shed.

"Stand back, lad," the Captain said.

With a rumble that made the wooden platform shake, a peculiar car rolled out of the shed on the rusty rails. Above wheels like those on a train, two rows of heavy posts, big as telephone poles, faced each other across empty space. The whole vehicle hit the water hard, sending up a huge splash. When it came to a stop the iron wheels were deep underwater. Only the tops of the timbers stuck up above the surface, like a double row of fence posts.

At the truck they picked up the Captain's other purchases and headed down a sloping gangway to the docks, which bobbed and rocked beneath their feet. Tomi made an effort to memorize their route as they passed from one float to another. At last they came to a slip at the very edge of the marina.

The *DogStar* proved to be a medium-sized sailboat. Two tall wooden masts rocked gently overhead and a trim wheelhouse glowed in the sun.

"Ever handle a line, lad?" the Captain asked.

Tomi nodded. Uncle Liam kept a boat on the Fraser River. The Tanakas often joined him for a day's outing.

Five minutes later they were chugging along inside the breakwater. Tomi stood at the rail, a wet length of heavy brown rope in his hands. *DogStar*'s deck rose and fell beneath his feet, like a slow breath. He drew sea air into his lungs and realized that he was grinning. The skipper had been right: that queasy "wrong place, wrong time" feeling was gone. It struck him that he hadn't had a thought about home — about Dad or Amanda or Obaacha or even the dreaded "family honeymoon" — for hours.

The timbers rising above the water just ahead reminded Tomi of the landing lights on either side of a runway. White foam boiled up along *DogStar*'s sides and she drifted to a stop, her rail bumping gently against one of the raised posts. Tomi dropped a rope over the post and knotted it around a deck cleat. *DogStar*'s engine died away into silence.

The Captain swiftly secured a few more ropes, then gave a thumbs-up to the stocky figure by the shed. A moment later a puff of blue smoke shot from a tin chimney.

There was a rattle and a sucking *sploosh*. A rusty cable rose out of the water and drew tight. *DogStar* shuddered and began to move again. Tomi got it right away: the cable was pulling on the sunken rail car, hauling its nautical cargo slowly toward dry land. Suddenly the bow tipped up and they were riding up the slope out of the water. With a gentle thud, the boat tilted to one side and came to rest against the right-hand row of timbers.

Their "voyage" was a short one. When the whole affair — rail car, timbers and boat — jerked to a stop, *DogStar* sat high above the tide. Water dripped from her sides and ran in small rivers along the platforms beside the rails.

Finn emerged from the shed carrying several thick wooden wedges. He disappeared out of sight beneath *DogStar*'s hull, then reappeared empty-handed. He returned to the shed and emerged carrying a ladder.

When the ladder rested against the side of the boat and Captain Harper had lashed its top rung firmly to the boat's rail, he didn't immediately climb down. Instead he dusted his hands and caught Tomi's eye. "What d'ye say to a bite of lunch, lad?"

Tomi had to lift his feet over a high sill to step into the small wheelhouse. It was warm with sunlight and smelled faintly of wet wool and diesel oil and tobacco. The Captain nodded for the boy to follow him and disappeared down a steep stair that led deeper into the boat.

For an instant Tomi flashed on all those street-proofing classes and "beware of strangers" drills he'd been given in school. But if what he'd come to believe was really true, it seemed a little late to be worrying about that stuff. *Or do I mean, "early"?* He grinned and stepped to the stairs.

These were more like a ladder than ordinary steps. Tomi had to bend backwards to avoid cracking his forehead as he descended. At the bottom he found himself in a small but tidy little room, as wide as the boat. Judging from the furnishings it was part kitchen, part dining room and part library. Motes of dust danced in the sun beaming through round portholes.

Dropping the paper on the table and gesturing Tomi to a built-in bench, the Captain wedged himself into the tiny space next to a sink. He pulled a half-eaten chicken from beneath a counter, ferreted out a jar of mayonnaise and began making sandwiches. When he was done, he put them on plates and reached back under the counter. He pulled out two green bottles, popped the caps off these and put one chilled Coca-Cola and a plate with a sandwich on it in front of Tomi. He placed the other Coke and sandwich in front of a chair but didn't sit down right away.

Turning to a small desk built into one corner of the room, the Captain opened a drawer. "I said I had something to show you." When he turned back, he held out a brightly printed little booklet.

Suddenly hungry, Tomi bit into the sandwich. The fresh sourdough was soft and tart around the mayo and mildly spiced chicken. *Quite the short-order cook, Skipper.* He put the sandwich down and reached for the booklet. On the front, grinning tourists lined the rail of a posh cruise ship. Then he felt *DogStar* seem to shift in her dry dock. The soaring white profile behind the tourists in the picture was Vancouver's landmark "Five Sails" cruise terminal. Flipping faster through the pages he found more pictures — ads for whale watching and heli-skiing and ship-board restaurants. He reached the back page. A mark at the bottom caught his eye. The words "Copyright 1998, Inside Passage Cruise Lines Ltd." were printed there. Someone had circled the words in pencil.

The Captain bit into his own sandwich and chewed it thoughtfully. His eyes stayed on Tomi.

Tomi swallowed hard and found his voice. "How …?" he started to say, but no other words came.

"I told you there have been others. Patsy Ann brings them from another time. Her very first visitor, Jeff, he brought that little booklet."

"Where is he now?"

A shadow crossed the old man's face. "I can't say. None of our visitors stay forever. They all find their way home eventually. So will you, I expect. When you're ready."

"When I'm *ready*?" Tomi erupted. "I'm ready now!"

The Captain's beard twitched in a faint smile. "Oh, no, you're not. Patsy Ann brought you here for *something*. I don't know what. And you may not either, for a while. But there's always a reason why she brings who she does."

Tomi looked from the crisp, colourful brochure to the newspaper with its streaky black headlines. *So there's a king now, instead of a queen. TV really is news.* What else was news in 1939?

"Penny for your thoughts?" the Captain said at last.

"I … I was beginning to think I was crazy," Tomi admitted.

"That's what I thought the first time too," the old man chuckled. "This may not be normal, exactly. But no, we're not crazy."

"How long do the … visitors … usually stay?" Tomi asked.

"Hard to say. As long as it takes to figure out why they're here, and then do whatever it is they need to do," the Captain said. "I guess the hard part is mostly the figurin'.

A few weeks. Sometimes a few months."

A few months! Holy crap! Suddenly Tomi felt like laughing. Here he'd thought he was in trouble for failing history and geography. He could barely imagine the kerfuffle if he flat-out vanished for a couple of months. Yet he couldn't deny how much better it felt having someone else who *knew*, someone to share his sense of strangeness with.

"Only a few, a very few, of us know anything about this," the Captain was saying now. "Patsy Ann and me and one or two others," he ended vaguely. "It's much better we keep it that way. Try not to attract too much attention to yourself."

Right. Well, that was working well so far. He thought about the FBI and Agent Nichols.

"And, if you can," the Captain fixed him with a level look, "keep your own counsel about what's to come. We have enough on our hands with the present."

Gotcha. He'd seen enough TV shows where the hero travelled through time and then caused some huge disaster by trying to improve on history. *But there's something I'm supposed to do.* Jeez, this was like a test where you have to guess the questions *and* the answers.

The Captain eyed Tomi's feet. "All of our other visitors had funny-looking shoes too," he said.

Tomi frowned down at his sneakers. They were nothing special, just your basic runners from Wal-Mart.

"Buck Rogers is the only fella around here who wears boots like those," the Captain said.

Buck who?

"Wait here while I see what I can do," the Captain said.

When the old sailor returned, he dropped two pairs of sturdy leather boots in different sizes in front of Tomi. "See if any of those fit ye'."

Tomi examined them skeptically. "Did they belong to other visitors?"

"Aye. They left them behind when they went home. So you see, you'll be walking in the footsteps of those who came before ye'!" The grey eyebrows shot up as though this idea struck him as very witty.

The first pair of boots Tomi tried was obviously too small but the second fit reasonably enough. He laced them up tight, feeling the unfamiliar stiffness of the leather. He wondered what had happened to the last kid to wear them. *Maybe the captain'll tell me sometime.*

But all the Captain said was: "Patsy Ann will let us know when it's time for you to go. You can change back then."

Us. He liked the sound of that. *At least I'm not alone anymore.*

The old man straightened. "Now, let's get you back to Mizz Sanderson."

TOMI WALKED down the hall toward the dorm room. His "new" boots made much louder footfalls on the hard floor than his old sneakers had. In his pocket he felt three quarters tap against his leg — the share Miss Sanderson had let him keep from the $1.50 that Captain Harper had paid the orphanage for his time.

He still felt out of place. But if he couldn't explain *how*, it was good to know there must be a *why*, even if he wasn't yet sure what it was.

From the room at the end of the hall came the sound of music. Some kind of band, the sort Obaacha listened to sometimes. His hand was on the doorknob when he heard an angry yell, a thud, and the music skidding off into a painful chalk-on-blackboard *scrreeech* that ended with a crash. Someone swore.

He opened the door in time to see Charley Ramsey's fist connect with JP's shoulder. The smaller boy went down and Charley landed on top of him, arms flailing. "You stupid, clumsy ..." the white boy was yelling. "You broke it! I *told* you to be careful and now it's bust!"

The fight disappeared behind a knot of other boys. Some egged the pair on, saying things like "Give it to 'im!" and "Hit him back, JP, hit him!"

Upside down on the floor was a wooden box, with its hinged lid gaping open. Near it was a flat black disc, as big around as a dinner plate.

"Hey!" Tomi pushed his way into the circle of boys. JP was curled on his side, knees to his chin and his arms over his head. Charley was sitting across his hips, methodically punching JP in the arms and shoulders.

"Hey, leave him alone!" Tomi grabbed the white boy by the shoulders and pulled. Charley tried to pivot and swing at Tomi, but Tomi grabbed his arms from behind and held on. "Chill! Just chill!" he panted into the white boy's ear.

"He bust the music box!" Charley shouted. "He's an idiot,

ignorant Indian and now it goes too slow. We lost our music!"
He swung a kick at JP that only missed when Tomi yanked
Charley away at the last moment.

The circle of faces around them darkened. Tomi could
hear words passing in the language he'd heard before.

"Whadaya mean, he bust the music box? What music box?"

"The record player," Charley wriggled and swore. "Son of
a bitch was goofing around and he hit it to the floor. Now
look at it." He raised his chin toward the box on the floor.
"It's wrecked." Tomi could see tears starting down Charley's
pasty cheeks.

"Hey man, cool it," Tomi tried to sound calm and
soothing. "Maybe I can fix it. Just chill out and let me try."

"Screw you!" Charley doubled over and pulled sideways,
trying to pull Tomi off balance. But Tomi saw it coming and
let his knees go slack, putting his full weight on the other
boy. JP was on his feet now. Charley twisted hard a few more
times then gave up, his fury finally seeming to drain away.

Tomi relaxed his bear hug. Charley scrambled to his feet,
turning a spiteful look on the newcomer. He muttered
something that ended in "… Jap!" and Tomi felt a splatter of
spit hit his shoulder.

Now Tomi's own blood raced. He felt a hot energy rise in
him and pulled back his fist. A voice from somewhere inside
him spoke softly: *Remember* when *you are.* He breathed in
deeply and tried to let his temper flow out of him along with
the exhausted air.

Watery green eyes stayed locked on intense dark ones a

moment longer, but the fight seemed to be over for now.

Careful not to turn his back on the white kid, Tomi stepped sideways and squatted to examine the box on the floor. The lid was just a lid, but in the deep part of the box was a round platter like the turntable inside a microwave. Beside it, what looked like part of a trumpet or a bugle was bent at an odd angle. He picked up the black disc and centred it on the platter. In the middle of the disc was a round paper label. On the rest of the surface, fine grooves cut into the black material reflected light in rainbow colours.

So this was what an old record player looked like up close. He carried it across the room to his bunk.

Tomi pulled his backpack from his closet. Silently thanking Agent Nichols for only taking his mp3 player, he got out his little tool kit and opened the leather case. With JP hovering at his shoulder and Charley Ramsey scowling from across the room, he set to work.

It took a while to figure out what was wrong: a belt that connected the wind-up motor to the turntable kept slipping off. Just when he'd twigged to that, the dinner bell interrupted him. But Tomi made short work of the gluey stew that was on offer that night, and it was the girls' night to clean up. Even so, it was almost lights-out before he had the record player back the way he thought it was supposed to go.

He could feel Charley's pale eyes on him when at last he put the black record on the turntable. He dropped the arm on the outside edge, flicked the little lever to "play" and held his breath. The record began to turn and the threadbare dorm room was filled with the raspy sound of a cheerful dance band.

Tomi looked up and met JP's delighted grin with one of his own.

THAT EVENING, Patsy Ann trotted up the gravel path to the log house just as the sky was fading to purple over the distant mountain. She barked once, twice, then a third time before the door opened, splashing warm lamplight out onto the porch.

"Come on in, then," Mizz Alex called.

Patsy Ann rushed the steps and trotted across to the door. She stepped into the kitchen, rubbing her plump white side across the woman's legs on the way in.

Mizz Alex spooned the last of the soup from a pot into a bowl, and put it on the floor. She took her mug of tea back to the table, which was spread with papers. She picked up a pen and returned to the notes she was making on a lined pad.

Patsy Ann sniffed at the bowl. With a grateful little grunt, she began eating. When she was done, she walked over to the woman and stretched out near her feet. Her little black eyes watched the woman intently.

"Yes, dear, I know," Mizz Alex said, catching her eye. "You were right and I was wrong. I'm going down to see Judge Burns first thing in the morning to see if I can set it right."

Patsy Ann let her head drop to the floor. Her dark eyes closed. In a few minutes the first gentle snores rose from the white muzzle.

Thirteen

THE MUSEUM

SISTER AGATHA rapped on her desk. Today's Bible verse was from someone named John: "We know that we live in him and he in us, because he has given us of his spirit." That works, Tomi thought. Obaacha was always reminding him to listen to his "Buddha in the belly."

He let his mind wander. Things didn't seem nearly so weird now that he knew for sure where — and, more importantly, when — he was. In fact, 1939 felt pretty normal. *Now, that's strange!* He smiled to himself.

The dorm thing wasn't that different from the summer three years ago when he'd gone to camp. Except that was sixty-four years from now! It was a little weird not to have a computer to jump on, but no one seemed to miss it. *Well uh, goofus, why would they?* Yet everything seemed to get done.

He felt the presence of the other boys sitting on either side and behind him. JP had kind of adopted him. Charley Ramsey was a pretty unhappy camper. Maybe it was being the only white kid in the dorm. Whatever it was, Charley seemed determined to make up for his misery by running down everybody else in the world.

And school, how could that really be any worse in 1939 than in 2006? He should know all this stuff — *I mean, it's already happened!*

Besides, he had more important things to think about. *There's always a reason. Wasn't that what old Captain Harper said?* Tomi looked around the small classroom. Through the thin wall he could hear the younger kids reciting the alphabet in the room next door.

So what was his reason for being here, violating every law of physics and nature? Something to do with the orphanage, maybe?

He caught the words "… visiting Canada." The nun was holding up a newspaper.

His heart jumped. "Tomi Tanaka," Sister Agatha said in a voice as cheerful, as friendly, as nice as possible. "You can probably tell us his name, can't you?"

Tomi sat frozen. *Who?* He tried to read the headline but Sister Agatha had put the paper down on her desk.

"Tomi? Who's visiting Canada?"

Eh? Who's visiting Canada? How the … Wait … I know this … It had been in the paper yesterday. He had it: "The King!"

"Yes, of course the King, Tomi." Sister Agatha smiled encouragement. "But which king?"

How should I …

"You're Canadian, I'm sure you know this. Don't you?"

King? There was a queen. What kings did he know? *Tut? Too Egypt. Elvis? Too rock'n'roll. Burger? Get serious.* "George?"

"Why no," the nun gave Tomi an odd look. "No, not George.

Can anyone else tell me his name?"

The eager girl in the front row waved her hand. The nun's face fell, then took on a resigned look. "Yes, Zoe," she said.

"Edward, it's King Edward!"

From his seat two desks over, JP winked and shot Tomi a thumbs-up. In the corner, Charley Ramsey slouched low, pale eyes on the new kid and a thoughtful look on his face.

By the time the noon bell rang, Tomi had established that his knowledge of geography and history hadn't improved at all by being sent back, oh, about seven decades. He was glad to discover that other things hadn't changed. Math was the one subject he usually aced and 3,506 times 43 was still 150,758. And when Sister Agatha made him read aloud from a story about a husky dog, she complimented him on how well he pronounced the English words, like it was a surprise.

At the sound of the bell, books slammed shut and a hubbub of voices erupted. Sister Agatha shouted to make herself heard: "Don't dawdle back. Remember it's Thursday, and we have a field trip!"

THE CAR, high on its spoke wheels, rocked wildly as the driver veered at the last minute toward the sidewalk. Brakes squealed and the vehicle lurched to a stop with its bumper just clearing the high curb. A door opened and a tall woman in a dark suit got out. A moment later a white dog followed her, dropping heavily to the dirt. The woman brushed at her sleeves and skirt, then stepped onto the sidewalk and looked up.

The building was the biggest in Juneau, rivalled only by the Baranof Hotel itself. The hotel may have looked down on its neighbours from the eminence of its five floors, but the United States Federal Building had the edge in volume: its two brick floors extended over a full block. Most of the important offices for running the Alaska Territory could be found under its roof.

A chatter of young voices brought the woman's eyes back to street level. She stepped into the shelter of the car's high bumper as a chattering mass of boys and girls, ranging in age from no-longer-small to early teens, streamed past. A pair of boys trailing behind the rest brought the woman forward a step but then she stopped herself. One of the boys had the strong features of a local native. The other shared his black hair and broad cheeks, but there the resemblance ended. The second boy's head turned as he walked past, giving the woman a long, neutral look.

The woman squared her shoulders and pushed against the tall, heavy door. Patsy Ann followed her in.

A broad staircase dominated the small lobby. Behind glass on one wall was a directory. The tall woman consulted it, then climbed the stairs to the second floor, the dog accompanying her. At the top of the stairs she paused, then turned right down a wide hallway. Patsy Ann's toenails tapped loudly on the polished floor.

They came to a door on which, in gold letters, were the words: U.S. FEDERAL COURT — TERRITORIAL DIVISION.

The woman took a deep breath and stepped inside. A woman at a desk was sorting papers. At her elbow were a telephone and a spray of wildflowers in a waterglass. She looked up. "Miss Kasilof?" She tipped her head toward an inner office. "Go right in."

Mizz Alex disappeared through the second door. Patsy Ann stepped up to the woman at the desk, giving her an affectionate nuzzle.

"How're you keeping, old girl?" the woman said, rubbing her knuckles along the furry back toward Patsy Ann's tail. Patsy Ann stretched happily into the caress. The woman opened a drawer, withdrew a square of waxed paper and unwrapped a berry-scented pastry. Breaking it in two, she offered the larger half to the white dog.

A moment later, the clickety-click of hard canine toenails could again be heard echoing down the polished hallway. After a few turns and another flight of stairs, the sound stopped in front of a pair of glass doors. The letters on these doors read: FEDERAL BUREAU OF INVESTIGATION.

A gentleman in pinstripe trousers reached over the white dog and held the door for her. "Ma'am," he murmured.

Patsy Ann stepped around a reception counter into an area laid out with rows of desks. She shivered gently and got down to work: a half sandwich here, a muffin remnant there, a sliver of candied salmon after that. At the far end of the room she paused to catch her breath.

Ahead of her was an office where a thin man with a narrow face and cold eyes pored over papers on a desk. Patsy Ann cocked her head and watched him concentrate on something he was working out with a pen on paper.

"Ha!" the man exclaimed at last. "Gotcha!" He held up the sheet he'd been working on. Printed on it were lines of numbers. Above them, often scratched out and overwritten, were letters in Avery Nichols' own hand.

The FBI agent lifted a phone receiver to his ear and tapped twice on the cradle. "Get me Ingrid Sanderson," he barked. Long fingers tapped impatiently. Then his head shot up and in a quite different voice he said, "Ingrid, it's Avery."

Nichols leaned over the phone. "I think we have a live one. I just got this, direct from J. Edgar's desk: *coded!* These so-called *nissei*, these second-generation Japs? The Emperor's using them as spies." He paused to listen, then erupted. "He did *what*? For *Harper*?" The agent's brows knitted over close-set eyes. "That man has some very suspect associates." He listened some more. "Well don't lose him, whatever you do."

The agent returned the phone to its cradle and swivelled away from the desk. At the sight of Patsy Ann, the agent exploded out of his chair. "Hey you! Get out! Outta here!" Heads turned to the red-faced man standing in the office door. "What's that mangy mutt doing in here?" Nichols demanded.

The white dog gave a prim little shake. Tail high, she turned away and walked off without hurrying.

"Don't worry, Avery," came a sarcastic voice from an adjoining office. "She didn't hear any of your high-security secrets. Don't you know she's deaf!" The voice laughed.

"There's no dogs allowed on federal property," Nichols fumed.

"She's a city official," came the deep chortle from the next office.

YOU JERK! *You shoulda said something!*

But he'd been listening to JP tell a joke, something about spelling "Canada," and they were halfway down the block before he connected the woman in the suit with lasso-wielding Mizz Alex of the lumber yard.

"'N'-eh? 'D'-eh?" JP said, doubling over in laughter. He gave Tomi a "get-it?" nudge with this elbow.

"Hey, yeh," Tomi faked. *Sorry, guy, try me another time with that one.* At the corner he turned to look back and caught a flash of white fur as Patsy Ann followed the woman into the big brick building.

"Boys and girls! Boys and girls!" Sister Agatha gathered her little flock around her by a door framed in stone carved in a vaguely floral pattern. A brass plaque read: ALASKA STATE MUSEUM.

It wasn't at all like other museums Tomi had visited. Those were imposing edifices. This was more like a big house. Still, glass cases lined every wall, and more cases, set on tables with glass tops, filled the floors. The first exhibits told how prospector Joe Juneau and his buddy, Richard Harris, found gold at the foot of a river here in 1880. A wall of axes and shovels and miners' lamps dramatized how Juneau had been built "from the ground up" on the discovery of gold.

Who knew? Tomi mused as he drifted from room to room. Russia used to own Alaska. An exhibit devoted to whaling made him feel queasy. When he looked at the gun — more like a small cannon — that had actually been used to kill whales "until recent years," he shivered.

He heard Sister Agatha clap her hands. "Everyone. Everyone! Gather up and follow me."

Tomi found her in the small lobby, standing at the foot of some stairs. "I think you'll all find this next exhibit something special," Sister Agatha said, and turned to go up.

The museum's second floor held more rooms like those below, but Sister Agatha did not head for these. Instead she turned down a narrow hall that led to the back of the building. It ended at a heavy door. Iron straps bound its thick planks. The door stood open. Past it was a windowless room hardly bigger than Tomi's bedroom at home.

The room was a well filled with light. Sunshine fell through a skylight onto a single glass case, like an upended aquarium, that stood alone in the middle of the floor. As the class filed in and flowed around the exhibit, there was a rippling intake of breath.

In the glass cage stood a boy. The figure was perhaps a metre tall; it resembled a large doll with a face like a cherub and curly hair. It wore the hard trousers and roughly stitched wool shirt of a Klondike prospector. Hands hung loosely from the sleeves. A frozen gaze stared solemnly out of the glass prison.

But that wasn't what caused everyone who saw it to draw

in their breath. Even in the watery light from above, there was no question. The figure's hands, head, face and hair were all fashioned from the same yellow metal. The boy was made entirely of gold!

"His full name," Sister Agatha read from the cardboard notice propped at the figure's feet, "is 'The Golden Boy of Lost Creek.'"

Tomi craned to read the rest: "A Bequest for the Prosperity and Enjoyment of All Juneau Citizens, donated by the estate of the late Mr. Michael Alexander (b.: Mikhail Elexei, St. Petersburg, 1814 d: Juneau, 1907), Juneau Businessman and Public Citizen."

Sister Agatha explained how "Russian Alex" had been one of the first prospectors to follow Joe Juneau, becoming a giant in local lore. "Some people believe Russian Alex found the other end of Joe's gold seam, a vein of ore running right under the mountain," the nun said.

Someone snorted in disbelief. Looking past the golden figure, Tomi saw the scornful expression on Charley's face, wavering through the layers of glass.

Sister Agatha gave Charley a disappointed look. "Of course, no one else ever found it, so it is just a legend." She straightened and smiled in a shaft of light from above. "But some people like to believe the story anyway."

"At least the gold part," someone said. A sly chuckle ran around the little room.

Tomi gave JP a "what's-up?" look.

"The gold mine they got is running out of gold," JP

explained, leaning in at Tomi's shoulder. "Soon even white people ain't gonna have jobs."

"Don't say that!" a bright voice protested.

Tomi turned to look. The speaker wasn't any of the kids from the Home. This girl was almost dark enough to be native, but her hair was straw-blonde. He recognized the girl from the soda counter. Yesterday she'd worn mauve. Today she had on dark blue pants and a cream blouse under a vest. Her pretty face was flushed with anger, or hurt.

Another ripple ran round the small room. Then Charley sneered, "I bet Russian Alex made it up!"

"Then where'd the gold come from for the boy?" JP asked in his soft voice.

Sister Agatha coughed loudly. "They also say," the nun began firmly. "They also say," she dropped her voice to a near whisper, "that once upon time, the Golden Boy of Lost Creek could dance!"

This time there was no ripple of indrawn breath. Instead, a shuffle of feet and one or two stifled snickers suggested that the class thought Sister Agatha was beginning to pile it on just a bit.

But Tomi had noticed something that no one else gave a first glance to, let alone a second look. The floor of the Boy's case was fenced in wooden sides that rose to the figure's knees. Tucked down there was a cardboard box with broken sides and in it, dozens of large and small rods, levers, cogs, gears, springs and screws.

The golden face with its pursed lips, blind cherub's gaze

and ringlets worked in precious metal exerted a powerful fascination. But after a while, the boy's silent and unflinching stare became, well, a little creepy. Sister Agatha's flock began to drift away from the boy in the glass box and out to the other rooms on this floor of the museum.

But Tomi remained rooted in place. His eyes flicked back and forth between the Golden Boy and the box of cogs and gears. In his mind he considered them first as separate pieces, then together. Working together. *I wonder …*

Tomi leaned close to the glass. A second card had fallen down into the darkest corner of the case. He squinted and read aloud: "Michael Alexander, who trained as a clock-maker as a boy, built the Golden Boy over several years and presented the …" — he took a moment to work out the word — "… the *automoton* to his family in 1884. According to legend, a clockwork mechanism inside the Boy could be activated to make him perform. Sadly, Golden Boy was taken apart for cleaning after Mr. Alexander's death and was never reassembled."

"Isn't that sad?" The blonde girl produced a notebook and a pen and began scribbling. "He used to dance and now he's just a box of old parts."

"What's that for?" JP gave the notebook a suspicious look.

"Oh, I have to do a project for school, something about Juneau's history and, well, there it is." The girl nodded to the Boy. "'Russian Alex and the Lost Mine.'" A thoughtful look came into her blue eyes on the last word.

The watery sunlight had moved on. The golden face

seemed to have lost some of its glow. But something new and hot burned inside Tomi's chest. "I bet I could make him dance again."

It slipped out without thinking. And without any doubt. It would be the ultimate project. This would be even better than the machine!

"You think so?" the blonde girl asked with wide eyes.

"You bet he could!" JP spoke up stoutly. "He fixed our record player after it got all smashed up. Made it work better'n ever."

The girl gave Tomi a new look and the tall boy felt himself blush.

"Sophie? Sophie Carr?" A woman's voice — a *mom's* voice — reached them from the hallway.

"In here!" the girl called back.

"Who are you talking to?" A short woman bustled into the small room. She had waved blonde hair and a load of papers under one arm. "Sophie Carr! How many times have I told you about talking to strange boys." She cast a look over Tomi and JP and reached her free hand out for her daughter. "And orphanage boys at that! What are you thinking of?"

Sorry! Sophie mouthed the word, rolling her eyes for emphasis. To her mother she protested aloud, "But you talk to strange people all the time!"

Sophie's protests faded toward the stairs. A minute later, from the same direction, they heard the clapping of Sister Agatha's hands. "Everybody! Everybody!"

Tomi pulled himself reluctantly away from the glass case. *You're gonna dance again, little dude, I promise you.*

OUT ON the street, the nun counted her little flock and started them back toward the Orphans and Indigents' Home. Soon the class was scattered along a block of sidewalk.

Tomi and JP walked together. Tomi's thoughts were racing. You could do almost anything with enough gears. He'd seen some amazing toys that twirled and kicked and bowed by clockwork.

Then there was the girl, Sophie, the blonde with skin as dark as his own. Could there really be a lost vein of gold?

"Do we go to the museum a lot?" he asked JP.

"Not really. That was the only time," JP said.

"I'd like to get back there."

"There's Sunday."

"Sunday?"

"After lunch, we can do what we want. Sometimes families visit. Or there's a baseball game. Or if we have some money we can see a movie. You could go then."

Sunday. Today was Thursday. What if the museum was closed Sunday? *Arrgh.*

ORPHAN LIFE seemed much less bleak that night. Almost as soon as they got back to the dorm, the record player was out and wound up and playing the half-dozen records the dorm owned in tight rotation. *It's even worse than Top Forty,* Tomi groused when some guy began warbling about "Rosalie" for the fourth time in a quarter-hour.

After a supper of sausages and fried cabbage, with more Jell-O for dessert, his mood lifted further. The boys who regularly played cards got their decks out. A few read, helping each other past the harder words. JP's cousin Willy Paul unwrapped a knot of soft cloth to reveal a grapefruit-sized piece of cedar wood, then opened a pocketknife and whittled away at the wood, which he was gradually transforming into the shape of a turtle.

Tomi pulled out the only thing he had to read and kicked back with Superman's latest adventure. *Holds up pretty well, considering it's set sixty-seven years in the future.*

"Tomi?"

He looked up. It was one of the younger boys, who was holding a hand out. In it was a toy not much bigger than the boy's palm: a racing figure riding a motorcycle. "Can you fix this?"

"What's wrong with it?" He took the toy out of the boy's hand. It was made of tin, with rubber tires on wheels that turned. Where the motorcycle's motor was, it had a place for a wind-up key.

"Won't go," the boy said, a serious look on his round face.

"Let me see," Tomi said. He pulled out his travelling tool kit and positioned the motorcycle toy in the best of the bad light that reached his bed. Forty minutes later, he sent the little bike whirring across the floor to a shriek of delight from its owner.

Five minutes after that, another boy showed up at Tomi's bunk. He was a little older and a lot bigger than the last kid, but even shyer. He stumbled over his words as he held out a small wooden box for Tomi to look at.

It was barely bigger than two decks of cards held together. When it opened, scarlet cloth and a mirror inside the lid created a private stage for the dancer who was meant to pop up and twirl there. But the tiny dancer stuck at an awkward angle as though frozen in the act of falling to the floor. *It's a music box.*

"It was my mother's," the shy boy finally managed to get out.

Tomi felt something clench in his chest. He rubbed a sleeve across his face. "Yeh. Let me see what I can do."

Fourteen

LOCO PARENTIS

THE HALL echoed with teasing laughter and the scuff of leather soles on hard linoleum as the boys jostled to breakfast the next morning. JP was telling Tomi about his uncle, who made masks that could change their appearance from one face to another, when Miss Sanderson stuck her head out of the office door.

"Ramsey," she called. The white boy turned, a nervous scowl on his face, and started walking back toward the office.

Tomi peered at the open office door and got a shock. The FBI guy, Nichols, was in there. *What's he want with Charley? Is he an "alien" too?*

He felt JP's elbow in his ribs. "Guess they caught him," the other boy grinned. "Whatever it was."

But when Charley sauntered into the cafeteria twenty minutes later, he didn't look like someone who'd just been dressed down. The last watery eggs had long since been consumed and only a few heels of bread lay beside scrapings of pale butter. It didn't seem to bother Charley. He even wore a smirk of secret pleasure as he took a seat facing Tomi and JP a little way down the table.

Charley's good humour carried through to the morning's classes. When Sister Agatha read the day's "lesson" — a verse to the effect that "a little sleep, a little rest, and poverty will come on you like a bandit" — Charley's hand was the first up to offer his take on what the verse meant.

"You gotta grab every chance you get," he declared.

Sister Agatha looked like this wasn't quite what she had in mind, but thanked Charley for speaking up anyway.

Later, during the part of the morning that Sister Agatha always spent discussing the day's headlines, Charley was again more talkative than usual. Germany's Chancellor, whatever that was, had given a speech. For once, Charley seemed to be on top of the news. "Hitler's gonna give the Jews what they deserve," he said. "Clear 'em out and make Europe for the real Europeans!"

Tomi heard Willy Paul's voice behind him. "Maybe they'll all go back there then." Beside him, JP stifled a snicker.

Charley's mirth only began to melt away when Sister Agatha put the paper aside and started writing fractions on the blackboard for them to add. Tomi liked fractions; once you figured out the trick, they were really pretty easy. "You gotta get the bottoms the same, then it's just like adding regular numbers," he explained to JP.

The door at the back of the room banged open. "Tanaka!" It was Miss Sanderson's voice, and she sounded *P'd-off!*

Tomi rolled his eyes. *Sheesh, what now?* He turned. The woman's normally grey face was flushed almost scarlet. Her jaw worked back and forth.

"Come!" she commanded sternly, as though Tomi were a bad dog.

Tomi caught JP's eye. The other boy lifted a brow in sympathy, or warning. Tomi shrugged in reply and got to his feet.

The furious woman marched ahead of him, hard heels almost striking sparks from the worn lino. At the door to the office, Miss Sanderson tipped her head for Tomi to enter ahead of her.

He turned in the door and nearly doubled over as a furry white face pressed hard into his crotch. "Patsy Ann!" he coughed. "What are you doing here?" The stocky white dog pushed against his knees, thin tail whipping hard enough to take the rest of her back end with it.

Fending off the black nose and wet, lapping tongue, Tomi looked up into the face of Mizz Alex.

Captain Harper stood at her elbow.

"Here he is then," Miss Sanderson was saying, sounding very cross.

What did I do now?

But neither the lumber yard owner nor the Captain seemed to be calling him down. In fact, Mizz Alex looked almost sheepish. "Mr. Tanaka ... Tomi," she began. "I'm most grateful for your help with the mill and I ..." She seemed at a loss for the right words.

The Captain came to her aid. "It seems that Mizz Alexandra's discovered your talents in the mechanical field," he said. "She feels she could use them up at the yard, if you're agreeable."

Say what? Was this another hire-an-orphan-boy gig, where Sanderson took half the money? "You mean, now? Today?" he asked.

"Well, yes," Mizz Alex nodded. "But not just today." Her head came up and their eyes met. "I know you must feel that I ... I'm responsible for you being here." *Well, yeeeeah.* "But I have plenty of room and I can afford a salary — a small one — for a hand around the place. If you're interested, that is. And meals, of course. And you can sleep in the bunkhouse."

Tomi hesitated. He'd just begun to feel almost at home here. On the other hand, being out from under the watchful eye of the orphanage staff might give him a clearer shot at the Golden Boy. And for sure it meant better food.

"I have an order, a court order," Mizz Alex was saying. "It means the home has to give you up. But I won't make you. It's up to you."

He looked to the Captain. The old man winked and Tomi thought his head dipped in the faintest of nods.

"Unless you'd rather stay here?" the lumber yard owner asked.

There was a bark. Patsy Ann nuzzled his hand, then went to sit at Mizz Alex's feet. Her small dark eyes stayed on Tomi. Suddenly he was sure. "No! No way!"

Mizz Alex's face fell.

"No," Tomi blurted. "I mean, yes! Yes, I'm good to go, for sure."

The Captain beamed and Mizz Alex broke into a smile.

"I can't argue with an order from Judge Burns," Miss

Sanderson sniffed. "But he's received clothes that will have to be paid for, to say nothing of meals and —"

"Will ten dollars cover it?" Mizz Alex cut her off.

The director of the home made a sour face. She placed a form on the counter and pointed a pen to a space for the other woman to sign. To his amazement, Tomi thought he saw a blush creep up the tall lumber-yard owner's neck as she bent over the paper.

"Tanaka," Miss Sanderson said. "Go get whatever else you've got. You can take the change of clothes as well, so long as you also take those filthy things you were wearing when you arrived."

"Don't go anywhere," he almost shouted to the waiting adults. "I'll be right back!" He bolted out the door.

Tomi ran to the dorm, getting juice out of ignoring the "house rule" against moving faster than a polite walk. He pulled his backpack from the closet and stuffed in his toothbrush, paste and few new clothes. From the wicker bin near the door he reclaimed the jeans, sweatshirt, socks and underwear he'd been wearing when he arrived. A bell rang and a flash hit him: *This is all I own in the world.* Suddenly, the hoard of toys and videos and games and the overflowing closet of clothes he'd left at home in the distant future all seemed so … *too much.*

Voices in the hall signalled the end of morning classes and the arrival of the other boys. JP's face lit up at the sight of Tomi, then clouded over. "What happened?" he asked. "What're you doing?"

"I'm outta here!" Tomi crowed. Almost immediately, he felt bad for sounding so happy to be going. "I mean ..."

But JP seemed only to be pleased for him. "Hey, that's good," he said in his soft voice. "Did your parents come get you?"

"Uh-uh. But someone else did. I ... Someone I helped out, I guess. Anyway, they're getting me out."

"Maybe I'll see you again, eh?" JP suggested.

Tomi's gut clenched. He knew he would miss JP. The quiet boy had quickly become his closest thing to a friend — and not only here in the present. *Or the past ... or whatever it is.* "For sure, yeah! Maybe the weekend?"

"Good," JP said as they shook hands.

"Cool," he said. "Saturday, for sure."

"Good luck," JP's voice followed Tomi to the door.

TOMI CLIMBED into the back of Mizz Alex's car, a big, boxy green four-door. The back was roomier than the front, with way more window than Dad's Accord. But the cloth seats were hard. As Mizz Alex took the rutted road past the marsh with a reckless, pedal-to-the-metal gusto, Tomi found himself missing the security of lap and shoulder straps.

As they drove, the two adults filled Tomi in on what had happened after Nichols and Miss Sanderson took him in. That had been Tuesday. It wasn't until the next day that Patsy Ann had led Mizz Alex and the Captain to the repaired mill. Even then, its owner could scarcely credit her senses at first.

"I'd really given up hope," she said. "I'd tried everyone,

all the mechanics in the territory, I swear, and even a few off the ships. Half of them took one look at it and walked away! I had to go back half a dozen times and try it, to be sure I wasn't imagining it."

At the main road, Mizz Alex swung the wheel hard without noticeably slowing down. The car's back wheels slithered across the gravel and steadied with the vehicle pointing uphill. Mizz Alex put her foot down and the car rocketed forward with a roar. Tomi gulped and braced himself against the door.

"Not that it changes other things," Mizz Alex shouted over the engine. "I just hate to saw up all that lovely timber so the town can ship itself away in packing cases."

What was it that made Sophie cry out yesterday? A joke about even white people losing their jobs. Tomi risked a question. "Are things really that bad? Everything here is made of wood. Don't you need wood for, like, *everything*?"

"I'd like to think so." Mizz Alex's head dipped to one side. "But only when things are growing." She geared down as they came to the first of the turns that led higher up the mountain slope. "Juneau's a boom-and-bust town, Mr. Tanaka."

He broke in. "It's Tomi, Mizz Alex."

"Tomi," Mizz Alex nodded. "Well, for years the Prospector Gold Mine kept us booming. It got bad other places but it's been good here. Jobs, families, building — lots of building. Now our boom's gone bust. The mine's tapped out. Everyone knows the company's going to admit it any day now. We're looking down a barrel."

The car shook and tires rumbled as Mizz Alex accelerated across the timber bridge and swung into the rising turn beyond it.

"*Two* barrels," the Captain said, "if we include letting you loose on the roads!"

The big car rocked as Mizz Alex wheeled to the left. Hitting the brakes at the last possible moment, she brought the vehicle to a hard stop inches away from the squared stone holding up one corner of the log house.

"Yiiii!" Tomi flew forward off the hard seat and came down painfully on the even harder floor.

"Welcome home," Captain Harper said into the sudden silence.

OVER CRAB chowder and sweet tea, Mizz Alex produced a sheet of heavy paper from her purse and smoothed it out on the table. One corner of the page bore the raised imprint of a stamped seal. Tomi leaned in to read.

The paper was a court order, awarding "custody of the juvenile alien" to Alexandra Kasilof. Until his "natural parents" turned up to claim him — *like that's going to happen anytime soon* — or until "attaining the age" of fifteen, or until "the future disposal of this court" — *"disposal"?* — Tomi was to live with Mizz Alex. She was to provide "all that support, guidance and discipline as a person *in loco parentis* ought to."

All parents had to be "loco," Tomi thought. *Hey, wait a second. "Parents"?* "You're adopting me?" He wasn't ready for that. Rory was a pain sometimes, but he *had* a family.

"I should think not!" Mizz Alex said, somewhat sharply. "No. But I am, I suppose, taking responsibility for you. I hope that it's not a mistake."

That sounded more like the lady he'd come to know.

Mizz Alex laid down the ground rules. Tomi would come on as general help in the lumber yard. That meant she'd have chores and odd jobs for him to do, in return for room, board and five dollars a week. From what Tomi had seen of 1939 so far, that sounded like it might go a long way. He'd sleep in the bunkhouse, eat with Mizz Alex in the kitchen, and on Monday, they'd see about enrolling him in what was left of the school year.

"Do I have to?" *What do I have to do to get out of school, go all the way back to 1000 BC?*

"That's what the law says and what Henry Burns' order says," Mizz Alex said firmly. "So, yes, you do."

Gee, but I'm already violating the laws of physics, what's wrong with breaking one more little rule? He kept this to himself. School might not be so bad, especially if that blonde girl was in his class.

"I think it was Patsy Ann who actually tipped the balance," Mizz Alex said.

"Patsy Ann? She was there? In court?"

"Not technically, no," the Captain said. "But she is very friendly with Judge Burns, so she's often in his chambers."

"I just don't think old Henry Burns can say no to that animal," Mizz Alex agreed.

Could she actually be giggling?

SISTER AGATHA held the side door of the orphanage open for the white dog to come in. She reached into the folds of her brown robe and bent down to offer something to the dog. Patsy Ann sniffed: bread, a whiff of cheese. Gently, she took the little sandwich from the woman's fingers.

A flick of the tongue and Patsy Ann set off along the echoing hallway. At the corner she turned right, and at the pair of swinging doors she put her nose down and pushed. She stepped across the narrow lobby and started down the hall on the other side.

A gust of ill-temper blew out from a door on her left.

"You're kidding?" Avery Nichols sputtered.

"Don't blame me! It was a signed order. I didn't have a choice."

"Damn it, Ingrid," the agent said. "This was working out perfectly. I knew where he was all the time. You were keeping an eye on him. He was safely out of circulation. Now ..."

Patsy Ann paid no attention as she carried on down the hall. At the end of the hallway, one of the double doors was open. She stepped through into a boisterous babble of boys horsing around after supper. The air was full of their assorted smells: unwashed socks, gravy, soapy hair. For the next several minutes she was busy accepting pats and scratches behind the ear, corners of cookies and dusty squares of twice-melted chocolate.

When the welcome wore down at last, she doubled back to the first set of bunks by the door. A boy sat on the lower bunk, reading a comic book. On the cover was a man flying.

Patsy Ann lowered herself into a crouch, tensed once or twice, then launched herself heavily into the sagging bunk. The boy's face lit up.

Patsy Ann curled herself into a half-moon and settled in with her back to the inside of his knees. She was still there half an hour later when the lights went out.

Fifteen
NICKEL MOVIES

AFTER CAPTAIN Harper had departed in his own truck, Mizz Alex invited Tomi to join her in what she called the "sitting room."

It was well named: the chairs were deep and comfortable, and a large cabinet in a corner proved to be a radio. It turned on with a hum that faded as a news broadcast began. The news seemed to Tomi to contain all the usual mayhem, just in different places. When the news ended, the broadcast switched to a baseball game.

Mizz Alex perched a pair of reading glasses on her nose, picked up a magazine and settled in. Tomi tried to get interested in the game, but without any action to watch he found the play-by-play hard to follow.

"Hmph," Mizz Alex snorted at something in the magazine.

"What's that?" Tomi asked.

"This new radio thing they're writing about, sending moving pictures over the air ..."

"You mean television."

"Is that what they're calling it? It's all the rage in New York, I guess, but I just don't see it catching on. With radio you can read, work, cook. But this thing, you'd have to just sit there and watch this little screen or whatever it is. Idle as cats on a windowsill."

"Couch potatoes."

She gave Tomi a dubious look. "Well, cats or potatoes, it's all a waste of time as far as I can tell."

Yeah, that's what Obaacha says, too. "Maybe, Mizz Alex. But trust me, it's gonna catch on!"

"Hmph. We'll see."

Yup. "Say, Mizz Alex?"

"Mmm?"

"You know the Golden Boy?"

Mizz Alex's head came up. She seemed to stare into space for a moment, then turned to Tomi. "What about him?"

"Is it true he danced?"

A shadow crossed Mizz Alex's face. "That's what they say."

"Pretty complicated way to make a puppet's feet dance."

Mizz Alex sniffed. "You're right about that. But back then, there wasn't any radio, weren't so many newspapers, magazines. People had to work harder to amuse themselves."

Tomi smiled. *Obaacha says* that, too! Still. It was a lot of work just for a toy. Unless there was something more. He flashed on the box of gears and cogs lying forgotten in the Boy's case. A strange lightness came over him. It's almost as though they were waiting … *waiting for me.*

"You know," he said. "I bet I could fix him."

Mizz Alex's grey eyes probed his dark ones a moment, then turned back to her paper. "I doubt it. It's been tried. Probably missing half its innards. And you said it yourself, it's an awful lot of work to make a boy dance. There are better uses for your talents."

Hmm. "So what about the gold mine? You think Russian Alex really found it?"

Mizz Alex frowned. "That's just a nursery story. Fireside tales."

"But wouldn't it be good for Juneau if there *was* another mine?"

The fierce grey eyes fixed Tomi with an unreadable look. "I'm sure it would. But Juneau's sent enough brave young men, and even a few young women, up into the mountains looking for one motherlode or another. Too few of them ever come back, and too few of those come back sane. Wishful thinking will kill you sooner than a mama grizzly will."

Ouch.

A few minutes afterward, Tomi said good night and retreated to the bunkhouse. After his nights in the dormitory it seemed quieter and more private, but also a little lonely.

He didn't go straight to bed. His mind buzzed with the developments of the last two days: the certain knowledge of where — and *when* — he was; the challenge of the Golden Boy; being out from under the thumb of the orphanage. Then there was Mizz Alex's strange negative vibe toward anything to do with the Boy or Russian Alex. *What's that about?*

This was like playing a new computer game for the first time, he thought — like that moment when you first "got" how the world of the game worked, and what you had to do to survive in it and win. Tomi always spent a while checking out the game world, trying to learn as much about it as he could before trying to conquer it. Now his gaze drifted to the bunkhouse walls and their unconventional covering. *No time like the present*, he told himself. *Or is it the past?*

He chuckled as he got to his feet and carefully lifted the lamp from the table.

"Ticker-tape welcome for 'Wrong Way' Hero," read the caption under a picture. It seemed some pilot named Douglas Corrigan had been told not to fly his small plane from New York to Ireland. "Too far for reasonable safety," authorities said. Corrigan filed a flight plan for California, took off and made a hard left. He landed in Ireland next day, and blamed his "faulty compass." *Yeah, right.* He lost his plane and pilot's licence, but got a parade. Tomi checked the date: 1938. *Try that today, dude, and they'll take you out with F-18s before you hit Newfoundland.*

He moved along the wall. A word leapt out at him. "Japs …" He looked at the rest: "… Defy Ultimatum." This one was harder to make sense of. It seemed that the U.S. and Britain wanted to know where Japan's navy was and Japan wouldn't say. *Well, d'uh.* But then …

Ohmigod! It hasn't happened yet! Something very like an electric shock went through him. *The big bombing. Pearl Harbor, the first 9/11.* It hadn't happened yet!

The room seemed to shiver for a moment. Should he tell someone? Who? Nichols? *Then he'd really be sure I'm a terrorist.*

Who'd believe him? Captain Harper? But what was it the captain said? *"Keep your own counsel about what's to come."* And besides, what could he tell them? Japan was going to bomb Hawaii? Could he even tell them when? *Oh, jeez. Missing data.* He could hear Obaacha's voice in his head, scolding him for not knowing a date this big.

He came to a part of the wall where newer pages had been tacked up over old ones. November 1938. *Last fall.* CHOPSTICK SPIES was the headline over several inches of text. "Diplomatic sources" and people "close to events," it said, warned that Japan had a spy network in the United States and Canada.

This accounted for some of the reactions he'd gotten. It also made his situation a lot scarier. *It's what they believe. Who do they think I am?*

"HE'S AN agent, no question," the thin man with eyes the colour of smoke leaned toward the woman across the table. "We're just not sure what kind."

"But dangerous, you think?" Ingrid Sanderson's eyebrows went up.

"No doubt, no doubt." Avery Nichols looked around and spotted a waitress. His fingers snapped and he pointed to their wine glasses. "The best kind," he gave a wolfish grin.

"How do you mean?" Miss Sanderson put a hand over her glass before the waitress could refill it. "Surely we don't want a dangerous spy wandering loose."

Nichols leaned back and took a deep drink from his own glass. "Of course not," he smirked. "Which is why there'll be such a stir when I … when *we* wrap him up. Him and his network."

"Network?"

"Of course, they never work alone."

Miss Sanderson looked impressed.

"I bet it makes headlines all the way to Washington!" the agent declared. He looked around the half-full dining room. "Yeah, I should think they'll be pulling me out of this dump pretty smart once word of this hits the director's desk."

"Oh." The woman's face fell. Before her companion could turn back to her, she managed to get a smile back into place. "Why, that's wonderful for you, Avery."

A soft expression came over the man's narrow face. He slid a hand across the white linen tablecloth and put it over the woman's dry fingers. "Might be good for both of us, Ingrid," he suggested.

A retching sound came from somewhere. Nichols turned in his seat and Miss Sanderson craned her neck in search of the noise. Behind the man's chair, a pair of swinging half-doors led into the hotel kitchen. A white dog was just visible beneath them. Its mouth was wide open and it was hacking like an animal that had changed its mind about swallowing something when it was already halfway down.

"That's disgusting." Nichols turned back to the table, scowling. "Animals in the kitchen."

"Well, she *is* the official town dog," Ingrid Sanderson said.

"It's uncivilized."

Patsy Ann hacked a final time, gave herself a shake and

turned away. Her toenails rattled across the hard kitchen floor. She pushed at the screen door with her nose, letting herself out.

In the lane behind the hotel she snuffed deeply, glad for the smell of honest vegetable peelings and cold meat scraps. She put the sour, dank smell of the two humans huddled over the little table out of her mind, and trotted off into the purple dusk.

FREE! Free, and feeling good. Free of the fear of being crazy. Free of the home. Free of school, at least until Monday. And free, for the moment, of Mizz Alex's list of things around the yard that were "just waiting for a strong young back."

Morning had been more bacon, fried bread and eggs. *So, my arteries ...* he shrugged. *But sooo goood.* Especially washed down with the hot milk and coffee that went along with it.

Afterward Mizz Alex had kept him moving all morning. First she gave him a basket the size of a washtub, showed him to a small hill of scraps and end bits of wood left over after bigger pieces had been sawn, and told him to fill the basket. Two basket loads filled the bins by the fireplace and four more filled the ones beside the woodstove in the kitchen.

Then she had him carry large beams of wood, one at a time, from various piles out in the yard to a ramp near the saw. The individual beams weren't so heavy, but after a couple of hours the skin on the top of his shoulder was raw and his muscles ached. *If this is the deal,* he began to think, *is it too late to go back to being an orphan?*

His outlook brightened over lunch. Crumbly pieces of cold salmon mixed with plenty of mayonnaise on fresh white bread. There was brown apple cider from a big glass jar, sweet and crisp at the same time.

"That was a good start this morning," Mizz Alex had said. "Later on, we'll rip those down to strapping lumber."

Tomi examined her over the edge of his glass. The way the light fell he could see the spray of thin lines raying out from the corners of her eyes. *Older than Mom,* way *older than Amanda. Not as old as Obaacha.* The tall woman reminded him of a movie star, the one in the old movies who could look classy up to her neck in leeches with that other guy, Bogie.

She tossed her head, got to her feet and began collecting the plates. "But we can't make a single cut with that blade. It'll take me the rest of the day to put an edge on it." She gave Tomi a nod. "The afternoon is yours."

Mine? His heart soared. *I think I'm …*

"Just be back for supper. We eat at six."

… free!

TOMI CHECKED his pocket. The seventy-five cents Miss Sanderson had left him from working for the Captain were still there. His new boots fit well enough for a hike, even if they were a bit more Doc Marten than he usually wore. He headed for town.

It no longer gave him brain-shock to come around the curve and see the view widen out. It felt more like a sudden, 3-D diorama of a familiar scene. To the left was the road to the Captain's marina, lined with cottages. Hidden behind a bare hill to the right was the Orphans' Home. And straight ahead down the long hill, just beyond the tall brick building with BARANOF HOTEL painted on its side, was the museum. Between here and there stretched a kilometre or so of houses and cabins on large lots.

Fifteen minutes later he came to where a side road led off past rotted stumps, sunken grasses and green-speckled stretches of dark brown water. He slowed his pace. What had JP said about free time at the home? They got some, he knew.

He raised his head at the sound of a bark. Something white flashed between the stumps on the far side of the pond. Then an animal galloped into view from around the bend. Its pink tongue bobbed foolishly beneath a black nose, and it was panting like an out-of-shape locomotive.

"Hey, Patsy Ann!" He stepped aside in time to avoid being bowled over, then buried his fingers in the damp fur around her neck. Patsy Ann licked his hand once, then stood wheezing through her nose in deep, grateful breaths.

When she seemed to have her wind back, Tomi straightened up and turned to go. "Coming?"

Patsy Ann barked sharply and abruptly dropped her hips to the ground.

Say what?

"Hey!" JP's voice somehow kept its soft note even when he was yelling. Tomi looked up to see the other boy wave from the end of the pond.

"Hey," Tomi called out.

"Howzit goin'?" JP said.

Tomi shrugged. "Not bad, I guess. The food's better. The work …" He stretched his shoulder painfully. "You?"

JP shrugged back. "Where you going?"

"To the museum. I want a better look at the Golden Boy. Want to come?"

JP's face brightened. He shrugged his agreement. Now Patsy Ann stood and gave herself a shake.

"JP," Tomi said once they were walking. "I have to tell you something."

"Okay."

"I think …" *How to put this?* "I really think I can fix him. No. I think I'm *supposed* to fix him."

JP nodded.

Tomi waited for more, but no more came. "You don't think I'm crazy?"

"Probably." A light flickered in JP's eyes where the corners twitched.

"Be serious. It's only levers and gears. I bet I can work it out. If they'll let me."

"Let you what?"

"Fool around with the Golden Boy's insides 'til I get him to dance the night away."

JP chuckled. "Yeh, you're crazy all right."

They stepped onto the first of the plank boardwalks that served as sidewalks for downtown Juneau. Neither boy noticed the lanky figure hovering in the middle distance behind them.

PATSY ANN walked ahead. At the carved facade of the Juneau Territorial Museum, she stopped, turned and waited for the two boys.

How does she know these things?

Tomi put his shoulder against the heavy door to push it open. The museum was much quieter without a class of kids milling about. Their footfalls — and, even more, Patsy Ann's hard toenails — struck sharply on the polished plank floor.

They reached the foyer that led upstairs to the second floor. As they did, a girl appeared from behind the staircase — the same girl he'd met twice now.

"Hi!" he said. *Go for it, dude*, he told himself. He held out his hand. "I'm Tomi. This is JP."

"Hi," the girl smiled back. "Sophie." They shook hands. Hers felt small and soft. *Wow, nice.* She shook JP's hand, then reached down and gave Patsy Ann a scratch behind the ears. The white dog made a sound almost like purring.

"So, do you, like, live here or what?" Tomi asked.

Sophie laughed. "Of course not! But I'm here a lot. Ma's on the historical society. They run this place. It's almost as good as the library for projects for school. Better, 'cause no one ever thinks to come here."

Patsy Ann flopped heavily to the floor. There was a silence. "Anyway," Tomi fumbled for something smooth to say and failed to find it. "We're on our way upstairs," he ended, lamely. He put a foot on the bottom stair and started up.

"Yeh? What're *you* doing here?" Sophie asked, keeping up with him.

Clearing the head of the stairs, Tomi looked down the hallway ahead. *Yesss!* The door to the small room at the back was open.

"He's gonna make the Golden Boy dance again," JP volunteered.

Sophie's eyes opened wide. "No fooling? Do you really think you can?"

"If I can just get my hands on him."

They reached the end of the hall. The lights in the small room were off and the figure in the glass case was almost lost in shadow. Tomi groped for a switch, then flicked it on. Light reflected on golden curls. Tomi's heart raced. He could feel blood pounding in his ears.

He stepped into the room and walked slowly around the case. The Boy's hands hung limp, but his lifted head seemed to watch the door through open eyes. The golden lips were pursed, as though caught in the act of blowing a kiss. "Your Mom's on the historical society?"

"Uh-huh," Sophie said. A door opened and closed somewhere below them in the building.

"D'you think she knows anything about this guy?"

"I dunno. I can ask."

"Anything you can find out." His mind was working, trying to picture how the Boy moved. *Danced ...* but how?

Heavy footsteps mounted the wide staircase, the sound echoing along the empty upstairs hallway.

The back of the case was built like a door, with hidden hinges and a little brass ring that pulled out for a handle.

He slipped a fingernail under the ring and lifted it up. He tugged and tried to turn it. It didn't budge.

"What are you up to back there?" A man's voice, sharp with alarm.

Tomi looked up through the glass walls of the case. A man in shirtsleeves and tie stood at the door. His plump, clean-shaven face was flushed and curly hair stuck up from his head like a brush.

"Nothing." Tomi pulled his hand away from the case and stuck it in his pocket. "Just looking. Do you know —"

"You were here the other day, weren't you?" the man asked. He stepped around the side of the case, watching Tomi closely. His eyes bulged from shallow sockets. "You're from the home."

"No," Tomi said. "That is, yeah. I mean I *was*. But —"

"What are you doing with Miss Carr?"

Say what? Tomi's dark eyes blazed. *What do you mean "doing with"?* "Nothing! She just was here."

"Does your mother know where you are?" the man demanded of Sophie. "Are you all right?"

"Of course I'm all right!" the girl answered him. But another voice cut her off.

"Sophie?" a woman called from the head of the stairs. "What are you doing down there? Mr. Bartlett? Is my Sophie down there?"

Oh, jeez. Tomi's guts clenched.

Sophie's mother half trotted down the hall, toes and heels tapping brightly on the hard floor. "You again!" she said at her first sight of the two boys.

"Mother!" Sophie cried out in protest as the woman gripped her hand fiercely and pulled her toward the door.

"Can't you even wait for me without getting into some kind of trouble?" the woman scolded. "And as for you," she turned a sharp look on Tomi and JP, "if I find you two bothering my daughter one more time …"

"Lady!" Tomi protested. "We didn't do anything. She started talking to us!"

"I'm not interested. One more time, and I'm reporting it to the police."

Tomi's jaw hung open. *Are you people* insane?

"All right then, move along out of here," the man was saying now. "You've seen everything you need to."

"But I —"

"Come along, before *I* call someone." The man had his hand on Tomi's shoulder now, turning him toward the door. JP was already heading for the hall, eyes on the floor.

"All *right!*" Tomi shook the man's sweaty hand off his shoulder angrily. He stepped into the hall in time to see the woman dragging Sophie to the head of the stairs.

Just as they started down, Sophie snuck a look back over her shoulder. Her left eye gave a broad wink. Tomi saw that she was grinning. A key turned behind them.

He saw Mr. Bartlett step away from the door to the Golden Boy's chamber, now shut and apparently locked tight.

This has gone well.

"Walk," the man ordered.

They retraced their steps to the front of the building. Patsy Ann had vanished, and Tomi felt a pang.

At the heavy front door, Bartlett sent them off with a final warning. "Miss Sanderson's going to hear about this! Don't come back," he waggled a plump finger, "and I won't have to take it any further than that."

THEY STOOD on the boardwalk, adjusting to the bright afternoon following the gloom of the museum.

JP broke the silence. "See, what did I say?" he said with a note of satisfaction. "You're crazy. They're not going to let a Jap fool with anything in there."

"I'm *not* ..." He gave up. "If I could just explain, *show* him."

They turned and walked a while, not going anywhere. They stopped at a poster showing soldiers in antique uniforms fighting in a desert.

"You got any money? Want to see a movie?" JP suggested.

"I only have, like, seventy-five cents." The last time he'd been to a movie it cost eleven bucks just to get in the door.

"Hey, how'd you get so rich?" JP laughed. "Don't you know it's only a nickel on Saturdays?"

"Yeah?" *This whole price thing ...*

Why not. Tomi paid for JP's ticket and his own. For another nickel they got a big bucket of popcorn and took it with them into the darkened theatre. A black-and-white cartoon was showing, the animal characters drawn with arms and legs like spaghetti. The theatre was more than half full, but they managed to find a row with empty seats toward the front.

People were still drifting in. Neither of them noticed when a tall youth settled into a seat two rows behind them and began stuffing handfuls of popcorn into his pinched, oddly flushed face.

In the darkness, Charley Ramsey leaned forward and tried to catch the voices speaking in low tones in front of him. Only disconnected words drifted back to him.

"... get to him ..." the Jap was saying. "... what I'm here for ..."

"... army ..." the Indian was laughing. Something, something "... locked up."

"... get someone to talk ..." the Jap spoke again. "... Juneau ..." something, then ... "gone."

A splash of colour burst across the screen and the music swelled, drowning out everything else.

THE MOVIE was a not-bad thriller. When it ended, Tomi stood and stretched and looked back. With something very like an electric jolt, he met Charley Ramsey's pale eyes, which were watching them from a couple of rows back. It creeped him out a little.

He put Charley out of his mind and determined to enjoy the rest of the day. If he couldn't get to work on the Golden Boy himself, he could at least scheme about how he was going to do that.

That night Tomi combed the newspapers on the bunkhouse walls for anything about the golden statue. There was nothing, and soon his eyes began to tire from squinting at the close blocks of text in the dim light.

But that's got to be it, the reason I'm here, he told himself as he pulled the blanket to his chin in his bunk. He closed his eyes and imagined the boy coming to "life," hidden gears making his arms lift, his torso turn and his feet dance. He drifted off to sleep.

All around him was a maze of machinery and clockwork. It was his machine, but then it wasn't. The machine over his head was coming apart. Everywhere he looked parts were slipping, gears no longer meshed. He was in a forest of mechanical trees and wind-up lumberjacks who looked too much like the Tin Man. He was racing a motorcycle, chasing somebody through an alley lined with wet lumber. He looked over. Obaacha was riding the motorcycle, but he was running so fast he was keeping up with it. He looked forward again and a figure running ahead of them turned its head to look back.

Tomi's eyes shot open in the darkness and he was greeted by the ash-and-mouse smell of the silent bunkhouse. The laughing, golden face faded very slowly from his vision.

Sixteen

BUSY TONGUES

THE MIDSUMMER sun rises even earlier in Juneau than in Vancouver. For a while Tomi turned to the wall to create an illusion of darkness and managed to fall back to sleep. But soon the gathering light forced him into wakefulness.

He checked his watch. It hadn't completely stopped, but it seemed to crawl forward impossibly slowly. It said quarter to eight, but he was sure it was earlier than that. Unable to keep his eyes closed, he got up and dressed.

He stepped out into the yard. The air was fresh and moist. The damp smell of moss on gravel mingled with the sharper smells of juniper and pine drifting down the mountain. Birds made a twittering racket in the branches and he could hear the restless splash of water falling into the pond.

It was the kind of day when you really had to work at it not to feel good. And Tomi didn't feel like working that hard.

A few minutes later, loaded down with small-bore cuttings of wood, he bummed open the door to the kitchen. A welcome aroma of cooking bacon and coffee met him as he carried the kindling to the basket by the stove.

They were soaking up the last of greasy yellow yolks

on crusts of warm sourdough when Mizz Alex cleared her throat and said, "Now, Mr. Tanaka."

Mr. Tanaka? Did I do something? Had he farted?

"It's Sunday, you know." She seemed more nervous than annoyed, unsure how to proceed. "Well, I don't know your religious persuasion, but I'll be attending service at Saint Nicholas' later this morning. I'm sure you'd be most welcome, if you wished to join us."

Tomi kept a straight face. "That's ... thank you. Really. But I thought maybe I'd go check out Juneau a little more, maybe hike down the shore a bit." He flashed on his secret thinking nook by the Fraser River. The vision brought with it a stabbing glimpse of his father's upset face. He gave himself a shake. The fastest way back to *then* was to do what he needed to *now*.

"Well then," Mizz Alex seemed neither upset nor relieved, "you can ride with me as far as town, if you like."

He liked, of course — until they were actually on their way. The big green car reared backward into the road, turned and launched itself downhill, and he recalled Mizz Alex's heedless delight in the gas pedal and her near-total ignorance of the brake. His well-fed stomach rolled over.

Twenty minutes later, the car squealed to a last-minute stop in front of a curiously pretty building, built with six sides and topped by an onion dome. Tomi unlocked his knees from where he'd braced himself against the passenger seat and opened the door. He stepped shakily to the ground and took several deep breaths to centre his *ch'i*, his energy-flow, the way Obaacha had taught him. Opening his eyes, he considered the church and offered up a silent "thank-you" to whatever power kept Mizz Alex between the ditches. Barely.

Taking his bearings from the mountain and the stubby brick tower of the Baranof Hotel, Tomi headed off in what he hoped was the direction of downtown. He was rewarded a few minutes later with the squat mass of the Federal Building. Just past it was the museum block.

He took the corner at a run, banked hard into it and thanked his karma when there was no one there to run into. Breathing hard, he pulled up in front of the heavy doors in their ornate frame.

Mr. Bartlett, I really think … He ran over what he wanted to say in his mind. *"You can ask Mizz Alex …"* The guy just had to listen for once. He willed his heartbeat to slow down. Then he reached out for the door. He pushed. It didn't budge.

Knew it! He turned to go and noticed the small piece of cardboard pinned to the left side of the frame. CLOSED SUNDAYS. *Idiot.*

But that was okay. He had a backup. Just go to the ocean and hang a left.

After a few blocks, downtown Juneau fell away behind him and Tomi walked past boxy wooden warehouses between the road and the shore. Gulls wheeled above the warehouses, their purpose made plain by the pungent smell of fish. The row of warehouses came to an end and the view opened up. Tomi recognized the cottages that sheltered between the road and the flank of the mountain. Ten minutes later he was looking down the slope at the little shed.

Below it the *DogStar* leaned unnaturally against its timbers, ungainly and forlorn-looking out of the water. As he got closer, Tomi could see gaping wounds where entire planks had been pulled away from her side, revealing thick ribs that rose from below and reached up toward the deck.

The Captain had set up sawhorses on one of the wooden platforms beside the steep railway. His back was to Tomi, as he bent over a plank. The tool he was running along it pulled up a shaving so thin that it let the light shine through and curled like an auburn ringlet.

"Ahoy, Captain!" Tomi called.

The old man straightened and turned, one hand working the muscles of his back. "Mr. Tanaka! Tomi! Now there's a man I could use right now!"

Tomi looked about. New planks lay amid nests of shavings on the wooden platform. "You need a hand?"

The blue cap dipped. "Unless I can figure out a way to hold both ends of a two-fathom plank at the same time, I do," he said. "But I don't imagine that's why you're here, is it lad?"

"Not really. But I don't mind. Better than church."

The old man grinned. "A good shipwright would say it *is* church, in a way, turning trees into boats."

Tomi smiled. *Nice idea.*

"But let's have a cup of tea first, and you can tell me what you really came for."

DogStar's galley was as trim and functional ashore as afloat. The Captain produced a tin of shortbread cookies to go with the hot, milky tea. When they were served, he fixed a keen eye on Tomi. "Well, then?"

"I think I've got it."

"Got it?"

"The reason I'm here."

"Go on."

"Sister Agatha, at the home, she took us to the museum. I saw this exhibit. It's a boy, a golden boy."

"Aye," the Captain nodded his head. "The Golden Boy of Lost Creek. What about him?"

"I can fix him, Captain, I know I can."

The Captain's look grew dubious. "They've tried over the years, they sure have." He shook his head. "He's been in pieces for so long, no way of knowing whether he's even all there. For that matter, it's only legend that he ever did dance. I don't know of anyone who can say they saw it with their own eyes."

"But what else are all those pieces for? If he fit together once, he can fit together again."

The old man shrugged. "But even if you could fix him, I don't know what difference that would make to anything. He's just a toy."

"Captain, I know this is crazy, but I think the Golden Boy has something to do with Russian Alex's mine."

The Captain shot a hard look at the boy. "So you've heard that old story? I wouldn't hang a lot of sail on it, lad. Old Alex's tales have broken plenty of hearts before yours."

"That's kind of what Mizz Alex said."

"She would know," the old man said softly.

Tomi waited for more but nothing came. "Okay, well, I haven't got that part figured out yet. But putting the Golden Boy back together is what I'm here for. I'm sure of it. It's the only thing I'm any good at, for one thing."

"You do seem to have a knack," the Captain said.

"Besides, I just feel it in my bones. I can fix him. I know I can!"

"Well, things that are lost can sometimes be found," the old man said. "I should know. And there's things you can't know 'til you test 'em out." The Captain raised an eyebrow. "Though in truth, it would be something of a miracle for Matt Bartlett to let you try."

Tomi felt his anger rising. "Is it because I'm ..."

"Your race, you mean? Oh, I don't think so, not with Bartlett. He's a stickler for professional privilege. Doesn't think anyone below a full Doctor of Philosophy ought to lay a hand on his precious artifacts. Then there's the value of the piece. The Boy's real gold, you know. There'd be hell to pay if he ever went missing."

"But I don't want to *steal* him," Tomi objected. "I want to *fix* him." *Why does everything have to get so complicated?* "It's his guts I need to get my hands on, not his head."

"Well, it's Bartlett's head you'll have to deal with first," the old man said. "And it's a complicated one."

PATSY ANN nosed the big double doors. Through the crack between them came smells: rolls fresh from the oven, eggs and sausage, ham steaks, halibut browning in butter, floury biscuits, pancakes drenched in maple syrup.

A couple stepped up behind her: a flushed fellow with hair like a brush who held the hand of a woman in a flowered dress. The man reached over the dog to open the door, enveloping Patsy Ann in the disagreeable smell of unopened cupboards. Gratefully, she stepped inside and trotted down the broad hall.

It was Sunday, the day that everyone who was anyone in Juneau attended brunch at the Baranof Hotel as faithfully as they did their various churches and chapels. Patsy Ann trotted briskly to the far end of the hall and slipped through an open door. The air was filled with appetizing aromas.

She dodged a moving forest of legs across the big kitchen to where a set of swinging doors led to the dining room beyond. Waiting by the doors were two white bowls. One held water and a bright twist of yellow lemon peel. The other was placed where waitresses entering the kitchen from the dining room could most easily direct the better scraps that patrons left on their plates.

Tucking herself into the cave-like space beneath the counter, Patsy Ann dropped to the floor. From here, she had a clear view beneath the swinging doors out into the dining room.

At a table near the centre of the room, the musty fellow with the stiff brush of copper-coloured hair was holding a chair for the flowered woman. He took his own seat. A waitress handed them menus. The man's eyes slid across the page and his mouth tightened. The woman patted his hand.

She leaned close and whispered, "Now, honey, remember the lesson. We're supposed to enjoy the day!"

"That's all very well for Pastor Petrus. He's not trying to get a new building from City Council. If the mine closes, we'll be lucky to keep what we've got. If the city can't afford the museum they sure can't afford a curator."

"Oh, honey," Doris Bartlett said. "It hasn't happened yet. Maybe it won't happen at all."

A waitress with a notepad appeared at his elbow. He ordered without looking up: "A muffin. Plain. Thank you."

Doris sighed and asked for eggs over-easy with ham and fried potatoes.

Patsy Ann's gaze drifted to a table closer by. For once, Agent Nichols looked almost relaxed and Ingrid Sanderson was almost smiling.

"No, no, of course not," the agent waved his hand as though brushing away a fly. "You had no choice, I know that. What can you do when the judiciary is against you?" He shot a baleful glance at an older man seated by the window.

"Completely out of step," his companion agreed warmly.

"To be honest," the agent leaned closer to Miss Sanderson, "the home's been more help than anyone. That communicator of his, that mp-something he called it, won't even get to the lab boys for another few days. The Canadian authorities cabled to say there are Japanese by the name of 'Tanaka' living in Vancouver, but none missing and no one named 'Tomi'."

"You think …?" Miss Sanderson's cold eyes opened wide in a creepy imitation of girlishness.

"Oh it's a cover name, absolutely. And thanks to our young friend," he smirked, "we know he's not here by accident." Nichols leaned toward the woman. "Told an associate he's 'here for a reason.' Exact words!" The agent leaned back with a triumphant look on his narrow face.

A waiter in a black jacket led a tall, proud-looking woman to a seat. The agent and his companion followed her progress with sidelong glances. As she passed their table, Miss Sanderson's chin nudged forward and her face became flushed. "Miss Kasilof," she greeted the other woman stiffly. "I hope you're not regretting your decision."

A look of contempt swept over Mizz Alex's handsome face. "Quite the opposite. Tomi's very helpful. My mill's turning again, thanks to him." She surveyed the room at large. "That means we're sawing again."

The agent gave her a sharp look. "You say the Jap fixed your mill?"

"Japanese–*Canadian*, I believe. But, yes, indeed he did." Lifting her chin, she added in a louder voice: "Put us right back into business, cut to order, any size."

"Isn't he the mechanical one," Miss Sanderson's voice dripped sarcasm. "Even my boys miss him. He fixed a number of personal items for them. They're always breaking anything anyone gives them."

Mr. Bartlett popped to his feet to push aside the black-jacketed waiter and seize the tall woman's chair. "That's wonderful news about the mill, Miss Kasilof," the curator gushed. "Wonderful." He shot a nervous glance toward the agent's table and lowered his voice. "But do I understand you've engaged one of Miss Sanderson's boys? An *Oriental* lad?"

"Yes, that's right. What of it?" Mizz Alex sat down and pulled her chair closer to the table.

"Nothing. Nothing at all. A very charitable impulse. Very."

"Charity had nothing to do with it," Mizz Alex snapped. She cocked an expectant eye at the waiter.

The curator stepped back. Speaking over the waiter's shoulder he went on, "Still, I do hope we can count on you for this year's drive."

"We'll see," Mizz Alex accepted a menu. "'Open for business' doesn't mean open for handouts."

"No, no. Of course not." Mr. Bartlett took a step backward, cheeks flaming. He sat back down and glared at the muffin that stood alone on his plate.

"'Charitable,'" Avery Nichols sniffed. "That's one word for it. 'Reckless' might be another. Whoever this character is, it's clear he's received special training. Putting him in a position to sabotage a key industrial plant. There really ought to be some consideration for public safety."

A weathered-looking man pushed back his chair by the window. He gathered up the several printed journals he'd been dining with and got to his feet. A black suit hung loosely on his wiry frame, the square toes of trail-worn boots peaking from beneath stovepipe pants. He started toward the door, then turned aside to pass closer to the table where the tall woman sat.

"Judge," Mizz Alex rose slightly in her chair.

"Alex," Henry Burns offered his hand. "That's wonderful news. Let's hope it's a sign of better things for Juneau." He focussed a withering look on the FBI man. "As for Mr. Tanaka, surely a federal agency can think of better uses of its time than hounding a mere boy whose sole act of 'sabotage' has been to get our only sawmill back to work."

A red blaze rose up Nichols' neck and spread across his pale cheeks. Ingrid Sanderson took a sudden interest in adjusting the sugar balance of her coffee.

Patsy Ann heaved herself to her feet, shook in a business-like way and made for the door. Ten minutes later, she poked her nose under another set of swinging doors — the main entrance to the Red Dog Saloon. Its clientele being generally a harder living and less church-going group than the Baranof's, Sunday "brunching" here usually got a much later start. But today's crowd was especially grim. At a few round tables men with hunched shoulders nursed glasses of yeasty ale and shook their heads at each other's worries and bad news. Fear flowed like cold water across the sawdust floor. The white dog moved on.

The Gold Dust Café was Patsy Ann's usual last stop on a Sunday. She followed a young couple in the door, walked the length of the counter and back, then dropped to her haunches in the middle of the floor. Regulars smiled and began pushing sausage ends and bread crusts to one side of their plates. It wasn't long before the first savoury morsel soared across the room. Patsy Ann fielded the pop fly with perfect timing.

Booths ran along the window. Halfway down, a girl sat with her parents. It was easy to see where her striking good looks came from. A powerfully built man with a proud profile and a complexion like well-polished oak faced a petite woman with fair skin and blonde hair the colour of straw. Looking past his wife and daughter, he dipped a piece of toast in a pool of egg yolk. Catching the white dog's attention, he gave the greasy twist a one-two-three windup and let fly.

Powerful jaws snapped it out of the air with a grunt.

"Never misses a beat, does she?" He shook his head. "I'm going to miss the old girl."

"Don't say that, George!" Judy Carr protested. "You never know what's around the corner."

"Probably a bear," George Carr said gloomily.

"But the mine's not even closed yet!" Sophie erupted.

"Might as well be. Foreman says they won't be opening any new galleries. No new galleries means no more blasting. And that means they won't be needing me."

"Can't you get another job?" Sophie demanded.

The big man tousled his daughter's blonde hair. "Not much call for blowing things up outside a mine, honey," he laughed. "But don't worry, I'll find something. They're opening up new diggings down in Canada, I hear."

"But all my friends are *here*. I don't want to go anywhere else."

"Sophie," her mother broke in. "You know your father is a very talented man with a very special job. Not the kind of job you can find walking down any street. But really, it's too nice a day to spoil. Why don't you enjoy your pancakes and leave the worrying to us."

Sophie bit back a fresh retort and regarded her untouched food with disgust.

The bell over the café door tinkled. Patsy Ann gave a little prance and rushed over to nuzzle the hand of the tall, dark-haired boy who came in on the heels of an older man wearing a blue peaked cap.

"Judy," George Carr leaned toward his wife. "Isn't that your Oriental orphan boy with Captain Harper?"

"He's not *my* Oriental orphan," his wife objected.

"He's not Oriental either," the girl said. "He's Canadian. And he's a whiz at fixing things." Her sad face gave way to a fresh smile and she raised her hand to wave.

Taking a stool beside the Captain, Tomi gave her an answering smile. *Omigod, I think she likes me!*

"Sophie Carr!" her mother batted down her daughter's hand. "For heaven's sake. Don't you know nice girls aren't forward like that?"

"Sure about that, are you dear?" George Carr asked his wife with a heavy wink.

Across the table, Judy Carr blushed to her blonde roots.

Seventeen

SECOND TIME LUCKY

THE NEXT DAY was Monday and Mizz Alex was all business. School, it turned out, was included in her notion of business.

"Shouldn't I stay here and help out?" Tomi offered.

Mizz Alex gave him a "nice-try" look. "One: it's in Henry Burns' order. Two: you need an education," she said. "You've got a knack, I grant you. But a knack'll only take you so far."

Jeez, have you been channelling my Dad? The grown-up rant on education sure hadn't changed any in sixty-seven years.

Nor, he thought forty-five minutes later, after another hair-raising hurtle down the mountain in Mizz Alex's green fright-mobile, *had school smells.* The odour of paper and people and hallway disinfectant washed over them the moment they stepped inside the Juneau Middle School office.

A woman came to the office counter. Mizz Alex stated their purpose.

"Is he a resident of Juneau?" the secretary asked doubtfully.

"He is now," Mizz Alex replied, a little shortly. "But he's been educated in Canada to grade ..." She looked at Tomi.

"Seven, going into eight."

"You have your last report card?"

Tomi's chest pounded. Which was worse? F's in history and geography? Or the fact that his report card was now in the hands of the FBI?

"Any documentation at all?" the woman pressed.

Tomi shook his head.

"Well then, he'll have to take the assessment exam."

Tomi's heart fell. *Exams? I just took exams!* Then again, maybe he could improve his marks some. *Can I get the credit in 2006 if I do?*

The woman flipped open a ring-binder. "We're not holding another sitting until July. July 6. Nine a.m. Just come here and someone will tell you which room."

"But that's weeks away!" Mizz Alex objected. "The year will be almost over."

"Well yes, but we have to know which grade to put him in," the other woman smiled an apology. "There's so few new students these days, we only give the test twice a year."

Yessss!

BUT ANY HOPES he had of being quickly set free to take another run at Mr. Bartlett were soon dashed.

"What are you grinning about?" Mizz Alex asked as they walked back to the car. "Don't imagine you've got three weeks to lollygag."

Lollygag?

"I've started getting the word out that we're back in business, but there's plenty more to do to get ready for customers."

Mizz Alex's meaning became clear once they were back at the lumber yard. It took the form of a tool she called a "peavey." Tomi thought it looked like something out of a warrior quest. A long handle ended in a spike that the person wielding the tool speared into a log; a steel hook then swung down on a hinge to grab it tight. Under Mizz Alex's directions, Tomi wielded the peavey for the next three hours, rolling logs onto one of the handcarts and delivering them one by one to the saw shed.

By lunchtime, an impressive number of logs waited to be turned into planks. Then he discovered another benefit of his labours. *Guilt-free gluttony*, he revelled, as he layered a thick slice of cold ham on a slab of sourdough. *I can work with this!*

"So when do we start sawing?" he asked.

"Tomorrow," Mizz Alex answered. "I'm going down to the *Alaskan* and the *Empire* this afternoon, place some ads, make sure word gets out that the Kasilof mill has wood for sale again."

"And me?" If he had to load any more logs, Tomi thought he might actually run away *to* school.

Mizz Alex broke into a rare smile. "You've earned your board today I think," she said. "And I don't expect a grown man's hours from a boy. If there's something you'd like to do, the afternoon's yours."

"Can I get a lift into town?"

TODAY WHEN he pushed on the brass plate, the heavy door swung ponderously open. Tomi straightened the collar of his fresh shirt and stepped into the museum.

The offices, he seemed to remember, were off the hallway behind the big staircase. The second door he came to bore the word CURATOR in small black letters. A male voice answered his knock.

Tomi stepped inside. The man with the brush of upswept hair sat behind a desk. Before him was a large book filled with columns of handwritten numbers. The flushed face looked up and scowled.

"Mr. Bartlett?"

The man nodded impatiently.

"Sir, I know we got off on the wrong foot. But my name is Tomi, Tomi Tanaka, and I —"

"You're the lad who got Miss Kasilof's mill working?" His tone was skeptical.

"Yup, that's me." Tomi forced a smile. "And I think I can do the same with the Golden Boy. I think I can make him dance again."

"Did she send you over here?"

"Who?"

"Miss Kasilof." The curator searched his face.

"No, why would she send me here?"

"Nothing, never mind." The man leaned back in his chair. "You know we've tried. I don't even know if all the pieces are still there."

"I've got a knack for these things." *Wasn't that what everyone said?* "And if no one else can make him work, what have you got to lose?"

Mr. Bartlett frowned. "Do you have any idea of the Boy's value? It's an irreplaceable artifact."

"But think," Tomi said with heavy emphasis, "think how much *more* valuable it would be if it worked!" On impulse he added: "It might even get a few more people to come in here."

The plump face flushed a deeper red. Mr. Bartlett opened his mouth to speak but then his eyes dropped to the book on the desk and he seemed to lose his thought. He shook his head. "I appreciate your interest, Mr. ... Tonka. But I'm afraid I can't just turn the Golden Boy over to a ... a youthful amateur, no matter how precocious his mechanical talents."

"Not the whole Boy." Tomi tried his last card. "Just the clockwork parts."

The curator's brow furrowed. "Just the ...?"

"The parts in the box. That's all I need for now. If I can put the pieces together, get them to work, then we can put them in the Boy."

The flushed face gave a little. "Just the parts."

"Look, let me show you what I mean," Tomi pressed. "One chance, that's all I ask. You watch me, see if I know what I'm doing. Then decide."

The curator was silent a moment. "You're very persistent, Mr. Tonka."

Yesss! "Tanaka ... Sir."

"Tanaka." The florid man heaved a heavy sigh and got to his feet. "Wait here."

Tomi listened as Mr. Bartlett's heavy footsteps mounted

the stairs and echoed along the upstairs hall. Now that it looked like he actually had a chance, his own doubts came alive. *You better be able to pull this off, dude.*

Steps sounded again on the stairs and a moment later the curator reappeared carrying a dusty cardboard box. Stepping to a table, he elbowed a pair of Native masks to one end and dropped the box beside them. It clanked dully as it landed. "So, show me."

Tomi stepped to the table and got his first clear look at the Boy's metal innards. His own insides did a sullen somersault. A dozen or so brass rods lay on top, stacked like miniature versions of the logs in Mizz Alex's yard. Beneath them was a jumble of cogs, gears, springs and cams; more rods bent at different angles; things he didn't recognize at all. Pushed into one end of the box was a larger piece: two flat brass plates with a blue spring coiled between them.

Shivers and stink! Had he only imagined he could do this, that this was why he was here? Hadn't other people, real experts, already tried? It didn't help to have Mr. Bartlett hovering over his shoulder. *Probably wants to make sure I don't pocket some "irreplaceable" nut!*

But it was too late to back down now. Tomi began to remove pieces one by one. First he laid the rods out in a line. Beside them he placed the bare brass frames. Next he made several rows of gears in different sizes. He could feel Mr. Bartlett beginning to fidget. *Okay, okay.* He breathed deeply, willing his *ch'i* to find its centre.

Wait a minute.

He selected a brass plate. Small posts stood up from its smooth surface. He chose a brass gear and held it up to one of the studs. He pressed gently and the gear slid easily onto the post. A smaller gear fit the next post, its teeth meshing smoothly with the first. Excitement rising, he ran his fingers down the row of cogs to one shaped like a cylinder instead of a wheel; a groove ran around it like the stripes of a candy cane. It fit perfectly between the last set of posts.

"Watch," he said, and held the pieces up. With his thumb, he began rolling the grooved cylinder. As he did, the smaller gear began to turn, its movement transferring to the next. He turned to face the curator. "Just give me enough time. I know I can make this work."

A hearty bark startled them both.

"Patsy Ann!" Mr. Bartlett exclaimed. "Who let you in?"

"I did," said Captain Harper, stepping around the door. "We were passing and she set to barking as though we were steaming full-on into an iceberg." He looked at Tomi and raised an eyebrow in question.

The curator followed his look. "You know each other?"

"Tomi's given me a hand down on *DogStar,* aye."

"Well he's been trying to convince me that he can fix our Golden Boy."

"Now, that I do not know," the Captain said. "But, he does seem to be handy at fixing things." *Thank you!* "And I'll vouch for his honesty." *Double thank you!*

Mr. Bartlett frowned. "I still don't … The Boy's worth as much as the rest of our exhibits put together."

"I don't need the Boy's outsides, the gold," Tomi said, frustration sounding in his voice. "I just need his gears, and some time."

"What can it hurt to let him have at a lot of old gears?" Captain Harper asked. "The Boy can't get any more broken than he is now."

Another bark came from the vicinity of their knees.

The curator looked from the Captain to the white dog. "Well …" Tomi held his breath.

"… all right."

"Yesss!" Tomi pumped his fist in a victory salute. "You won't regret it, Mr. Bartlett, I promise you."

"I hope not," Mr. Bartlett said, looking faintly alarmed. "You can work in the basement; there's a spare table. It will have to be during regular hours: noon to five, Monday through Saturday."

"Can I start now?" He was already replacing the gears and rods in the box.

Eighteen
THE GOLDEN BOY

THE MUSEUM basement was a cobwebby place, stacked with boxed and crated artifacts that lacked room for display upstairs. Mr. Bartlett led the way past a full-length war canoe to a corner where a stuffed bear stood upright, peering into the gloom through eyes of glass. He reached up and yanked a string. A bare bulb glowed into life over a wide workbench. "Here you go," he nodded. "But check in with me on the way out."

"You got it," Tomi said, and put the box down on the bench. He pulled up a crate and began to lay the pieces from the box out where he could see them.

He did little more that first afternoon than clean and organize the pieces into matching items: long rods, gears and screws and cams, the small brass plates that once held the gears together. It took no time at all to recognize the heavy steel spring coiled tightly between two pieces of brass, like meat in a sandwich. It was the Golden Boy's heart, the mechanical "battery" that would hold and release the energy to make him move.

But four other pieces mystified him. Each of these looked like a stack of thirty or forty brass pancakes with deeply fluted, uneven edges. No clue. He put those aside.

Instead he concentrated on finding pieces that fit each other, like a very complicated 3-D jigsaw puzzle. He'd hardly begun when Mr. Bartlett appeared at the basement door to tell him it was almost five o'clock.

Reluctantly, Tomi pulled on the string to turn off the bare overhead bulb.

THE NEXT DAY began with a roar — literally. As soon as breakfast was over, Mizz Alex led Tomi out to the mill. The fearsome teeth of the big saw blade now gleamed bright and sharp. A score of large timbers and logs waited to be cut.

The cutting itself was both thrilling and scary. Mizz Alex handed Tomi safety goggles and donned a pair herself. Then she threw the lever that brought power from the water wheel to the saw blade. When the blade was spinning so fast the deadly teeth were a blur, they rolled the first log off the platform. A moment later the shed was filled with the roar of steel teeth ripping into solid wood. A fountain of light yellow chips filled the air.

By the end of the morning, they had transformed half a dozen large timbers into smaller boards and planks. "That'll do for today," Mizz Alex said.

Tomi's ears rang as they walked back to the house for lunch. The moment the last plate was washed and dried, he headed out, swinging by the bunkhouse to collect his backpack and the tool kit inside. From the bale of rags in the lumber yard workshop he pulled a few of the least filthy; they joined the tool kit.

Taking the long hill at a steady, hike-for-distance stride, he pictured the Boy and tried to fit the bigger pieces from the box into his mental image. On the way through town, he stopped at the drugstore and bought a small jar of brass cleaner and a little tin of machine oil.

By the time he reached the museum, he was already deep into the gears, levers and cogs, the rods and cams of the problem.

THAT BECAME his pattern over the days that followed.

Mornings began at the mill, either pushing logs into the roaring, spinning saw or stacking fresh-cut planks while Mizz Alex waited on customers in the office. There were more customers every day, and the increase in their numbers seemed to coincide with a steady improvement in Mizz Alex's spirits.

In the afternoon, under the bear's glassy gaze, he tackled the problem of the Golden Boy's mechanism from both ends. Wherever two pieces seemed to match, he fit them together. Some cogs spun loosely on their studs; others had tiny screws that gripped their axles tightly. Many pieces had grit and dried gunk stuck to them. These he carefully scraped clean. The little tool kit got plenty of work.

But he also tried to reason things out. The long rods must be the Boy's "bones" — his spine, arms and legs. These Tomi laid out on the work table as though reconstructing someone's skeleton.

The hours flew by. Too soon each day he heard the heavy

tread of Mr. Bartlett's feet on the basement stairs. Later, when he drifted to sleep in the bunkhouse, cogs whirled and gears spun in his head as he tried to make sense of what went where.

ON THE third day, after checking in with Mr. Bartlett, he headed as usual for the basement. A familiar voice caught him at the stairs.

"Tomi!" Sophie Carr called.

The Golden Boy could wait. Here was a real girl.

"Hey!" Tomi answered. "What's up?"

"I've been researching." She made it sound like fun. "There's lots of useful stuff here, old newspapers and maps and things. Mom showed me how to find things for school. Now it's my secret weapon," she grinned. "How about you? I thought you were banned."

Should I tell her? Sophie's smile melted any doubts. "C'mon, I'll show you."

He led the way to the back stairs.

"Gee, look at all this stuff," Sophie marvelled, as he led her past the war canoe under the glassy glare of the grizzly. "It's too bad they don't have these up where people can see them."

"I guess." He'd been too involved with the gleaming gears and brass rods on the work table to give anything else down here much thought. He pulled on the string and the bulb blazed into life.

Sophie looked over the array with a blank expression.

"Uh-huh," she said. "It's ... What is it?"

Jeez, girls! "It's him! The Golden Boy! Mr. Bartlett's letting me put him back together."

"He is? That's super!" She scanned the disconnected pieces on the table. "So, how is it coming?"

"Not bad. See," he pointed. "There are his arms, his middle. There's his neck." He picked up the coiled spring between its brass plates. "This is what makes the whole thing work. And these," he lifted two long rods that were now joined at one end into a curved bar, "I think these are parts of his legs."

"Huh. And what are all those?" She pointed at several large families of additional rods and unassembled gears that still lay on the table. "And those?" She peered closely at the close-packed piles of brass pancakes.

You would notice those. "I'm not really sure yet." *Like, I don't have any freaking idea.* "It's weird. He's supposed to dance, but the pieces that go down his legs are pretty simple. And there's all these other pieces that must do something but they don't seem connected with his legs at all. I'm still working it out."

"Good," Sophie said. "I've been working too."

"Eh?"

Sophie's face crinkled into a grin. "You must be Canadian, eh?" she teased.

Har, har. "I mean, what do you mean you've been working?"

"I told you, I've been researching. I've been reading up on Russian Alex."

Tomi felt the back of his neck tingle.

Sophie turned to rest a hip against the edge of the workbench. The movement put the light behind her, turning her blonde hair into a kind of halo. Tomi had to force his attention back to what she was saying.

"Joe Juneau and Russian Alex were rivals," Sophie explained. "Alex never had a share in Joe's mine, but he always had money, lots of it. Gold. But I guess he never told anyone where he got it. People used to follow him and try to figure out where his lode was, but no one ever managed to."

"So, there is a mine somewhere?"

Sophie's eyes sparkled. "I think so." She sighed. "If only we could find it."

Tomi's eyes fell back to the collection of gears and disconnected rods scattered across the workbench. A new determination flowed through him. "I think it's right here."

"Don't chizz me!" The dark cheeks flushed. "What do you mean, 'right here'?"

"I mean here on this table. What are the two biggest mysteries about Russian Alex?"

Sophie shrugged. "I guess the Boy and the mine. So?"

"So think about how much work he put into making the Boy." Tomi couldn't help himself. These were the thoughts that had been wearing tracks in his mind for days. "It must have taken him years. What was worth that much work? And what was the most important secret he had? The gold. There's got to be a link."

"But the Boy's just a toy."

"I know. I know that. I don't know *how* they're connected. I just think they are. The only way that makes sense is —"

"If the Boy knows where the mine is!" Sophie pounced. The girl's face glowed with excitement now. "If you're right, and if you can make him work again, maybe he can tell us." Her blue eyes blazed.

"I don't think it's an 'if.' I think it's the reason I'm here."

Sophie frowned. "Here?"

Yikes. "I mean ..." *Cover, dude.* "I mean this is my talent, my knack. This is what I do."

A strange, on-the-edge-of-creeped-out look formed on the girl's face and she glanced away. When she looked back at him, her bright blue eyes held a challenge. "Then you'd better get working on it, hadn't you?"

Something I said?

"And I better not let anyone catch me down here." With a toss of her golden bangs she turned and walked back toward the stairs, hips swinging a little as she ran past the end of the big war canoe. "Abyssinia!"

Abyssinia? Giving his head a shake, Tomi turned back to his project.

It wasn't until that night, in the half-world between waking and sleeping where memories shift and words play games with the mind, that their conversation came back to him. Now he heard it end with a promise: "*I'll be seein' ya.*"

He smiled as he fell asleep.

THE WHITE DOG lay in a hollow. An overhanging fern hid her from the gravel road. The strong jaws opened wide to gnaw on the beef knuckle held between grubby paws. The small space was filled with the smells of meat and marrow.

Suddenly the white head lifted, pink tongue flicking over white-whiskered chops. Beyond the green curtain, a boy walked past. His face reminded Patsy Ann of Huk-sing, the laundryman who never forgot to leave a pot-sticker in a small blue-and-white bowl at his back door. Dark eyes blinked, but she made no move to get up, and Tomi disappeared from view.

Patsy Ann nudged the knuckle into a new position and turned to get a better grip on it. Another movement caught her eye. This boy was taller, with fairer skin. Charley Ramsey walked in the same direction as Tomi, stepping lightly as though trying not to scuff the gravel with his boots. His head craned forward on his thin neck, and Patsy Ann's black nose wrinkled at the unwashed smell that followed him.

A *craaack* echoed around the small cave. The dog's long tongue probed newly exposed marrow. A third boy passed. This one looked more like the first, with darker skin and jet-black hair. JP walked even more lightly than the second boy, keeping to the grassy edges of the road. On his feet were soft moccasins. The sun flashed off bright beads sewn into their tops. But he too walked with his head forward, eyes alert to the road ahead.

Patsy Ann rose heavily to her feet. She scrabbled a hollow for the bone and scuffed it over with sand and gravel, then pushed through the curtain of fronds and stepped out onto the road.

Tomi kept to his quick pace, dodging around slower-moving men and women who blocked his way. At the corner opposite the Federal Building he turned out of sight toward the museum.

At the same corner Charley slowed his pace. He leaned forward to peek past the edge of the building before stepping around it. Half a block back, JP walked faster.

Charley came back around the corner just as JP reached it. The two boys collided squarely. A block away, Patsy Ann winced.

Both boys staggered but kept their footing. Dark eyes holding pale ones, they moved carefully around each other. Charley stepped off the sidewalk, darting past an oncoming car, yelling as he went: "Stupid moron, can'tcha watch where you're going?"

JP observed the other boy sprint down the length of the brick edifice that occupied the opposite block. Halfway along, Charley turned up a short flight of steps and entered the Federal Building.

JP reached the same steps a minute later. Patsy Ann galloped across the street to meet him. "Hey, Patsy Ann." JP scratched her affectionately behind the ears. "You following him too?"

He reached over her head to push the door open. "You go on then. I think I better wait out here."

Patsy Ann had no trouble finding the scent, part overripe

adolescent boy, part macaroni and cheese, part scuffed ox-hide and road tar. Hard toenails tapping like gravel on tin, she followed it along a corridor, round a corner, through a pair of doors and down an alley of desks to a row of office doors that ran along the back of a big room.

The smell drifted through from the fourth door. The pale boy slouched in a wooden chair. He smirked at Agent Nichols across a desk and stuffed something in his pocket.

At sight of the white dog, Agent Nichols' face went red. He rushed to the door and put his head out. "Who keeps letting this mutt in here?" he yelled. "Rules! Doesn't anyone here even *read* the rules?"

The door slammed shut.

Two feet away, Patsy Ann gave herself a prim shake and turned her back on the closed office. Her mouth opened wide in a generous, dismissive yawn.

She began walking back along the rows of desks, stopping wherever she had earlier brushed past a kindly offered snack.

FOR THE twentieth time Tomi pressed the ball at the tip of the brass rod into the hollow socket. For the twentieth time it slipped right back out.

AAAAaarghhh! He threw his head back and glared in frustration into the yellow glass eyes of the grizzly bear. How could it be?

He'd finally figured out what the stacked pancakes were for — he thought. They were like the program cards for a game box: they controlled the Golden Boy's motions.

It was almost the same idea as the little music box he'd fixed at the dorm, which had used a cylinder with carefully arranged studs to plink out a tune on little brass keys. This gizmo captured motion in the ripples around the edges of the pancakes. When everything worked, the turning pancakes would push and release a cam. That movement, carried along through various rods and levers, would — he hoped — control the figure's hands and feet.

All very well in theory. But the Boy was supposed to dance. That meant the stacks should control the long rods down his legs. But every way he tried to fit the Boy's leg "bones" in to reach his "game" stacks ran into some obstacle. The rod didn't reach. Something got in the way. It was driving him crazy.

So close ... so far!

He could see how the spring drove everything else, how its energy was divided and distributed. He could see how the stacks of pancakes guided the automaton's actions. But there was just no way to make the darn thing *dance*.

"Aaaaarrrrghhhh!!" This time he said it right out loud.

Nineteen

A GOLDEN GIRL

"GOT TROUBLE?"

Tomi turned to see Sophie swinging past the end of the big war canoe. His mood brightened. "Hey!"

"Hey. Sounds like something's not working."

"Well … yes and no. I'm seeing how the parts go together, just not how they go together to make the Boy dance."

"Maybe I can help."

Tomi's brows went up. *Yeah?*

"C'mon."

He followed Sophie to the lobby of the museum and then up to the second floor. She led him down the hallway to the small room at the back of the building. The golden face gleamed inside his glass box. Just as it had that first day, something about the blind golden eyes and cherub's kiss caught in Tomi's chest.

"Don't look at his face," Sophie said. "Look at his hands."

Tomi leaned closer. On his earlier visits he'd been too dazzled by the Boy in his entirety — or fascinated by the problem of his clockwork — to devote much attention to his hands. But now he noticed something odd. One hand was held out flat. The other — his right hand — was curled closed.

Not fisted, but with its thumb touching its fingertips. *Weird*.

"Now come here," Sophie said, taking Tomi's hand and pulling him back out into the hallway.

An electric charge went through him. For a moment, the Boy, his purpose, the whole impossible strangeness of being here in 1939 faded into the background. All Tomi was aware of were the small, soft, warm and incredibly smooth fingers holding his own. *Oh ... my ...*

"Here, look." Sophie let his hand go.

Say what? For a moment Tomi wasn't quite sure where he was, like coming to the surface after a deep dive. He felt an urge to shake his head to clear his eyes. "Huh?" he said stupidly.

They were in one of the side rooms on the second floor, a room lined with bookshelves and wooden cabinets. A book lay open in front of him.

"Here," Sophie pointed to a passage in the book.

Tomi leaned forward. The handwriting was old and the paper yellowed, but he could make it out:

"After the meal, Peter Alexei demonstrated his most recent automaton. A remarkable little man, barely the size of a small boy, when set into motion the creature put pencil to paper and, in the most lifelike manner, executed a drawing of exceptional artistry. The entire company was taken with his performance and required that it be repeated several times. Further exciting our zeal for the little man was the richness of his costume and workmanship of his features, these last composed entirely of purest gold. Mr. Alexei jokes that he has entrusted the secret of his riches to his automaton, even above his own flesh and blood."

Ohmigod! "It's him! It's got to be!"

"It is," Sophie said, just a little smugly. "It took me until just now to find it. This is a journal. One of the first Americans in Alaska wrote this after a banquet with this Peter Alexey-whatever."

"But ..."

"Exactly! He didn't dance. He drew!"

"Holy," Tomi gaped. Drew? That was way more complicated than just moving his feet. But suddenly everything he'd been struggling with made sense. The ripples on the pancakes guided the Boy's *hands*, not his feet. "Sophie, this is great. Fantastic. It's exactly what I needed. I've been so close, but sooo wrong."

Sophie was grinning now. "And," her blue eyes blazed, "I think he knows where Alex was getting his gold!"

Tomi reread the last line of the account. "'The secret of his riches.'" *Sure sounds like it.* "But how could he?"

Sophie raised her shoulders and shook her head.

"A map? He could draw a map."

"A treasure map?"

Sophie was practically buzzing with excitement now. Tomi wanted to get back downstairs right now and start over in light of this new idea. Cogs and gears were already turning in his mind.

Somewhere on the floor below a clock began to chime. *Three ... four ... five.*

Aargh. The museum was closing. It was Saturday already.

His whole body itched to get started and not stop until he had the Golden Boy working again. *Dang, dang, DANG.*

He met Sophie's look. The golden brow and cherub kiss of Tomi's imagination faded in the warm presence of real blonde curls and a righteous full-on grin. He still had a couple quarters in his pocket.

"Say, want to go down to the drugstore and get a pop?"

"A what?"

"A pop. You know, Coke, Pepsi, Dr. Pepper?"

"Ahhh." Understanding dawned. "A soda! Sure, I'd love to." *Soda, right. I'm in America now.*

At the drugstore they found seats at the long counter. Tomi could see himself reflected in the mirror that ran behind the drink fountains and bottles, his dark hair beside her blonde. They ordered Coke floats.

The youth behind the counter filled frosty glasses with ice cream and soda and presented them with a flourish that reminded Tomi of the barristas in the coffee shops at home. His eyes went to the reflection in the mirror.

"Hey." He tried to make his voice as soft as JP's. "What's the matter?"

Sophie took a deep breath and let it out. "I just had such a sad thought."

His brows knitted. *Coke floats, I think we've cracked the Golden Boy. How is this sad?*

"Sad?"

She turned to look at him. Her blue eyes shone with near tears. "You're the most interesting person I've ever met."

Woah! "*Back at'cha,*" he wanted to say. But something held him back.

"But if we're wrong," her voice trembled a little. "Or you can't do it, can't fix the Boy, then I may never see you again."

Okay, they say girls are impossible to figure out. Go with that. "How's that?"

"The mine. My father's a blaster. He only works when they're digging more galleries. They already told him they won't be needing any more galleries. Ma and Papa told me the rest last night. Papa says there are jobs on Vancouver Island. We've got tickets on the *Stella* next week." A thought struck her and her face brightened. "Vancouver Island, isn't that where you're from?"

"Near there." *But not "then" — or do I mean "now"?*

"And it's not just you, it's everyone I know here." Sophie shook her shoulders and sucked on her float. "I'm okay. I just don't want to move. Especially now."

"I hear you," Tomi replied. "That's kind of what got me here."

"How?"

"My mom died a couple years ago." Sophie's head tipped and her eyes saddened in sympathy. "My dad and my new step-thingy want to move to a new house. I don't. We kind of had a blow-up. I blew off and, well, kinda just ended up here."

"So you wound up moving anyway."

"Yeah, I guess." *Then again, there's moving, and there's moving.*

"Was it a brodie?"

"Say what?"

"A brodie, a good idea? Or not?"

Well, it's sure been different. He drew a fizzy mouthful of cold, creamy Coke float into his cheeks and thought about that. In the mirror, he saw himself bowed over his drink. Her head suddenly bent next to his, her tongue reaching out to pull in her straw. Blue eyes met his in the mirror. Then Sophie winked.

Tomi was so shocked he inhaled his Coca-Cola and when it came out of his nose, Sophie's question got lost in their laughter.

IT WAS past seven when he got back to the lumber yard that evening.

Mizz Alex insisted on an explanation, and was only somewhat mollified by his account of having floats with a girl. "Carr, is it? Sophie Carr? I think I've met her mother. Spirited." It wasn't clear whether she considered this a good thing. "There's a hash in the pan on the stove. You know where the plates are. Just make sure they're back and clean when you're done."

"Sure."

With the smallest of nods, she went through the door that led to the rest of the house and closed it firmly behind her.

MIZZ ALEX seemed to treat Sundays differently from other days of the week. That made it hard to know whether her formal tone the next morning meant Tomi was still under a cloud or simply that she was preparing herself for "service." The green car roared off to church shortly after breakfast.

A little later JP showed up. Tomi met his friend in the gravel yard.

"How's it goin'?" JP asked.

"Okay. Better than okay. I think I've worked it out."

JP gave him a look. "You're still crazy over that Boy."

"Not crazy. I've almost got him figured out!"

"I thought you weren't allowed in the museum no more."

"He changed his mind."

"*He's* crazy then." JP grinned.

"Maybe a little," Tomi laughed with him. "But that's where I've been. And really, I'm getting it together. Only he doesn't dance, he *draws*. That makes a huge difference."

JP shrugged like someone willing to take a friend's word on that.

"And I think he's got something to do with Russian Alex's gold."

"The gold he's made from?" JP asked.

"The gold from Russian Alex's secret mine, the other end of the Juneau gold vein."

JP squinted in puzzlement.

"I think the secret of the mine is hidden in the Golden Boy somehow. But not hidden out in the open, in among his parts; hidden in whatever it is he does. I can't know for sure until I put him together."

The other boy gave Tomi an affectionate slap on the shoulder, then waggled his finger in a circle beside his own head. "Crazy. Definitely crazy."

The day was warm. Puffs of white cloud chased each other from one mountain peak to the next across a pale blue sky. Together they explored up the pipeline that ran up the hill behind the Kasilof watermill.

There was a small lake up there, in the valley between the mountains. Holding it back was a wall of timbers made from some of the hugest logs Tomi had ever seen. Whole trees had been squared off to make a palisade of wood breasted with bands of iron, flaking red rust in the sun. The water ran back, clear and cold, until it disappeared around a distant shoulder of the left-hand mountain.

They scrambled all over the dam. Tomi showed JP how he thought it worked. They spent the rest of the day exploring along the lake behind it. JP told Tomi the names in his language of the things that grew there. All the names sounded sort of like coughing though, and Tomi almost began to appreciate how simple Japanese was to understand. *Don't let Obaacha hear me say that*, he teased himself.

Where a stream chuckled into the lake from the slopes above they paused, each finding a different water-scooped hollow of stone in which to lie back.

For a while they lolled in the sun, enjoying the sounds of small waves lapping on rock, the gurgling stream, the fresh breeze dancing across the water, tart with the scent of the distant cedar slope. Tomi watched clouds go by overhead, playing the game of finding animals and faces in the flossy masses.

After a thoughtful silence, JP spoke up. "Does Charley know?"

Say what? He hadn't thought about the twisted and unhappy Charley Ramsay for almost a week. Not since leaving the home. "Know about what?"

"The Boy. Russian Alex. What you're thinkin' 'bout his gold."

"No, I don't think so. Why would he even care?"

"I dunno. That's what's strange."

Eh? "I don't get it, what's Charley got to do with the Boy?"

"Maybe it's just you."

"Say what?" This was too confusing.

"Maybe he just doesn't like you, for sticking up for me that time."

Aargh. "What? Is he saying stuff about me? I don't get it."

"He's following you."

A chill shadow fell over them as the leading edge of an especially thick and bulbous cloud swept across the sun.

"You're kidding."

"Remember the movie show?"

He was there, sitting right behind us. A creepy sensation walked cold feet up Tomi's spine.

"A couple times since, I noticed him acting strange. So I followed him, and he was going where you were, watching you."

Holy crap!

JP rose from his stone sofa to look across at Tomi. "You better watch out for him, Tomi. Charley, he likes to get back at people. Even when they don't do nothing to him, he likes to get back."

My very own racist stalker. Nice.

The cloud across the sun had stalled there. It was cool in its blue shadow and they were both ready to get moving again.

MIZZ ALEX'S mood had softened somewhat by the time they got back to the yard. She'd been cooking, and invited JP to stay for supper.

The meal was a deep-dish pie full of onions and potatoes and carrots alongside big chunks of flaky white halibut in a buttery rich sauce. *Fish pie! Who'd a' thunk it could be so good?* Tomi and JP raced each other to the bottom of the pot, but Mizz Alex snuck in and snatched the last spoonful.

Afterward, they had milky tea and macaroons.

Tomi's thoughts drifted to Coke floats and the difference between dancing and drawing.

"Tomi?" Mizz Alex broke in. She held the plate of macaroons toward him, and it seemed she'd been holding it there for a while. "Your mind's somewhere else, my boy. What is it? That young lady?"

"Sophie? No, ma'am," he suppressed a smirk. *Actually, it's a boy.* "But I've been working on something, and I think I've almost got it licked."

"Have you now? And what's that?"

"You know the Golden Boy?"

Mizz Alex's face froze. "Yes."

"Mr. Bartlett's been letting me work on the insides."

The strong face closed like a window being slammed shut. "Waste of time. He shouldn't have agreed to it."

"But it's not! Or at least, I don't think so. I think I've got it figured out."

"Hmph. Nothing but trouble that thing. Trouble and a waste of everyone's time." She got to her feet and began gathering up the dishes.

JP gave him an "uh-oh" look across the table.

Tomi got a sharp elbow when JP left a little later, with a wink to let him know his friend was still in the game, whatever Mizz Alex thought.

Twenty

STAR OF WONDER

HE WOKE UP thinking about the Boy. *Drawing.* That changed everything. He could already see that the medium-sized rods, the ones he hadn't been able to figure out, must work like biceps to make the arms move. He leaped from the bunk.

But Mizz Alex's efforts to get the word out were paying off. A steady trickle of customers came by the little white office. Tomi was kept busy fetching small orders to the gravel parking lot or directing patrons' cars and trucks to the right stack to pick up larger ones.

It was well past three that afternoon before Tomi at last got to the museum. By then he was burning with impatience. He eagerly set about rearranging gears and cogs.

Parts that before had stubbornly refused to fit now fell into place easily. With each new cog that dropped smoothly onto its post, teeth meshing neatly with a neighbour, Tomi saw where yet another might go. The long rods and their extensions snicked without protest into sockets. It was almost eerie to watch as the legs, waist, torso, neck, shoulders and arms of the mechanical boy took form in front of him.

By 4:30 he had the Boy almost together. But as he tightened a small screw that held the last piece in place, he was aware that he was not yet there. He'd looked in every fold and corner of the cardboard box, and he had used every cog and cam. But there were still four or five studs where gears were missing — breaks in the chain of radiating teeth that carried power from the Boy's clockwork heart to his hands and arms.

And something else he had not found: a key to wind the spring tight.

He leaned back. There was one other thing. What he'd built sure *looked* right. But he could never really know until the mechanism was where it belonged: inside the Boy.

First things first.

The five chimes of the clock striking the museum's closing hour echoed in the lobby as Tomi walked to the door. He pulled it open and stepped into the sunny street.

His toe hit something solid but yielding. He spun across the sidewalk, struggling to regain his balance. Looking to see what tripped him, he saw a white dog stretched across the sun-warmed stone of the museum step.

"Darn you, Patsy Ann," he sputtered. "That's a stupid place to lie."

The white dog blinked mildly.

"Who you talking to?"

Tomi spun at the sound of Sophie's voice. She stood a little way along the sidewalk with a fellow a couple years older than himself. Not bad looking either. *Does she have a boyfriend?*

Sophie smiled. "Don't you know she can't hear you?"

"Say again?"

"She's deaf. Patsy Ann can't hear," Sophie said.

Tomi turned to the dog and without warning shouted: "HEY, PATSY ANN." The white ears didn't shiver and the dog didn't blink.

"That's what makes it so swingy that she hears the ships coming in," the older boy said.

"Never mind that she always gets the wharf right," Sophie nodded.

"Maybe she reads lips," Tomi suggested. The other two laughed, but Tomi wasn't so sure he was joking. *She can do a lot of things you guys don't know about.*

The boy gave the dog a scratch behind the ears and turned to go, saying to Sophie as he went, "Okay, see you at seven."

Omigod, it is her boyfriend. I am such a doofus.

"That'll be kippy!" Sophie said, waving him goodbye. "Bring your test, the one you got the E on. We'll pick it up from there. And I charge twenty cents an hour."

She's his tutor! Relief and embarrassment flooded over him.

Sophie watched her student walk away. When he was out of earshot she turned to Tomi, her face eager with anticipation. "So, how's the Boy?"

"Almost there. Hey, is there a thrift store in town?"

"What's a thrift store?"

"A place where you can buy things used, second-hand things."

"It's hard enough finding first-hand things in Juneau.

What kind of things?"

"Old clocks. Or maybe a big watch. I need some parts."

"Levi's Pawn Shop has watches in the window."

They found the shop's narrow front window under a sign with three gold-painted balls hanging from it. A cluster of bells tinkled above the door as they pushed it open. Tomi could have spent hours checking out the shelves. On racks behind the counter were more rifles and handguns than he had ever seen outside a TV screen. On a shelf in a corner he found an assortment of wind-up alarm and mantel clocks.

He chose three with cogs about the size he needed. Turning them over, he made sure there was a winding key taped to the bottom of each one. *One of these has gotta work.*

He took his selection over to the ornate cash register. A man wearing purple suspenders over a white shirt with pink pinstripes eyed the two suspiciously. "What do you kids want with all these clocks?"

"School project," Tomi said smoothly.

The guy behind the counter pushed up his lower lip and bobbed his head. "Fifteen cents then."

Tomi counted out the change. The man put the clocks in a paper sack.

They stepped back out to the sidewalk, and for the second time that day Tomi was nearly knocked off his feet. This time the offender wasn't Patsy Ann, but Charley Ramsey.

"Hey, watch where you're goin'," Charley scowled. "Or can'tcha see outta them slanty eyes."

Tomi's temper flared and he rounded on the taller boy. But he felt Sophie's hand on his arm.

"Oh, Tomi, don't mind his booshwash."

Tomi glared at the sour smirk on Charley's face. He breathed deeply. "Booshwash" was one word for it. Meeting Charley's eye, he tried to sound tough. "Learn some respect, dude." Then he stepped back and began walking stiffly away down the boardwalk.

Sophie trotted to keep up. "That was brave of you, Tomi. There's no point getting into trouble."

Yeah, sometimes there is. "There will be if he keeps that up."

"Oh, Tomi, he's just a pill. And a scrub too. Forget about him."

No idea what you just said, Soph, but I think you just called him down. His breathing began to calm. "I'd be happy to forget him. It's Charley who's not dropping it."

"What do you mean?"

"JP says he's been following me."

The bells tinkled behind them as Charley pushed open the pawn shop door and went inside.

"Lay off!" Sophie turned to look over her shoulder, but the sidewalk was empty.

They walked a little faster.

THE NEXT morning seemed to crawl by.

A week of slicing logs and timbers into smaller planks had turned the mill into a fragrant wonderland of sawdust. Pale drifts of wood chips filled the corners. "It's all got to be swept up and carried back to the waste pile," Mizz Alex said, handing Tomi a broom and a dustpan.

It took what felt like forever. Dust was everywhere. At last he had every visible surface clear, but even then they weren't done. "Now," Mizz Alex handed him a thick tube as long as Tomi's forearm with a hinged lever and a stubby hose off one end. "Ever use a grease gun?"

Tomi shook his head.

"Mmm." Mizz Alex looked disappointed. "Nor I. But when my brother was alive, he used to go 'round once a week and grease every bearing. I'm figuring you'll have a better idea where it goes than I do."

Tomi took the gun and worked the handle. A greenish-grey worm squooshed out of the hose. *I get it.* He regularly oiled his machine at home. This must be the industrial-strength version of the same thing. For the next hour he barely thought about the Boy. He crawled through the massive mill mechanism, tracking down little fittings and squirting a shot of grease into each.

When he was done, he threw the lever that sent water onto the big wheel. Slowly at first, then faster, the wheel began to turn. He felt a gentle rumble beneath his feet as the rest of the machinery awoke. The great machine seemed more ... relaxed, almost. *Smooth*, he thought.

But that only reminded Tomi of the other cogs and gears waiting for him down at the museum. He threw the lever back and let the big wheel come to rest once more. He put the grease gun in the shed.

He raced across the yard to the house. Impatiently he scrubbed the worst grey-green grease smears from his face and arms and scarfed down a salmon sandwich, eating so fast that Mizz Alex warned him against forgetting to chew. "I'd hate to have to explain how you choked to death," she said, sounding just like Obaacha.

"I'm good," Tomi assured her, guzzling a glass of milk. "Gotta go. See you later."

Paper bag of pawn-shop clocks under one arm, he headed downtown.

Hot and sweaty, he pulled up at the stone facade. Automatically, he grabbed for the door handle and pulled. But the big doors were locked tight. *Must be early.* He could do nothing but pace the boardwalk, stomach churning in frustration.

The curator arrived after what seemed far longer than just a few minutes, ambling up to the door with a half smile on his face. "Aren't you the eager beaver," he remarked, bending to fit a key in the door.

Tomi felt himself blush. *Just wait*, he told himself. *This is going to be totally awesome, you'll see.*

The Boy's brass skeleton stood where he'd left it. It looked raw, almost clinical — like a teaching aid for showing off the bones and muscles beneath the skin — but incomplete. The upright torso lacked a head. The upraised arms ended at wrists without hands. *Soon, little guy.*

Tomi upended the paper bag onto the table and set about dismantling the old clocks. It didn't take long to find four or five gears to replace the ones missing from the Boy.

By the time he had them in place, Tomi could feel his chest tightening with excitement. Breathing deeply to steady his hand, he inserted a screwdriver carefully into the Boy's chest. He pressed the tip against the big cog beside the coiled spring and gave it a gentle push. The wrist at the end of the Boy's right arm jerked upward.

Something like a balloon felt like it was getting ready to explode in Tomi's chest. This was it! There was only one last test to try before he tracked down Mr. Bartlett and demanded that the Boy and his insides be reunited.

He picked up the windup key that had come with the first clock and inserted it into the small hole in the Boy's spring casing. The key barely entered the hole before something blocked it. *No sweat.* This was why he'd bought several. He tried another. It went in a little farther, but when he turned it, the key simply spun uselessly.

He picked up the last key. One try and he threw it down in disgust. This one was fatter than the others, too thick to enter the small keyhole at all.

Dammit, dammit, DAMMIT. This was the last thing he'd expected.

He examined the three keys more closely. Each ended in a slightly different-sized version of the same thing: a square socket that should fit over a square post to wind the clockwork spring. Cradling the brass skeleton in his arms, Tomi moved it about until light from the overhead bulb shone in the tiny keyhole. It was hard to see in without getting his head in the way of the light, but at last he managed it.

Oh, man! Every other windup clock or toy he'd ever taken apart had been just like the pawn shop clocks: You used a key with a square socket to turn a square peg to wind it up. This peg was star-shaped, an irregular, five-pointed star.

Crap.

Tomi fell back in the chair and blew out a breath. The Golden Boy might as well have been back in pieces. Without a key matching the star-shaped shaft, there was no way to wind him up. *So close and yet …*

Three muffled *tings* sounded through the floor from above. Over the past couple of weeks, Tomi had learned that these signalled the three-quarter mark of each hour. *Nearly five.* He thrust a hand in a pocket. *Yeah!* He still had a few coins. Maybe he could find a key to match.

One more day, little guy, he breathed to the headless figure on the bench. *Don't give up on me.* Reluctantly, he turned off the light and headed for the stairs.

At the first floor he turned toward the back hall. A quick check-out with Mr. Bartlett and he could make it to the pawn shop before it closed. He had his hand on the knob of the curator's office door when he heard a harsh voice behind the frosted glass. "A spy, maybe a saboteur, we're not sure."

It was Nichols, the FBI agent. The man's tone had lost none of its bullying edge. "… some kind of transmitter, top-drawer stuff. We sent it to Washington," he was saying.

The FBI agent was the last person Tomi wanted to see. He stepped away from the door. Hopefully Mr. Bartlett wouldn't mind him leaving without checking out this once.

Nichols' next words stopped him cold. "We're shadowing him. We know he's acquiring parts. Could be for another transmitter, or maybe a bomb. We just don't know." The agent's voice dropped again and Tomi could make out no more.

There was some kind of terrorist loose in Juneau. *But why is Nichols talking to Bartlett about it?* Maybe the curator was a spy too, an undercover agent working secretly for the FBI?

Man oh man this is too freaking Big Brother. Another thought struck him, a really nasty one. *Charley!* Could *he* be part of this?

Naah, you're way too paranoid.

Yeh, but just because you're paranoid, doesn't mean they're *not* out to get you, the old joke line came to him. Besides, it wouldn't be the first unbelievable thing he'd had to accept since chasing Patsy Ann in among the lumber piles.

Whatever was going on in the curator's office, Tomi was pretty sure they didn't mean to include him in it. He was in Nichols' bad books enough already, without getting pegged as an eavesdropper on top of everything else.

He stepped quietly to the lobby and slipped out of the building.

DINNER THAT night was a spicy red stew, swimming with chunks of chicken and sliced onion. Mizz Alex called it "goulash" and encouraged Tomi to add dollops of sour cream that nicely took the edge off its fire. After washing up the dishes, Tomi retired to the bunkhouse.

A restless energy possessed him. His stop at the pawn shop had been fruitless. Every single clock key he looked at had the same square-shaped socket, the only difference being the size. None would work to wind up the Golden Boy.

Tired of thinking in circles he pushed the problem to the back of his mind. There was still enough light in the late northern dusk for a little "wall reading" before he turned in.

A newspaper stapled near the front door was yellowed with age. A half-page picture went with a screaming head-line: ST. VALENTINE'S DAY MASSACRE! A gang dressed like policemen had surprised a rival mob in a garage. The killers had machine-gunned their victims. *That black stuff, it's blood all over the floor.* Afterward, the fake policemen had flashed their badges to convince the neighbours that everything was normal as they made their getaway. *Sneaky.*

The other stories on the page were all politics and wars and crises. He soon lost interest. His thoughts kept drifting back to the Boy, all put together and no way to go.

He flopped into bed and stared at the springs of the bunk above. His eyes closed and his waking mind fell asleep still tugging at the problem like fingers at a loose thread.

HIS MOTHER was sitting at her vanity. She seemed to be getting ready to go out. Lamplight shone warmly on her bare shoulders. Tomi was in pyjamas. She turned to smile at him and a bolt of love and loneliness shot through him. The light danced in her grey eyes, so unlike his own. Where had he seen eyes like those? But now she was rooting around in the little tray where she kept her favourite jewellery. She held up a gold chain. The brooch that hung from it was a funny shape, like a short, squat lollipop. Then Tomi was downstairs. Dad was opening the door. It was the babysitter. The babysitter was a man, a man in a suit, wearing a fedora. His pale eyes were set close together and he had an eager, hungry look.

Tomi awoke with a start and sat up in his bunk. It was dark, but he was glad to have awakened. His dream had felt like it was about to turn into a nightmare. *Yuck.* Nichols in his dreams! What was even worse, in the same dream as Mom. *Yeee-yuck!* He gave his head a hard shake and lay back on the pillow.

He tried to recapture the part where Mom had turned around and smiled at him. A sharp pain cut into his chest along with the old unanswerable question. *Why?* And why did her face seem to fade away so fast? He felt that hot, familiar burn in the corner of his eyes.

Then ... *Ohmigod.*

Tomi leaped from the bunk and stumbled to the table. Groping in the darkness, he found the box of matches and pulled one out. His hands shook so much it took him three tries to strike it. He held the guttering little flame up near his chest.

With his other hand he lifted the key hanging from its fine chain around his neck. It was the key he'd rescued from the box in the garbage, the one Mom used to say, with a laugh, was "all that's left of my family fortune." He held the key sideways and brought the match up close, trying to get the weak light in line with the business end of the key.

"Ouch!" The flame had reached his fingers. Hastily he flicked the match out. But before the light faded, he had his answer. The inside of the key's round shaft was hollow. In cross-section, it formed a perfect, five-pointed star.

Holy crap. Cold electricity ran over Tomi's skin, setting the hair at the back of his neck on edge. *This* is *why I'm here! It's got to be.*

It took him a long time to get to sleep again. Part of him wanted to race down to the museum right then and there. The rest of him couldn't let go of the coincidence — if it really was coincidence.

Desperately, he combed his memory for anything Mom might ever have said about her family, anything that might explain ...

HE WOKE with a start. It was bright in the bunkhouse and Mizz Alex was standing in the open doorway.

"Daylight's wasting." She sounded annoyed. "Coffee and eggs are up. Shake a leg."

When he reached the kitchen and glanced at the clock he was shocked to see how late he had slept. Should he tell her? Ask to be excused from his morning's chores? Something held him back. Mizz Alex hadn't seemed to think it was such a good idea to try to fix the Boy at all. Not that it was any of her business, really. She was his boss, but nothing more.

He needed to *know*. After the other setbacks, he needed to be sure he hadn't been jumping to conclusions in the middle of the night.

The morning seemed to drag by even more slowly than the last. Once more, Mizz Alex had him shifting large timbers to the saw shed. For some reason today the peavey kept slipping in his hand, the hand-truck bucked and resisted going where he pointed it. More than once Tomi had to jump to avoid being kneecapped by a swinging timber.

When Mizz Alex finally declared the morning over and hung her "gone to lunch" sign on the lumber yard office door, Tomi could wait no longer. "I'll grab a bite later, Mizz A," he said. "If that's okay."

She gave him a sharp look — *Where have I seen eyes like that?* — but let him go with a nod.

He took the road to town at a run, slowing down only when he ran out of breath. He made the distance in record time, alternately walking and jogging.

He pushed open the heavy museum door and headed directly for the basement stairs. He was halfway there when Mr. Bartlett shot out of his office. "You!"

"Hey, Mr. Bartlett," Tomi started to say. "I think I've almost —"

"You can stop right there."

Say what? "What the … What's happened?"

"Nothing yet, and that's exactly what's going to happen. *Nothing.* Not if I can help it." The curator seized Tomi's elbow and steered him forcibly back toward the door.

"But what did I do?"

"The FBI came to see me." *Nichols!* "I don't need that kind of trouble."

"But ... let me explain."

Without letting go of Tomi's shoulder the curator pulled the door open. "Don't bother. This experiment's over. Out you go." He shoved the boy roughly down the steps onto the sidewalk. "I never should have let you in to begin with."

Tomi wheeled. "Hey! I'm not a spy, Mr. Bartlett."

The curator's cheeks blazed. "How did you hear that? Have you been eavesdropping?"

"No sir. I just came to say goodbye last night. You were in your office. I heard Agent Nichols talking. I couldn't help it. But I'm not a —"

"Sorry," Bartlett cut him off. "No dice. Deal's off. Can't risk it. Shoo." The door closed with a heavy sigh and Tomi heard the snick of a bolt shooting home.

Double Holy Crap! His head spun with furious thoughts. He kicked hard at the stone step. *Yeow!*

He heard a snicker. Charley Ramsey leaned against the corner of the building, hands in pockets and a smirk on his creepy face.

Fury boiled up in Tomi. His eyes blazed and for a moment his arms itched to haul off and pop the taller boy. Barely in time, a voice spoke in his head. *"Don't mind his booshwash."*

Swallowing his temper, Tomi gave the white kid a last glare and turned away.

Sophie. I need to find her. And JP. *There's got to be another way.*

Twenty-one

TURNS OF THE KEY

PATSY ANN lay sprawled in a patch of sunshine in front of O'Doule's barbershop. She scrambled hastily to her feet when the tall youth came striding up the hill, his face a study in concentration.

"Hi, Patsy Ann," Tomi said, without breaking pace.

With a quick shiver that barely hinted at a proper shake, the white dog broke into a trot to keep up. Where the track to the orphanage broke away from the main road, they turned. As they skirted the swamp Tomi made out Sister Agatha in her dark robes, standing against the weathered planks of the building. Afternoon recess was still on.

Most of the girls stood around in twos and threes and fours chatting; a few more skipped rope.

At one end of the yard a line of boys was forming up. A smaller group of three stood in the middle of the hard-packed ground. With a chorus of yells, the boys in the line began to run, pelting across the schoolyard. The kids in the middle tackled two of the runners, bringing them to the ground. When the line formed again at the far end of the yard, the two had joined the three in the middle. Tomi recognized the game; it was forbidden at his own school.

JP was still among the runners. But the moment he spotted Tomi and the white dog he abandoned the game and walked over to them. "Hey," came his soft greeting.

"Hey." In a few sentences, Tomi told him what had happened at the museum. "It's so crazy too, 'cause I'm so close," he said. "Like, an hour, max, and I'd have him together again and doing … whatever it is he does."

"No kidding. So what are you going to do?"

"I need your help."

JP looked over his shoulder. The group of boys in the middle of the yard had grown to eight. An equal number were lining up ready to run. Charley Ramsey was in the second group, but his eyes were on the two boys talking by the road.

A bell rang and the line of boys made one last rush across the yard. "Wait for me down the road," JP said, his voice even softer than normal. "Under the bent cedar, the big one. You can wait out of sight there."

Tomi locked eyes with him a moment, nodded and turned away.

JP WAS grinning when he came along the road beyond the green curtain of Tomi's hiding place fifteen minutes later. "That's gonna be the longest bathroom break anyone ever took," he laughed.

They set off for town.

"So what're we gonna do?" JP asked.

"We're gonna go over Bartlett's head. We're gonna put the Golden Boy back together."

"How? We'll just get thrown out again."

"Not if he doesn't know we're there."

"You mean, break in?"

"Not break. More like sneak."

"Oh, boy. I dunno. We're gonna get in trouble."

"No we won't. Once the Boy's working again, no one's going to care if we bent some goofy rule to do it."

"I dunno," JP said again, shaking his head. "Sure sounds like trouble to me." But he kept on walking.

By the time they reached Juneau Public, classes there were letting out. Sophie spotted them as soon as they waved from the park across the street. She ran over to join them.

"You're going to do *what*?" she said when Tomi unveiled his plan. Her blue eyes were bright with excitement.

"We're going to sneak into the museum and put the Boy back together," Tomi said.

"What if he doesn't work?" JP said.

"He will," Tomi said. "I'm sure of it."

"How d'you know?"

"Don't ask me how, or why, 'cause I swear I don't know how I know. But look." He lowered his voice and the other two leaned in to listen. He pulled the small key on its chain from beneath his shirt. "This belonged to my mother. It came from our family somehow. But, here's the thing: It's the only key that fits the Golden Boy."

Sophie frowned. "What about the clock keys?"

Tomi shook his head. "Nope. I even went back and looked at some more. There's not another key in Juneau that'll fit."

JP was looking at Tomi through half-lidded eyes. "You're really not from 'round here, are you," he said.

"Well, I'm in." Sophie bobbed her blonde head. "I can't wait to see the look on everyone's face when the Golden Boy comes back to life. And if he really does know where old Russian Alex hid his mine, we'll be heroes!"

"Yeah, I guess," JP said. "But there's gonna be trouble."

"Not if we do it right," Tomi said. "I just need, I don't know, maybe an hour to get the Boy's insides inside him."

"I have an idea." Sophie's face glowed with the light of battle. "Let me go in first. I'll ask Mr. Bartlett to help with my history project. He loves to give advice." She smirked. "Trust me, I can keep him busy for a hour."

"You're sure?" Tomi's stomach was doing somersaults as the reality of what they were planning sank in.

Sophie rolled her eyes. "Have you ever heard that man get started about history?"

FIFTEEN minutes later Patsy Ann stood beside the eager blonde girl as she tapped on the frosted glass of the curator's office door.

"Come in." Mr. Bartlett's muffled voice came through the glass.

Sophie took a breath and opened the door. "Hi, Mr. Bartlett," she said in her sweetest good-girl voice. "Can you help me with something?" She stepped inside, pulling the door closed behind her.

JP followed Tomi down the staircase that led to the basement. Past the rows of crates and the war canoe, the child-sized mechanical body lay where Tomi had left it. With its head-less torso and brass limbs ending at wrist and ankle, it might have been an unfinished meal waiting for the stuffed bear's appetite to return.

Tomi's heart pounded as he took the small figure into his arms. Carrying it in front of him, he headed back to the stairs. JP cracked open the door at the top. Along the hallway, the frosted glass door was open. They heard Sophie's voice coming from one of the rooms toward the front, followed by Mr. Bartlett's deeper one.

"Let's do it," Tomi said. Stepping as lightly as he could in his leather boots, and followed by JP moving silently in his beaded moccasins, he hurried to the big central staircase and started up to the second floor.

He breathed a sigh of relief when they reached the top and looked down the upstairs corridor — the door to the Boy's chamber was open.

Inside the small room, Tomi came to a stop, struck as always by the golden radiance of the cherub face and its life-less body. JP pulled the door nearly shut, then stood with his eye to the crack. Tomi placed the clockwork figure gently on the floor. *Almost, little guy*, he thought. *Real soon.*

From the distance, he heard sharp footsteps cross the downstairs lobby and for a moment Tomi's blood froze. He glanced over at JP, who shook his head.

"It's okay. They're not coming up," he whispered.

Tomi stepped around the glass case and tried the door at the back. *Locked. No worries.* He pulled the small screwdriver from his tool kit and inserted it where the door latch met the frame of the case. He looked up and met JP's dark eyes.

The other boy nodded. "Do it," JP said.

Taking one last, deep breath Tomi pushed hard on the driver. With a crack that sounded loud enough to be heard in the lumber yard, the door popped open.

He reached into the case and very gently lifted the little figure in its rough prospector's clothes. As he did, the golden head sagged backward and the clothes seemed to collapse in on themselves. Without his mechanical insides, there had been nothing holding the Boy upright inside the case except a bare cross of wood. Even so, Tomi was startled by the weight of the sculpted head and delicate gold fingers.

PATSY ANN'S nose wrinkled as the FBI agent walked toward them.

"Gee, Mr. Bartlett," Sophie was saying. "These are great." She surveyed the half dozen books that lay open in front of her. "But don't you have anything more? Maybe something actually written by a woman? That's my topic you see, Alaska's early —"

The man in the fedora cut her off. "That Jap come by here?"

"He's Canadian," Sophie corrected him.

"Miss Carr!" the curator exclaimed. "I'm sure your mother doesn't condone rudeness." He raised a weak smile to the agent. "No, Agent Nichols. I turned him away just this morning. I 'preciate your speaking to me. We don't want any trouble here, we sure don't. What do you want with him?"

"My informant lost him. Last we saw of him he was with an Indian — could be another operative."

Sophie snorted.

Nichols' eyes narrowed and he looked again at Sophie. "And we think there are others. The Russian, for one."

"The who?" Mr. Bartlett asked in a voice that wavered slightly.

"Kasilof."

"You mean Mizz Alex*andra* Kasilof?" The curator gave a nervous laugh. "She's hardly a spy. Why, she's lived here longer than either you or me. She's one of the benefactors of this museum, for heaven's sake."

Nichols gave him an icy look. "We have sources. And she may not be the only one." His pale eyes turned back to Sophie. "What about you, Miss? You seem to know who I'm talking about."

Sophie's look grew stubborn. "It's still a free territory," she retorted.

The colour rose in Nichols' cheeks. "He been feeding you that kind of leftist talk?" His voice was hard. "They're planning something. If you figure in it, Missy, you'll see how far that attitude takes you."

All three of them jumped at the sharp bark that came from their feet.

In the silence that followed, Sophie's whisper came out very clearly. "They're down in the basement." She kept her head low, watching Nichols from the corner of one eye.

"What?" Nichols voice cracked with excitement.

Patsy Ann barked again.

"Down ..." She paused and sighed theatrically. "Down in the basement. Working on —"

But Nichols wasn't listening. He had already turned and was racing toward the basement stairs, Mr. Bartlett on his heels.

Sophie was only a heartbeat behind them.

TOMI FROZE. A moment later he heard it again: an urgent bark echoing up from the lobby below.

Busted!

But not yet, not quite. Mind racing, Tomi folded the Boy's empty suit of clothing in on itself, wrapping it over and around the gleaming head and hands. He put the rough bundle on the floor beside the brass torso and ripped off his work shirt, silently thanking the karma that made him throw it on over his T-shirt this morning. Hastily he wrapped the shirt around the mechanical skeleton and the bundled Boy. Carefully, he lifted the whole package to his chest.

Tomi felt way past the need for caution. This was what he'd been sent across time for; he knew it. That singular thought justified whatever they had to do now. "Let's go."

Footsteps pounded in the corridor one floor down. *They're not coming up. They're heading for the basement. We've got a chance.*

Looking down the grand staircase to the lobby, he saw Patsy Ann near the front door. Her dark eyes were turned toward him. She barked. He started down the stairs, JP close behind.

As his foot hit the lobby floor, Tomi ran sideways to look back down the hall in the direction of the basement stairs. Sophie raced toward him.

"Go! Go!" Her blue eyes were ablaze and she was out of breath. "I locked them down there!" she gasped. "C'mon, let's make tracks."

All three were pelting full-out as they banked into the alley beside the Red Dog. They pulled up behind a tower of wooden barrels. "Woooo!" Sophie whooped, gasping for breath. "That was too wacky!" She broke into nervous laughter.

"I told you there was gonna be trouble," JP said, shaking his head with a grim sort of satisfaction.

"But not for you guys," Tomi panted. "Seriously. It's me they'll be looking for. You guys should split."

"What about you?" Sophie asked.

Good question. He looked around. "Where's Patsy Ann?" The white dog was nowhere in sight.

"She must have stayed behind," Sophie said, "back in the museum."

Damn. Somehow he'd been counting on her to figure out what came next. This was getting hairy. *Where … ? Yeah!* "Okay, I've got it," he said. "I've got to get to the marina."

"The marina?" JP and Sophie spoke as one.

"The boat docks." *And the* DogStar.

"Gee, I don't know," Sophie said. "They'll be looking for you, or for anyone who might have the Golden Boy."

"Then I better get going." He stepped out into the alley.

"Wait," JP gripped his arm. "Not that way." He grinned.

"There's ways they don't know. I'll take you."

"'Kay," Tomi agreed. "Soph, if they get you, stall! I don't need long. Then everything's going to be cool."

"Cool?"

"Good. Fine."

"Jake!"

"Yeah, Jake." *Whatever.* "C'mon JP, let's go."

Twenty-two

KIDNAPPERS

PATSY ANN had stayed behind at the museum. She sat, skinny haunches pressed against the bottom of the big double doors, and gazed calmly back across the empty lobby. She shuddered when a splintering crash toward the back of the building sent shock waves through the plank floor.

A moment later Agent Nichols came pounding out of the back hallway, turned and raced up the broad stairs. The breathless curator followed more slowly. His face was bright red and his hair looked like he'd stuck his finger in a light socket.

At the top of the stairs, Mr. Bartlett barrelled into Nichols, who was already heading back toward the main floor on the double. "Gone!" the agent said. "Your Boy's been kidnapped."

Mr. Bartlett actually screamed. "No! My God! I knew it! I *knew* it! All he ever wanted was the gold!" He sagged at the knees, slumping on the top stair. "I knew it! This is the end of me." He dropped his head into his hands and sobbed. "I'll never get another job after this."

Nichols hit the bottom of the stairs and swung left. The room where Mr. Bartlett had been working with Sophie was empty. "Gone, dammit!" he snarled. Nichols spun back and toppled over something low and heavy.

The agent was quick. He rolled and scrambled to his feet, hand reaching for his waist beneath his jacket.

If a dog could smirk, Patsy Ann was smirking.

"You," the agent snarled. "She's in on it," he spoke to himself, dusting his suit. "But that's fine. Plenty for a warrant now. Then I'll round up the lot of them. See if the director doesn't notice me then."

He yanked open the big front door and swung left onto the sidewalk. Striding fast down the boardwalk, Nichols didn't notice the white dog slip out after him.

TOMI doubted it was really the "old Indian trail" JP claimed it was, but they were certainly off the beaten track and out of sight of most of Juneau's busiest streets.

After they had emerged from the alley beside the Red Dog, JP led him across the street to where a saloon and a Salvation Army mission stood side by side. Between the two buildings was a gap just wide enough for a boy to slip through. The narrow space sloped sharply downward and quickly became muddy and slick. A rank smell of oil, dead fish and chemicals wafted toward them.

They came out at the shore. But where they were felt more like a damp cave. Straight ahead, the sun glinted on small waves. Directly above them loomed the heavy timbers of the town wharf.

JP turned left. It was rough going. Brown flats of smelly mud alternated with steep banks of boulders that were crusted with sharp-edged shells. To their right, green water lapped against tarred pilings. The sound of the water echoed loudly in the cavernous space. Tomi could hear people walking above. Wheels rumbled. Occasionally, the cracks between the timbers were wide enough to glimpse someone's legs. But the two boys were well hidden.

Where the wharf ended, they climbed up into a winding valley between ridges of shining black rock piled twice as high as a full-grown man's head. "Coal," JP said, answering the question in Tomi's eyes.

A sprint across another street led to a maze of back alleys that resolved into a path past the back fences of a row of houses. At the last of these they turned and headed back toward the water.

They had left Juneau behind them now. They dashed over open ground and across a road. Brush grew between the road and the shore. JP pushed a way through, holding back the branches so they did not slap in Tomi's face. They came out at the top of a steep bank and JP paused for breath.

The view was amazing. Deep blue water ran away from the foot of the bank toward the distant mountain. Far off to the right, Tomi could see the tall bulk of the Baranof Hotel rising above its neighbours. Straight ahead, half a dozen boats carved white wakes across the sparkling channel. Beneath his feet, a narrow game trail followed the top of the bank.

JP turned left, but their secret passage was almost over. No more than a couple of hundred metres farther on they rounded a small headland. Here the bank cut back again toward the mountain.

Ahead, Tomi saw the squat box of Finn's cabin above its short railway. Another boat now stood high and dry there. Beyond was the boat basin. Tomi thought he could even make out *DogStar*'s two brown masts bobbing at her slip.

When they reached the parking lot, Tomi called JP to a stop. "You should head back now. No one's seen you with me. No reason for you to get into trouble too."

JP looked up and down the shore road. It was empty in both directions. "You sure?"

"Yeah, no worries. I know where I'm going now. Go on, get back."

"I'm probably in trouble anyway," a grin broke over his face. "For taking too long to go to the bathroom."

Tomi had to smile back. "Yeah, I guess. But at least don't get yourself in trouble with the law."

"Yeah, okay." JP gripped his arm briefly as he passed. "Good luck, huh?"

"Thanks. You too."

"YOU!" Avery Nichols felt as though his frayed temper was about to burst apart altogether.

It had taken him barely twenty minutes to get to his office and draft a bare-bones application for an arrest warrant, and about ninety seconds to race upstairs to the second floor of the Federal Building where Judge Henry Burns had his chambers. But the blasted white dog had beaten him there. She lay curled on a braided rug in front of the fire, looking primly up at him.

"Are you speaking to me, Agent?"

Nichols turned to gape at the wiry man reading a paper with his weathered boots up on the desk. "No, your honour, no."

"Well then, don't waste your breath on Patsy Ann. The animal's quite deaf."

Nichols glared a last time at the dog and forced his mind back to the matter at hand. "Judge, we have a situation," he started. "A spy ring, here in town. We don't know their target, but it could be the Navy base. Could be something else. The kingpin is that Jap who's been passing himself off as a kid. But I think the Russian's in it too."

Judge Henry Burns swung his feet to the floor and put down his paper. "What 'Russian'? We have a good many citizens of Russian descent here in the territory."

"The one who runs the lumber yard."

"You don't mean Mizz Alex?"

"Kasilof. Alexandra Kasilof, you bet. That's exactly who I mean."

The judge sniffed and pulled off his glasses. "You're barking up the wrong tree."

"They stole the Golden Boy."

This got the judge's attention at last. "The Golden Boy of Lost Creek?"

"There's another one?" The agent's sarcasm was wide open. "Of course the Golden Boy of Lost Creek. I need warrants for them all. Here's the paper." He dropped several typed sheets onto the judge's desk.

Judge Burns read them quickly, then put them down again. "Just a minute," he said and picked up the telephone. "Yes, get me Bartlett, at the museum." The conversation that followed was brief. When he was done, the judge shook his head.

"I'll give you a warrant for the boy — only. And a tip: Mizz Kasilof is not involved, certainly not in the theft. And, frankly, if she proves to have anything even remotely to do with any 'plot,' I'll eat my hat." He pulled a sheet of paper to him and began writing. "There must be some other explanation."

Nichols was growing more agitated with each minute that passed. The moment the judge was done writing, the agent snatched the warrant from his hands. "I'm going to find that boy," he declared. "I'm going to put him together with the Russian and I'm going to roll the whole lot up!" He spun on his heel and left.

"Now *there*," Judge Burns shook his head sadly and looked over at Patsy Ann, "is a fellow who just doesn't listen." He picked up his paper, leaned back and swung his boots back onto the polished desk.

TOMI WATCHED JP start down the road to town. Then he shifted his burden higher in his arms and headed for the gangplank down to the floats.

Please, let him be home, Tomi thought as he picked his way over the rocking floats. *Or "aboard," or whatever.*

Five minutes later he found himself looking up at the *DogStar*'s masts, swaying gently against a cloudless sky. Hoisting the bundle onto one shoulder, he rapped loudly on the deck. "Hullo," he called. "Anyone home? Captain?"

A moment later the lean, bearded face appeared at the window of the wheelhouse. At the sight of the boy, a smile broke out.

It faded as soon as they were below decks and Tomi unwrapped his bundle.

"What on earth do you think you're doing?" Captain Harper demanded. "You've stolen a museum exhibit! Not only that, but a town treasure worth heaven knows how much money. And now you're asking me to hide you here?"

"Borrowed, Captain, I borrowed a museum exhibit. And I don't want to hide — not for long anyway. Just long enough to put everything together again. An hour — *half* an hour — then we can take him back."

The old man shook his head. "I've given you the benefit of every doubt, Mr. Tanaka," he said, his voice cold.

God, not the "Mr. Tanaka" treatment.

"For Patsy Ann's sake. But maybe I've been mistaken."

"No! No, Captain, please. Just look." For the second time that day, Tomi pulled the chain from beneath his T-shirt. "Look, this key fits the Boy! It's what winds him up."

"Yes, and so?"

"Captain, it was my mother's. I brought it with me. From … from *then*."

A new look came over the craggy features. "From?" the Captain's bushy white brows rose in a question.

"Exactly!" Tomi said. "Now do you see?"

The Captain cleared his throat. "Well then, yes, yes, I do see." He stepped to a porthole and looked out. Then he pulled a tiny curtain across it. "In that case, you'd better get started. There's going to be hell to pay when they find the Boy missing."

Yesss! I knew I could count on you.

After the excitement of the getaway and his furtive flight along the shore, the next few minutes seemed almost too easy. With the Captain's help, Tomi stood the mechanical skeleton upright on the saloon table. Unwrapping the bundle of doll-size clothing, he exposed the golden head. A shaft of late-afternoon sunlight caught the gilded hair and set yellow reflections dancing across the low ceiling.

Excitement rising, Tomi took the heavy thing in his hands and lifted it onto the brass torso. With a little *snick*, the head dropped into place on its mechanical "neck."

"There you go," Tomi murmured. "Back where you belong. Now ..." He lifted the gold left hand and fit it snugly onto the brass "wrist." With a twist of his driver, Tomi tightened the hidden screw that kept it in place. A minute later, the Boy's right hand was restored to its matching wrist.

"Okay, little guy," he said. "Now let's get you dressed." Feeling slightly foolish, but more excited than he could ever remember, he drew the Boy's sleeves up his arms and around the brass shoulders. For the first time, he noticed a small hole at the back of the rough denim shirt. The hole rested just where the key would go to wind up the Boy's clockwork "heart."

"Here, hold him up," he said.

Captain Harper gripped the Boy around the chest and lifted him. Tomi slipped the miniature trousers up the brass legs and buttoned them closed.

The Boy's "boots" were actually more like "feet" — solid pieces of iron, each with a hole drilled into the top. Tomi slid one onto the end of each of the Boy's brass legs.

"Voila!"

The Captain placed the Boy on his feet on the saloon table and took away his hands.

For a moment, neither one said a word. They just stood and looked in amazement at the little figure, rocking before them on the table, smiling its golden smile.

There was a sound outside. *DogStar* rocked abruptly and the Boy toppled. Tomi caught the clockwork child just before he rolled onto the floor. He heard heavy steps, then a rush of feet down the ladder behind him.

"Freeze!" a voice bellowed.

Tomi looked up. Nichols stood at the foot of the ladder. Then Tomi saw the gun.

Twenty-three
ON WITH THE SHOW

THE BLACK CAR smelled. That's what Tomi would always remember about the ride from the boatyard. It smelled of cigars and puke and something that might have been fear. The Captain sat stiffly beside him and said nothing the whole way. The Golden Boy rode with Agent Nichols in another car.

Outside the thick windows, the row of cottages, gulls wheeling over blue water, the coal heaps, the open doors of saloons downtown all seemed to go by like images in a video.

The driver turned into the curb. Through the window, Tomi recognized the block-long brick wall of the Juneau Federal Building. A second car pulled up behind the first. A police officer opened Tomi's door and he stepped out. Nichols emerged from the second car, a cloth-wrapped bundle in his arms.

"Judge Burns' chambers," the agent said to the officer, who nodded.

Tomi felt a hand grip his arm and turn him toward a door. Behind him, a second cop held the Captain's arm. *It's a "perp walk,"* Tomi thought. *At least we're not in handcuffs.*

Inside the building, the FBI agent led them along a corridor. Half a dozen men and a couple of women lounged against the walls. Now they straightened and pulled notebooks from pockets and purses.

Tomi stiffened when he saw Sophie's mom. Then he saw Sophie herself, standing with her back against the wall. Her face gave away nothing, but her blue eyes were large with excitement.

Then she winked.

Hey! Tomi staggered as the policeman gave his arm a yank to move him along.

They turned through a doorway. The room was one Tomi had seen a thousand times on TV — one of those windowless, book-lined chambers where the real deals were cut.

Sitting in an upright chair in front of a wide desk was a tall woman. As Tomi and the Captain were led to the far side of the room, he recognized Mizz Alex.

Nichols stepped forward and put the bundle on the judge's desk.

JP's words echoed in Tomi's head. *I am SO in the soup.* For the first time a really frightening thought occurred to him. *Could I go to jail for this?* He shook his head and tried to breathe normally.

A man in coarse wool trousers and soft buckskin shirt stepped into the room. His face was weathered and lean, his grey hair cut short. He lifted a black robe from its hook. While he shrugged himself into it, a white shape slipped in through the half-open door.

Judge Burns stepped behind his desk. Patsy Ann walked across the patterned carpet to where Mizz Alex was seated. She dropped her narrow haunches to the floor and leaned into Mizz Alex's legs.

"Your application, Mr. Nichols?" the judge said, adjusting his robe.

"Your honour, I demand that this alien be detained under charges of grand larceny, theft, breaking and entering and impersonation," the agent said. He paused for a breath. "And that the other defendant before you be similarly detained as an accomplice before and after the fact."

Captain Harper bristled.

The door burst open and Mr. Bartlett rushed in, face scarlet and a hand to his chest. "Have you found him?" His eye fell on the bundle of rags. "Is that him? Is he all right?"

"Mr. Bartlett!" the judge's voice cracked like a pistol shot. "Get command of yourself, sir. This is a hearing. Kindly take a seat and if we need you we'll call you. Now, Mr. Nichols, what is the basis for these remarkable charges?"

The agent puffed out his chest. His close-set eyes gleamed. "Your honour, not one hour ago, at the Juneau municipal boat basin, I executed a search warrant at the vessel *DogStar*, the property of Captain Ezra Harper, and there found and took into custody ..." Here Nichols leaned over the table. "The Golden Boy of Lost Creek!"

With a flourish, the agent pulled back the cloth that enveloped the child-size figure. Seizing the Boy by the waist, Nichols set him upright. The statue's bright yellow hair and face gleamed in the chamber lights.

"Upon questioning," Nichols went on, "I established that defendant number one, the alien identified as Thomas Tanaka ..."

That's Tomoyuki Tanaka, you creep. Tomi's stomach clenched.

"... transported the priceless artifact to Harper's boat earlier today. As clear a case of possession of stolen property as I've ever seen, Judge."

The judge turned a severe look on Tomi. "Mr. Tanaka?"

Tomi nodded.

"Stand up, please."

When Tomi was on his feet, Judge Burns fixed clear eyes on him. They were eyes it was hard to look away from, and harder still to lie to. "Well? What do you have to say for yourself? How did the Golden Boy come to be in your possession on the *DogStar* instead of at the museum?"

"I was trying to fix it, sir."

"Fix it?" The judge's voice was plainly skeptical.

"Yes sir. Mr. Bartlett let me."

"Is this true, Mr. Bartlett?"

The curator jumped out his chair. "Yes sir, your honour. But then, Agent Nichols informed me, that is, he —"

Tomi jumped in. "And I *did* fix him. I got his pieces all together. But then Mr. Bartlett wouldn't let me put his insides back in his outsides and —"

"Is that true, Mr. Bartlett?" Judge Burns asked.

"Yes. But, as I said —"

Tomi was losing it. If Mr. Bartlett had only listened to him for five minutes at the museum, none of this would be happening. "If you'll just let me show you," he interrupted again. "I got him *working*."

There was silence in the room. Finally the Judge broke it. "Young man, are you telling me, telling the court, that you successfully reassembled The Golden Boy of Lost Creek? And that he now functions in ..." Judge Burns seemed momentarily at a loss. "... In whatever it is that he does?"

Tomi gulped. "I think so, sir."

"And you can show us this?"

Tomi froze, then nodded. "If you want." *At least, I sure hope I can.*

"Mr. Nichols, do you have any objection to this demonstration?"

"Your honour, we're dealing with an alien here. His assertions have no credibility. There's no reason at all to delay —"

"Your objection is noted," the judge said dryly. "Does the Boy need any preparation?"

"I need to wind him up, that's all."

The judge nodded. "Wait one moment." He turned to the policeman standing at the door. "If the Golden Boy is going to come back to life, the Juneau public deserves to witness the event. Allow the press in."

Tomi's pulse raced as the gaggle of reporters trooped in and squeezed into a line along the back of the room. To his amazement, Sophie managed to slip in beside her mother. In a few words, the Judge explained what they were invited to witness. Pads came out and half a dozen pens and pencils began scratching in double time.

The Judge nodded to Tomi. "Go ahead," he said.

Tomi stepped across the room to the boy. *Please, please, please, God, Buddha, Vishnu, anyone.* Reaching under his shirt, he pulled the light chain over his head and wrapped his fingers around the small gold key.

A sharp intake of breath brought Tomi's eyes up. Mizz Alex had a hand to her lips, a strange look on her handsome face. His gaze shifted to the FBI agent standing behind her chair. The cramped face held undisguised hatred.

With trembling fingers, he found the little slit in the back of the Boy's cotton shirt and inserted the key. *Yesss,* he breathed, as he felt it snick tightly into place. He began to turn the key, gently but steadily, until he felt the spring inside grow tight. *Now ...*

Tomi looked out across the room one last time. Bodies filled every chair and stood along the walls. Grey eyes met his. *Mom? How ...?* He blinked and shook his head. *Ohmigod, Mizz Alex.* The jolt that hit him was so strong he almost tasted it. He knew now where he'd seen those eyes before.

His finger found the little button hidden in the folds of the Boy's shirt. He pressed.

A very faint whirring began inside the Boy's chest. For a moment, nothing else happened. Tomi's guts twisted at the thought of everything that could possibly go wrong, every cog and gear that might come loose or slip or fail to click on its neighbour. The room was so silent he could hear a pigeon land on a window ledge and stride back and forth.

The Golden Boy of Lost Creek began to move. Stiffly at first, then more smoothly, the clockwork child came to life. First he bowed. Then he swung his left hand in front of his chest. Then his right arm came up and moved jerkily back and forth, up and down, in front of his chest. The motion ended in a short flourish. Once again the Golden Boy bowed, then clicked to a stop.

There was silence for a few seconds. Then a faint *whoosh* as a score of lungs breathed out at the same time.

"Not much of a dance," huffed one of the reporters under his breath.

"He doesn't dance," Tomi burst out. "That was wrong. He *draws*. Sophie found that out." From the corner of his eye, he saw Sophie's mother look up sharply from where she stood with the other reporters. "He needs a pencil, and a piece of paper, something to draw on."

Suddenly everyone was talking at once. The reporter next to Sophie's mother held out a stub of a pencil. It fit tightly between the Boy's golden fingers. A clerk produced a reading stand and several thick, bound volumes to raise it up to the right height. The Judge handed over a tablet of blank paper.

Gently, Tomi moved the little figure to where the pencil gripped in its right hand was poised just above the paper. Again, he turned the key until the spring came tight. Again he pressed the hidden button.

Again: the whir, a gracious bow. But this time when the golden left hand swung low, its purpose was apparent as it smoothed the sheet of paper. Then the right hand rose, fell to the paper and began to draw. Quick, sure strokes moved briskly up, down, over and across the paper. The Golden Boy clicked to a stop.

Judge Burns pulled the sheet of paper from the tablet and examined it. His lean, weathered face betrayed nothing. Tomi's ears rang with tension and the room felt prickly with expectation. Surely no court in Alaska ever awaited a verdict more eagerly. Then the judge held the sheet up.

The astonishment this time was greater yet. On what had been a bare and empty sheet of paper was now a jagged but unmistakable sketch of a ship under sail.

"Well I'll be." Mr. Bartlett's complexion reddened a shade deeper. There was a commotion as two of the reporters pushed by the others and rushed out of the room.

"I don't believe it," Agent Nichols snarled. "It's some kind of trick. Let's see it again."

Again Tomi wound the Boy. Again he pressed the small button. Again the Boy bowed and smoothed his paper. Again his right hand dropped to the page and moved swiftly over it. But this time when the Boy clicked back into silence, a different image had emerged: forested slopes met in a mountain valley.

Unbidden in the silent room, Tomi wound the Boy again. Yet a third picture appeared: a crude doorway under a fringe of trees. When Judge Burns held this drawing up, Sophie's mother made a sharp sound. "That's a mine portal," she breathed in disbelief.

Tomi looked to the chair in front of the desk. Mizz Alex's face was rigid with concentration. Catching his eye, she gave the faintest of nods.

A fifth time, Tomi turned the key and wound the clockwork up. The same little bow, the smoothing gesture, but this time the Boy's pencil didn't move so grandly across the expanse of paper. The golden hand moved instead in tight circles and jerks, moving methodically across and down the page.

When the Judge held up the page, the lines of spiky script were clear from across the room. In an awed voice, the clerk read out the words they contained:

Of dust are you
Of dust am I
But if you'd know
What dust made me
Remember this
Art does not lie

Beneath the last line, the Golden Boy had signed the verse with the letters "MA."

There was a long silence now. The judge broke it. "Is there more?"

Tomi wound the Boy again and once more the little figure bowed and ran his pencil over the page. This time, however, the picture he drew was the first one they had seen: the sailing ship.

A sigh swept over the chamber.

But Nichols was indignant. "Cute, very cute." He stepped away from the wall into the centre of the room. "But beside the point. Makes no difference. The Jap stole the Boy. The ancient mariner there haboured him. They're both guilty. End of story."

"Hogwash!"

Mizz Alex?

The tall woman was on her feet now. "He stole nothing."

Thanks for sticking up for me, but what do you mean?

Nichols stuck out his jaw and took another step. He planted himself in front of Mizz Alex. "Sit down! Before I charge you as a co-conspirator."

Mizz Alex was taller than Agent Nichols. She looked coolly down at him, contempt in her grey eyes. "Say that again."

The agent took a step back. "I got him red-handed, holding museum property."

"*My* property!" Mizz Alex snapped back.

What? Your property? Howzat? "MA" for "Mizz Alex"?

"Everyone calls him Russian Alex, but Mikhail Alexei was my grandfather," Mizz Alex said.

"Order!" Judge Burns raised his voice over the sudden hubbub. "Stand down, Agent Nichols! These are my chambers, not the FBI's interrogation rooms. I will decide who is heard here."

The agent's narrow face twitched, but he stepped back.

"Now," the Judge collected himself. "For the record, Mr. Bartlett, is this correct?"

The curator's colour had returned. He rose and bobbed his head. "Yes sir, your honour. The Boy has been on kind loan from Mizz Kasilof, that's right. Generally, we don't name benefactors, but it's hers, all right."

"And Tomi removed him with my full permission," Mizz Alex said firmly.

Say what? The reporters' pens scratched.

The judge shrugged. "Then why are we here, Agent Nichols?"

Agent Nichols gaped.

Judge Burns shook his head. "There's been no crime here. The only purpose you've accomplished is to waste my time and these good people's time." His gaze fell on the Golden Boy. "Well, perhaps not entirely wasted. But we have your 'defendant' to thank for that, Mr. Nichols." He nodded toward them. "Captain, Mr. Tanaka, you are free to go."

Free to go. Tomi breathed out. Now that it was over, his knees felt like Jell-O. Beside him, Captain Harper gave a gruff little cough. *Whew.*

The noise in the room seemed to swell like an invisible fog. Through a daze he saw the judge hook his robe on the wall, nod in the direction of Mizz Alex — or was it Patsy Ann? — and retreat to his inner office. His clerk stepped forward and began trying to shoo everyone out.

Excited chatter filled the room and flowed into the hallway. Tomi heard Mr. Bartlett's wavering tenor rise above the other voices. "Let's get the Boy back to the museum," he was saying. "That is, if he's coming back?" He directed this hopefully to Mizz Alex.

"Of course," she replied without hesitation.

Mr. Bartlett beamed. "Marvellous, Miss Kasilof, just marvellous." He elbowed his way through the crowd and busied himself wrapping the Boy back up in Tomi's jacket. "Why, I bet the whole town will come to see him perform. This could wipe our debt right out, this could."

You're welcome, dude, Tomi thought. *But just try to make him go without my key*, he smiled secretly. Then his eye caught the FBI agent's livid face.

Nichols held his look. "You're all in this together," the agent snarled. "And I'm going to prove it."

Twenty-four

BOY OF THE HOUR

THE NEXT DAY was Thursday. Mizz Alex insisted on sticking to their routine of the past couple of weeks. Or, at least, she tried to.

A steady stream of cars and trucks pulled up to the small white lumber yard office. But there were few orders for Tomi to pull together from all the sawn planks waiting for sale. Instead, most visitors seemed to want to see him, if only to pump his hand.

At mid-morning, Mr. Bartlett called to ask if Tomi would visit the museum that afternoon and take the Golden Boy through his routine. Mizz Alex agreed to run him down in her car after lunch.

Tomi was hardly prepared for the sight that greeted them as Mizz Alex roared past the Federal Building, rocked the green car hard as it hurtled around the corner and slammed to a stop across the street from the museum.

Men, women and kids were lined up from the big front door all the way to the corner. The line continued out of sight around the block.

Mr. Bartlett, or someone, had been busy. A sandwich board near the door blazed: MECHANICAL MARVEL! HE DRAWS!

262 ❖ BEVERLEY WOOD and CHRIS WOOD

HE WRITES! ONE PERFORMANCE ONLY! Whoever had painted the notice hadn't forgotten to add that admission was five cents, NO EXCEPTIONS.

Tomi and Mizz Alex made their way along the line to the door. As they went, more than one voice said something like, "That's him there, the Jap-lookin' fella." Or: "You bet I know him. Why, I was talkin' to him just today." Even once: "Sure talks good, too, for a Jap."

"My, my," Mizz Alex said as they stepped inside. "You're certainly the town celebrity."

Or is that town curiosity, he wondered. *What's a guy gotta do to just be Joe Ordinary around here?* Still, he had to admit to a certain thrill at the attention. *If this were home, there'd be TV cameras everywhere.*

As it was, the first person he met in the museum lobby was Sophie's mom. "My daughter's told me so much about you, Tomi," she gushed. "I wonder if you'd give me five minutes for the *Daily Alaskan*?"

Bit of a change in attitude there, Mrs. Carr, he thought. But it was hard to say no. In fact, even without TV, it was fun being interviewed as though he were some kind of celeb. Even if he had to skate around a few questions.

"How'd I get to Juneau? Oh, just visiting." "When will I be going back? I'm not really sure. Soon, I expect." *I mean, my work here is done*, he added privately. *It's up to Patsy Ann now.*

Mr. Bartlett greeted them with a loud hello. His brushed-up hair seemed to flare even more than usual this afternoon, and his cheeks were bright red with excitement. "Mr. Tanaka, if you would?" He gestured them on toward the stairs.

A policeman in uniform guarded the bottom step and a table had been erected part-way up. The Golden Boy stood on the table. He was turned sideways to the audience. A small writing stand stood in front of him. "It was the best we could do," the curator bubbled. "So everyone can see. Not having a proper lecture hall, you know. Though maybe … perhaps with this new attraction." His jerked his head in an expression of hope, as though all things were possible now.

Tomi lifted the chain over his head and fit the key into the back of the Boy. As he wound the clockwork up, he asked himself the same question he'd been turning over in his head since yesterday: *How did Mom end up with the Golden Boy's key?*

But then Mr. Bartlett parked himself by the door and began letting in the crowd, making sure to collect their nickels and dimes as they filed past. By the time the last paying member of the public had squeezed in, the museum lobby was jammed from side to side and the flushed curator had to squeeze and elbow his way through the crush of people to reach the stairs.

"Ladies … gentlemen … young people of Juneau," he began. And for the next ten minutes — it felt to Tomi more like sixty — Mr. Bartlett laboured on. He gave the crowd a brief history of the Golden Boy of Lost Creek, but mostly he made it clear what a very important thing it was to have a municipal museum, one that was "adequately funded" and "well supported" by the town, that is. Only when the crowd grew audibly restless, and the calls to "shut up and show us the Boy" were becoming hard to ignore, did he finally wrap up.

"And now, thanks to our ingenious, nay, if I may say it, *illustrious*, guest, Monsieur T. Tanaka of Canada, our Golden Boy is fully restored to mechanical life. So, without further ado …" Hoots and hollers from the floor made it clear that there had been far too much already. "… I will ask Mr. Tanaka to activate the automaton."

Tomi reached forward and pressed the hidden button.

A gasp ran through the crowd as the Boy made his first, stiff little bow. When he finally clicked to a halt and the beaming curator raised his sketch of the ship under sail for the audience to admire, the packed lobby erupted in loud cheers and applause.

The reception was warmer still for the next drawing and the next. And when the Boy finally wrote out his brief poem and signed it with a flourish, Tomi thought the cheering and clapping and stomping might actually bring the museum's rafters down on all their heads.

It took some time for the crowd to drift away. Some loitered at the front, hoping in vain for another display of the Boy's clockwork magic. Others, who had been pressed to the back of the lobby, now pushed forward for a better look at the golden figure. Among these, Tomi spotted a boy with hair as black as his own and, with him, a blonde girl and a white dog.

"Hey, JP." He slid past the police officer to greet his friend. "Hi, Sophie."

"Murder!" Sophie said.

"Eh?"

"I mean, how darb!" The bright blue eyes shone with admiration. "You really did it, just like you said you would. That's sooooo juicy!"

"Thanks." *I think.*

"I thought they'd send you to the lockup for sure." JP shook his head in disbelief.

"Guess not, eh?" Tomi grinned. He cast a quick glance around the room. He lowered his voice. "So what's happening with you guys?"

"Nothing much," JP shrugged. "I gotta polish all the nuns' boots and shoes for skipping out yesterday."

Tomi looked up at the lobby clock. He grinned. "Aren't you kinda skipping out again today?"

"That's okay," JP grinned back and winked. "They got lots more boots and shoes."

There were several other kids from the home circulating. Charley Ramsey was one of them. He came up to the three of them and fixed a defiant look on Tomi. "Think you're pretty smart, don't you, Jap," he smirked.

Tomi gaped. *Is he for real?* Then his temper began to rise.

"But you're not smart enough," Charley spat out. "And we're gonna get you."

We? Who else had said something like that? *Nichols!*

The other boy's pale eyes looked past Tomi's shoulder. His scowl froze. Then he gave Tomi a final smirk, turned and pushed his way toward the door.

Mizz Alex and Sophie's mother stepped up behind him.

"There you are!" Judy Carr sang out at sight of her daughter. "You know," she gave Tomi a look, "Sophie's been very vague about her part in all of this."

"Oh, she …" Tomi caught the warning look in the blue eyes. "She was very helpful." He gave the woman a smile but bit back any further comment.

"I don't mean to tear you away from your moment of glory," Mizz Alex said. "But we need to be going. I thought we might swing by the docks and get something special for supper."

"Yeah, okay. See ya, JP."

"Later, 'gator," the other boy grinned.

"Are you teaching him this stuff?" Tomi asked Sophie as they followed the women toward the door.

"You shred it, wheat," she got out, before collapsing in a fit of giggles.

Oh boy. And Dad thinks I talk funny sometimes.

They reached the sidewalk and Mizz Alex paused. She turned to Sophie and her mother. "Perhaps you and Mr. Carr would like to join us at dinner as well? And Sophie, of course. We're already having Captain Harper. He boards with Miss Baker and she's away all week, so I thought we'd feed the poor fellow."

"That's very kind, Mizz Alex, but I'm afraid I've got a story to write," Judy waved her notebook. "And George is knocking together crates for the furniture."

Tomi saw a shadow fall across Sophie's eager face. He caught Mizz Alex's eye and dipped his head meaningfully in the girl's direction.

Mizz Alex looked doubtful, but hesitated only briefly. "Well then, perhaps your daughter could still join us?" she asked. "I'm sure Captain Harper could drop her safely home afterward."

Yay, Mizz Alex!

"Sophie?" her mother asked. Sophie's head nodded so hard her blonde bangs flapped up and down. "Well, that would be lovely, thank you."

THE "DOCK" where Mizz Alex pulled up a few minutes later was neither the downtown wharf where ocean-going ships called, nor the small-boat marina where *DogStar* lived. It was between those, hidden behind the black hills of coal JP and Tomi had snuck through yesterday.

After a short talk with a man wearing a long rubber apron, Mizz Alex had Tomi take charge of four of the biggest, longest-legged crabs he had ever seen. Each monster was as big across as a jumbo pizza. Black eyes like pomegranate seeds waved on short stalks and the long spidery legs creaked as Tomi hoisted the cardboard box the man provided to carry them in.

Back at the log house, Mizz Alex produced a pot that looked big enough to bathe in and sent Tomi to fetch one bucket of water after another. When the water bubbled, she had him drop the heavy-shelled creatures one by one into the pot. They drained the pot once, and used hammers to crack the bright red shells and split the spiny legs, pulling out thick ribbons of pink and white meat.

The result of all this preparation was that Tomi barely had time to scrub the fishy smell from his body and change into his only clean shirt before a newish-looking truck — *newish for 1939* — came into the yard.

Behind the wheel was a man with huge shoulders. Through the tall windshield, Tomi watched Sophie give the man a hug and swing away toward the passenger door. The man's eyes seemed to regard him with suspicion. Then Sophie stepped out in a sky blue dress and shiny shoes and he was glad he'd changed his shirt.

They sat in the kitchen while Mizz Alex tore a head of lettuce into a bowl. "Miss Carr," she said over her shoulder. "I understand you were a big help in putting the Boy together again."

"She found out I was going the wrong way trying to make him dance."

"And how did you realize that?"

"Research. My Ma says there's nothing you can't find out with a good nose and a library."

"Good for her," Mizz Alex nodded.

The Captain arrived soon after that. He wore a clean, if not new, white shirt with a collar that looked like plastic buttoned onto it. With him he brought a small wooden crate containing six green glass bottles of Coca-Cola.

Mizz Alex had turned the crabmeat into a rich casserole beneath a blanket of fluffy biscuit. Tomi's momentary qualms over the crabs' fate were forgotten as he wolfed down sweet chunks of meat in buttery gravy. Crab at home was occasionally a pigout straight from the shell, but more often it was a few shreds on *nigiri* sushi. *Obaacha should try this.*

"Mm, this is swell, Miss Kasilof," said Sophie.

"Aye, and we should savour it, too," said the Captain, taking a sip of his Coke. "Of all the gifts of the sea, this is the hardest won."

Eh? "Say what, Captain?"

"Well, they're a very fine feed, there's no doubting that. But fetching these fellas off the bottom of the north Pacific, that's one of the most dangerous jobs on earth."

"Catching crabs?" Tomi asked. "How can that be dangerous?"

"Never ask that of a man who's been out in Bristol Bay in the Kodiaks in dead winter, with waves kicking up the size of three barn doors, trying to lift those big traps from forty fathoms with frozen fingers. This is meat men die for," the Captain said, and presented the two younger ones with such a serious expression that they were taken aback. Then he brought a big chunk of crab to his mouth and smacked his lips. "Just say a prayer for the crabbers now and then."

"To the crabbers," Sophie sang out, raising her glass of dark brown soft drink.

They tapped glasses and drank.

Then Mizz Alex raised her glass for another toast. "To the Golden Boy," she said.

"And to the boy who fixed him," added the Captain.

Their glasses clinked another time.

"Mizz Alex?" Tomi wondered one thing. "Why did you give the Boy away?"

"I didn't, really. I loaned it to the museum. I just thought he'd be better off under their lock and key than here in this house." She sniffed. "Didn't realize he could be spirited away by one thirteen-year-old boy."

"Well, not —" *just one*, he'd been going to say, before Sophie's toe hit his shin. "That is … not that it was ever really spirited away."

Mizz Alex gave the two a sharp look. "In any case, he hadn't worked in years, not since before I was born. And no one knew how to fix him."

"I guess that's where the story got around that he danced," Sophie suggested.

"I suppose. The story in the family was that if things ever got very bad for us in Juneau, somehow the Boy would help."

"Then it's true!" Sophie's eyes blazed.

"What's that?" the Captain asked.

"What Russian Alex said, that he trusted the 'secret of his riches' to the Golden Boy."

"Where did you hear that?" Mizz Alex frowned.

Sophie gave the grown-ups the gist of what she'd found in the traveller's journal account. "So you see," she finished. "The Boy's not just a … a toy. He's like some kind of secret code. He knows where Russian Alex's mine is."

The Captain leaned forward. His tanned face was taut with interest. But Tomi's look went to Mizz Alex. She had slumped back in her chair. Her face was clouded.

"Are you okay, Mizz Alex?"

Mizz Alex straightened and took a long breath. "Of course." She seemed to reach a decision and her features relaxed.

"'Russian Alex's mine,'" she began. "You don't know how often I used to hear those words. Everyone had a theory about where it was. Too many people lost their senses over it." Her voice became heated. "They wasted their fortunes, even their lives, chasing that damn legend up one dry valley after another." A look of grief crossed the handsome face. "One of them was my sister."

The other three all spoke at once. "Alex ..." "Your sister?" "You mean a lady prospector? Swingy!"

"She was young, and madly in love. They were certain it was up Yukon way, some river no one had ever heard of."

Yukon?

"We had a letter or two. Then nothing. My father spent a whole winter working every back trail in the Klondike ..." The grey eyes grew distant. "Nothing." Mizz Alex shook herself and squared her shoulder. "So much for gold."

There was silence around the table.

Sophie broke it. "I hope you're wrong," she said in a small voice.

Say what?

"Miss Carr?"

"About the mine being a ... a legend. That's like a myth, isn't it? Not really real. And if it's not real, after all this, the Golden Boy and the drawings and ..." Dampness welled in the blue eyes. "Then what's the point?"

"You mean for Juneau?" the Captain asked.

Blonde curls tossed as she nodded. "Papa says nothing can save it now." Sophie looked around, her eyes coming to rest on Tomi. "We have to move, go wherever there's work, I guess. Papa's home packing up our table and chairs right now. Ma says I have to start packing too."

That's so unfair! Tomi seethed. "When?"

"Tuesday," Sophie groaned. "On the *Stella*."

"Oh my," Mizz Alex said in sympathy. "That *is* soon."

"There's work in Nanaimo, Papa says."

"That's near your home, isn't it, Tomi?" Mizz Alex asked.

"Maybe we could see each other?" Sophie's look brightened.

"Maybe." Tomi exchanged a glance with the Captain. *I think there might be a bit of a timing issue.*

Mizz Alex got to her feet and began picking up plates. "Well, I do believe you've got better odds of that than of finding Grandfather's gold." She made a face. "I always believed he won it off old Joe in a poker game, myself. Those pictures and bit of verse? Grandfather liked to dazzle people. It didn't always mean anything."

Tomi looked across the table. His eyes met Sophie's. Something like a promise passed between them. *Don't believe it! Don't give up!*

Dinner ended with homemade pecan pie and freshly whipped cream. The light outside had faded to pearly dusk as the Captain drove off, Sophie waving goodnight through the window of his battered pickup truck.

When they were alone, Mizz Alex invited Tomi to join

her for cocoa in the sitting room. By fiddling, she got the radio to bring in some music.

After rooting through several drawers, she brought a number of old photo albums to the sofa and invited Tomi to sit beside her. She opened the oldest album.

"There's Mikhail Alexei." She pointed to a big, strapping man in a full beard. He stood in front of a crew of other men, all of them wearing wide trousers and a heavy coat. Behind them a log building was under construction against a wall of forest.

Tomi remembered the card in the Boy's case. "He was a clockmaker?"

"He trained as a clockmaker in St. Petersburg. He never earned a living at it." She turned another page and stopped.

Tomi looked at the picture: a young woman in a long dress, somewhere outdoors. A chill ran through him.

"That's Renata, my older sister."

Tomi held his breath. *The woman in the picture, she could be Mom.* There was something in the eyes, a kind of joyful daring that made his heart go limp.

"Renata Mikhailovna. She certainly had Alexei's spirit. Swept off her feet by a dashing young buck and nothing would do but she had to follow him after Grandfather's gold." Mizz Alex was still for several moments. "Twenty-four years without a word."

He did some math. Dad's family he knew all about. Mom's, not so much. Only that they'd come from the North when it was wild frontier, and they had some kind of Russian connection. *Toooo spooky.*

Mizz Alex sat upright and levelled a sharp look at Tomi. "That reminds me, there's something I meant to ask you."

Tomi braced at something in her tone. He could feel her eyes on him.

"Where *did* you find the Boy's key? It's very unusual."

After the day's demonstration, Mizz Alex had agreed with Mr. Bartlett that the Boy's key should be locked in a museum safe. It had bothered Tomi to give it up — *"my only connection with my Russian family fortune"* — but it was her Boy, after all, so it was her key. Nor could he think of a good reason to refuse.

But now he was beginning to think he had a lot more of a connection with Mizz Alex than one old key. Still, he held back from telling her the whole truth. *"Keep your counsel,"* that's what the Captain had said.

"I bought some old clocks, and they had some keys with them. One of them fit the Boy." He made a silent apology for the white lie. "I just thought, you know, maybe back then there were a lot of different keys floating around for clocks." *Could have been.*

"No. That was the only one. After Grandfather died it disappeared around the same time as Renata." She frowned. "Very curious it should show up now."

You have no idea.

PATSY ANN followed Judy Carr back to the *Daily Alaska* offices. They were in a former fish cannery near the crab docks. The *Daily Alaska*'s owner found them cheap. Judy Carr found them pungently fishy. Patsy Ann found them cozy and agreeably full of interesting odours.

Gus McGreeley, the paper's editor, kept a small rug in the corner for whenever the stocky white dog dropped by for a strip of salmon jerky, a nap or a look-in on tomorrow's news. At a desk, Judy reread her story about the Golden Boy one last time. She dropped it on Gus' desk, looking up at the clock as she did. "Forty whole seconds ahead of deadline, boss."

Gus scanned it. "Nice," he grunted to no one in particular.

The office phone rang as Judy was putting away her notes. She gave Gus a look, threw up her hand and shook her head.

Gus grabbed his phone. "Desk." He listened for a few moments, then snatched up a notepad. He began scribbling. Cradling the phone on one shoulder he held up a hand to his departing reporter. She stopped at the door.

"For sure? You're certain about this?" he said at last. "Can we quote you?" He paused again. "How about 'sources close to the investigation'? That's always good." He nodded. "Right you are." He hung up. "Carr, get back in here."

Gus dialled a number into the telephone. When the other end answered, he said, "Stop the presses, Murphy. We're remaking the front page."

Twenty-five

THE WAY HOME

THAT NIGHT Tomi lay awake for a long time in his bunk, staring up at the bare rafters and thinking. Perhaps "wondering" might have been a better word.

There was always a reason why Patsy Ann brought her visitors to Juneau, that's what Captain Harper had told him. He'd been so sure 'til now that his reason had something to do with the Golden Boy. What Sophie found in the old journal had persuaded him that the lost gold must be tied in to it too. But could all that just be wishful thinking? Wanting things to work out for Sophie's sake? The Boy's drawings were neat all right, but they sure didn't amount to a treasure map.

Maybe it's something else entirely. The picture of Renata, Mizz Alex's sister, seemed to hover in the air before him. *Am I all off on the wrong trail?*

The verse that followed the three pictures pulled at his thoughts. Again, he ran it over in his head:

Of dust are you
Of dust am I
But if you'd know

What dust made me
Remember this
Art does not lie

Ashes to ashes ... dust to dust. People said that at funerals. But the Boy wasn't that kind of dust. Could he mean *gold* dust? Tomi thought gold came in nuggets or ore, but he made a mental note to check that one out in the morning. *Tomorrow,* he thought as he finally drifted off to sleep.

He was walking down the boardwalk — Juneau's boardwalk. Only it wasn't Juneau, he knew this somehow. There were mountains with snow and small buildings with false fronts like in a Western. There were horses and crude trucks and men in hats and thick moustaches and high boots. In front of him walked two people, a woman and a smaller woman. They wore long dresses and quilted jackets. The shorter one turned to look at him. It was a girl about his age. It was Mom, young mom. Or was it? The older woman began to turn around. She wore a broad-brimmed hat and her long hair was pinned up. Her face ...

... vanished along with the dream. Tomi lay open-eyed in the dove-coloured darkness of the Alaska summer night.

PATSY ANN'S head came up and she blinked lazily in the morning sun. This time of year in Juneau the sky grew light long before most people rose from their beds. But there were exceptions.

The white dog scrambled to her feet and began the day

with an extended bow-and-stern stretch, followed by an energetic nose-to-tail shake. Then she set off.

Her first stop was Bakers', where a sharp bark brought young Rose Baker from the kitchen in the back. A little pyramid of day-old cream puffs waited on a plate between the ovens. The white dog wolfed the pastries down in four or five grunting mouthfuls. She ran her pink tongue lavishly around her muzzle a few times, then buried it in the bowl of cold water sitting next to the plate. Thanking Rose with a quick lick to the ankle, she headed out into the back alley.

Her usual circuit took her next to the Gold Dust Café. Early-rising fishermen often stopped there for a warm breakfast. That usually meant that at least a few sausage-ends and crisp fried potatoes would be up for grabs. Meanwhile, the air was damp and fresh and full of morning smells — the powerful salt-rot scent of the morning sun on the low-tide mud flats, wood smoke, the strong note where cats had been fighting. Her small eyes almost disappeared in her white face as she squinted into the sun.

Then a particular waft caught her attention, out of place on a morning like this. She was still casting about, black nose lifting and probing for the source of it, when her path took her into a patch of shade at the end of an alley. Here she paused and looked across the street where the flat brick walls of the Federal Building rose behind a narrow strip of unhappy shrubbery.

A man with narrow shoulders in a dark overcoat was walking quickly away from the door. Behind him trailed a smell like unopened basements. Patsy Ann tipped her head and watched him start uphill.

Twice, the man turned to look over his shoulder and down the street. But it was still early; there was no one else around. The white animal in the darkness of the alley escaped Agent Nichols' notice. He didn't look back again, or he might have seen her step out from the alley and begin dogging his steps.

The FBI agent crossed in the middle of the block and headed toward Douglas Street. Two blocks along, he turned into the alley that ran behind the drugstore. From there Nichols slipped through the back of a lot where Ed Wheeler kept the carcasses of cars and trucks he was selling back to his customers one part at a time. This led to a footpath that skirted the mountain. Here Nichols stopped, head cocked, then set off again to the right, away from downtown Juneau.

Patsy Ann did not actually see him make this decision. A half-devoured rat carcass, several days old, had momentarily distracted her attention. But one cast of her black nose left and right on the path, and she trotted confidently in the direction the agent had gone.

This was a path used by the two-legged as well as the four-legged for far longer than Juneau had existed. It went a long way. And this morning, it began to look like Agent Nichols was off for a hike. He left Juneau behind in a matter of minutes and continued past the string of cottages just outside of town. Beyond their back gardens, the path turned up and inland, following the curve of the mountain.

Nichols looked back through the trees toward the blue water and white boats moored in the basin. He didn't spend much time looking, nor did he notice the brighter white within a patch of sunlight back down the trail.

Patsy Ann was starting to think that this was more exercise than she had planned for on a few light pastries, even if they had been filled with heavenly bursts of sweet whipped cream. She came around a bend and pulled up at a fence. It made no sort of barrier to the path. Time and insects had eaten away the ankles of most of the posts, and the grey weathered planks tipped and bent in a shaky line to the left and right. Where the fence crossed the path, two planks had been pulled off the rusty stumps of their nails and tossed aside.

Patsy Ann stepped through. She walked ahead slowly now, her head down and nose close to the earth.

In a few steps she came to an open space, a wide gravelled work yard like the one where Mizz Alex stacked lumber. This yard was much bigger, though. And rather than ending at a low row of sawn wood, this lot faced a building that might, anywhere else, have almost been mistaken for a mountain itself.

It was huge, rising slant-wise in terraces that seemed to slouch against the side of the mountain. It was boarded with grey planks. Many of these had lifted and buckled over the years while the frame beneath them sagged. The resulting impression was of some vast grey slug nibbling away at the mountain.

In some respects that's exactly what it was. This was the

main works of the Prospector Gold Mine. Here, men had been tunnelling and crushing the mountain in their search for that precious metal since long before Patsy Ann had come to town as a young puppy.

The dog's black nose lifted and cast about. Dark eyes searched the treeline around the bare yard. Her head came down and her whole body hugged the ground. Nichols had gone left, following the forest edge toward the wall of mountain. There, where the gravel yard met the cliff, crushed rock had been pushed roughly together to make a broad, untidy wall.

Nichols was nearing this, keeping close to the trees. His progress had a furtive air. He no longer checked behind him, but instead looked off across the open ground toward the mine. At this hour and this late in its life, the mine was as silent as the rest of Juneau.

Nichols disappeared behind the wall of broken rock. When Patsy Ann reached the same spot, she saw that the wall enclosed a small shed like those that some of Juneau's citizens had built to keep their cars in. The only door to the shed was closed. A padlock hung from it.

The man pulled a thin bar from beneath his coat and slipped one crooked end beneath the padlock. With a grunt, he threw his weight against the bar. The padlock ripped free and swung back at the end of a short metal strap. Nichols looked around one last time.

Patsy Ann stood motionless, but very little space separated them now. The agent's head pushed forward, drawing his face deeper into the shadow of his hat brim. The dog's steady black eyes regarded the man's restless pale ones. Nichols put his right hand to his hip. The air inside the rock enclosure was still and warm. Patsy Ann could smell the man's sweat. An insect buzzed.

Nichols shook his head sharply, pulled his hand away from his hip and turned into the darkness of the small building.

When Nichols came out again, he was carrying half a dozen round sticks in the crook of one arm. Squinting in the sunlight, his eyes probed the gap in the rock, but the white dog seemed to have gone off to scrounge somewhere else. Nichols closed the door behind him and arranged the lock more or less in its former place. He hurried back along the treeline toward the footpath.

After he passed the broad green skirt of one especially large cedar tree, the bough shivered. A black nose appeared from under the lacy green hem, followed by a pinkish-grey and white muzzle, and eventually the rest of Patsy Ann. She moved quietly and carefully, letting the man gain a little distance on her, but not so much that she lost sight of him.

IT WAS FRIDAY. As soon as breakfast was under their belts, the lumber yard was open for business. Fewer people dropped by just to shake the hand of the kid who resurrected the Golden Boy. But whether because of his exploit or Mizz Alex's newspaper ads, there were more people coming to buy. Tomi was kept busy helping them find the sizes and kinds of planks they wanted.

By lunch, Mizz Alex was smiling and her face had a cheerful carelessness about it that he hadn't seen before. "If this keeps up," she said, puffing out her cheeks and fanning her face theatrically with a hand, "I'm going to have to take on some *real* help."

What? I'm chopped liver? He gave her a hurt look.

"Well, I can't work you 'round the clock, now, can I?" She smiled and took a sip of coffee. "You've made very good use of your free afternoons, I grant you. But I need someone to package orders after lunch. And, between you and me," she leaned in to the table, "I'd rather have one of the old hands working the saw than either you *or* me."

Her face clouded. "But I can't ask them to work if I can't be sure I'll be able to pay them. And without some good news soon, this morning may just be a nice ripple on the way downstream." She gave her shoulders a shake and straightened her back. "But those are my troubles, not yours. Off you go."

That worked for Tomi. He still had that we're-not-done-here feeling. There was just too much connecting the Boy and Russian Alex's gold for it all to be in his imagination. It was like when he could see how each piece of the Boy connected to its neighbour one by one but still couldn't put them all together, like the answer to a test that he *knew* he knew but just couldn't bring to mind.

Sophie had found the answer the last time. If anyone could help him unlock this new puzzle, it was her.

He consulted Mizz Alex's telephone book. He'd seen thicker fliers for grocery stores. A "Carr, George, mng eng" was listed, with an address at "Cor. A & 11th." A map at the front of the book located a section of Juneau with numbered streets and avenues identified by letter. Sophie's address was at the north end of town, across the creek and past the Orphans and Indigents' Home.

The afternoon was sunny, the walk into town a pleasant one. Where a main road led north away from downtown, he turned right. The Carrs' neighbourhood turned out to be a new one built on the lower slopes of the mountain. The cleared forest was still raw; stumps and rocks stubbled the yards.

The small lot at the corner of Avenue A and 11th Street belonged to a square house, recently painted a fresh blue. Effort had gone into building stone-walled terraces and filling them with dirt to make beds where flowers sent up pink and purple spikes.

Tomi stepped through a wooden gate and up a gravel path. The front door of the house was open; beside it was a stack of trunks. Another trunk lay empty and open in the doorway. Tomi rapped sharply on the door frame.

A man came to the door. Tomi recognized Sophie's father by his broad shoulders and smoked-oak complexion. His movements were deliberate, almost dignified, but at the sight of the boy in the door, the long face grew alarmed.

"Hi, Mr. Carr. Is Sophie home?"

"She's here, but she's not receiving visitors."

Ohmigod. "Is she okay?"

"She's fine. But she's told us what really happened at the museum. You dug my daughter into a heckuva deep pit of trouble, sir. She's luckier than she deserves to be out of it as it stands. And so are you, if you take my drift." He raised one eyebrow and gave Tomi the benefit of a full-on glare from beneath it.

"She didn't do anything," Tomi insisted, eyes wide. "Whatever she told you." *What do you think?*

"I know exactly what my daughter did and did not do," George Carr said. "But that's plainly not the end of the trouble you're in. We've only got a few days left in town. We don't need to spend them mixed up in any federal investigation."

Federal investigation? *Boy busted for fixing wind-up toy?* Surely not, even in America. "What trouble?"

A bell jangled over the man's shoulder and he turned. Mr. Carr looked edgy and stressed. *See, that's what moving does to you.* The big man went to a small table in a corner and lifted the handset of a black phone. "Yeah?"

Tomi remained rooted to the spot. Somewhere out of sight he heard drawers being opened, and female voices too muffled to make out. But no footsteps came his way. No blonde head appeared around the doors opening into the small foyer.

"So's your old man!" Sophie's dad was saying into the phone. His colour was up, his voice thick with annoyance. "For the last time, Graham, you fired me, remember? You paid me out not two hours ago. Now, why would I need dynamite?"

Dynamite? Sophie had said her dad was a "blaster" in the mines. Tomi hadn't put that together until now.

"Are you insane? *No!* For one thing, they have all the TNT they need in Canada already. And for another, do you think I've had my head rattled so many times I'm going to pack a few sticks in the picnic basket while I sail off with my wife and daughter? ... No, I don't have any idea." He slammed down the telephone.

His head came up and he saw Tomi still standing in the door. He lifted his arm and he shouted. "Beat it! Hit the road!"

Tomi turned and walked stiffly back down the path, moving as fast as he decently could without actually breaking into a run.

The way "home" took him past the orphanage. He searched the playground and the bare windows for JP, but didn't see him. The marsh beyond buzzed in the late after-noon heat. He had to swat and fan the air to drive off the mosquitoes that swarmed from its brown water.

The walk up the long hill to the lumber yard seemed at least three times longer than it had earlier. Once or twice he heard an engine coming up behind him. On an impulse, he stuck out his thumb. Two cars slowed down, but when they came alongside, the drivers leaned close to their windshield to stare out and suddenly picked up speed.

By the time he got back to the log house he was tired and out of sorts. His feet hurt, too. He thought there might be a Coke left over in the strange-looking fridge from the "six-crate" the Captain had brought the previous night.

The moment Tomi stepped into the kitchen, he felt the tension. It was like those moments of still, bright sunshine in Delta just before a storm blew in from the water and bent over every tree. Mizz Alex sat at the table with her back to him. Her back was very stiff. Her hands held an open newspaper.

He jumped when she threw the paper to the table.

"She's done just about everything but call us by name." Mizz Alex turned on Tomi with a look all too much like the one he'd first seen on her when she had him at the end of a tight lasso rope.

"I've taken a lot about you on good faith, Mr. Tanak ... Tomi." Her eyes broke away and she looked out to the mill. "I've appreciated your help, all that you've fixed."

There was a scuffling near her feet and a white head emerged from beneath the table. Patsy Ann looked at him sleepily and gave her head a shake that left her ears flapping.

"Yes, and because of you." The old woman dropped her fingers to Patsy Ann's scruff. "Though then again, look at the riff-raff *you* consort with, eh?" She looked again at Tomi, and her eyes were searching. "And because there's something else I can't put my finger on. But look at this ... Have you read a newspaper today?"

Tomi walked over to the table and looked at the headline. The letters were tall and wide and black: SPY RING IN JUNEAU!

Say what?

He leaned in and read on. "FBI sources" revealed that a

"ring, or network" of "deep-cover" agents was acting on behalf of Japan, or Russia, or even possibly both. Their likely target was the Naval base just north of Juneau. "Stands to reason," the secret source said. What the FBI knew was that "individuals from both those communities" were involved, including some "prominent names in Juneau business" and other "personalities" in the city.

He checked the name at the top of the story: Judy Carr. He riffled quickly through the rest of the paper. On an inside page was a picture of the Golden Boy in action, and a caption about the museum's new exhibit. No mention of Tomi.

"I can't believe they would print such rubbish," Mizz Alex was shaking her head. "They have no right."

"Maybe they mean someone else. Aren't there lots of people with Russian names here, and other Japanese people?" Somehow it slipped out.

"That makes it no better."

Tomi walked back to the porch. Patsy Ann followed him. Together they drifted toward the rows of sweet-scented sawn lumber. The mountain cast its blue shadow over the yard, plunging the narrow alleys between the stacks into deeper shade. In the evening quiet he could hear the ruckling rhythm of the water wheel turning. *What a totally messed-up place.*

It seemed that ever since he'd gotten here, all he'd been doing was fixing things, making things work. And now some "secret source" — that freak Nichols, for sure — was making him out to be this Osama guy. He looked down at the white dog, now walking in step with him.

"What kind of a place is this anyway," he asked the dog, knowing she couldn't hear him. "And what's the good of my being here, eh? I was doing better back then." He thought about this. "Or forward then?"

They had reached the first row of piled planks and beams. The wood creaked as it cooled in the evening shade. He remembered their first meeting. "I was just trying to be a good guy and rescue a hurt dog. You tricked me, Patsy Ann. What kind of karma is that?"

Suddenly the dog's head went up and she turned her whole stocky body around to face him.

"I fixed the darn Golden Boy, why don'tcha just take me home?"

The white dog lowered her head again, but kept her dark eyes fixed on Tomi. She barked, then turned and took a few steps into the nearest alley between fresh-cut planks and weathered timbers.

What? All I had to do was ask? Right. That would be too easy. But he followed her anyway.

She was already a couple of turns ahead of him through the maze of lumber. After a few wrong guesses and a momentary panic, he saw her to the right a couple of piles. She was standing and seemed to be waiting for him. He went to her.

She sat on her haunches facing him. Then her head turned in profile. She looked deeper into the aisles of lumber. When she turned her head back, Tomi's eyes met hers. Pinpoints of light glimmered deep in the dog's black eyes. She turned again and looked away from him.

Tomi followed her gaze, and got a powerful shock. Between the rows of lumber in that direction, he saw a row unlike any that he had seen at Mizz Alex's lumber yard — and he had now seen all of them. Nowhere on her property was lumber covered in tight vacuum-sealed plastic. However, at River Side Lumber it was. Back home. Back then.

He looked quickly up at the mountain that cast its shadow at his feet and back toward the house. Yet when he looked back down between the stacks, he saw sunshine glowing on the plastic tarps.

Tomi looked at the white dog. Again their eyes met. As Tomi gazed deep into the black depths, he saw other images flicker there. Mizz Alex speaking up for him. The look on Captain Harper's face when Agent Nichols pushed him into the smelly back seat of the big black car. Sophie's fierce grin.

He put his head back, closed his eyes and breathed in deeply. The spicy smell of cedar tickled his nose. He opened his eyes and looked back at the dog. "I'm not finished here, am I? It's not time yet." He looked back down the row; the gleam of white plastic was fading into the evening shadows. "But you can do it, can't you? Take me back."

Patsy Ann barked.

Together they walked back through the gathering blue dusk to the log house. The smell of roasting chicken wafted through the air. "One thing I will say for this place," he admitted to Patsy Ann as they stepped onto the porch. "You can't beat the food."

"She can't hear you," Mizz Alex called out through the screen door.

"Doesn't matter." *Oh, yes she can.*

After dinner and clean-up, Mizz Alex needed to spend some time with her office books. "The bane of my existence. But it's good to have it back!"

Tomi smiled and headed to the bunkhouse. In the lamp-light, he took his mind off the day's dead ends with some more wall reading. A headline about how Adolph Hitler had just opened the Winter Olympics in Germany made him check the date: 1936. *That's just three years ago. But wasn't Hitler one of the bad guys?*

Another paper told him that President Franklin D. Roosevelt had given the FBI new powers to pursue fascists and communists and "foreign agents." *Maybe they should be chasing Hitler instead of me.*

He gave up reading the walls, they were just making him depressed. His eyes turned to the envelope on the table. Judge Burns had given him the automaton's drawings and his little poem. Tomi took them out of the envelope now and looked at them.

He leaned back and held the first one up. He looked for a place to prop it and rejected the lamp. *Too hot.* He swivelled and propped it on the ledge inside the front window.

A sailing ship. *Okay, you're going somewhere.*

He picked up the next picture and propped it on the ledge on top of the first. A mountain valley. *You take your ship to your mountain valley. Great! How many of those around here?*

A few thousand?

He picked up the last picture and put it over the others. A mine's front door. *Well d'uh. You take your ship to the mountain valley, and there's a mine.* That could be Juneau. Was old "MA" just recording the how-we-found-gold-in-Juneau story on a windup man because he didn't have video capture? *Naah. Then why'm I here?*

He put the last sheet up separately, beside the rest. "Of dust are you. ... am I ... What dust made me ..." *Gold, he's made of gold.* "Art does not lie."

Tricky dude, old Michael Alexei. Great, great, great ... how many would it be? ... great-grandfather Michael Alexei?

He left the pictures where they were, blew out the lamp and lay down in his bunk. Tonight he fell asleep quickly and gratefully.

Twenty-six

SEEING THROUGH IT

THEY WERE at Uncle Taka's cabin, deep in the rain forest on Cypress Mountain. They were playing hide and seek among tree trunks that soared several storeys tall toward a distant canopy of green. Tomi was curled up tight under the knee of a vast cedar root. He could hear voices — kids' voices — laughing. Then Mom's voice: "Come out, come out, wherever you are." She was laughing. Mom was "It" and she was getting closer. Tomi's heart raced as he hid, wanting to be found. Then a door opened — he'd been in a closet after all. A figure was silhouetted in the brightness. Mom! He leaped toward her arms.

Then there was only bright light, bright enough to make Tomi blink. He was sitting up in his bunk in Juneau where there was a demented cop who thought he, Tomi, was a terrorist, or whatever they called them in 1939.

As his eyes cleared however, he saw that *something* was partly blocking the early-morning sun from beaming through the window directly into his face. Groggily he got to his feet and made his way to the end of the table. *Oh, yeh ... right.* He had left the Boy's sketches propped against the window when he went to bed last night. They were still there.

Stupid. That'll make 'em fade.

He was about to pull the paper away from the window when something made him stop and step back — something he hadn't noticed last night. The paper the drawings were on wasn't very thick. In fact, it was so thin that when the sun shone through it, as it did now, you could easily make out all three images. But that wasn't all. *What is that?* He looked closely at the effect.

Here and there, the lines of one sketch lay over the lines in the one below. In a few places, all three sketches came together and these lines were especially dark. More than that. They seemed organized, not accidental.

Organized, but meaningless to him. Those near the top might all be in his imagination, just long wiggly lines. *Unless they're, I dunno, rivers?* But down at the bottom, some kind of weird early texting? *Three-becka wapnew-uh.* Didn't sound like any language Tomi knew. But it was like letters in Greek or Korean: they meant something to somebody. He turned his head to both sides, trying to place these.

заВеса Uарпuа.

Then he had it. *Russian!* His eyes widened. *Of course, Russian. Old Alexei was Russian.* So was Mizz Alex, distantly. The way he was Japanese — *and I guess Russian too.*

Maybe she would be able to read these letters. Tomi gathered up the sketches, brushed his fingers through his hair once or twice and headed for the house.

There was no sign of Mizz Alex yet. He glanced at the small clock over the sink and saw that it was only about a quarter after five. The summer sun rose early back home, but here the June mornings seemed to start at hours that should be the middle of the night. He put the pictures on the table and went out to collect some saw scraps for the box beside the stove.

While he filled the basket with kindling-size slashes from the pile behind the saw shed, he thought about the Boy in a whole new light. Granddad — or whatever he was — Alexei was one awesome clockmaker! Tomi recalled how the revolving brass "pancakes" transmitted their bumps and hollows to a cam, rods and levers that directed the golden hand. Like with plug-in games, the Boy drew whatever was "programmed" into the pancakes.

The Golden Game-Boy. What a wild way to code and hide a secret message.

He brought in his third load to find Mizz Alex in corduroy trousers and her favourite lumberjack shirt, squatting in front of the stove poking thin strips of saw slash into the fire box. She turned at the sound of his arrival. "I see you were up bright and very early," she said. "Couldn't sleep for the sun?"

"That too," Tomi upended his basket of slash into the kindling box. "But this is better." He dusted his hands and collected the Golden Boy's papers from the table.

Mizz Alex struck a match and put it to the furled corner of a newspaper. A fringe of orange ran along the frayed grey paper, consumed the heavy black headline and began to spread onto a sliver of wood. She closed the stove door and got to her feet.

"Here. Look." Tomi stepped back to the window beside the door. At this hour, the sun was still low enough to reach in under the broad overhanging porch and splash itself across the bottom half of the glass. Clutching the three drawings as one, Tomi held them in the middle of the largest patch of sunshine. "What do you see?" he asked.

Mizz Alex wiped her hands on her hips as she stepped closer. Her head tipped to one side and her brows knitted in thought. Her mouth worked, sounding something out in a language Tomi didn't know. "Just a moment," she said, and turned away toward the front of the house.

When she came back, she held a thick book in one hand, clutching it close to her chest as she leafed through it. "Yes!" She looked up in triumph. "I thought so! Of course it's Russian. It means 'Tsarina's Veil.'"

"Who's Tsarina?"

"She was the Queen, when Russia had kings and queens, before the Revolution. But I don't think it means her." She shaded her eyes against the sunlight with one hand. "Show me again."

He held the paper sheets up to the window and Mizz Alex looked hard at the merged images. "Uh-huh. There's the line of the channel, there's Douglas Island, Cooper Point …" She rocked back on her heels. "Well, I'll be …"

But Mizz Alex seemed lost in thought, or memories.

"Not the Queen. So who?" he prompted. "And why a veil? Is she a Muslim?"

Mizz Alex gave him an odd look. "No, nothing of the kind.

It's a waterfall, the loveliest lacy cataract down the side of the mountain. Grandfather took us there once or twice. We had to go by boat, I remember."

A *waterfall?* "Was there a mine there?"

"No. But Grandfather called it the Tsarina's Veil," she smiled. Then her eyes sharpened as a new light flooded them. "And!" She held up a finger. "And he used to take the boat right up to the falling water. He'd hold us on his shoulders, Renata and me, and he'd let us feel the spray from the falling water, and he'd say: 'There, that's what a queen's lace feels like. And behind it, a queen's fortune.' And then he'd laugh that huge great laugh he had. And we'd laugh too, just because he had." Her eyes were moist, and excited.

A *"queen's fortune," eh?* "Where is this 'Veil'?"

"Probably not over twenty miles in a direct line, but you could spend a week trying to get there." She gestured out the window. "It's on the other side of our mountain, this one here. Climb over that! It's easier to run a boat down around Bishop Point and back up the fjord."

"On the other side of the mountain. Isn't that where the gold vein comes back up somewhere?"

"That's what they say," Mizz Alex's head came up and her grey eyes met Tomi's. "'Somewhere' is the word."

"Can you find it again?"

"The Veil?" She glanced at the drawings on the window. "With these, I expect so. If we only had a boat."

Tomi narrowed his eyes and raised his brow. *A boat? We know somebody …*

For the third time in this conversation, he saw an "I-get-it" light come over Mizz Alex's face. He grinned.

PATSY ANN idled down Franklin Street, licking and relicking her pink-and-black lips and greyish snout and taking glad satisfaction in a tightly stretched tummy.

When a door opened halfway down the long block of the Federal Building, she was of two minds about whether to step inside. But she'd known Jefferson, whose hand was on the door, a long time. His molasses cookies were, she felt, the very best in Juneau.

She followed Jefferson to a small, windowless room. Vacuum cleaners and floor-scrubbing machines lined up against one wall. Another wall had shelves with pungent powders and liquids and waxes, Jefferson's arsenal in a life-long crusade against grime, dust and the other enemies of flawless shine. Beneath a bulletin board feathered in notes was a cluttered desk and a wine-coloured armchair with thick arms, wide back and four missing legs. Into this, Jefferson dropped.

Patsy Ann collapsed onto the blanket nested under the desk. She allowed herself to be talked into a molasses cookie. She was still licking sticky crumbs from her lips when a bell rang. Jefferson jumped off his chair.

He propped the door open. "Jus' let yourself out," he said. Then he grinned at himself and stooped down to rub her ears. She looked up at him fondly. "What kinda fool talks to a dog, eh, Patsy Ann? Never mind. You jus' take your time."

He went off in the direction of the ringing bell.

Patsy Ann burped politely and got to her feet. Her shake was short and lazy. She walked out into the polished corridor with nothing much on her mind. Even on a weekend, there was often someone somewhere in this big building, especially those people having to do with the police. She trotted around the corner. She nosed the double glass doors experimentally. They pushed open and she passed through.

The middle of the room was in shadow, the rows of desks silent. But through the hard wooden floor came a faint concussion, too uneven for machinery. An office at the back was lit. Patsy Ann looked in. Agent Nichols was on his feet, a phone to his ear. He was pacing, two steps up and back across the room, and irregularly kicking his heavy desk, gesturing into the air with his spare hand.

"Yes, Director ... Of course ... Uh-huh ... No question, sir. I'm sure they will. Absolutely. They won't be able to resist the story: attack on the Navy, the Jap angle, the Russian female, how they got what they needed from an ordinary pawn shop ..."

He listened. "Don't worry about that. I've got a lady scribbler I can count on to put it on the wires. It should hit the papers there first thing Monday morning ... Oh, imminent, sir, imminent is the word. We'll be snatching them up just in time. It's all in the statement for the press ... TNT, we believe, sir ... It was reported stolen just this morning by the day boss over at the mine."

Nichols chuckled. "Indeed I will, sir. That's a brilliant idea, have him ready for the cameras. I can do it today, a suspicious-alien beef." He leaned over the desk and made a note. "By the way, anything on that little radio I sent back to DC?"

He stopped his pacing and looked surprised. "No fooling, it's not? … They don't?" He shook his head and turned to lean against his desk. Agent Nichols saw Patsy Ann and his pale cheeks flamed.

"You blasted animal, get out of here!" He lunged toward her.

Before his foot could connect with the animal's side, the agent came to the end of the telephone cord. But then he stood stock still, his fury suddenly drained. His face went even paler than usual. "No, sir, not you. Director, no, not at all, no. There's this dog …"

Patsy Ann hadn't twitched an ear at Nichols' outburst. But the smell of sour dampness that now came off him made the whiskers on her arched nose wrinkle with distaste. She shrugged and walked away through the desks.

THE WHITE DOG walked along the low road beside the marsh. The sun was warm on the weedy water, bringing up smells of frogs and rotting bulrushes, marsh rats, mould under a fallen tree. She checked her pace. Someone on two legs was hurrying toward her, walking so fast as if to break out any moment into a run.

"Hey, Patsy Ann." JP chucked her ears on the way past. But he didn't stop or even slow down, just called back over his shoulder, "Gotta go."

The white dog looked down the road toward the home and back at the retreating boy. She turned and followed JP, jostling her breakfast cruelly in her effort to catch up with him.

"Good," JP said when she fell in beside him. "I may need you."

Twenty-seven

SWITCHING IDENTITIES

TOMI looked up from the lengths of wood he was piling on a hand-truck and caught the white flash against the deep honey of the house logs. His smile grew wider when he saw that JP was running alongside Patsy Ann.

"Hey dude, your dudetteness," he called out to them.

"Tomi." JP barely slowed down even now. He grabbed Tomi by the sleeve and hustled him between two rows of stacks. Patsy Ann worried herself around their legs.

"Hey man!" Tomi protested. Then he saw the look on JP's face and let himself be led. As soon as they were between the walls of stacked lumber, he shook the other boy off. "Okay, okay! So what was that about? Is someone after you?"

"No. You."

"Say what?"

"Charley."

"What about him?"

"He's been running his mouth, tellin' everyone how he's the FBI's 'secret source', showin' off all this new stuff he got. Boots, brand new ones with steel toes. And he got himself a new knife, one that's got a bunch of tools that fold up inside.

Says he got paid off 'cause it's almost over. All's left is rounding everyone up."

"And?"

"And that's *you!*"

Oh. *Oh!* "This is insane."

"You gotta get away from here."

"But I'm supposed to move these two-by-fours closer to the office."

JP rolled his eyes. "You don't get it. This is the first place they'll look for you. You can't stack the lady's wood from jail."

Patsy Ann had moved off a little way toward the saw shed. Now she barked. *Jeez. I get it.* "Okay," he said. "But what about Mizz Alex? They could be looking for her, too."

JP just looked at him.

"I have to warn her," Tomi insisted.

JP shrugged. "I don't know when they're coming."

Tomi plunged back toward the log house, JP stayed at his heels and Patsy Ann brought up the rear, barking as she ran. They arrived with so much commotion that Mizz Alex would have had to be deafer than Patsy Ann not to notice. The tall woman appeared from the hallway as Tomi burst open the porch door.

"Is someone hurt?" she demanded.

"No, but listen to this." Tomi pushed JP in front of him. "Tell her about Charley."

Mizz Alex planted her hands on corduroy hips, boots spread wide on the plank floor and listened to JP's account. She asked a few questions, then stood silent. "So Nitwit thinks

I'm plotting against America?"

"And he wants to take us down *today*," Tomi said. "If we're going to prove there's gold behind the Veil, we can't let him."

Mizz Alex looked around the room, then out the window at the silent lumber yard. "Right, then. Grab your jacket, toothbrush, whatever you need for a few nights on the trail. Meet me at the car as soon as you can." She spun on a boot heel and strode out to the hallway so briskly that Tomi stood gaping. Then he also spun around and banged out the screen door.

JP shook his head at the other boy's racket and followed him outside. He made almost no sound at all.

FIVE MINUTES later they were all in Mizz Alex's dark green Ford, hurtling round the bend onto the bridge over Gold Creek. Mizz Alex was behind the wheel, Patsy Ann beside her. The boys were in the back seat, a space so large and square it felt like a small room.

"It might be a good idea for you two to hunker down back there," Mizz Alex called over her shoulder as they started down the long hill into Juneau. "No need to advertise that we're off on a cruise."

The car bounced and shook. JP and Tomi braced themselves against the seats and doors. *One good thing,* Tomi thought, *the way Mizz Alex drives, no one'll notice anything different while we make a high-speed getaway.* He grinned.

"Cruise?" The question mark in JP's eyes was clear as a comic balloon.

"Later," Tomi mouthed back.

The car slowed, then proceeded forward in short furious bursts interrupted by sudden panicked stops. Looking up from the floor through the car's high windows, Tomi saw the tops of buildings tall enough to have upper storeys. Then they were picking up speed again. Tomi thought he could smell more wind and water in the air, a little less car exhaust.

A dead-fish aroma, carried on the back of a fresh salt draft, teased at their nostrils. The car tipped alarmingly and pulled hard to the right, then it skidded to a stop, its locked tires sliding across gravel.

Tomi and JP each took a breath and exchanged glances. They popped their heads up to look around. They were at the boat basin.

All four of them piled out of the car. Mizz Alex was already opening the trunk.

Tomi shrugged into his backpack and shouldered the duffel Mizz Alex handed him. JP had care of a sturdy cardboard box, hurriedly filled with cans and boxes and bags of food. Mizz Alex's own pack was larger than Tomi's, made of canvas and leather, well stained and scuffed from use. From it hung her lasso, and the rifle was lashed to the back.

It was a sunny weekend afternoon and the boat basin was a hive of activity. No one paid the slightest attention to three more people among the steady file portaging boxes and bags and duffels and fishing rods and bits of pipe and cans of paint and all the other countless things that get carried to and from boats when people are mucking about on them on a sunny day.

That was especially true once word got around that Patsy Ann was on the docks. She dawdled behind, greeting friends and admirers and gathering little knots of attention that brought sharp complaints from those trapped behind them on the narrow walkways.

But the two boys and the tall woman arrived unobserved at the rail of the last boat on the last dock in the basin. Only much later did Patsy Ann give a bark from the float to announce that she had caught up with them and was now asking permission to board. But it was well known around the basin that she and Captain Harper were special friends, so no one saw anything unusual in that, either.

WHEN Captain Harper held the three drawings up to the light pouring through the portholes of *DogStar*'s spic-and-span saloon, he quickly recognized the Russian letters. His finger traced the lines above them that had baffled Tomi. "That'll be Bishop Point, and Cooper beyond it. That must be Taku Gorge." He listened to JP with a little more skepticism.

"I remember Charley," the Captain said. "And not fondly. Are you sure he wasn't just spinning a yarn, making himself out to be bigger than he is?"

"He's been working for Mr. Nichols," JP said. "He's been following Tomi all over town, going into the Fedr'l Building, talkin' to Mr. Nichols in the street."

"And you know this how?" Harper looked the boy hard in the eye.

"I followed *him*." A sly smile fought for JP's lips and won.

"You saw what was in the paper, Ezra," Mizz Alex said. "I've no idea where this Nichols character gets his ideas, but he's the one spreading these absurd plot rumours."

The Captain stopped her with a gesture. "Let me be clear on this: You have not heard a single word, officially, from Mr. Nichols or anyone else that you are under the least suspicion or about to be invited in for questioning?"

Mizz Alex looked nonplussed. Tomi glanced at JP, then dropped his eyes to the table. "No, Ezra, that's true. I haven't," Mizz Alex admitted.

"Very good!" A fierce light ignited behind the grey eyes. "Then there's no reason at all for me to decline the proposal of a pleasure cruise." He grinned a little wolfishly. A sudden energy arose in the old seaman. "Stow those rations wherever you can find room."

He looked at the two teenagers a moment, and his brow furled in thought.

"Turn around, you lads. Let me see the backs of you."

Okaaay. Tomi caught JP's eye as they both turned in the tight space to present their backs to the old man.

"You're very much of the same cut, you know," the Captain's voice came from behind them. "Oh, that's all right now, you can turn back around."

Tomi's doubts grew.

The Captain looked from one to the other and back. "Think of it this way. Nichols is looking for Tomi Tanaka. He found Tomi here once. When he finds he's missed you at the yard, he'll come straight here. If *DogStar*'s gone, he'll find a fast police launch. We need to be out of the Gastineau Channel and out of sight before he does."

"But." The Captain raised a white brow. "If Nichols should happen instead to spend several hours pursuing someone who merely happens to *look* like Tomi Tanaka ..."

"Someone who knows all the routes he doesn't ..." A faint, sly smile played over JP's face.

"Those hours could be critical."

"But what about when they *do* catch him?" Mizz Alex objected. "I wouldn't want the boy in any real trouble."

"Well, now, we're none of us doing a single illegal thing at all, if it comes to that. The facts will catch up to Agent Nichols sooner or later. And it won't be any later than the moment we can get back here after settling this matter of the Tsarina's Veil. Fifty hours at the outside."

"You don't have to," Tomi said.

The other boy began shucking off his sweater.

The Captain disappeared toward the front of the boat. When he returned he had Tomi's sneakers in his hand. He raised a brow at Tomi, and nodded at the other boy. "What d'ye say?"

What the heck. "If they fit, sure. They'll cinch the deal for Nichols for sure."

A FEW minutes later, amidst the music of the marina, the slapping wires, the engines large and small, the cries of children unleashed on the floats, the curses of men whose tools had acted up and caused them to hit their own thumbs, amidst all these other notes, came a short whine. It was followed by a sharp cough and then a steady bass growl. A small puff of blue smoke drifted away from a boat moored at the very edge of the marina.

A moment later a tall teenager or young man, with very black hair, jeans, a backpack and sneakers dropped down from the same boat onto its remote float. The float rocked wildly when a white dog landed heavily beside the first figure. The youth on the dock untied the boat's mooring lines while a fellow who might have been his brother went along the deck pulling the ropes aboard. The boat pulled away, its forepeak rising and falling as it met the first waves in the fairway that led to sea.

On the dock, the boy and the white dog turned and began following the floating maze back toward shore.

Twenty-eight

THE GETAWAY

TWO BREAKWATERS curled their protective arms around the boat basin. Where their tips came close together, a gap created a passage for boats to enter and leave. On each breakwater, posts supported lights: green on the right as *DogStar* motored out, red to the left. Tomi watched them slip astern.

Captain Harper spun the little outside wheel and *DogStar* leaned into the first wave. She headed left, away from town.

Looking back, Tomi could see the buildings of Juneau lining the waterfront and rising a little way up the sides of the eastern mountain. There was the tall Baranof Hotel, with its name blazed across the side. Beside it, he glimpsed the low bulk of the Federal Building. He even thought he could see the tarpaulin flapping on the roof of the home.

Captain Harper pushed a lever and the rush of water quickened along *DogStar*'s flanks. The Juneau waterfront steadily shrank in the blue distance behind them.

Turning forward, Tomi saw mountains ahead that rose steeply on either side from blue-black water. For a long time, he was lost in the sheer bigness of the scenery. It was like the *Lord of the Rings* but real, as real as the rough brown rope he gripped for support and the cold spray when a wave struck the boat.

Hey Dad, he penned a mental postcard. *Hi from Alaska. Pretty here. Looking for gold. Oh, btw, I'm wanted by the FBI. Not really sure where I'm going. Actually, no idea. But having a great time. See ya soon. Say, in about seventy years. Love, Tomi. PS: You're not born yet.* He grinned into the warm salt air.

A sudden collision of wind, wave and hull sprayed cold water across Tomi's face and shoulders. *Yeah, well, meanwhile …*

What would Nichols do when he found *DogStar* gone? *Do these guys have, like, Nighthawks or whatever?*

He flashed on those eye-in-the-sky, helicopter gunships that TV cops pulled out in moments like these. He'd seen plenty of seaplanes around Juneau, not much different from the ones that buzzed regularly into and out of Vancouver … *back in the next century.*

WALKING ACROSS the maze of docks, Patsy Ann stuck close to the boy's heels. Most *unusual* heels, more than one passerby would later remember.

Shortly after gaining the shore, JP ducked back toward the water along the path he had earlier shown Tomi. He followed the same route in reverse now, emerging eventually where the black valleys of coal petered out and the downtown steamer wharf began.

Today there was no need to sneak down to the echoing caves under the wharf. To the contrary: JP stepped confidently out onto the timbers and began to saunter toward downtown.

Now and then he stopped to admire the ships tied up alongside: the tug and slap of cables and cranes; the restless loading and unloading that marked the freighters; the passenger ships calm as floating hotels.

Patsy Ann slowed down, nosing along the portholes at dock level. At more than a few, a hand reached out with a cookie, a peeled egg, a piece of toast smeared with sardines.

Opposite the second ship in line, two men in blue uniforms stood outside a small building with the words u.s. customs over the door. jp veered toward them. Before he reached them he cut away again, passing a few metres in front of them with his face turned away, as though his attention were fixed on the comings and goings at the ship.

The shorter of the men in blue elbowed his taller partner and nodded at the dark-haired boy. The taller one ducked through a door behind him.

jp strolled on a little farther before casting a look back over his shoulder. The taller policeman burst out of the door, tagged his partner on the arm and began striding quickly through the crowd toward the teenager. From a great distance, but distinctly nevertheless, came the rising whine of a siren.

Patsy Ann reappeared at jp's heels. Reaching down he flicked a finger over her right ear. "Hey, lady, want to play?" he said in a low voice. "Let's show the law what it's like to chase a *real* wild goose."

Abruptly he turned and stepped into the alley beside the Red Dog. Behind him a whistle sounded.

jp was running now, his feet falling nearly as quietly in

Tomi's sneakers as they did in his moccasins. The white dog galloped beside him.

"Police! Stop!" a voice bellowed from behind them.

Ahead, a side lane, barely wide enough to roll a barrel through, ran down the back of the Dog. The running boy ran past a garbage can, pushed himself off a side wall, spun left and sped into the laneway. At his heels Patsy Ann scrambled through the same turn, panting heavily, her red tongue lolling loosely from her open mouth.

"This way!" the voice from behind sounded muffled. Then, more clearly again: "Stop! Stop, in the name of the law!"

But JP did not stop. The side lane came out at a street. JP turned and peeled along a boardwalk, dodging passersby. A stream of curse words followed him, some directed at the "damned Indian," others at the "damn dog." Neither dog nor boy paid them the least attention.

At the corner JP turned. Halfway down the block he turned yet again, into another alley. This time as he stepped into its cool shade he saw ahead a flash of navy blue as the shorter of the two lawmen appeared from a side alley on the right and disappeared into another on the left without looking to either side.

Stifling a snort of laughter, JP slowed down. Catching up to him, Patsy Ann gratefully did the same. Less than a minute later the dark-haired teenager and the white dog, still breathing hard, emerged from the alley, made two quick turns and stepped inside Juneau Drugs. They adjusted their pace as they strolled the aisles, each marvelling at the variety of products and smells on display.

They were standing with particular admiration and interest in front of a pyramid of boxes containing "Ganong's Most Refined Hand-Dipped Selection" of chocolates, when the sirens raced by outside.

ARE WE *there yet?* Tomi laughed at himself. He'd never think about that question in the same way again. Still, how long would JP need to stall Nichols? Tomi would have to look at a map.

He peeked into the wheelhouse and made out the big main wheel. There were levers that he knew controlled the engine, a compass. But no hovering screens, no microphone. *No radar, no radio. Bet there's no GPS.*

The narrow channel led out into a broader reach. Here, the waves picked up and the wind veered around. For a few alarming moments *DogStar* rocked violently through an area of steep, criss-crossing waves. The growl of the engine rose to a shriek then dropped back to a growl as the propeller bit into thin air more than once. Through the porthole from the saloon came a staccato stream of very colourful language.

Mizz Alex! Tsk tsk, Tomi smiled.

The boat steadied as they reached the main stream of the new channel. Their course still carried them downwind, with the waves coming up behind them. Each swell gave *DogStar's* stern a shove this way or that, then ran away ahead of them. The boat surfed forward in a regular rhythm. The breeze was just strong enough to notice, a welcome relief from the heat of the sun.

Tomi yawned and took in a long, deep breath, drinking in the wildness and salt and whale's breath on the air. He locked his lips and held the breath in for as long as he could. Finally he let it go in a long, whistling release. There was a lot more he'd like to see in this place and time. A lot.

How much longer do I have? What a funny question, really.

What was happening *there*? He'd been *here* for two weeks now. Had he been gone that long? How did that work? When the Narnia kids went through the wardrobe, time pretty much stood still. No one back "home" ever suspected a thing. *Maybe Dad's not even back from his layover flight. Or maybe they're holding press conferences and giving TV interviews and I've really, really messed up the honeymoon.*

He felt a lump of guilt. *Hey, this wasn't my idea. Blame the dog!* He smiled. At the same time he made a mental note to try not to be so negative about travelling in future. *In the future.* The smile became a grin.

He turned and looked back. The Captain steered easily with one hand. The other shaded his eyes as he looked from one tall mast to the next.

"Hey, Captain."

"Aye?"

"Do they ever come back?"

"Eh?" The Captain dragged his attention away from the rigging. "Who?"

"Those other 'visitors' that Patsy Ann brought. Did anyone ever come back a second time?"

The grey eyes raked over him, then returned to the masts.

"No, lad." A shadow crossed the old man's face. "At least, not yet." He leaned out over the rail and peered ahead, then straightened. "Have you ever helmed a boat?"

"You mean ... steered?"

"Aye."

"No. Not a boat. Only a quad. That's sort of like a car."

"Well, see if you can't get the hang of it." He motioned for Tomi to take the wheel. "Keep her running more or less downhill for just a short while. I'll get some canvas up and we'll get as much out of *DogStar* as she can give us."

Tomi quickly realized that the classic wheel spokes were not merely for decoration. Each time a wave came up under the back of the boat, the water gave them a huge push to one side or the other. Tomi had to spin the wheel very fast in the opposite direction to counter the motion.

DogStar rushed forward in a series of wide swoops, alternately surging toward the mountainside looming on the left or straight out into the channel. He was doing this very badly.

But the Captain beamed. "That's it, lad. Just keep her generally headed thataway and you'll be fine." A few moments later, a pair of wooden poles swung out from above the saloon roof to hang out over the right-hand rail. Sailcloth bagged between them.

Jeez. Tomi spun the wheel as hard as he could to the right, but not in time to stop the boat's back end from swinging the same way. The whole boat leaned to the right and with horror Tomi saw the tips of the poles catch the top of the wave.

This, however, served to slow the boat's onward rush.

With the wheel turned hard, it soon came back on its course. A fresh wave already loomed astern, but now the top pole began to rise up the mast. Soon the sail billowed out and both poles were safely above the surface of the sea.

The Captain secured a rope at the bottom of the mast, then came back along the deck with another. When this was tied, the sail stretched tight. The throb of the engine through the decks did not change but Tomi could feel the boat pick up speed beneath his feet.

The sail seemed to steady the boat as well. *DogStar* became easier to keep in a straight line. Tomi wished Rory could see him now, or Obaacha. Even Amanda.

He remembered snow boarding at Whistler 'til their skins burned and muscles melted. Really, they could be a lot of fun, his new family, in the right place and time and the right frame of mind.

Mizz Alex appeared, carrying a basket.

Tomi gave up the wheel and accepted a waxed-paper package. Hooking his own arm around a vibrating rope, he unwrapped a sandwich.

The sun shone. The water sparkled. The wind was at their backs. The boat had settled into a long, slow up-down-sideways routine that was almost sleepy. Tomi bit into a thick cut of pink ham sharply laced with yellow mustard.

Blissout.

THE TALL teenager and the white dog were on the move again. Once more, JP led Patsy Ann up an alley. Past several back doors that reeked of beer and tobacco smoke, they came to a row of steel drums filled with food scraps. Beyond them was a street. Patsy Ann's nose lifted to the smell of well-aged bacon rind and sandwich ends that still smacked of enough egg-and-salmon salad to be promising.

JP had already gone ahead, stepping out into the street and turning along the side of the building. Patsy Ann snuffed appreciatively a last time and followed him. At the corner of the building, the boy turned again. Now they were heading back in the direction they had just come.

Along this block were the swinging doors of several saloons. At each, JP idled by the door long enough for Patsy Ann to make a circuit of the tables, accepting a pickled egg here, a chew of jerky or potato fry there. At the end of the block they entered the alley a second time, retracing their steps. When they came to the row of trash barrels a second time, they sprinted across the street and disappeared into another alley.

North of town a paved road crossed the creek on a concrete bridge, then climbed a hill. At the top the ground levelled out enough for the ball diamond, where a game was underway.

As the bleachers came in sight JP looked back. He could still see the saloons, gaudy signs hanging out from false fronts. While he watched, a big, square, black car sped out of a side street and pulled up in front of them. Several men got out and went into different saloons.

A roar erupted from the ball diamond. Patsy Ann's nose lifted and caught the smells of hot dogs, mustard, popcorn and beer. JP watched the men come back out of the saloons, huddle, then pile back into the black car. It made a U-turn and sped away south.

JP grinned and headed for the bleachers.

Making a wide circle around the back, he took advantage of the washroom and lingered in the greasy air drifting off the hot-dog grill. It was getting late. JP's stomach rumbled. At any moment the cafeteria bell would ring for dinner.

Past the baseball field the road ran through open country. Green pasture ran up a slope to a forest on one side. On the other, marsh grasses glowed vibrant green and copper, and mud flats gleamed brown in the late sun. A flurry of white birds wheeled over a thin band of blue water in the distance.

Patsy Ann trotted a little way ahead of the dark-haired boy, her nose rising and falling as she followed the mosaic of smells blowing past. Back toward Juneau, a siren rose up through the register. The hair on JP's neck bristled and his step faltered. Patsy Ann carried on unmoved.

The boy with the backpack kept walking steadily even after the big black car came slewing to a stop fifty metres ahead of him. Two men in suits jumped out of the car and strode back to intercept him. A second black car pulled up behind him and its doors flew open.

"Stop right there," one of the suits in front said.

JP stopped.

The thinner of the two suits stepped up to the dark-skinned, dark-haired youth and looked him closely in the face.

"Damn," Agent Nichols spat out. "It's not him." He stepped back. He looked JP up and down. "It's the Jap's clothes though, and look at those shoes. Those sure aren't from any Sears catalogue."

From near JP's knees came a sound he'd seldom heard from Patsy Ann: a deep, throaty, hair-raising growl.

Nichols stepped back. "And he's got that animal with him."

"What, Patsy Ann?" one of the other suits asked.

"She figures in more than half the sightings we have of conspiracy members."

The other suit looked like he was about to laugh, then stifled it. "Really? Don't try to get an Alaska jury to convict her." He fought to suppress a smile.

Patsy Ann's growling continued. Her lip curled and she paced in a stiff-legged circle around Agent Nichols' feet.

"Though I gotta say," the same suit added, "She sure doesn't agree with this collar. You sure you got the right guy? This fella's just an ordinary Indian, not your, what'd you call it …"

"Suspicious alien!" Nichols snarled. "Take him in, anyway. He knows something." He stalked back to his car and slammed the door closed behind him.

Twenty-nine

THE VEIL

A COLD SLAP of Pacific brine stung Tomi's face, breaking the bliss.

Ahead he could see a much wider body of water. The channel they had been sailing down met three others of its own size or larger, a vast crossroads of whitecapped water many kilometres wide. Peaks loomed in all directions. Through them ran a labyrinth of smaller channels.

"It's going to be a bit lively where the willawaws meet," the Captain said. "Stand by the wheel again, would you, Tomi?"

Tomi moved back to the wheel. Their route, it seemed, ran around the high cliffs to their left, where the mountainside formed a sheer drop to the water. A wider seaway to the right ran south.

The Captain tipped his cap down the southern reach. "That's the way to Canada, lad," the old man said. "Maybe you remember it from your passage up." He gave Tomi a heavy wink.

Back at the boat basin *DogStar* had seemed big, nearly a ship. Now it felt small, a tiny chip in the immensity of sky and mountain and water. As they came around the headland, the wind seemed to lose all sense of direction, buffeting them this way and that. With Tomi at the wheel and Mizz Alex gathering in the canvas, the Captain dropped sail.

The wind whistled directly into their faces. Hard spray blew back from the bow like cold, wet sand. Turning the corner, they had also sailed into the late-afternoon shadow of Mount Juneau. The wall of mountain was blue and indistinct in its own shade. The air was sharply cooler.

Tomi was glad to escape into the shelter of the wheelhouse.

They made way more slowly now, the engine alone pushing them against wind, wave and — so the Captain said — tide. But it was warm in the small cabin, and after a while Mizz Alex produced thick, hot and darkly flavoured cocoa.

As late afternoon slipped toward evening the wind faded. Soon they were motoring evenly over little more than ripples. In every direction, it seemed, a towering mountain peak raised its head. The nearer ones were green and shaggy to the summit. Those beyond were bare and craggy, snowcaps blushed with sunset.

Tomi turned and looked back. An expanding chevron of wavelets rolled away to either side of their passage. Canada was down that way. The idea of home tugged at him, but he remembered Obaacha's stories. *Yeh, Canada 1939, not 2006. It's probably not much different down there right now.*

A flash of yellow brought him back to the present. "Hey Captain, you got any binoculars?" he asked.

The Captain supplied him with a pair and he focused back over the boat's wake. It took a moment, but then he had it: the yellow splash of a fuselage, flying down the channel they had taken hours earlier from Juneau. As he watched, the plane banked and became no more than a dot, slowly fading as it made south toward Canada.

Yellow. Back home that was the colour of search planes. He turned his back on the wake and looked thoughtfully ahead.

THE SHADE under the mountain was deepening. *DogStar* motored across flat water. A wall of green moss and grey rock slipped past, not more than a short toss away to the left. All aboard were quiet as the boat skirted the winding shoreline.

Around a small headland the rock wall fell away. Tomi looked ahead and upward, then up some more. His jaw dropped as his gaze swept over an astonishing vertical wound in the side of the mountain. It was as though a giant axe had sliced down through the rock when it was still soft, opening a deep wedge between the crags above but cleaving the cliffs below in a narrow gash that left a gap barely metres across at ocean level. From deep within the narrow entrance came the sound of falling water.

The break in the cliffs was barely wider than *DogStar*'s length. The Captain took her in very slowly. Tomi smelled moss and wet lichens. The walls that enclosed them echoed with the slap and flush of small waves on stone.

Just ahead the narrow passage made a sharp dogleg to the right. The Captain spun the wheel and *DogStar* put her bow cautiously around the blind corner. Past it, the crevice in the mountain opened out.

The Captain cut the engine and *DogStar* drifted very slowly forward. Walls of rock, moss and ferns rose all around them. The higher reaches were cloaked in cascades of smooth green leaves, the feathery wings of hemlock and cedar. The sea pool in which the *DogStar* floated was a well of clear, deep jade. Tomi breathed deeply, awed into silence by the beauty of the hidden cove.

The cove itself was anything but silent. The rush of falling water, echoing and re-echoing from the encircling cliffs, filled the green shaft of moist air with a noise that thickened the air. They stood on *DogStar*'s deck and gazed, open-mouthed, at the back wall of the cove.

Suspended in perpetual motion before them was a dancing curtain of sparkling water. It fell from somewhere unimaginably high above, not a roaring torrent of solid water, but a rippling surface of freefalling droplets, a diamond veil undeniably fit for a Russian queen.

Captain Harper stepped to the front of the boat and released an anchor. A splash echoed off the surrounding rock walls, followed by the rattle of chain and then the slither of rope racing over the side. A moment later, the rumble of the engine faded away. The only sound was of water falling endlessly into this hidden pool.

Mizz Alex seemed lost in her memories. "Nothing has changed. This is where he used to bring us. He would turn the boat into the cataract and we would reach out to touch the Veil." Her grey eyes scanned the shore. "There was a landing place. We could step ashore and work our way around to the falls or climb up to the top."

The light was fading. The lowest reaches of the cliff, where ferns and outstretched branches hung over the water, were in near darkness. "There," she pointed. "See that big root coming down like a snake? There's the beginning of a beach below it enough to pull up a tender."

Tender? Tomi looked at the Captain quizzically.

"Dinghy," he said, hoisting a thumb at the small boat suspended over *DogStar*'s transom.

"Who's dingy?" Mizz Alex demanded hotly.

Landing was for tomorrow. For now, they took a last look around the tranquil little harbour and trooped down the steep ladder into the saloon cabin.

Captain Harper busied himself with the lamps. Soon the small room was warm with yellow light. Mizz Alex cracked eggs into a bowl and put a match to the stove. In far less time than Tomi thought possible, they were sitting down to steaming, thick pieces of omelette studded with bacon curls and oozing melted cheese.

Breakfast for dinner, Tomi thought and dug in with a will. The hours on the water had brought everyone's appetite to a rare peak. It wasn't long before all hands had visited the stove to load second helpings onto their plate. Only then, with plates bare once more and the pan undeniably empty, did conversation resume.

Tomi leaned back into the settee and let his eyes wander around the cozy cabin. For the first time, he noticed a small leather belt buckled around the base of an oil lamp.

"Is that Patsy Ann's collar?" he asked, nodding at the lamp. "I've noticed she never wears one."

The Captain looked in the same direction and smiled. "No, that's my old Maddie's collar. Gone twenty years now, but another way, not gone at all," he said.

"And Patsy Ann will simply not wear a collar," Mizz Alex said. "Goodness knows the town's tried. Why, when the tagging bylaw came in, people took up a collection and bought her the most lovely collar, her name on it and everything. But she wouldn't wear it. It was forever coming off and turning up in this gutter or that. In the end the mayor had to proclaim her Official Town Greeter, so she wouldn't need a licence."

"Diplomatic immunity," chuckled the Captain.

It was after eleven by the time the supper dishes were done. The Captain gave Mizz Alex the spare cabin forward, unshipped a blanket and musty pillow to turn the main-cabin settee into a bed for Tomi, then retired to his own berth in *DogStar*'s small stern cabin.

Try as Tomi might, he could not make sleep come. Tomorrow kept pushing itself into his thoughts. *Gold* ... He somehow imagined it littering the ground like cast-off candy wrappers. *Or maybe not.*

It suddenly felt like an awfully long stretch from three sketches and the words they might spell. *Or not.*

What if I'm all wrong? Would Patsy Ann still take him home? Or what if the FBI really did scoop him up? Would he disappear into their dungeons forever, lost in Gitmo, or wherever they were keeping people back then. *Back now.*

The more these thoughts whirled around Tomi's head, the further away sleep seemed. He tossed and turned until his restlessness got the better of him. Pushing aside the blanket, he got up and made his way up the ladder and across the wheelhouse out to the deck. *Maybe some fresh air will make me sleepy.*

He slipped out the door on the left — the side the Captain called "port" — and took a step or two along the side deck. The rush of falling water filled the cool darkness. The boat had turned on its anchor line and now rode with its bow to the dogleg entrance of the cove. Looking up was like looking up from the bottom of a well: dark walls rose all around, a vertical tunnel up to a keyhole-shaped patch of sky.

That sky, however, was an endless depth filled with the most brilliant stars he had ever seen. *I've never seen so many, or so bright.* He knew it wasn't possible, but somehow the stars seemed closer tonight than on any other night of his life.

"Studying the heavens?"

The Captain's voice made him jump. He grabbed the rail and steadied himself. "You scared me!"

He realized he was whispering, not from secrecy but because the water-filled night seemed to demand it. "I've never seen the stars this close before. This is awesome!"

"Aye." The Captain spoke barely above a whisper himself. "That's what we are meant to feel when we look on God's handiwork: awe. I fear that in these modern days, too few look, and even fewer feel."

That's for sure, and it's only gonna get worse. But Tomi kept that to himself. Instead, he asked: "Is there really a 'dog star'? Can we see it?"

"Yes and no," the Captain said. "Its proper name is Sirius. But no, we can't see it tonight. Sirius drifts deep into the southern sky in this season. In any event," he tipped his head back and looked up, "these cliffs cut off the view. But in other seasons, aye, it's a sailor's prayer — the brightest star in the heavens. That's the Dog Star."

"I thought the North Star was brightest," Tomi said.

"So do many landsmen," said the Captain. "But look you," he pointed at a star just above the mountain rim. "That is Polaris there, and you can see it is not even the brightest star in this little patch of sky."

The Captain was right: there were several brighter lights amongst an infinite depth of lesser-twinkling points. "Why, do you suppose?"

"The scientists tell us Sirius is closer," the Captain mused. "The closest star in heaven to Earth, though how they know that, I cannot say. I'm a simple sailor with a simpler understanding. I believe it's the light of the souls of all the departed dogs, that's what keeps the Dog Star bright."

I like that. He looked again at the cliff edge. *Hey, wait, I know those other stars!* "Captain, isn't that the Big Dipper?"

"So it is." He was silent a moment. "Look at the Dipper's handle, look close and tell me what you see."

Eh? Is this a test?

He stared hard at the line of stars. "Hey, that one is brighter than the rest, bigger." He blinked and narrowed his eyes. *Could it be?* "Is it … are there … The one in the middle … is it really *two* stars?"

"Aye, lad, good eye," the Captain spoke approvingly. "The ancients of Araby, great stargazers that they were, called them the 'horse and rider.' They used to call the smaller one '*al Sadak*' — the riddle."

"Like the Golden Boy!"

"Much like. For so many years we saw his golden face but could not imagine his heart. We looked at two stars and saw only one." The Captain was thoughtful. "The wise man never forgets how much he does not know."

"'And keeps an open mind,'" Tomi said softly, the words not his but Obaacha's.

"Aye," the Captain said. Then he winked in the darkness. "But not so open that your brains fall out. We should be to our bunks. Tomorrow will be a full day."

"Aye, aye, Cap'n." Tomi couldn't resist it. He let his eyes circle the glimmering carpet overhead one last time before he ducked into the wheelhouse. *Tomorrow is going to be great. It's in the stars.*

WHY, come in, old girl," Judge Burns greeted the white dog at his door. "You're welcome company. I was just setting out on a long and tiresome trail." He lifted a thick document from his desk and let it drop in disgust.

Patsy Ann nosed his hand agreeably for a while, then stepped over to the braided rug near the unlit stove.

She made several circles around the rug, searching for the just-so spot, but looking as if she were chasing her tail. The Judge smiled and returned to his papers.

The white dog tucked her nose into the crook of one paw and dozed. Her dark eyes, small in that wide head, disappeared altogether into white fur. Soon, a small snore arose.

Ten minutes later Patsy Ann's head came up. Five seconds after that the door burst open with the force of a blow.

"You!" Agent Nichols' temper exploded at the sight of the white dog. "How did *you* get in here?"

"Kindly moderate your voice!" Judge Burns snapped. "Patsy Ann is my guest. And a good deal more welcome than some others I could name."

Nichols seemed to deflate. But then the agent gathered himself. "Judge, I need a broad mandate, open warrants."

The judge leaned back in his chair. "Whatever for?"

"I believe a dangerous espionage ring is operating right under our noses, and we need to sweep it up while we still have time."

"A what? A spy ring?"

"Exactly, Judge. I already have one conspirator in custody."

The rawhide hand reached for a pen.

A noise like bones being ground up came out of Patsy Ann. Judge Burns looked over at her, then back at the agent. His look was sharper now. "Who is that?"

"Gives his name as John Paul, says he's a Tahltin Indian. But you never know. We got a report of stolen dynamite just before we arrested him."

"Do you have anything — *anything* — that ties the Indian to the theft?"

"We'll see what he tells us."

The judge frowned. "And who are the rest of your 'conspirators,' Agent Nichols?"

"That's why I need you to cut me a warrant. They hit the road."

"Well, they won't get far then, will they?" the judge said dryly. He squared a sheet of paper on his desk and leaned over it.

"The press tipped them off. They took a boat. Probably headed for Canada. I've got a plane up looking."

Judge Burns leaned forward, his high forehead wrinkling. "Who did you say these suspects are again, Agent Nichols?"

"Why, the Jap of course. And that Russian. And the washed up old smuggler who goes by the name of Harper. Washington can't even find him in the national files. I'm not even sure he's American."

"Do you mean Captain Ezra Harper, Mizz Alexandra Kasilof and young Tomi Tanaka?"

"Who else?"

"Then say so." He gave Nichols a look of distaste and dropped his pen. He leaned back, lamplight etching the lines deep in his tanned face.

"Captain Harper was born on an island off the coast of Maine, Agent Nichols. I'm not surprised you can't find a record. It was probably kept with a quill pen." He brought his back up straight. "Miss Kasilof and her family are among the founding fathers of this part of 'America.' As for the young Canadian with the mechanical knack, he's been more boon than bane to Juneau so far, wouldn't you say? Do you have the least shred of evidence against these people?"

"Certain items seized from Tanaka. I'm not at liberty to reveal what."

"Well, when you are, perhaps we'll talk again. But you've given me no reason to let you arrest anyone." The judge waved his hand in dismissal. "And that includes the young Tahltin lad."

"But Judge, he's my best shot at the others."

"What do you have on him?"

"He was wearing clothing earlier observed on another suspect."

"They traded clothes?"

"That's my understanding."

"If trading's become a crime we'll have to give back Manhattan."

"I'll get more out of him. We haven't really begun to interrogate."

"And you won't!" Trail-hardened eyes regarded the man standing in front of the desk much as they might a cougar or a rattlesnake, both of which Judge Burns had encountered more than once in his long life. "If working over a helpless prisoner is the best shot you've got, Agent, you need to find a better target. You will confirm this young man's release to me personally within the hour, are we clear?"

Nichols swallowed hard and turned toward the door.

By the stove, Patsy Ann's hackles rose. Her growl followed Nichols down the hall.

"I know I'm an old-fashioned kind of lawman," Judge Burns said, looking after the retreating agent, "but I'd go after whoever lifted the blasters first."

Thirty

ALEXEI'S LADDER

THE SUN came late to the hidden cove. By the time the first rays touched *DogStar*'s deck, the sky above had been light blue for several hours. Tomi awakened to the thought that he might be too excited to eat, but Mizz Alex insisted on hearty bowls of oatmeal porridge all around, fortified with thick sprinkles of brown sugar.

"You'll need your energy on the trail," she said.

Now all three were finishing mugs of steaming sweet coffee made creamy with canned milk. *"On the trail"? But the Veil is right* there. Tomi could look over the table out the porthole and see the silver-grey cataract rushing endlessly from the cliff heights down to the sea.

They gathered on *DogStar*'s tiny afterdeck. White wisps of mist drifted and circled around the cove like a family of ghosts asking directions to the next world. Sounds seemed larger than life: Tomi could hear dew dripping off branches into the sea, wavelets licking the rough corners of the surrounding rock, the coarse passage of rope against rope as Captain Harper loosened the ties holding his small rowboat. When it landed on the water, the splash echoed off the cliff walls around them.

Tomi sat in the stern of the little boat, then helped Mizz Alex into the bow. She had her wicker basket over one arm. Next the Captain dropped lightly into the middle seat and unshipped a pair of oars. "Where away to the landing?" he asked over his shoulder.

"Over that way," Mizz Alex gestured through the silvery air.

The Captain dipped an oar and swung the bow in the direction she had pointed. Tomi stretched in his seat to look down into the water. Its surface was like glass, and where it was undisturbed by the oars the sunlight slanted into the green depths without revealing a bottom.

It was only a short way from where they had anchored to the tiny beach beneath the twisted root. They were nearly upon it before Tomi saw the blue and green shapes of fallen rock rising from the depths at the very edge of the cliff.

The prow of the boat bumped gently against rock. With an agility that surprised Tomi, Mizz Alex stepped ashore, the dinghy's bow rope in hand. As she did, the little boat's transom, where Tomi sat, dipped deep into the water. He was glad to follow the Captain in scrambling ashore.

The Captain tied the dinghy's rope firmly to the hanging root, then they set out. No one spoke much. *No one will say what we're all thinking.* A lot was riding on today's expedition. *Juneau's mine, Mr. Carr's job, Mizz Alex's lumber yard, my ride home.*

"Here's the way," Mizz Alex said with relief. "You can still see where old Alexei cleared some of the brush — see the axe marks on the stumps?"

He had to look closely, but Tomi could indeed see that

someone, a very long time ago, had cut a path through the dense growth of ferns and alder that sprouted around the larger trees. Two paths, in fact. One went straight up, really more like a ladder than a path, with footholds cut in places into the softer portions of the rock.

The other hugged the bottom of the cliff, finding its way from a narrow ledge to a spot where falling rocks had plunged into the sea, piling up until they broke the surface of the cove. Beyond that, the path might almost have been carved into the base of the cliff, which arched out above it in an alarming overhang.

That was the route they followed.

It took a good deal longer than covering the same distance over smooth ground. Each step demanded care. At first, there was just room to put one foot ahead of the other, while they clung to any root or branch that offered a handhold.

What came next was more rock climb than hike. Now and then one of them would trust their weight to a boulder that proved poorly rooted and it would slip and roll away into the depths. When that happened they all stood deathly still, feeling more than hearing the loosened rock tumble and grind down the submerged cliffside, setting off other mini-avalanches below the water's surface, until the rumbling faded away at unimaginable depths beneath their feet. Only when silence returned did they feel safe moving forward again.

At last they each perched on separate boulders and examined the final stretch of the "path" to the foot of the waterfall.

"That's what we're looking for." Mizz Alex pointed to a spot a little off from the silvery hem of the Tsarina's Veil.

Tomi saw nothing but rocks and lichens. His heart sank. "There's nothing but moss," he objected.

"That's what we're looking for," Mizz Alex said. "And just like that, too: off to one side of the main stream, where it will catch the occasional high flood without being rinsed clean all day long."

What? "But I thought we were looking for gold. What's moss got to do with gold?" Tomi asked.

"We'll see," Mizz Alex said. She handed the basket to Tomi and stepped out onto a shelf of rock that ran along the cliff a hand's breadth above the water, silvered by drops from the Veil.

"Be careful, Alex," Captain Harper called from the rear. "Or wait until I can get the dinghy and bring it round."

The woman snorted. "I'm fine." She crouched low so as not to bang her head on the rock overhang. With each step, she leaned against the cliff, keeping her weight on her inside foot. Tomi and the Captain watched her slow advance with their hearts in their mouths. By the time she came within reach of the moss bank, Mizz Alex could just as easily have stretched out her other arm and bathed it in the falling water of the Veil itself.

With infinite care, she selected a piece of moss from the larger mass and pried it loose. From a distance, the clump looked like a small green animal curled in her palm. She hefted it once or twice in her hand, judging its weight.

Turning gingerly, she made a gentle underhand toss.

Tomi snatched the clump out of the air and peered closely at it. He could see nothing more than a densely packed cushion of small light-green tendrils. "Heads up!" Mizz Alex called. He lifted his head just in time to grab another piece of moss out of the air.

When Mizz Alex had broken off several more pieces of moss and thrown them back to Tomi, she turned with great care and made her way back to the rocks.

"My," she said when she had regained the relative safety of the rockfall. "That's almost as exciting as riding a log downriver!" Her cheeks were flushed and her spirit had something girlish about it. "Let me see one of those."

The Captain held up the basket.

She lifted out a chunk of moss. Carefully she broke it apart, exposing the dense mat where green tendrils rose from dark brown roots. "The moss acts like a filter. If there's any gold up there," she tossed her head in the direction of the mountain, "it has to wash down here. And when it does, a little of it will end up in the moss."

Tomi's chest tightened. Again Mizz Alex broke the moss apart, exposing more of its roots.

At that moment, a ray of sunshine found a gap in the cliffs. Shooting past the needles and leaves and creepers that hung from the sheer walls, it cast a bright radiance over the three humans in this remote place. In the damp, sandy roots of the moss, the sun found an answering golden sparkle. Yellow grains were packed tightly amid the brown strands.

"*Of dust am I.*" *Huh* ... Somehow he'd imagined something a little more, oh, Fort Knox. Actual solid nuggets of yellow metal.

But beside him he heard a sigh escape Mizz Alex's lips. "That's what we're looking for," she breathed. "When we get back aboard I'll dry these and separate out the gold. That will give us a better idea how much has been washed down. But if this is any sign, it's more than a trace. Much more." She looked up to the heights above the cataract. "Somewhere up there is a motherlode."

Tomi leaned back and followed Mizz Alex's gaze. The view up the vast chimney of green and blue made him dizzy. *The other path!* It went up. *Up to the "motherlode"?* There was only one way to find out for sure.

They made their way back to the small beach and placed the precious moss in the boat. Then Tomi hooked Mizz Alex's basket over one shoulder and pulled himself up onto the snake-like root — the first rung of Alexei's ladder.

LONG BEFORE Tomi made it to the top he began to regret his enthusiasm for moss-hunting on the Veil's upper reaches.

The long scramble was an endless clutch at vines for handholds and at grub in the dirt for toeholds. His palms were scratched and fingertips raw. His calves ached and he hardly dared look down. When he did, he could no longer see the little beach at all. Even *DogStar* looked like a toy boat floating in a bathtub far below. He tried not to think about the return trip.

Instead, when the cliff relaxed a little and became merely a steep hillside, he began to move across it. Picking his way through wildflowers, he neared the cleft where the stream that fed the Veil leaped and tumbled down the side of the mountain.

Reaching it, Tomi turned up the slope and climbed some more, casting about, as Mizz Alex had told him he should, for other streams joining this one. There were several of these, and in little more than an hour he had gathered moss from the banks of each.

He reached the top of the steep meadow. Vivid green grasses, dusted with scarlet and purple wildflowers, bent like waves before the breeze. The basket was filling up. Looking ahead and still higher, he traced the milky tumble of the Veil's water with his eyes until he lost it in the wisps of cloud clinging to the higher peaks. He could see no more streams joining the main course. He settled the basket over one arm and had turned to begin the descent when something caught his eye.

He hadn't seen it on his ascent, tucked as it was into a side gully. He might not have seen it at all, had he not climbed so high. Only from this vantage point was it hard to miss: the squared angles and straight lines of a man-made structure, a grey frame around black emptiness.

Sliding and leaping from rock to grass tussock to root, Tomi scrambled to the bottom of the gorge and found a place where he could step across the rushing channel of the Veil. Finding the opening of the side canyon he began to climb once more.

It was noisy here. The steep valley echoed with the chuckle and splash of water finding its headlong way down the mountain. He didn't focus right away on another sound until he heard it again and felt the hairs on the back of his neck rise. It was a deep, bubbling growl, as though the mountain itself were clearing its throat.

He looked back, searching the far ridge. He froze. Moving across the bank of wild blossoms was a huge, shambling form the colour of cedar bark. As Tomi watched, the shaggy shape rose onto great back legs. Compared to this animal, the stuffed creature in the museum basement was a junior pee-wee.

A brown head the size of a champion pumpkin lifted its black-tipped snout and cast about in the air. Tomi imagined he could hear the bear snuffling in the wind, searching for boy scent. Blood rang in his ears. He tried to breathe without actually breathing.

The bear dropped to its four paws and turned away from the gully where the stream tumbled. But it did not move away. One massive forepaw scraped at patches of vivid green, exposing dark earth beneath. The black nose hunted around in the exposed roots and rose up, great jaws chewing on something.

Tomi's stomach felt like it might melt into something hot and runny. Somewhere behind him now, higher up the side gulley, was whatever it was he had seen from the vantage point of the meadow — the angular lines that spoke unmistakably of a human presence here. Far below, and across the exposed lower reaches of the slope, was the head of the "trail" that led back to the beach, the boat and relative safety.

A sudden feeling of release rushed through Tomi. This was your classic rock-and-a-hard-place, but all he could feel was a kind of fierce calm and excitement. *"If we're treading on thin ice,"* he heard his mother's voice, singing some old song while she held his hand and coaxed him out with her onto the trembling diving board, *"then we might as well dance,"* until they toppled off into the cool water only to burst back a moment later into sunshine, laughing and shrieking with delight.

Screw it. I'm here now and I probably won't be back. He turned and began to make his way once more up the side canyon.

He tried to move the way JP did, how he seemed to put each foot down only where the ground was ready to receive it. He chose only the biggest rocks to take his weight, the ones least likely to slip and roll. His eyes searched for roots moored to something solid, lest one should come loose and send him scuffling for another handhold.

He could feel sweat beading on his neck, running down his skin under his shirt. His arms and legs were beginning to feel more like rubber than muscle. Somewhere behind and above his ears, a tense ache was gathering. He looked over his shoulder and breathed out more easily. For several metres here, an exposed sinew of mountain cut off the scene on the far side of the Veil. Another steep turn in the gorge would bring him back into view of the meadow. But as Tomi pulled himself around a shoulder of rock, he forgot all about the burly presence prowling there.

Just ahead of him across the narrow stream, opening onto a natural patio barely bigger than a dinner table, was the image in the Golden Boy's last drawing: the low portal of a mine shaft.

Heedless now of the stones that flew from beneath his boots to skitter noisily down the gulley, Tomi raced the last few metres. On the small patio of rock he stood a moment, grateful for level footing.

The portal was smaller than he'd pictured it. He would have to get down on his knees to venture inside. With a jolt, he realized that Russian Alex — *great, great-whatever-Granddad* — must have carried each timber here by hand, packing them up the same way Tomi had just come. Over time the wood had turned grey, with cracks where small insects crawled, crumbling with decay at the bottom where it met the earth.

Tomi slipped to his knees. His body in the portal blocked most of the light. He wished he had a flashlight, but as his eyes adjusted to the gloom he realized it wouldn't have done much good. No more than a couple of metres in, another timber frame was even more decayed than the one at the entrance. Beyond it a tumble of fallen rock blocked the low passage completely. There was no way to know whether the tunnel continued deeper into the mountain, or whether that was as far as Russian Alex had dug.

Every sense tuned for a creak of rock or timber giving way, Tomi leaned into the tunnel. He crawled forward into his own shadow. He smelled mould and insects and roots. The trickle of a few grains of rock down a wall snapped his head around and made his heart race.

This is dumb. The freaking roof's gonna fall in and no one'll ever find you. He could reach out and touch the fallen clots of rock and earth now. The collapse had left a rough dome in the roof of the tunnel. Water seeped from it. *Get out, dude, just back out.*

He was about to, when his eye caught the heap of broken rock. Where a large piece of tunnel roof had flaked off and fallen to the floor, something tawny glowed. He scrambled forward again. Across the rock, he saw now, was a line of what might have been drippings from some primeval candle. He reached out and took one in his fingers. It broke off with only a little more effort than if it had really been wax.

He held the object in his hand, turning it to the light. As thick in places as a pencil, it reached from one side of his palm to the other. But it was heavy. Heavy, hard and unmistakably metallic. And even in the dim light, its dull shine was the colour of the Boy.

Hastily he pulled off the rest of the "drippings," four or five more thin, knobbled strands of metal. He put all the pieces into the breast pocket of his orphanage shirt and buttoned it closed.

Then he backed gratefully out into the light of midafternoon.

Spinning on his knees he searched the meadow opposite for the moving mountain of brown fur. *Gone. Whew.*

Yeah, but where?

He bent to pick up the basket with its no-longer-so-vital samples of moss. *Omigod.* His stomach did a little lurch.

The cove below now looked like something seen from an airplane. With a shiver, he recognized the bird making lazy circles many metres below him as a bald eagle. For a moment he felt frozen, paralyzed by the thought that he might just step off the mountainside ledge and fall, fall, fall into the distant postage-stamp of water where a boat the size of a fingernail shaving turned slowly on its anchor. He swallowed hard and looked toward the horizon to steady himself.

Oh. ... my ... this really must be God.

Spread out in front of him was range upon range of mountains, disappearing into a blue and white haze in the immeasurable distance. Between the nearer peaks ran channels of dark blue water laced with white.

There were no more excuses, and still only one way down. The basket again over his shoulder and using his outstretched arms more for balance than to grab onto things, he made his way as swiftly and as quietly as he could down the gulley.

Where the smaller stream joined the Veil, he crossed again, reaching the upland meadow just above the point where it dropped away in a sheer plunge to the water below. Keeping a respectful distance between himself and the cliff edge he crossed back to the head of the precipitous trail.

He looked up one last time. Wherever the bear was, it was out of sight. But now a new sound caught his ear, the growl not of an animal but of an engine. An *aero* engine.

Tomi turned carefully and looked out. The view from here was only a degree less spectacular than it had been higher up. In the distance to his right was the wide channel heading south to Canada. In the other direction the channel narrowed and turned out of sight among the mountains.

There! Sunlight flared on a bright yellow fuselage. A moment later the aircraft turned and seemed to fly directly toward him. With a shock, Tomi realized he was looking *down* on the plane.

He shrank back into a patch of giant ferns and kept still as the plane droned down the channel, a sunflower-yellow cross against the deep blue sea. *DogStar!* How tall were her masts? Could they be seen from the plane? He tried to judge the concealment offered by the cliffs around the cove.

Perhaps the cliffs were high enough. Or perhaps the people in the plane were looking the other way as they flew past the hidden harbour. Or perhaps they weren't looking for a boat at all. In any case, Tomi was glad when the yellow plane droned past and began to dwindle in the hazy sky to the south, never altering its course.

Basket over his shoulder, he turned to face the mountain and let his lower limbs slide over the edge, groping with his toes for a hole or cranny.

The trip back down Alexei's ladder-like trail went faster than the trip up. As he reached bottom, he felt the Captain's strong hands grip his lower back to help him down onto the narrow beach.

"Thank God," he thought he heard Mizz Alex say. More clearly he heard, "We were beginning to worry."

"That engine." The Captain was already untying the dinghy.

"The yellow one again," Tomi said.

"They're looking for us. That's Nichols' work."

"Let them find us," Mizz Alex said defiantly. "We've got what we came for." She put the moss from the waterfall of the Veil with the samples Tomi had collected and stowed them in the front of the boat.

"More." Tomi couldn't contain himself any longer. "I *found it!* Just like in the picture. The portal!"

The Captain broke into a grin and slapped him warmly on the back. "Well done, lad!"

Mizz Alex straightened. She stood silent a moment, gazing up toward the distant peak. The grey eyes seemed to strain to see something that wasn't there. "Well," she said at last. "That's that."

"Oh, yeah, and there's a bear up there."

"What?" two sharp voices asked at once. Both adults were looking up the steep trail now.

The Captain turned back to the dinghy. "Shall we?" He steadied the little craft for the other two to climb in, then followed them.

Thirty-one

SILENT VOYAGE

BY THE TIME they were back on *DogStar*'s solid deck and the little dinghy was tied securely aboard, the evening dusk was thickening over the hidden cove.

The Captain fired up the galley stove. While he set about supper, Mizz Alex separated the moss into batches, asking Tomi to identify those that came from different upland streams. Heating each batch in a black skillet until it crumbled, she used a wooden mallet to crush the dried moss and its gravelly contents into powder.

As she worked, Tomi recounted his adventures on the upper slopes. When he produced the wax-drippings of yellow metal he had collected in the tunnel, Mizz Alex gasped.

"Native gold," she shook her head in wonder. "Grandfather used to talk about it, but I've never seen it. Nature makes it raw and massive like that. When the first man finds it, that's usually what he takes before he digs for more."

She tipped a batch of powdered moss and dirt, from the foot of the waterfall, into the biggest plate in *DogStar*'s small cupboard. She ladled a scoop of sea water into the plate. Flakes of dried moss floated to the surface. It took only a little careful swishing to wash away the lighter sand and gravel as well. In the bottom of the plate glowed a thin crescent of yellow.

By the time she was done, Mizz Alex had panned enough gold to more than half fill a tea mug. The greatest amounts had come from the bottom of the waterfall and a fist-size knot of moss that Tomi had collected where the stream from the portal met the Veil. But every other batch had produced gold as well.

"You'd think the whole mountain was made of it," Mizz Alex marvelled.

They were a festive crew that evening. Over corned beef from a tin, cooked with onion and potatoes into a salty, savoury hash that amply met their hearty appetites, they toasted Russian Alex with more rounds of hot, sweet, milky tea.

Tomi had to describe more than once his foray into the tunnel past the crumbling portal. Captain Harper and Mizz Alex couldn't help guessing how the discovery might revive Juneau's fortunes.

"I imagine they'll want to push a road over the mountain," the Captain suggested. "Easier than building a way up from here."

"Plenty to do, even before they sink the main shaft," agreed Mizz Alex. "They'll need shoring, bridging, timbers." She looked over at Tomi. "Any amount of work for an eager young man who can keep the mill turning," she smiled.

Tomi had fallen quiet. A curious disappointment was

settling over him. This really did feel like it might be "mission accomplished."

Captain Harper caught his look and brought everyone's thoughts back to the present. "First we need to get this cargo back to Juneau and straighten that Nichols fellow out." He got to his feet and began clearing away empty tea mugs and plates. "He could still cause trouble if we fall afoul of him before we can file claim on our gold or explain ourselves to someone with more sense."

"Our" gold?

PATSY ANN spent her day in perfect satisfaction with the world and all that her maker had provided in it. Her morning rounds of the Gold Dust Café and the hotels had set her up nicely for a ramble.

She passed a pleasant early afternoon exploring the banks of the stream that flowed into Juneau from the valley above. Nosing among damp logs and mossy boulders, she followed the river to the quiet pond beside the sawmill.

The lumber yard, with its log house and orderly stacks of scented lumber, was quiet, empty of the usual restless energy of its humans. The white dog followed the vast iron pipe that snaked higher up the valley on its short timber legs, up to where grey timbers like iron-bound trees held back a lake.

There she was surprised to encounter the man who made her black nose wrinkle with his damp, basement smell. He crouched over something at the bottom of the wall of oozing timber. When he saw her, the man threw rocks at her until she slipped away into the bushes along the creek.

Now she gazed out beneath the half-doors of the Hotel Baranof kitchen. Sunday night in the dining room was generally quieter than the after-church crowd. But Patsy Ann's exertions had sharpened her appetite, and the Baranof's end-of-weekend leftovers were always reliable.

She put her nose down on her front paws and dozed. Suddenly, the white nose wrinkled and her head lifted.

Agent Avery Nichols held a chair for Miss Ingrid Sanderson at a table along the wall. He had changed out of the dungarees and plaid shirt he'd been wearing earlier, into his more familiar dark suit. Miss Sanderson had on a mauve dress with a little spray of flowers at the lapel. They smelled sweet, but not sweet enough to hide the rancid odour flowing off her companion.

"We're celebrating tonight," Nichols said, taking his own seat.

"Well, that's always nice," the woman said, her plain face striving for a smile. "But what? I thought Hizzoner turned you down, wouldn't give you a warrant."

"After tomorrow, it won't matter." Nichols looked smug. "He'll look like a fool. And I'll be on my way to a promotion."

Miss Sanderson's face clouded. "Does that mean ..." Her voice trailed off and her final words were spoken barely above a whisper. "You'll be leaving?"

Nichols had perhaps not heard. He leaned back and puffed out his narrow chest. "You're dead right, we're celebrating.

Whatever you like — the filet, the lobster. Tonight, anything."

A scuffling noise from beneath the door to the kitchen caught the man's attention. He craned to look past his companion and a curse slipped out.

Patsy Ann shivered and went out the back way.

MORNING dew soaked *DogStar*'s deck and rigging.

Tomi and the Captain took turns cranking a brass handle to retrieve the dripping rope, chain and, at last, the anchor. As it let go the bottom, *DogStar*'s prow swung gently into the tide.

The Captain pushed a lever and Tomi felt a *ka-thunk* from below. Water rushed astern and the boat surged gently toward the dogleg entrance.

Mizz Alex produced hot coffee and frying-pan biscuits, with berry jelly and yellow butter. They reached the junction of seaways, once again passing the great headland, and this time turned right — "starboard," the Captain called it.

Two days earlier they had run lazily down this channel. Now they pounded uphill into breezy whitecaps. Inside the cozy wheelhouse it wasn't unpleasant, but the distant "V" in the mountains that marked the channel to Juneau drew closer at a snail's pace.

It left too much time to wonder how Juneau would greet them. They had no radio. The Captain couldn't call ahead with the news. And who knew what "Nutbar" might have set up. Would the FBI be waiting at the marina with guns drawn? Tomi had seen that a zillion times on TV.

Maybe they'd been wrong all along and Agent Nichols never had planned to arrest them. They hadn't committed any crimes. Maybe it had all blown over.

Or maybe it hadn't, and JP was in some jail cell somewhere. Tomi wondered how far Avery Nichols might go to get JP to snitch on whatever it was the agent thought they were up to. The idea brought a sudden knot to his stomach, along with a stab of guilt for letting his friend play decoy.

The distant roar of an engine intruded on his thoughts. Sliding open the wheelhouse door, he stepped out onto *DogStar's* deck. Waves rushed by at his feet and the wind cut through his shirt. He grabbed a rope for safety and looked behind them.

The yellow plane was flying low over the water, tracking *DogStar's* wake. The Captain and Mizz Alex had also noticed. They watched the yellow wings dip, tip and straighten as the plane climbed to overtake them on the right, its two big propellers roaring. They could see into the cockpit where two white faces looked down at them.

The plane had barely pulled ahead of them when it banked into a turn across *DogStar's* bow. They watched as the plane made one complete circle around them, right wing dipping tremulously toward the water, before it levelled off again and resumed its course up the channel.

Tomi saw the Captain and Mizz Alex exchange a look. *So much for the element of surprise.* The plane's passing had reminded all three of them of the confrontation waiting ahead.

Keeping their fears to themselves the two adults quickly agreed on a plan. If all was quiet at the dock, they'd proceed into town like the law-abiding citizens they were and report their discovery at something called the "claims office."

"We'll put all three of our names on it," Mizz Alex said. After that, she thought they might go over to the *Daily Alaska Empire* and give that Carr woman a *real* story.

"Aye," said the Captain, dryly. "Or maybe we'd best keep our cards close to our waistcoat 'til we see how things lie with the law."

Mizz Alex shrugged her grudging agreement and the crew of the *DogStar* lapsed into silence.

It was late morning when Juneau finally came into view. Tomi was surprised by the warm thrill he felt at the sight of the familiar downtown and the scattered homesteads climbing toward the wooded valley where the lumber yard hid among the trees.

But aboard the little boat he could feel the tension rising. Each wave that slipped beneath their stern brought them closer to whatever Agent Nichols had in store. No one spoke.

THE ARMS of the breakwater reached out to welcome them. They slipped between the two lights, green to the left, red to the right. The captain sent Tomi to the foredeck to "man the bowline." He cut the throttle and nosed *DogStar* into the gap in the breakwaters. When the lights were clear astern, he put the wheel over.

The boat glided forward through the water into its slip.

As soon as he was sure he could make the jump, Tomi leaped onto the float. The engine died away.

"Home and dry," said the Captain, stepping away from the little outside wheel.

They made the boat secure in silence, listening to the creak and slap of wood and rope, the distant voices, someone working an engine throttle up and down, all the usual marina sounds. Nothing seemed out of place.

As they trooped along the floats toward shore, Tomi scanned the cars and trucks in the parking lot for signs of a stake-out. *Nothing. Unless they're hiding on us.*

They were stowing their packs in the trunk of Mizz Alex's green Ford when a hoarse voice hailed them.

"Ahoy, *DogStar*." Finn's unshaven face and permanently grimy shoulders appeared, hurrying up from his shed. "Ahoy, there!"

"Finn," the captain greeted him. "What's the flap?"

"Is Mizz Alex with you?" The man peered near-sightedly at them.

"Yes, Finn," Mizz Alex stepped away from the car into the light.

"Thought so. Seen yer car and I heered you took a cruise with the skipper and the young fella what figured the mechanical boy." He patted his chest with a greasy hand to settle his breath. "There's some kind of trouble over to the yard."

Mizz Alex's brows came together. "What kind of trouble?" she asked anxiously.

"Not sure pro'zactly. Something 'bout the dam. An incydent, the FBI man called it. Said if you was to show up, you should make for the yard full ahead, that's all. I been keepin' an eye out for yez, watch-on, watch-on."

"I see," she looked thoughtful. "Thank you, Finn." She searched a pocket, then dropped a coin in the man's hand.

"Thank yez, ma'am. Thank yez," Finn said, and turned back toward his cabin.

The Ford's engine roared and gravel rattled against its undercarriage as Mizz Alex reversed out of the parking lot. Tomi was thrown forward in his seat, then back, then back again as she shot backward out into the road, braked and launched the vehicle at full speed up the road toward town.

"Ezra, you take Tomi and register the claim," Mizz Alex shouted over the motor. "I'll run up to the yard."

"You're sure that's wise?" Captain Harper gave her a concerned look. "It could be a trick."

Mizz Alex considered this a moment. "I suppose. But it's my mill. If something is wrong I should be there. Besides," her grey eyes narrowed, "if that moose nugget thinks he's got the drop on me, it'll be a downright pleasure to set him straight!"

Attagirl Mizz Alex! But then something occurred to Tomi. "I'd better come with you, Mizz Alex. In case anything needs fixing."

A shadow flitted over the woman's face, but then she nodded. "All right. But Ezra, you'd best get our business done. The sooner that claim's on the record the happier I'll be.

And you know," she gave the Captain a sideways smile, "there's no one I'd trust more with a load of gold!"

Say what? But Tomi's curiosity was swept aside by the need to grab onto something solid as the big Ford rocketed round a curve on what felt like two wheels. Ahead loomed the black ranges of coal.

"Pull up a moment, Alex," the Captain said suddenly.

Mizz Alex stood hard on the brake and the car skidded to a stop. Letting out a relieved breath, the old man continued: "Best I slip into town on foot from here. Let you two attract any attention the law wants to pay!" He pulled on the handle and got out, holding the door for Tomi to take the front passenger seat.

For a moment the two stood at the side of the car. Tomi leaned forward to whisper something into the Captain's ear. The old man gave him a surprised look. But when the tall boy nodded firmly, he dipped his head in assent.

Tomi climbed in beside Mizz Alex. She put her foot to the floor and Tomi found himself wishing seatbelts had been invented sooner. *Airbags, too.*

PATSY ANN planted her front paws and pushed her nose toward the open truck window. Black nostrils flared into the breeze. Even without the scents of sea-salt and soda biscuit and diesel oil, she would have known the pea-jacketed figure striding down the shoulder ahead of them.

Suddenly the white dog barked, paying not the least attention to Judy Carr's "oofs" and "ughs" and her sharp warning to "Watch your dirty great feet on my clean skirt."

The truck pulled to a stop and George Carr called across his wife and the dog, "Hey, skipper, give you a lift?"

"Why thank you, George," Captain Harper said, fending off Patsy Ann's slobbery affections. "Perhaps I'll just put her ladyship in the back with your trunks." He took the wriggling dog in his arms, grunting with effort to hoist her over the pickup's side. He nearly dropped her again when a blonde head popped up from behind the pile of crates and suitcases.

Sophie Carr threw her arms around the dog's neck and snuggled her into a corner of the truck bed.

"You're not sending Miss Sophie away to school, are you?" the Captain asked, squeezing in beside Judy Carr.

"No," George sighed. "No, it's all of us. We're just taking everything we can ship on ahead to the *Empress* now. We're out ourselves on the *Stella* in two days."

"Things that bad?" the Captain asked.

"Nothing left for me here," George shook his head heavily, "and they're blasting down south. No choice, really."

"Well, now," Captain Harper said. "I don't know that I'd be so sure about that."

"Fine for you," George said gloomily. "But I don't see any light at the end of the tunnel for us underground lads."

They were nearing the centre of Juneau now. Ahead of them a two-storey brick edifice took up a full block.

The Captain tipped his head toward the Federal Building. "I'll get down here, George, thank you." He paused a moment.

"But tell you what. If you could see your way to waiting for me, I might just be able to show you where you're wrong there."

"How's that?" George sounded skeptical, even a little testy. "I've been round and round this with Judy and the little one. They'd both stay if they could. So would I, come to that, but —"

"Ten minutes, George, no more." The Captain stepped out and closed the door behind him. Through the open window he added, "It might save you a voyage!"

The Carrs exchanged looks. "What have we got to lose, dear?" Judy asked her husband. The latter shrugged and turned the key to kill the motor.

Behind them, Sophie peered between two sharply pointed white ears at the retreating back of Captain Harper's pea jacket, a frown of intense concentration on her face.

Thirty-two
SHOWDOWN

MIZZ ALEX swept wide around the turn onto the timber bridge over the creek. *Please, no log trucks*, Tomi prayed. Luckily, the road was empty. Coming off the bridge she put her foot to the floor once again and the big green car roared up the gravel hill. The car tipped alarmingly as Mizz Alex wrestled it around another bend. She clamped her foot hard on the brakes and the heavy vehicle skidded sideways into the lot in front of the white office.

Do not try that at home, Tomi told himself, getting down a little shakily from the passenger-side door.

The engine ticked beneath its high hood. A flock of birds chattered in a tree. But otherwise the lumber yard, office and log house appeared silent and deserted. As Tomi watched, Mizz Alex stepped over to the small white building and checked the door: it was locked.

A hard look on her face, she strode up the gravel path to the log house. Both its doors were similarly locked tight. "At least it doesn't seem we were robbed," Mizz Alex said with some relief.

"He said it was the mill," Tomi suggested. "Maybe something wrong with the saw?"

Mizz Alex reached into the car and pulled her lasso from her pack. She nodded. "Let's find out." She headed across the yard toward the low, open building at the far end.

Tomi fell in half a pace behind her.

IT WAS closer to fifteen minutes than ten, but the Carrs were still waiting when the Captain came back out. He wore a satisfied look.

George leaned his lanky body against the fender of his truck, arms crossed. Judy's face in the open window was a study in poorly suppressed curiosity. In the open truck bed, young Sophie's face was mugging her impatience openly: "Well?"

"Okay." George pulled himself off the fender. "So what's the big deal?"

"Good news, George. The best," the Captain beamed. "It seems old Russian Alex was more than a tinkerer, and his Golden Boy was more than a pretty face." He dropped his voice to a confidential note. "Those drawings, they were a ... a kind of a code. Young Tomi figured some of it out; Miss Alexandra the rest. And once we'd seen the way of it, they led us straight to the other end of the vein."

"Hot *dawg!*" Sophie's voice crowed from the back of the truck. "I knew it, I knew, I *knew* it!"

George tipped his head, disbelief showing in his face. "The Juneau mine vein? The gold vein? But it's been given up on!"

"So it has." The Captain very nearly smirked. "By most folks.

But I tell you George, my business inside was with the claims registrar."

"My God," breathed George. "If this is true, why, there'll be more work than before."

"Yippee!" Sophie whooped, pumping her arms high over her head. "We don't have to move!"

"Wait a minute," Judy broke in. "Does anyone know about this?"

The Captain shook his head.

"Will you give me an exclusive?" She brought a purse up from the floor and pulled out a notebook. "George, where's my camera?"

"I'm not the one you want to be talking to, Mrs. Carr," the old seaman said. "The real story is with Tomi and Alexandra Kasilof, up at her lumber yard."

"Then let's go," she said. "Get back in here, George. You too, Captain Harper."

TOMI AND Mizz Alex walked forward.

At the entrance to the saw shed they stopped and listened. Birds chirped and twittered in the forest beyond the shed. Insects buzzed in the rows of stacked wood. A soothing rush and burble of falling water filled the air. Yet the hair on the back of Tomi's neck was rising.

They walked into the shadow of the tin roof together. All around, everything seemed as it usually was: the fierce teeth of the saw blade gleamed in the half light, yellow saw shavings covered every surface with a fine dust.

Nothing seemed amiss. Looking through the open far wall, Tomi could see the big wheel, motionless against the green glow of the sunlit forest beyond.

They worked their way past the cutting floor to where the corner of the shed was enclosed for storage. They stepped out on the catwalk that ran along beside the wheel.

"Freeze! Against the wall!"

Eh? Tomi looked up. Avery Nichols' voice had come from somewhere over their heads. *Whoa, dude!*

The FBI agent sat on the big mill wheel, braced between two of the iron buckets. He held a pistol. The barrel moved from Tomi to Mizz Alex and back. "Nothing stupid, or I'll shoot," the agent shouted down at them. "Back against the wall, both of you! And put your hands up!"

Tomi raised his hands to his shoulders. Beside him, Mizz Alex did the same. *This is insane,* he was thinking. *How can I go home if this nut-job shoots me?* He squinted up at the agent. *The guy is demented.* The look in Nichols' face reminded him of the villain in an old movie.

Evidently Mizz Alex thought so, too. "This will hardly advance your career, young man," she called up to the agent. "Whatever you may think, we have done nothing, *nothing*, to bring charges on."

The agent laughed. "That's what you think, babushka." He smirked. "But don't worry." Keeping the gun on them with his right hand, he flicked out his left wrist and glanced at his watch. "By the time this afternoon is over, there'll be plenty to charge you with. And all the evidence in the world."

"You're talking nonsense."

Way to tell him, Mizz Alex!

The agent's face flamed. "You're both under arrest, for espionage, sabotage, conspiracy, false statements, evading arrest." He seemed to be thinking. "And very likely, attempted murder."

Murder? Pistol or no pistol, Tomi could no longer contain himself. "You're crazy!"

"Am I?" Nichols' face was contorted in a mask of vanity and triumph. "Tell that to a jury once this dam blows."

"Say what?"

"The spotter plane let me know you were on your way back. I didn't expect you quite so soon. But this is even more perfect, because in just …" Nichols shot his wrist out and consulted his watch again. "… twenty minutes — give or take — that bomb you made is going to blow the Kasilof Dam sky high."

"What bomb? There's no bomb."

Nichols laughed his cracked laugh again. "Oh, yes there is, little chum, yes there is."

Mizz Alex glared at the man with the intensity of someone staring down a viper. "Are you entirely mad? If the dam goes, it could take out half of Juneau! The people —"

"A wake-up call," Nichols smirked. "Make them damn glad the Bureau's here to protect them."

Tomi could hardly believe what he was hearing. Without thinking he took a step forward.

There was a bang and something ricocheted off the machinery behind them. A white puff of smoke drifted away from the agent's pistol.

Holy shrimp-stains, that was a bullet!

"I said don't move!" Nichols shouted.

Tomi stepped unsteadily back against the wall separating the catwalk from the closet.

"You've got no evidence for any of this," Mizz Alex said.

The agent chuckled. "Think so?" He waved his gun to the path behind the pond.

They followed where the pistol pointed. Tomi's back-pack, the one he'd loaned JP, leaned against the side of the shed. "All the evidence I'm going to need is in that rucksack. Clockwork fuse, one you bought from D'arcy's Pawn, your prints all over it. As for the dynamite, well it'll be blown to perdition. It won't matter whose fingerprints are on it, will it?" A deranged peal of laughter rang out over their heads.

Omigod. The pit of Tomi's stomach turned to ice. This fruitcake nut-bar crazy-man just might get away with it. *Blow up the dam and frame us!*

Nichols shifted into a more comfortable position. "You're done like dinner, Jap. Sigh-oh-nar-ah."

Okayyy. Time for Lassie to come over the paddock fence and save the day. Where are you, Patsy Ann?

But no white dog appeared. Atop the big wheel, Nichols sat and smirked. At Tomi's side, Mizz Alex fumed. Minutes passed. The loudest sound was the rush of water shooting out of the nozzle and falling endlessly out into the pond right behind where the agent sat.

Right behind ...

Tomi knew that the gushing nozzle was the business end

of the whole water wheel set-up. Water from the dam farther uphill coursed down the long iron pipe to jet out of the nozzle with the force of a fire-hose. That provided the energy that turned the great wheel and all the heavy machinery it drove. And it was turned "on" and "off" by the simplest possible means — by turning the nozzle to or away from the wheel.

Turned to the side as it was now, all that vast energy roaring out of the nozzle just fizzled off into the pond. The wheel stood motionless. But shift the nozzle ever so slightly, so that it hit the wheel instead, and …

An idea burst into his head. Turn the nozzle, and the fire-hose will hit the wheel right where he's sitting.

Tomi leaned very gently backward. A prod to his lower back confirmed what he had suspected, and what he needed to know. The lever that moved the nozzle was at his back, just behind his right arm.

He watched the agent's face. The midday sun was strong and the man was sweating beneath his fedora, pale eyes blinking. Nichols raised his left arm to wipe a sleeve across his face.

For the split part of a second, Nichols' arm covered his eyes. Tomi twisted right, arm rising and chopping down on the lever. He threw his weight downward, feeling the iron linkage shift.

There was a gunshot, and splinters flew off a wall.

Nichols yelled. The jet of water hammered into the base of his spine knocking him off balance. There was another bang and puff of smoke, but the pistol was now pointed aimlessly into the sky.

The jet of water was beginning to do its work, transferring its relentless energy to the huge wheel and the agent perched on its rim. Agent, gun and great iron water buckets all together began to turn.

Frantically, Nichols tried to scramble to his feet and get free from the buckets and the fierce spray. "Woaaaaahhhhh!" the agent shrieked, the sound abruptly cut off by a loud splash as he plummeted into the water below.

Mizz Alex snatched the lasso from her belt and sprinted away through the saw shed. She reappeared beside the pond just as Nichols bobbed to the surface, splashing and thrashing in the water. His pistol was no longer in his hand. The brown rope spun in a lazy circle, once, twice, three times, then soared out over the pond. With a sound like a sigh it landed over the flailing agent. With a look of fierce satisfaction, the tall woman began reeling in her catch.

Tomi was on the move, too. He dashed away through the saw shed as well, but in the other direction.

He came out at the path. Three steps carried him to where his backpack lay. He fell to his knees, and hesitated. He could see a pair of wires coming out the top of his backpack, black and white. He followed them with his eyes to where they disappeared into the weeds alongside the pipe that carried water to the nozzle. *Those must go back up the pipe to the dam, and to the dynamite.*

IT WAS QUIET under the trees. The sound of an old-fashioned clock ticking was very loud. What had the nut-bar said?

Twenty minutes? When had that been? How much time was left? He had no idea. But he had no choice either.

Gently, he pulled at the zippered edge of the pack, opening it wider. Leaning in, he saw a battery, one of the big, boxy kind with two posts sticking up to provide the current. Dad had a camping lantern that used one. The white wire from the dam was twisted around one of the posts and taped in place. The black wire disappeared deeper into the pack. Another black wire was twisted and taped to the other post, but it too looped out of sight under the battery.

He didn't mean for this to get blown up, or washed away, Tomi told himself, *so we should be safe here even if the dam does go. I hope.* The rest of Juneau was something else. He put that out of his mind and tried to get his *ch'i* straight.

He reached inside the pack and very, very slowly lifted out the battery. Both of the black wires went to a small and complicated mass of cogs lying in the bottom of the pack. *It's one of the clocks,* one of the three he'd bought at the pawn shop. It lay face-up.

Gotcha! One of the black wires was taped to the clock face, its bare end sticking up an inch or more. The other wire was taped to the minute hand, the entire length of which had been stripped to bare copper. As the seconds ticked by, each one brought closer the inevitable moment when the bare copper along the minute hand connected with the bare copper standing like a sentry from the clock face. When it did, electricity would flow, the circuit would close.

With a jerk, Tomi yanked the black wire off the battery.

He waited. Birds twittered. The water burbled and the water wheel creaked. There were voices behind him, Mizz Alex, Nichols ...

He breathed again. He tore the other wire off the battery for good measure and let it fall harmlessly to the ground beside its mate.

He stood. Someone over by the pond was shouting. There was a pop and a flash. *Omigod, the gun.* But there was no bang.

He carried the battery back through the saw shed. As he stepped out the other side another flash caught him full in the face.

When he could see again, Judy Carr was fiddling with the flash pod on top of a big black camera. Nichols lay sprawled on his stomach on the bank of the pond. His hands were tied behind his back with a rope that bound his knees as well.

Thirty-three

TIME

TOMI TUCKED into a second round of fried sourdough and eggs. He was thinking he'd have to turn Obaacha on to them as a breakfast option — *the heck with my arteries*. A rap sounded at the door and JP peered through the screen, packages in his arms.

These turned out to be a paper bag containing the clothes he had "borrowed" from Tomi, now washed and folded, and a newspaper. Tomi and Mizz Alex both pounced on the latter.

"That's a terrible picture," Mizz Alex protested the moment she saw the front page. Across most of the top half was the photo of Agent Nichols on the bank, hog-tied, with Mizz Alex holding on to her lasso as though she'd just roped a wildcat. "I look like Annie Oakley's wicked sister."

"No way! You look like Batwoman!" said Tomi, before he remembered that Michelle Pfieffer probably wasn't even born yet. "I mean, you look great!"

"Like an old bat, is that it?" But in fact, Mizz Alex seemed not entirely displeased.

"Bat*woman*?" asked JP. "I know about Bat*man*."

"It's coming, just wait," Tomi said. *You may be about sixty or so, but it's coming.* His eyes went to the second picture on the page: Tomi himself, carrying his backpack. *I look stunned.*

He began reading, getting a new sense of the events that had turned into a blur after yesterday's showdown.

George Carr had followed the wires, finding the dynamite Nichols had planted at the foot of the dam. "Fool didn't know what he was doing," the story quoted Mr. Carr. "He used enough to take out half a mountain. There'd have been a tidal wave right through the middle of town if it ever went off."

"'Agent Nichols has been relieved of his duties and his badge'," Mizz Alex read aloud. "And a good thing too."

"Looks like that Marshall guy agrees," Tomi said. A telephone call yesterday had brought a tall, broad-shouldered lawman with several deputies racing to the lumber yard. "'We'll investigate thoroughly,' Marshall Al McMann stated," Tomi read from the paper's account. "'But I anticipate charges.'" *Well, d'uh!*

"He's just being duly cautious," Mizz Alex murmured. "Better that than go off half-cocked like Nichols."

Despite all the attention given to the drama at the sawmill, the other news — their gold discovery — wasn't entirely ignored. Several business types were quoted, saying how good it was going to be for the town.

"I suppose I could retire now," Mizz Alex mused. "But there'll be so much to do." She looked up and her grey eyes met Tomi's. "They'll certainly need a lot of wood."

Yeah … hmm. He had an idea. "You should hire JP!"

The other boy gave him a surprised look.

"Seriously," Tomi said. "You're going to need more help,"

more than you know, "and you know you can trust him."

Mizz Alex nodded, giving the idea consideration.

"Hey, look there," JP nudged Tomi. "I think they're going to throw a party for you!"

Under the headline MUNICIPAL HOLIDAY TODAY was a story. "'This young man has now saved our town twice,' said Juneau Mayor Harry Benson. 'We owe him a civic debt of gratitude and we intend to show him that.'"

"Goodness, that reminds me," Mizz Alex jumped up and began collecting the breakfast dishes. "I offered our yard for the big do. We need to lay out some horses with planks for tables."

For the next hour, Tomi and JP were kept busy carrying sawhorses out to the open gravel yard in pairs, and laying planks across them to make long trestle tables. Shortly before noon, Captain Harper arrived. He had Finn with him, and the two men set about constructing a low stage at one end of the yard. ("No shortage of lumber, that's one blessing," Finn said more than once.)

While they were doing that, Tomi, at Mizz Alex's suggestion, washed up and changed into clean clothes — his own clothes from home which JP had brought.

He returned to the yard in time to see a truck with big loudspeakers mounted on its cab roll up. The driver produced a large, lozenge-shaped microphone on a stand, and set it up on the fresh-built stage, running a cable back to the truck.

Next came an old bus converted into a snack stand. It pulled over in the yard, dropped one of its sides to make a counter, and began pumping out the irresistible aroma of potatoes frying.

Behind it came a car ancient even by Juneau standards: tall, faded black, with spoked wheels and a canvas roof like a buggy. Out of it stepped a very fat man the colour of dark coffee followed by a skinny fellow with Asian features and a long pigtail down his back, a short guy in a black suit and top hat and the driver. The last was as big as the other three put together and wore a plaid shirt and overalls. All four carried cases. They trooped to the stage where they unloaded a trumpet for the fat man, a clarinet for pigtail guy and a stand-up bass for the chap in the top hat. The mountain man produced the smallest instrument of the bunch, a harmonica. With no more than a one-two-three, they began to play a rousing Dixieland tune.

Next to arrive were several cars bringing ladies laden with platters of sandwiches and bowls of potato and macaroni salad and urns of tea and coffee. Last to arrive were the young women from Bakers' Bread & Pastries, with an older lady who pecked Captain Harper on the cheek over a tray of squares and small tarts.

Soon after, more cars and trucks began to pull up, releasing a steady stream of men, women and kids. A particularly large and shiny black car carried an important-looking gentleman in a suit with a gold chain around his neck, who promptly began shaking hands with everyone who would hold still for it. Yet more people arrived on foot, including what looked like the entire Orphans and Indigents' Home led by Sister Agatha (although Miss Sanderson had apparently decided she had other things to do). JP took it upon himself to organize tours of the water wheel and the pond where Agent Nichols had met his comeuppance.

A taxi deposited Judge Burns with Patsy Ann at his heels. The leathery old jurist came straight up to Tomi and took his hand in a firm grip. "Well done, young fellow," he said with a small smile. He stepped a little closer, turning to put his back to the gathering crowd. He pulled a folded white card from an inside pocket. "We went through ex-Agent Nichols' office last night," he said. "We found this."

Judge Burns held up the year-end report card from South Fraser Intermediate School, clearly dated May 31, 2006. He produced a pair of frail-looking glasses and put them to his nose. He opened the card and shook his head. "Disappointing, Mr. Tanaka, disappointing. That history mark, especially." Judge Burns clucked sorrowfully.

Tomi wondered if that wasn't a quiver at the corner of the dry lips.

"I see that the space provided for a parent to sign and prove they have read this report is still empty." The judge looked at Tomi over his glasses. "You'll wish to attend to that, no doubt." He handed the card to the boy and now Tomi was quite sure he saw the beginning of a smile.

"Sitting on a water wheel, was he?" The judge turned to look toward the mill. He shook his head. "Sometimes I think the Feds send them up here as a test, to see if they'll go crazy. Unfortunately, most of them do."

He winked and passed on to greet the Captain. Tomi heard him ask, "Patsy Ann bring this one too?" The Captain nodded once.

How much does he know?

Tomi had little time to wonder. Mizz Alex and the Captain insisted on giving Tomi the credit for just about everything, with the result that he was kept busy shaking a lot of other hands as well. With the handshakes and the smiles came a steady stream of "You saved my job, sir," and "Now we can keep our store open," and "We're so glad we're going to be able to stay" — an outpouring of goodwill and gratitude that very nearly had him tearing up.

One of the last to find him was Judy Carr, who shook his hand first then threw her arms around his neck in a big bear hug. "You're about the biggest story to hit Juneau in years," she gushed. "And thanks to you, I'm associate editor at the paper as of this morning! I owe you a big apology, I shouldn't have judged you so quickly."

Behind her was Sophie, looking unusually shy. When she stepped closer, Tomi could see that her blue eyes were shining. "Hey, hero," she said.

"Hey."

"You were great!"

Tomi shrugged, hiding his embarrassment behind a smile.

"No, really. And now we're not moving, so, maybe …?" She looked at him with an unspoken hope in her blue eyes.

Ouch. Tomi cast his eyes around. Wherever he looked,

people were smiling. Whenever he caught someone's eye, they tipped their hat or gave him a little salute. *I wonder, do I have to go?*

Then something totally unexpected happened. Sophie leaned forward and Tomi felt a warm breath, smelled a trace of lavender and — *ohmigod* — warm, soft lips that for just a moment — *ohmigod!* — had brushed his cheek.

The music died away and someone in a cloth cap came to the microphone and began saying, "Test ... test ... test." He handed the mic over to the fellow in the gold chain to "say a few words." The "few words" went on a remarkably long time.

Tomi stopped paying attention and joined a line of people who were filling up paper napkins with sandwiches.

"... and so will you please join me," the suit in the chain was finally working up to his big finale, "in giving a warm Juneau hand to the young man who's done so much for us, our own 'golden' boy ... Tomi Tanaka!"

Tomi winced but the yard erupted into applause and cheering. For the next few minutes it was all Tomi could do to keep smiling and nodding and shaking the hand of everyone who hadn't done so already, and a good few who had.

In time the handshaking petered out, the music picked up again, those who hadn't yet filled their stomachs began lining up along the tables, and a few daring couples even began forming into pairs and twirling around the gravel yard.

Mizz Alex stepped up behind him. She gave a small cough, like someone clearing her throat, and her grey eyes drifted toward the sawmill. "I've been thinking," she said, looking at her napkin, "that I've never properly thanked you myself. I had pretty much given up hope, when you arrived. So much has changed, thanks to you."

"I just did what I could," Tomi mumbled.

"And when I think how I treated you ..."

"You didn't know."

"It was wrong of me to judge so cruelly."

"Things aren't always the way they look."

Mizz Alex nodded. "I asked your friend, young John Paul, and he's going to come on to help."

"That's great."

"But, I do hope ..." Mizz Alex seemed to be trying to find the right words.

Tomi got there first. "I think I might have to be getting home, back to my family. They haven't heard from me in a while."

The tall woman nodded. "Of course. A smart lad like you, there's certainly more opportunity in a big city like Vancouver. Still, I hope you know, there'll always be a home for you here."

Home. He nodded. "Thanks, Mizz Alex." *Auntie Alex.*

Then it happened. He hadn't seen Patsy Ann since she had wandered off into the melee with Judge Burns much earlier. He recognized her sharp, ringing bark at once.

He looked around. Everyone was having a good time, eating, chatting, dancing. No one else seemed to be paying any attention to the barking.

No, that wasn't quite right. Through the crowd Tomi caught the Captain's eye. The old man gave him a smile and dipped his head once.

Patsy Ann barked several more times. Tomi traced the sound to the edge of the lumber piles. The white dog stood between two stacks of timber. Her head was down and she was looking at him. As he watched, her mouth opened and she barked again, a sharp, urgent percussion.

Tomi surveyed the crowd. *Nobody else hears her.* Nor did anyone seem to be paying any more attention to him. Across the yard, he saw JP lead a little group of younger kids from the orphanage toward the water wheel. Judy Carr stood by the mayor, taking notes. Judge Burns sat on a log, his eyes on the musicians and a smile on his lips, one toe tapping. Mizz Alex was — *holy cow* — dancing with — *no kidding* — Mr. Bartlett!

But to Tomi the laughter and music seemed to have become muted and faint, as though heard from a distance. *Not yet,* he suddenly wanted to shout. *Just a few more minutes.* But the barking continued, its note rising almost to a painful edge.

Then the Captain was at his side. "Aye, Tomi, it's time," he said. He handed Tomi his backpack. "You may need this. Something about a parent's signature required." He winked.

Tomi shrugged his pack over his shoulder and looked at his new old friend. "Captain, did you …?"

"Aye, lad. I claimed the mine in equal shares in three names: Alexandra Kasilof's, mine and JP's."

Perfect. "Thanks. And Captain, I ..." He couldn't finish.

"No need to say anything. You've done well. Now it's time. For her," he glanced over at the tall woman holding court by the iced tea, "and for Juneau, thank you."

"No, thank *you*."

"Godspeed, lad."

Patsy Ann barked, a hard, almost frantic sound. Tomi turned and started walking.

The white dog waited until he had left the crowd behind before turning away into the shadows between one stack of lumber and the next. Tomi broke into a run, reaching the alley just in time to see her white tail round a corner ahead. He followed Patsy Ann into the maze of lumber.

Thirty-four

TADAIMA

TOMI PEELED round the corner of the lumber pile. Patsy Ann stood a few metres away, where two damp gravel alleys between the stacks met. She looked back at him, the fur at the corners of her open mouth wrinkling in a grin. "Here I am," he said.

Patsy Ann trotted out of sight down one of the alleys.

Tomi reached the spot in time to look down the way she had gone. Her white rump and thin tail were disappearing around another turn. He set out in pursuit.

Left and right, right and left she went, ever deeper into the maze of high-stacked wood. Walls of sweet-smelling sawn lumber were high on either side, muffling sound. The music coming from the party soon faded. Then Tomi heard a new sound: the whine of a big diesel engine working its way up through the gears.

He came around another corner into a broader alley. Patsy Ann was no longer anywhere to be seen. But the lumber stacks on the far side of this alley were tightly wrapped in white, vacuum-sealed, plastic sheeting.

An unexpected reluctance brought Tomi to a stop. *Is this it? Or can I turn around, spend another day there and go back tomorrow?*

From somewhere up ahead he heard a bark, the same urgent note coming more faintly now. Something like panic seized him. *Holy cow, it is now or never!* He took off again in the direction of the sound.

He never did catch up to Patsy Ann again. Instead, he veered this way and that, following the fading echoes of a dog barking until suddenly he turned a corner and ran smack into a wire-mesh fence. He bounced back, staggered and stepped forward again, rubbing his nose.

He looked right: a gap where the fence ended left room to squeeze through. Beyond the mesh was a narrow strip of crushed rock, then a ditch where reeds and grasses were mowed into a military stubble. The ditch followed a paved road.

The place where Tomi stood was deep in shadow. Across the road, the last beams of a setting sun glowed on the faded paint of used cars. In the clear end-of-day rays, even the bare aluminum building behind them was beautiful. He looked up and around. No green mountain loomed overhead.

There was a rising sound of engines. A stream of cars, released by some distant traffic light, came around the far turn: *modern* cars. He felt a surge of regret. *I'm going to miss them.* But it was quickly washed away in a new and complicated set of feelings. Excitement — it would be good to see Dad and Obaacha again. And he had to admit, even Rory and Amanda. But also a little fear. *I wonder how much trouble I'm in?*

Even as Tomi stood there, shadows advanced across the scene in front of him. The sun was setting. The used cars ceased to glow. In the deep shade of the stacked lumber it was getting chilly.

When the last car had passed, Tomi squeezed out through the gap at the end of the fence and jumped the ditch. He sprinted across the road and began walking south along the cement sidewalk. He shifted the straps on his backpack. He spun around. In the distance, far beyond the lumber yard — the River Side Lumber Yard, he was now certain — lights twinkled over a splash of white on Mt. Seymour.

He turned his back on the mountain and resumed walking. *Okay, I'd better figure out what my story is.* It would help if he had any idea how long he'd been gone. He glanced down at his watch. It said 9:35, but who knew? It hadn't been working for as long as he'd been in Juneau.

He was passing the school when a car pulled to the curb ahead of him. It was a silver Accord like Dad's.

The driver's door flew open and Johnny Tanaka leaped out. "Son!" he shouted. "Where have you been? We've been out looking for you. Amanda's ready to call the RCMP!"

Wow. I could have been wanted by the FBI and the Mounties in the same week! Over his father's shoulder he saw Obaacha climb out of the back seat of the car.

"Tomi?" Johnny Tanaka took his son by the shoulders and looked hard at him. "Where have you been?"

"Around," Tomi skated. "With friends."

"What friends? And why now of all nights? We're out of the house tomorrow and you haven't even started to pack." Tomi's dad turned back to the car and opened the passenger door.

Tomi took a step forward and Obaacha stood in front of him. She looked in his face for a long time, and differently. Deeply. Not so hard.

"*Tadaima, Obaa san.*" I'm home, Grandma.

The tiny woman enveloped him in her arms and held him as tight and as high as she could. "*Okaeri nasai.*" Welcome home. Tomi leaned over to hug her back, his nose brushing the top of her grey hair. He smelled tea and Obaacha's peculiar ginger ginseng soap. He hugged her back harder.

They broke apart and Obaacha got into the rear of the Accord. Tomi slid into the front. His father pushed the door closed.

Oh, yeah, right, packing. But that meant he hadn't been gone so long after all. *It's still today.*

His father got in behind the wheel.

"But we're still … That is … it's still on, right? The trip?"

"Of course it is." Johnny Tanaka looked more closely at his son. "Are you all right? Have you been *doing* anything?" He reached for Tomi's backpack.

You mean, like, drugs? Nope. Just a little time-travel. Tomi couldn't suppress a smile. "Nope. Just …" *What?*

His father pulled Tomi's lunchbox out of the pack. He flipped open the lid; it still smelled of old banana. Next came his Superman comic, and his report card. Johnny Tanaka glanced at the card. "I'll look at that later. Where's your player? Your mp3?"

Fruitcakes. Like, Washington DC, in some secret warehouse. "Uh, yeh, I swapped it."

"Your second-most prized possession? What on earth did you trade it for?"

Please let it be here. Tomi thrust one hand in his pocket. It had been there just this morning ... *sixty-odd years ago. Yesss!* He pulled out the dripping of raw, native gold, a nubby bar as thick as a pencil and nearly as long. "I traded it for this."

Johnny Tanaka's face showed his doubts. "What? For a rock?"

"It's gold."

"Yeah, and I'm an Inuit." He put the car in drive and they pulled away from the curb.

Things aren't always what they seem, but sometimes they are!

"Ya never know!" *Who'd a thunk this face was Russian!*

"Hey, who doesn't have his belt on," Tomi's dad demanded. The little bell was dinging and the alert flashed on the dashboard.

Oh yeah. "Sorry." Tomi grabbed the belt and snicked it closed. *Whoa. Mizz Alex wouldn't last twenty minutes on these streets.* He smiled through his own reflection at the darkened streets of Delta. "Listen, Dad ..."

"Uh-huh?" His father's voice was held in, cautious.

"I was thinking. I know it's a little late for input, but you said, if there was any place *I* wanted to visit on this trip ...?"

His father gave Tomi an odd look. "Well yeah, a little late. But what are you thinking?"

"Could we maybe make a stop at Juneau?"

"Alaska?"

"Yeah, but Juneau."

Johnny Tanaka looked puzzled but tipped his head like someone giving the idea a chance. "It's on our way, sort of. And I did say we could make it up as we go. Let me get on the internet when we get home and see what I can do."

Way cool! I can see what's been happening since I left. He grinned privately. They stopped at a light. Halfway along the next block, Dad spun the wheel and turned into the lane. The sun was well down now, the lane darker than the surrounding streets. "You're going to need to hustle your buns though," his father said.

Headlights swept across a pyramid of garbage bags. They turned into the garage. It was a tight squeeze beside a row of cardboard boxes stacked several high. Tomi's eyes followed the boxes.

"Was that what set you off?" His dad turned off the engine.

"Say what?"

"Something must have set you off," his father probed. "Was it seeing your machine in boxes?"

Tomi thought back, trying to remember. "Yeah. Yeah, I guess so. Amanda was throwing it out."

"She wouldn't do that, Tomi." Johnny Tanaka reached out a hand and put it on his son's shoulder. "It *had* to come down, you knew that. But we've saved every piece. These boxes are for storage. You can put it together again in the new place if you like, bigger and better than ever."

Tomi looked out the car window at the brown stacked boxes. The machine in his bedroom had been cool, no question, but it couldn't hold a candle to the Golden Boy. Somewhere there was something else, waiting. "Naah," he said. "That's okay." He pulled on the handle and squeezed out the door. "They're not that important. We can put them with the garbage if you like."

Johnny Tanaka sat staring with his mouth open.

Tomi hefted the first box into his arms and carried it out to the laneway. He placed it beside the pile of garbage bags. There were five boxes in all. Johnny Tanaka helped Tomi carry them to the lane.

Tomi dropped the last box with the rest of the garbage and was turning back to the house when headlights blinded him. The car braked to a sharp stop and both front doors popped open. Rory and Amanda flew out and rushed over to him.

"Tomi!" Both women wrapped their arms around him in a fierce hug. Amanda pulled away and Tomi saw lamplight glisten on her wet cheeks. "I was so worried," his stepmother said. "I thought I'd done something, said something, that you'd run away."

Well, yes, and no.

They tried to tug him indoors.

From the corner of his eye he saw something flash at the end of the laneway. Tearing himself from the embrace, Tomi stepped back into the lane and looked toward the street.

There, framed between the fences at the end of the laneway, a white dog stood. In the pool of streetlight, the animal seemed almost to radiate light herself. The big head was turned toward him. Little wrinkles curled at the corners of the open mouth. The dog tossed her head and trotted out of sight.

Tomi raced to the end of the laneway and looked in the direction she had gone. Under the orange glow of the street-lamps the sidewalk was empty.

He turned back into the lane. For a moment he looked up. The sky was now fully black. The stars that had carpeted the northern heavens were outshone here by the city's glow.

But not entirely. He picked out the curved handle and square bowl of the Big Dipper.

Happy trails, Patsy Ann, and thank you.

Tomi walked back to where his family stood in the lighted garage.

PATSY ANN

is a real bull terrier who lived in Juneau, Alaska, during the 1930s. Stone deaf from birth, she somehow "heard" the whistles of ships long before they came into sight and would trot purposefully to the wharf to greet them. She became so famous that her likeness appeared on postcards. In 1934, the town's mayor bestowed upon her the title of "Official Greeter of Juneau."

In 1992, on the fiftieth anniversary of her death, a bronze statue of Patsy Ann was erected on the Juneau waterfront. There the little dog sits watching and waiting with eternal patience, forever fulfilling her duties as "Official Greeter."

The authors are donating a portion of their royalties to the Friends of Patsy Ann Society, an organization set up in conjunction with the Gastineau Humane Society to promote understanding of and kindness to animals. Patsy Ann's statue was created by noted artist and dog show judge, Anna Harris.

For more about Patsy Ann, log on to her website:
http://www.patsyann.com

BEVERLEY WOOD is a writer and marketer. Her husband **CHRIS WOOD** is a journalist and the author of fiction and non fiction books. Their dog, Cato, is a bull terrier. After a decade of living afloat on a boat in Vancouver, they all recently moved ashore to a home within sight of the sea on Vancouver Island.

SIRIUS MYSTERIES
by Beverley and Chris Wood

Look for these adventures starring Patsy Ann

DogStar

Juneau, Alaska, 1932. This is where thirteen-year-old Jeff Beacon is stranded when his parents take him on an Alaskan cruise to help him get over the death of his beloved dog, Buddy. The problem is that Jeff is a 21st-century kid, with a laptop computer and hightop sneakers. Why has he been transported in time to the Alaskan frontier? And how can he find his way home? Jeff must answer these questions quickly — and his only help is the town's bull terrier, Patsy Ann.

1-55192-638-5 • *Available*

Jack's Knife

Jack Kyle's 21st-century mom wants to break up his friendship with a retired policeman. But when Al McMann is taken to hospital and Patsy Ann spirits Jack back to Juneau, Alaska, in the 1930s, Jack finds himself embroiled in the controversial hunt for endangered whales and in pursuit of a daring bandit. The outcome could change his old friend's life as well as his own.

1-55192-709-8 • *Available*

By printing *The Golden Boy* on paper made from 100% recycled, 40% post-consumer recycled fibre rather than virgin tree fibre, Raincoast Books has made the following ecological savings:

- 46 trees
- 4,334 kilograms of greenhouse gases (equivalent to driving an average North American car for ten months)
- 36 million BTUs (equivalent to the power consumption of a North American home over four months)
- 26,555 litres of water (equivalent to less than one Olympic sized pool)
- 1,622 kilograms of solid waste (equivalent to a little less than one garbage truck load)

RAINCOAST BOOKS
www.raincoast.com

ANCIENT FOREST
FRIENDLY